VICTIMS AND SAVIORS

Joe—raised in a well-to-do family, never before had he been exposed to the utter desperation he witnessed daily at Jefferson. He soon realized that it would require much more than brilliant surgical skills to provide a doctor's care at this hospital.

Elena—the beautiful young nurse raised in the depths of the ghetto that surrounded Jefferson. Embittered by the recurring nightmare of the sexual savagery in her past, she refuses even the token affections of any man . . . until Joe walks into her life.

Ino—king of the streets, leader of the Young Toros. He has conquered every gang in the community. Now he is ready to threaten the highest level of city government to get what he wants—a better life for his people and direct control over Jefferson Hospital.

They're all under the knife in

THE
CUTTING ROOM

THE CUTTING ROOM

ETHAN BARNETT

BANTAM BOOKS
TORONTO · NEW YORK · LONDON · SYDNEY

THE CUTTING ROOM
A Bantam Book / January 1982

ISBN 0-553-20413-0

Published simultaneously in the United States and Canada

Bantam Books are published by Bantam Books, Inc. Its trademark, consisting
of the words "Bantam Books" and the portrayal of a rooster, is Registered
in U.S. Patent and Trademark Office and in other countries. Marca Registrada.
Bantam Books, Inc., 666 Fifth Avenue, New York, New York 10103.

PRINTED IN THE UNITED STATES OF AMERICA

0 9 8 7 6 5 4 3 2 1

Never go into an operation with the idea of doing the most amount of good. Rather, go in with the idea of doing the least amount of harm.

—Benjamin Gold, M.D.

Introduction

Jefferson Hospital has for many years served as the only treating facility for the five hundred and fifty thousand people of the South Bronx. As the area skidded into abysmal decay, the local doctors fled to safer, prettier places. The flood of impoverished people from Harlem and Puerto Rico continued. They crammed into primitive apartments, often without heating or plumbing. As disease slowly depleted their ranks they gave up hope. Their youth turned on each other in an explosion of violence fired by hunger and frustration.

Municipal officials watched, powerless, while the city hospitals they funded staggered under the malignant increase in need. The city first tried to combat the terrifying poverty by reallocating funds, only to realize the futility of their efforts. In desperation they turned to the huge successful medical centers to bail them out. City Hall would match a fixed amount of money, and in return the private institutions agreed to accept responsibility for the supervision and maintenance of these problem facilities. New York University took over Bellevue and Columbia took over Harlem Hospital. With considerable reluctance, Hirshorn Medical Center agreed to take over the care of Jefferson Hospital.

The transfer had taken place five years ago, but many of the same problems continued, and new ones had been added. Jefferson Hospital was faced with an imperative need to expand. But, with taxes skyrocketing and inflation rampant, the city could no longer meet its obligation. And by itself, Hirshorn Medical Center could not handle the awesome burden of providing for the destitute inhabitants of the South Bronx. The board of directors looked to the city, the city looked to the state, the state looked to Washington and all plans to expand Jefferson Hospital (and all plans) returned to the bottom drawer.

PART I

1

"The war goes down at ten. I just spoke to Hernandez, their chicken-shit warlord, and the place is the parking lot over by the Viejo on Fox Street. We've got to move ass. We got a day and a half."

Inocencio Sanchez paced back and forth in front of the twenty-eight young Puerto Ricans. Though they squatted and sprawled on the concrete floor, their attention never wavered. They all wore identical denim jackets with *Young Toros* studded on the back. There was a small number high on the sleeve, designating each man's rank. Only Sanchez had no number. He was el Jefe, the Chief, as he had been for ten years.

Never would the Young Toros fight a more important battle. The Five C's controlled the entire Hoe Avenue section of the South Bronx. They were older and better equipped than the Toros. Only two days before, they had invaded Sanchez's territory and rubbed out his number three man, his own young cousin, Jiminez.

Sanchez stood before his men as he always did—supple and relaxed on the surface, but inside, as taut as a bowstring. His black hair glistened in the early morning sunlight that beamed through the narrow window in the vacant warehouse. The light accentuated his pallor, exposing the deep lines and sharp planes of his face. A thick, six-inch keloid scar trailed behind his left ear.

"Paco." Ino addressed his first lieutenant. "This time we'll need real guns. Those homemade pipe jobs can't cut it. Go uptown to Torrez, the fence, and try to get two of them for about a hundred and fifty. It's all we got left in the treasury.

"Rico, we'll need some cars. Four-door and nothing flashy.

3

Take six men and head up to Riverdale. Don't forget to change the plates the minute you get them back.

"Juanito." He spoke more gently to the fourteen-year-old boy. "We need spotters. Get your friends off the playground and let them hit all the points. I want to find out where they're meeting before the war. We know that, and we're golden."
Juanito nodded.

"Paco, if we can't get that down, I want you and the Grand Council to stay out for the first few minutes of the action. Either we hit them first, or we surprise them at the end. We'll need an edge in this one."

Ino paused, troubled, then looked up. "I'm going to talk to the Vegas brothers. I'm sure I can get them to help us."

"The Vegas brothers can't fight for shit," boomed a strong voice from the back.

"I know that!" Ino glared coldly at Angel, the most aggressive member of his gang. "I'll take them in with me on the first line. The Five C's will be so busy tearing them apart, they won't even notice the Grand Council."

"But, Jefe, that means you go in without protection." Paco's voice had a slight quiver.

"I have the strength of the Young Toros." Ino smiled. "I will be okay."

He began to pace again. The shadows transformed his face into two large black hollows that seemed to bore into his men. A glint of light escaped from the chain hanging from his belt.

"No chippin' and no booze. Comprende, Angel?"

"I heard it, Ino. But does that go for you, too?"

"Fuck off, Angel. Smack to me is a happy vacation."

Ino strode into the center of the room and faced his men in silence for a long moment. When he spoke it was in a deep reverberant tone.

"The screwing off is over; it's time for battle. Time for work. We are all Young Toros. We live for each other." Ino clenched his right fist high; his men returned his salute. "And we are prepared to die for each other."

The phrase signaled the end of the meeting, but the ritual farewell was ominous. Today, they were talking about real death. The men filed out silently.

Sanchez stood alone, the haughty expression gone, his shoulders drawn up in tension. He lit a cigarette, flicking the match across the floor. He had been the neighborhood hero for too long, and it wasn't turning out the way he had hoped. Why did it always come down to this—another battle where he or his brothers could be killed or hurt bad? Years ago it had all seemed so clear. He was going to lift his people out of the ghetto, like a fucking Moses. Slowly, painfully his dream had faded.

He stood in the vacant warehouse, and for the first time since becoming a Toro he realized he was afraid. He had to act. Those shit-faced punks had sniped his own cousin in his own territory. He had to avenge the loss. But this would be a bad one. The Five C's were the toughest gang in all of New York City.

Worse, over the last few months Inocencio Sanchez, the man who at fifteen had taken charge by clearing the neighborhood of pushers, had himself become solidly entrenched in a three-cap-a-day habit.

2

Joseph Ruskin knocked on the door of the surgical office of the Hirshorn Medical Center in midtown Manhattan. He stood in front of the secretary, a small plain brunette in her early twenties.

"Hello, I'm Dr. Ruskin. I was instructed to report here."

"Hi. Take a seat," she replied, flipping through a small stack of papers. "Here, this will explain everything." She handed him a sheet and continued typing.

Joe scanned the paper. He had to pick up his uniforms, get a parking sticker, and go to the cafeteria to have his picture taken. As he left the office he was almost knocked over by a tall resident shuffling down the hall.

"Do you know where I might find the uniform department?" Joe asked.

"Medicine or surgery?" asked the doctor.

"Surgery," replied Joe.

"All right! Welcome to the club! My name is Matt Zilk, and

I'm a third-year surgical resident," the man said loudly as he pumped Joe's hand twice. "Married or single?"

"Single."

"All right!"

Zilk was at least six foot two. He had small shoulders and most of his two hundred forty pounds were packed into his hips and funneled down to his knees.

"Sorry about running you down. Who are you?"

"Joe Ruskin. I'm an intern."

"Where are you supposed to report tomorrow?" Zilk asked, grabbing the paper out of Joe's hand. "Shit! Jefferson Hospital. That's my rotation, too. You're going to take the longest seven-mile drive of your life. Yeah, you're in for a real show. Jefferson in the summer is one hell of a place to break in. It'll be the hardest four months of your entire year. Why the hell did you pick this program?"

"I was at Buffalo," replied Joe. "There weren't enough patients to go around, and I didn't want to learn by just watching for five years."

"Well, you got your wish. You're going to learn by doing all right. And if you fuck over a couple of bums, no one really cares. That's the one good thing about Jefferson. You're really lucky, Ruskin. I'll be over there to show you the ropes." He paused, smiling. "One more good thing there."

"Yes?" Joe questioned.

"Ass!" Joe shook his head, and Zilk seemed to enjoy his confusion. "All right. You can have a ball. The women down there are unbelievable. They're hot as hell and will do anything you tell them to."

"What women?" Joe asked hesistantly.

"All the women . . . staff, patients' relatives, junkies drifting through the ER. They all want something. Once I traded a junkie spic ten syringes for one great weekend of humping."

"Patients?" Joe asked, drawing away.

"Why not? They're not real people, they're animals. Treat 'em like dogs." A half smile crept over Zilk's lips as he continued to study Joe. "What's the matter. Don't you ever get hot for a little piece?"

"I do," Joe stuttered. "But patients?"

"Listen. They do it to themselves, anyway."

"What do they do to themselves?"

"Everything!" said Zilk laughing. "You'll see." He placed

6

his arm over Joe's shoulder. "Relax. We'll have a ball. Take it slow. I'll see ya tomorrow morning in the cutting room." He walked down the hall, still laughing.

Joe had a sudden queasy feeling in the pit of his stomach.

He returned to his small studio apartment, only a block away from Hirshorn and spent the rest of the day unpacking. He laid out the huge, weathered medical texts on the carpeted floor. There was room for less than half of his books on the three shelves of the small bookcase. Looking around the L-shaped room, he decided to stack the rest of the books behind the sagging sofa until he could pick up a couple of two by fours.

He tried to make the barren room look like home. A picture of his beaming parents, his dad's arm cradled about his slender mother, taken two years ago under the old maple in their backyard, found its place on the radiator cover. A junior high trophy, its small wooden base incongruously capped by a pair of cast-iron Greeks locked in a wrestling pose, went on the windowsill. He studied the faded photograph taken on his high school prom night. Blond hair, shy blue eyes, tiny, even teeth—she had married a restaurant manager when he was a junior in college. He thought of their fervid, exploratory lovemaking and shrugged, putting the picture in a bureau drawer. He placed his new white uniforms, neatly folded, on top.

Night came. He tossed and turned on the uncomfortable bed. He was afraid of the morning. He knew the books cold but had never had an opportunity to apply his knowledge. His ignorance would be discovered. Worse, it might go unchecked, and he might hurt someone by his mistakes. And who could he turn to for help? Certainly not Zilk.

At two A.M., he began fumbling through the high, stuffed cartons, looking for something that might help him sleep. All he found was an old bottle of cough medicine, half-filled. It didn't help. At four A.M. he wrapped himself tightly in the thin sheet and finally fell asleep.

Joe stared at the alarm clock in disbelief. It was only after he had watched the thin red hand complete a full revolution that he was ready to accept the truth: the clock was working. It was 6:06 and he was already late.

He leaped into the uniform he had laid out, cursed the slowness of New York elevators, and ran down the street to his car.

The '72 Mustang was easy to spot. In his last year at Buffalo he had bought four different colors of paint and allowed the neighborhood kids to paint anything they wanted on the old heap. One aspiring artist had painted a huge red elephant on the rear trunk. The car was wedged tightly between a green van and a small Volkswagen. Joe nudged the Volkswagen backward into a signpost. He turned the Mustang's wheel sharply, released the clutch, and the car jerked forward. A loud snapping sound from the right front axle shook the car violently. It stalled.

"Shit!" Joe turned the key again and nosed the Mustang into the street.

He raced up the FDR Drive, weaving through the early morning traffic. He was already fifteen minutes late. What if a cop stopped him?

"I'm an intern and I'm late for an emergency operation," he rehearsed in a booming voice. He smiled sheepishly as a passenger in a passing car stared back at him.

He rechecked the time, grabbing a cigarette from the visor as he waited in line at the toll at the Triboro Bridge. The air was heavy and he began to sweat.

He twisted the rearview mirror. He looked too young, he decided, with his new haircut and the white jacket two sizes too big. He shifted his right shoulder to study the red emblem on his sleeve. There was a large snake coiled about a staff, separating the equally spaced *D* and *H*—the Department of Hospitals of New York City.

In the intern matching selection Joe had gotten his first choice, Hirshorn Medical Center. It was clearly one of the giants, a fifty-million-dollar complex sitting complacently among the posh establishments of Fifth Avenue. It seemed strange that during his interviews at Hirshorn, Jefferson had been mentioned only briefly in passing. It seemed stranger to find that he would be spending six months of his internship in a place Zilk had referred to as "the cutting room."

The neighborhood along the Bruckner Expressway changed drastically as Joe sped along. The buildings had broken windows and wash hung from the fire escapes. Mounds of unbagged garbage littered the sidewalks. He turned off at 169th Street and drove down the block. There was a sparkling sea of broken glass and a small run-down diner.

Joe looked up the street. At the top of a steep hill stood Jefferson Hospital, a somber concrete slab five stories high with chain gates on all the lower windows. A hundred years of swirling dust and dirt had caked a brownish coat over the facade. Black soot belched from the chimneys. The heavy Gothic architecture on the roof top was blurred by the smoke making its slow descent to the street. Only the graffiti scratched on the walls of the decaying building brought it into the present.

Joe drove up the steep alleyway to the parking lot. He leaned out the window and called to the attendant.

"Hi, I'm Joe Ruskin. I'm a surgical intern, and I'm half an hour late—"

"I don't give a crap who you are. You can't park here. The lot is full and you don't have a sticker." The sweaty black man turned and started to walk away. "Park on the street," he called.

Joe squealed back down the hill and drove around the block. There were cars everywhere, half of them had no tires. The sidewalk was cluttered with abandoned furniture and debris. Suddenly, one of the garbage cans in the entrance of a burnt-out building fell over and began rolling down the hill. A huge rat grabbed a last piece of decaying meat and disappeared into the brick wall.

Joe pulled into a spot two blocks down. There was a hydrant. He printed "Doctor on Call" on a sheet of looseleaf paper and folded it around the windshield wiper.

He ran down the street, quickly finding the rhythm that had carried him to five touchdowns in his senior year of high school.

He cut to the right. There was a thin battered metal sign in the corner—EMERGENCY—and an arrow. He ran up the two-hundred-yard ramp that ended in a massive, flattened platform thirty feet off the ground. A black and white police car was parked against the far wall; both front doors were open, and the swirling red bulb on top turned aimlessly. Joe pushed against the large steel double doors and entered a huge waiting room flanked with long wooden benches. Joe noticed three bums sleeping soundly in different corners. One had immense red legs, and his feet were wrapped in rags.

"Where does the Department of Surgery meet?" Joe asked a towering Hispanic guard, who was twirling his mahogany stick. The guard pointed to the left.

Joe ran down the hall. As he swung the cafeteria door inward he was greeted by a husky, dark man with a heaped pompadour and piercing brown eyes. He wore a green scrub suit, and the black tubing of his stethoscope hung out of his jacket pocket. His eyes scanned Joe's name tag.

"I'm Mike Barilla, your chief resident. You're thirty minutes late. Looks like you screwed yourself out of breakfast. We have a meeting with the Chief of Surgery right now. Follow me."

Joe fell in behind the others. A thin brunette in a heavily starched white skirt turned around and smiled at him. She was cute, with a short pixie haircut outlining soft, refined features.

"Hi, I'm Susan West. I'm the second-year surgical resident on your team."

"I'm sorry I'm late," Joe blurted out.

"Relax. You didn't miss anything."

They continued down a labyrinth of decrepit halls. The place was poorly lit, and there were balls of dust in the corners.

"This place looks like it's going to fall apart."

"Don't worry, it's lasted this long," said Susan. They climbed two flights of stairs.

"It's hot as hell," Joe said. "Isn't there any air-conditioning?"

"Only in the emergency and operating rooms."

Joe looked about in dismay.

"You'll be okay." Susan reassured him. "You start in the pit. You'll be cool for at least two months. Cool and busy."

They entered a large conference room and found seats around a long library table. There was only one empty chair left, opposite the head of the table. Joe took it.

A heavyset man in a long lab coat stood looking out the window. He was bald, except for a thin silver border that continued forward around his ears. He leaned over the radiator, oblivious to the group. Benjamin Gold, Chief of Surgery, Hirshorn Medical Center, Jefferson Division, was not happy.

Dr. Gold had accepted the position of chief at Jefferson because, at fifty-nine, he didn't have the strength to battle the medical hierarchy. Now, five years later, he no longer had the strength to battle the community that had been entrusted to his care. How could they have done this to him? How could this have happened? He had worked harder and published better papers than any of his colleagues, and he deserved to inherit the job of director of Hirshorn. When Tabot died, Gold had readied himself. He was fifty-six and had a world-renowned reputation. But the board of directors had gone outside their own ranks and chosen a young hotshot from The Mayo Clinic. When William Boise arrived, the gulf only deepened. Gold found himself constantly upstaged by the slick, political maneuvering that was second nature to the young director.

When the Department of Hospitals, under Mayor Finch, turned to the huge medical centers, Hirshorn was pressed. Bolstered by the support of the Jewish philanthropies and the Rockefeller Institute, Hirshorn had in ten years created a first-rate medical school from scratch. Their exponential growth had created a lack of patients in proportion to their increasing staff, and they urgently needed a teaching hospital. Bellevue and Harlem were already taken, and the only other hospital busy and large enough to accommodate them was Jefferson. With typical youthful confidence, they accepted the challenge and assumed responsibility for the running of the decaying hospital.

Gold remembered sitting in Boise's large, modern office, sinking into a thick leather chair:

"I've recommended you to become Chief of Surgery at Jefferson. It's the most important responsibility Hirshorn has ever accepted. Imagine taking over two metropolitan hospitals within a year. We'll use Jefferson as our major teaching hospital. That's where you come in, Ben. You're the best surgical teacher we have. Everyone at Hirshorn knows it. That's why the residents respect you so much. I must admit even I envy your enthusiasm and your rapport with them. I just wish my job could be as simple as that."

"Why not Metropolitan?" Gold asked, fighting to hide his anxiety.

"We can't dismiss their old chief just yet," Boise countered. "It's part of our agreement with the Metropolitan staff. Besides, we need you at Jefferson. Everyone on the board agreed you're perfect for the job."

"But I've given twenty-eight years to Hirshorn." Gold's mouth was completely dry.

"Everyone!" Boise repeated.

"Then I accept," he said softly.

Boise was elated. He was finally going to get rid of his rival. Gold's ill-matched dress and impolite manner were enough of an embarrassment. The fact that Gold still commanded so much respect was a constant bewilderment. Boise pressed his manicured finger to the intercom.

"Get me the office of the board of directors," he ordered his secretary. "Congratulations, Ben. I know you'll make Hirshorn proud, and I'll give you all the help I can."

The help rarely came, and when it did, it was never enough. In his first year his response to the chaos was an unexplained zeal he had not known since his early years in training. The two years at Hirshorn under Boise's authority had been humiliating, but here, he was free once again to stalk about as the absolute chief. In fact, he was more of a chief at Jefferson where his power was not controlled by the board or the other ambitious professors. Here he had only to contest with a single administrator. And even if his requests for budget advances were denied, on the wards he was the sole authority. Within months he had managed to bring the level of care to a new standard.

But the job was overwhelming, and he found his strength slowly dissipating. He found himself having to rely more and more on the energy of the young staff he trained. They alone could manage to bridge some of the catastrophic gaps in medical care that existed due to the primitive facilities and inadequate number of personnel.

He was anticipating the next three months with dread. It took the summer heat to fully fire the black and Hispanic blood. The use of the Emergency Room increased thirty percent in the summer, making it the fourth busiest in the country. And despite the fact that he had a good resident team with Barilla and Susan, he had failed in his bid to have Zilk transferred off the Jefferson rotation.

He suddenly straightened and turned. A large hook nose dominated his jowly face. He dabbed nervously under his chin with a handkerchief clenched in his fist.

"Good morning Mike, Susan, and Team A of the surgical division. I'm sure you are aware that the great Hirshorn Medical Center has deemed it proper to supply this department with only seven people. We are missing a first year resident. I argued that this is the busiest time of the year for us, and with new interns to break in and a flock of medical students under our feet, it is hard enough. As usual, they could give a damn. Susan, you are going to have to double up and help the two interns starting in the Emergency Room. I just don't understand why they always do this to me in the summer. If things get bad, we'll have to cancel the rule about an intern having to ride the ambulance. If someone dies on the way over, maybe they'll wake up to the fact we really need help. Ruskin and Hautman will start down in the Emergency Room."

"Dr. Gold, I have a stomach resection set for eight A.M."
interrupted Barilla.

"Isn't he the diabetic?" asked Gold.

"Yes. Susan just got him stabilized. His upper GI shows a
large fungating mass."

"I better help you with that. Susan, take Ruskin and Hautman
down to the ER and get them oriented." The group broke as
Gold headed out the door.

"Come gentlemen, you better follow me." Susan strode briskly
down the hall.

3

Over the last fifteen minutes the hospital had come alive. Stretchers
and wheelchairs and groups of patients flooded the halls. Joe and
the other intern got caught behind a stretcher that was being
wheeled into a side room and almost lost Susan, who was
rushing ahead of them. Joe looked at his compatriot and extended his hand.

"I'm Joe."

"I am Arnost," said the thin, boyish-looking intern. They
began to run down the hall to catch up with Susan.

"Where are you from?"

"My homeland is Hungary, but I escape. I work as scrub
nurse at the North Shore Hospital, until Dr. Star and I become
friends. The university would not send my graduation papers,
but he arrange for an extra spot in the internship class. I have
very good fortune. I will work very hard."

By the time they reached the Emergency Room, they were out
of breath. Susan had stopped at the reception desk.

"There is only one real entrance to Jefferson Hospital"—she
began—"and that is up the ramp. Anyone who is really sick will

come through here.'' She pushed open the large swinging doors. ''The ER is in the shape of an H. There is a surgical side and a medical side. The short corridor in the middle connects them. At the far end of the medical side is X-ray. This whole area is ours. We have a trauma room and two suture rooms on either side of the nursing station.''

Susan went into the first room on the left. There was a six-inch thick sliding steel door guarding the entrance. ''This is the trauma room.'' A single stretcher stood in the middle. ''The room is equipped with every piece of machinery to keep a patient alive. We always stock several units of plasma, and when things get bad, a couple of units of O negative blood in the fridge.''

Susan paused and then walked over to a large Formica table with heavy rubber wheels. ''And this, doctors, is the max cart. It cost twenty thousand dollars, and we don't use it. It comes complete with a volume respirator and a sophisticated cardiac massage arm. It's too heavy. Once you hook a patient up, it takes three men to wheel it around.''

She waited to see if there were any questions, then went on. ''Your job will be to stabilize the patients as quickly as possible and then get them up to the OR, or transfer them over to Hirshorn. Either way, you'd have to disconnect the patient from this cart if you were using it. It's also noisy. When you turn it on, you have to shout to be heard.''

She walked over to the far wall. ''On this wall we have taped every different size chest tube. The ones on the bottom row are designed so you can slide the tube directly over the trocar.''

''What is the trocar?'' asked Arnost.

Susan picked up a metal, spear-shaped rod covered with a thick plastic tube and handed it to him. ''Here's one. You make the hole with it, then slip the tube over it into the wound. You can drain a chest in a couple of seconds with one of these. But be careful. Unless you're really in a rush, I'd advise you to use a thoracotomy set. It takes a couple of extra minutes, but you can see what you're doing. If you have to use the trocar tube, aim for the middle of the rib. That way you'll be less likely to bag the lung.

''On a normal weekend, we get ten to twelve stabs of the chest,'' Susan said. ''That's our specialty. A few years ago one of the residents did a study. We get six stabs of the chest for

14

every stab of the abdomen. In Harlem, the ratio is directly reversed.''

"What causes the difference?'' asked Arnost.

"Our patients are mostly Spanish. Their violence is emotional, triggered by passion. They come overhead and stab down. The blacks are more controlled. They hold their weapons at the waist and slice forward.''

"Which is worse?'' Joe asked.

"I don't know.'' Susan laughed. "Six of one. But if it's just a simple stab of the lung, we usually don't have to admit them. We put the tube on drainage, keep them down here overnight, and clamp it in the morning. If the lung stays up, we pull the tube by noon and discharge them a couple of hours later. Saves a lot of beds.''

"Shouldn't they be kept for a few days?'' Joe asked.

"We don't have the beds or the nursing staff. You cut corners where you can. The motto here is 'treat 'em and street 'em.' '' Susan studied the interns' stunned faces. "Don't worry, you'll get used to it. We all did.''

They moved to another area. "This is the first suture room,'' she said, as they walked through the connecting doorway. Hanging from the wall was a simple bunk stretcher.

"Use 4-0 or 5-0 nylon on the face. You can probably get away with 3-0 nylon on the extremities. Infiltrate with Xylocaine from the wound out. The suture clinic is every other day. Always be sure to follow up on the patient on your next clinic day. Don't send the patient to the other team's clinic.

"It will take you quite a while to get any sort of rapport with the patients. Until that time, if anyone acts threatening, call a guard. Some of our patients are extremely volatile. Most are armed. Just three months ago an intern at Bellevue got stabbed. That mustn't happen here. Just get the guard and have him stay in the room. He might try to embarrass you, but protecting us is his job.''

She opened the next door. "And this is the nursing station. Joe, Arnost, meet Elena.''

Joe faced a voluptuous Puerto Rican woman in her mid-twenties. Her thick black hair fell halfway down her back. She had huge almond eyes, bordered by long lashes. She wore a green OR dress with a string tied at the waist. "Welcome to Jefferson,'' she said, flashing a brilliant smile.

15

"Elena is the head nurse on the day shift," said Susan. "Usually she has two other nurses to help her. She has been working down here for five years and has seen just about everything."

Susan continued through the nursing station into the adjacent room. As Joe started to follow he was forced to turn sideways to squeeze past Elena. He felt her large, warm breasts pressing against his chest. He stopped and their eyes met. Embarrassed, Elena took one step sideways as Joe rejoined Susan.

"This is the second suture room. We use it as our dirty room, for draining abscesses and handling any other infective process. All the aides have gone through a twelve-week intensive training program supervised by Dr. Gold. They all speak English and Spanish fluently. In a pinch, they can even start IVs and sew simple lacerations. Luis is on duty for this shift. He's the best." There was a note of pride in Susan's voice. She glanced at her watch, then walked back to the nursing station.

"Elena, I have to run. Please finish showing them around, and then you'd better put them to work. Page me if you have a problem."

"Gentlemen, if I can leave you with one message, it's simply that this ER is an unpredictable place. Expect anything."

Elena brought Arnost and Joe into a back hall. They entered an empty room approximately eighty by a hundred feet. A row of curtain rods extended from the far wall, dividing the space into eight cubicles. Only one curtain hung in place. Cartons were piled in a far corner. Taped on the wall was a small yellowed newspaper photo of John F. Kennedy. Above Kennedy's picture hung a larger black and white photograph of Martin Luther King. Someone had taken a black marking pen and drawn an *X* across both faces.

"This place looks like a hangar," said Joe.

"It's just a storage room," said Elena, working her way around the piles of boxes.

"But's it's so large," said Joe. "What was it intended for?"

They were in the center of the room. Elena stopped and looked up at the decaying walls. "This, gentlemen, was your original 'cutting room.' "

"What is 'cutting room'?" asked Arnost.

"Before Hirshorn took over, this was the entire surgical ER, if you could call it that." She shook her head sadly. "There were eight stalls against the wall. If someone was really hurt, they'd

16

be wheeled into the center. Everyone would drop what they were doing and pitch in. There were no white tower doctors here then. Jefferson Hospital was a whole different place.''

"So why do they not use it anymore?" asked Arnost.

"Oh," said Elena, suddenly snapping out of her reverie. "There's no air-conditioning and no windows. On really hot days you could die here." She walked slowly through the room.

"When did Hirshorn take over?" Joe asked.

"About five years ago."

"Were you here then?" The question caught her off guard.

"Why, yes," she said. "I was here then. Why?"

"Just wondering what it was like."

"You want the truth?" Her clear dark eyes seemed to challenge him. "I hated it. Jefferson was just an independent city hospital. No supervision and no equipment. The foreign interns and residents didn't understand English or Spanish. The people were right—it was a slaughter house."

"So Hirshorn made a big difference," said Joe.

"I'd say." She smiled. "About three million dollars worth." She led them to the plaster room for a quick cup of coffee. On the counter was a large urn and a plastic cup filled with wooden tongue depressors. One had been snapped in half and was lying on a bed of sugar crystals. Its edge was stained brown.

"Where are you from?" she asked Arnost.

Arnost jumped up on one of the stretchers, carefully balancing his cup of coffee. "My homeland is Hungary."

"He escaped from behind the Iron Curtain," Joe said.

Elena stared at Joe. She let her eyes wander up his five-foot-eleven-inch frame to the soft, curly brown hair that fell just over his ears. He looked uncomfortable in the starched white shirt and striped tie. A small cleft in his chin accentuated his full lips.

"And where are you from?" Elena asked.

"I grew up in Levittown. I left Amherst after three years and went to Buffalo Med."

"A very sheltered life," she snapped.

"I guess so," he continued. "My biggest problem in school was getting up enough nerve to ask a girl for a date."

"Looks like you've managed to overcome your nervousness." Then she spoke to both of them. "We'd better get you guys into greens. You can't work in those uniforms." She went over to one of the cabinets. Piled high were green OR scrub outfits.

"You will find that you have to change two or three times a day, especially at the beginning. Dr. Gold has a thing about clean uniforms. If you have valuables, don't bring them anymore. It's impossible to keep these doors locked. For now, give me your wallets and I'll leave them with the nurse at the desk. We'd better get to work. The patients are piling up." Elena closed the door behind her.

Joe stared at Arnost. "Sensational, huh? I think it's her eyes."

Arnost smiled. "Her physique is not too bad to look at." They glanced at each other with mutual understanding.

"I'm exhausted already. I couldn't get to sleep last night, nervous about today," Joe confided.

"Me, also," said Arnost as they started to change into the greens. They walked out to the rooms already filled with patients.

Joe draped his arm on Arnost's shoulder. "Well, here we go."

"I have hope that Susan comes down soon."

"Don't count on it," Joe replied. "I think we better get used to relying on each other. Susan looks like she has more than enough to handle. Hey, don't worry. I have a *Merck Manual.*" Joe let his right hand rest on the edge of the small blue book in his pocket.

Elena was waiting in the middle of the corridor. She pointed to his pocket and asked, "What is that?"

"It's a *Merck Manual.*"

"It's not going to help you much down here."

"What do you mean? It describes every classical medical illness."

Elena laughed. "Unfortunately, Mr. Merck never made it to the South Bronx. We have our own classic illnesses. The aides can help you a lot more than that book." She grabbed Joe by the elbow and led him into the first suture room.

Lying on the stretcher was an eight-year-old boy, wide-eyed, his arms restrained by a canvas wrapping with Velcro fastening tape. He had a two-inch laceration over his eyebrow that had already been washed by Luis, the burly Puerto Rican aide. Joe took one step toward the child. The boy let out a piercing scream. Joe stepped back.

"Get me twenty-five of Demerol." He motioned to Luis.

"What?" asked Luis.

"The child is frightened, and I plan to sedate him before I do the repair."

18

Luis looked at him questioningly. "Right away, Doc," he answered. The wound only needed three stitches and could be done in a minute and a half. Sedating the child would mean keeping him for several hours. Luis came back and administered the Demerol. As the needle plunged into his upper buttock the child started to kick his feet. He lay sobbing until the analgesic took effect.

Joe slipped on the surgical gloves and sat down on the stool. He looked at the instruments laid out on the tray.

"Where are the scissors?" he asked.

"We don't use scissors. They're always being stolen. It's easier to use a fifteen blade. But since it's your first day, I'll let you use mine." Luis grabbed the smooth gold scissors from his pocket and quickly sterilized them.

"Be careful. Don't lose them. They're a graduation present."

Joe stared at the wound. What had Susan said? "I'll take some 4-0 nylon," he said with faked assurance.

Luis had already turned and grabbed the aluminum packet from the middle row. From his response, it was obvious to Joe that he had made the right choice.

What had she said about infiltration? From the wound edge out, he remembered as he brought the plunger down. The skin edge became thickened and white. He clamped the needle directly at the bevel; his hand began to shake. The needle did not pierce the skin, and as Joe began to twist his wrist the needle bent. He glanced at Luis, who was arranging packages on the shelf. Joe turned the needle on its side and attempted to lead it through the skin. It snapped in half. "Fuck!"

Luis did not even glance down. A new silver package appeared on the tray.

Joe's next attempt was smoother. He found that if he held the skin perpendicular, the needle did not bend. Luis was studying him. Another clumsy intern who didn't know shit. Well, at least this one knew how to tie. Joe's fingers moved swiftly as he tied the square surgical knot that would not slip. He had practiced this for over a year; on the edge of his favorite chair in medical school hung hundreds of strands of threaded silk sutures.

Joe looked at the clock. It was ten-thirty. It had taken him half an hour to sew up a two-inch laceration. He examined his handiwork. The area closest to one edge was definitely uneven, and a small blob of tissue rose from the wound edge. The skin edges did not really fold out, but at least they were together.

Luis leaned over Joe's shoulders. "Great, Doc. Do you want me to dress the wound for you?"

"Yeah, thanks." As Joe got up from the stool Luis began to paint the edges of the wound with a thick brown solution. Joe watched as the aide waved his hand over the painted margin. "Hey, thanks again. And not just for dressing the wound."

Luis seemed embarrassed. "My pleasure, Doc. It only takes a couple of days."

The long, loud whine of the siren suddenly filled the room.

"Uh, oh. We better move," said Luis as he grabbed the child and began pushing him out the door.

"What's that?" asked Joe.

"Ramp code. If the ambulance brings in someone who's really hurt, they'll sound it for a full minute to warn us in here. We'd better get to the trauma room pronto."

Two ambulance attendants came running down the hall, pushing a stretcher. As they brought the patient into the room Elena grabbed the woman's arm and slapped a blood pressure cuff on it.

"Ay, he cut me! My man cut me!" the middle-aged woman wailed in Spanish. Joe listened to the woman's chest. "She's not in shock, but I better start an intravenous, just in case." He drove the exposed metal tip of the angiocath beneath the skin and flipped his index finger upward. Then, reintroducing the tip, he slid the plastic tube into the vein at her wrist. As he lifted the sponges that had been taped over the wound, a stream of bright red blood pumped onto his shirt. He tried to grab at the area with the hemostat but succeeded only in clamping an edge of the skin. The woman jerked and screamed loudly.

"¡No te mueble!" Luis yelled at the woman.

The laceration had laid her wrist completely open. The tendons, like taut leather quills, ran up and down as she jerked her arm. The clamp, holding a useless glob of fat, fell over onto the floor. The white moist wrapping around the nerve had been nicked, and the small meandering artery, flashing its brilliant red with each pulse, lay ominously on the cordlike structure. Then, there was just blood, pouring out, covering everything. Joe frantically pushed down with the sponges.

"It must be an artery," Elena shouted.

"I know, but I can't stop the bleeding long enough to find it." Joe swallowed hard. He looked helplessly at Elena.

20

"Just push harder," she encouraged. "Keep the pressure on for at least two minutes. It should stop."

Joe did as directed. Checking the clock, at exactly two minutes he slowly lifted the sponge. The blood shot up, splattering the overhead light. Joe pushed down.

"Now what do I do?" he asked, his face ashen.

The steel door slid open and Benjamin Gold stood in the doorway, dabbing at his face with a handkerchief. The exertion he had just undergone—running the two flights from his office—had caused a thin layer of sweat to collect on the undersurface of his sagging chin.

"What do you have, son?"

"A laceration of the wrist. I can't seem to get control of the bleeding."

"Okay, let's see what she's done." Gold took off his long white lab coat and slipped into the gloves Luis had prepared.

"Have you anesthetized the area?" he asked.

Aware of his lapse, Joe looked up at the ceiling. "No sir. I guess I forgot."

Gold slapped the twenty gauge needle onto the syringe and forcibly injected some air.

"Why did you do that, sir?" asked Joe.

"It creates pressure in the bottle so you can aspirate quicker."

Gold administered the anesthetic and explored the wound. "She's lacerated her ulnar artery. Elena, blow the cuff up to two hundred fifty, and then give her a shot of two cc's of Valium to quiet her down."

Within seconds Joe saw the whole situation change. There was only a trickle of bright red blood oozing out of the proximal part of the wound, and the patient seemed to be resting comfortably. Gold laid out four blue towels. Then he began to fumble through the suture tray.

"Where are the Senne retractors, Luis?" he asked.

"I'm sorry, sir. We'll have to call the OR for them. They're not routine on the suture tray."

"Not routine on the suture tray!" roared Gold. "What do you mean, not routine on the suture tray?"

Luis went over to the phone and dialed the OR number. "We have an emergency down here. Dr. Gold needs some Senne retractors, stat!"

Gold turned to Joe, disgusted. "How can anyone do a decent job around here without the proper instruments?"

21

Luis covered the receiver with his hand. "Dr. Gold, there are only three in the hospital."

"Well, we need at least twenty!" shouted Gold. "Tell the nurse to order seventeen new ones."

Luis relayed the message. "The nurse says that's not in the budget."

"Look," yelled Gold, "we need seventeen of those retractors, one on every suture tray. Tell her to order it, and I'll pay for it myself." He turned to Joe. "I've never heard of anything so ridiculous!"

Luis spoke softly into the phone. "Order it and tab it."

"Need any help?" Susan asked, coming into the room.

"No problem, Susan. Joe and I have this under control. Oh, by the way, there are no Senne retractors on the suture trays."

Susan smiled. "Frankly, Dr. Gold, I doubt if there are two of them in the whole hospital."

"No, there are three. I just ordered seventeen more."

Susan left the room, shaking her head. After three years she had come to accept Gold's obsession with instruments as just another of his idiosyncracies. He was as intent on stocking his shelves with the best instruments possible as he was on staffing his surgical team with the best residents he could steal from the Hirshorn rotation.

"You only have to look at the edge of this vessel to know that her radial artery will be enough circulation for the hand." Gold snapped the clamp down and twisted it. The distal tip showed brightly in the OR lamp. "Let's tie this vessel, Joe. One more throw on that suture ought to do it."

Suddenly, Gold's demeanor changed. Now that the emergency was under control, his temper flared. He began throwing four-by-four gauze pads on the floor, striking his head on the overhead light as he stood up. "Where are the goddamn scissors?" he growled.

Luis gasped. He was already running into the other room and returned in a moment holding the handle of the scissors in a sponge clamp.

Gold's face had turned scarlet. Beads of perspiration covered his forehead. Joe looked up.

"Dr. Gold, I dropped the scissors on my first attempt to clamp the bleeder," he said.

"Oh, okay, Joe," Gold said. The red began to drain from his face, and Joe was glad he had lied. "Actually, that's not your fault. They ought to have two sets of suture scissors on every tray. Here, you better clamp the distal end." Gold slapped the curved clamp into Joe's palm. Joe took the hemostat. Gold's hand suddenly covered the wound.

"Wrong side down, Joe. Concave toward the wound," he instructed.

Joe turned the hemostat over and proceeded to clamp the vessel in exactly the same spot as Gold had. He threw down the square surgical knot, this time putting in three throws without stopping. "Hold the ends up," directed Gold as he cut above the knot. "Okay, let's see what we've got. Elena, release the tourniquet."

There was no bleeding. "Be sure to irrigate it with at least two hundred cc's of saline before you close, Joe." Gold was already removing his gloves. He started buttoning his lab coat. "Not bad." He smiled. "Where did you say you trained?"

"At the State University in Buffalo." Joe proceeded to relate the history of his schooling. He needn't have bothered; Benjamin Gold wasn't listening. With the intensity of a baseball manager going over his starting lineup, Gold had studied the records of all his new interns. He had chosen Joe to start in the Emergency Room because of his superior record. He had chosen Arnost because he had six months of OR experience working as a surgical nurse.

As Joe grabbed for the large pickups Gold came rushing back. "You need some Adson forceps," he said, gesturing to the far corner of the suture tray. Joe picked up the small fine pickups. "Not like that," said Gold. "Hold it like a fountain pen. A surgeon is an artist. Use your instruments as an artist would. Don't squeeze with all four fingers, just use the tips of your index finger and thumb. Slowly press together. And, the whole thing in throwing a suture is twisting the wrist. Use the index finger for control."

Gold began to put on another pair of gloves. As he got his left glove on he saw that Joe had already understood. The needle didn't bend. The suture was easy to point and place at the right distance from the edge of the wound. When Joe brought the first suture down into a knot, he was excited. The wound edges everted. "Better, son. Finish closing and we'll admit her. Give her at least one day of IV antibiotics."

"Thank you for giving me a hand, sir."

"No problem at all. I was just walking by the ER anyway. Oh, by the way, you'd better change your shirt." He pointed to the large blood stain. Joe smiled as he watched Gold walk out of the room.

Luis caught Joe's eye. "Well, Doc, it looks like I owe you a thank-you."

"I thought it was the best thing at the moment, but now what do I do? When Gold finds out there aren't any suture scissors he'll kill me."

"Let Susan tell him. She's his pet. Gold treats her like she was his own daughter."

Joe walked over to the phone and dialed "O." "Hi, this is Dr. Ruskin."

"I've already heard about you."

"You heard about me?" Joe was surprised.

"Well, not really about you, but I heard about your curly hair," the operator flirted. The hospital underground looked forward to the first of July. Were the new interns kind, or were they mean? Were they skilled or were they poorly trained? Most important of all, were they handsome or were they ugly?

"You simply have to come down and visit us." The voice went on. "We're on the first floor, behind the cafeteria. We always have a tray of fresh cookies."

"Well, I'll try to get down and say hello. What's your name?"

"Lucy."

"Well, Lucy, could you please page Dr. West to the Emergency Room?"

Elena returned. "Can't you ever learn to throw the containers into the trash?" she asked.

"I already paged housekeeping to clean up," Luis replied.

"Lunch?" Joe asked.

"In half an hour, I'll come and get you," Elena said. Joe studied her swinging hips as she walked down the hall.

"Who's Lucy?" asked Joe. Luis was looking at him strangely.

"Lucy who?"

"Lucy, the telephone operator."

"Oh, that Lucy." Luis laughed. "Did she make a pass at you?"

"She offered me some cookies."

"Well, you should see her. Four feet one, two hundred pounds."

"Just my luck." Joe smiled.

"Wait a while," said Luis. "There are some real knockouts around here."

"They couldn't be better than Elena."

"I wouldn't waste time on her, if I were you," Luis snapped.

"How come? She isn't married, is she?"

"Well, no." Luis hesitated.

"You're going with her?" asked Joe.

"No, that's not what I meant."

"What do you mean?" he pressed.

"Elena is not into men, Doc."

"She's a lesbian? Come on."

"She's not a lesbian, but don't get hot on her tail. You'll just hurt her and she'll say no."

"How do you know?"

"Because she's never said yes."

"That's crazy."

"Not really. She has her reasons," Luis stated abruptly. "But they're her reasons."

Susan entered and Luis looked relieved. "We've got a problem down here, Susan," he said. "Gold says we have to admit her."

"That's impossible. We're already two over quota."

"He says we ought to admit her for a day of antibiotics," said Joe.

"No can do, Joe," answered Susan promptly. "Look, leave the patient down here for at least twelve hours. Give her an intravenous bolus of two grams of Keflin and we'll give her two more doses. Then we'll load her up with IM Kefzol and check her in a couple of days in the clinic."

"What if Gold finds out?"

"Gold won't find out. I'll tell Barilla and we'll both cover. Okay?"

"There's another problem. Apparently there are only three suture scissors in the entire ER. All the rest have been stolen. I didn't have the heart to tell Gold, so I lied and told him I dropped them."

"No problem, Joe. I'll take care of it."

"Well, what are you going to do?"

"I'll just call the OR and order seven suture scissors, and put it on Gold's bill. He'll think he ordered them. Gold would gladly donate his entire salary to stock this place with instruments." She paused. "It's too bad the one thing he can't buy is an extra bed. That's the real problem with this place. We need at least three times as many beds. Look, I have to run. Joe, make sure that patient gets a tetanus shot.''

Elena came back just as Susan was leaving. Joe gave the patient the Keflin, and Elena began to wheel the stretcher down the hall. ''You know,'' she said, ''on some weekends we keep ten patients on stretchers down here. They've been promising us a holding ward with a separate nurse, but then they've also been promising us a new hospital. Oh, well, it gives me a chance to do some floor nursing. Listen, there's one more in the next room. If you knock him off quickly, we can sit down to a nice lunch. Say ten minutes.''

''Ten minutes to finish the patient or ten minutes for lunch?'' Joe asked.

''For the patient. I don't think you'll have to sedate this one.'' Elena laughed.

4

Mike Barilla and Matt Zilk walked down the hall, and Joe rushed toward them. They were still in their surgical greens, their masks hanging down around their necks. ''Hi Mike, Matt. How'd the case go?''

''It was a real bitch,'' said Barilla. ''He had a nodule in the upper lobe of his liver. I didn't want to waste time with a frozen section, but I'm sure it's a metastatic spread.'' Barilla turned to Zilk. ''Make sure we get an oncology consult.''

''So they can push their poisons,'' Zilk sneered.

''Come on, Matt,'' said Barilla. ''I don't have much more faith in the oncologists than you do. But if we don't do everything exactly by the book, the chief will act like we gave the guy the cancer.''

"He's the biggest pain in the ass around here anyway."

"He may be a pain in the ass, but without him this place would be a total disaster," said Barilla. He turned to Joe.

"He knows as much as any surgeon you'll ever meet. But putting it in strictly selfish terms, I need Gold because he keeps me out of trouble."

"That's bullshit," said Zilk. "Gold causes more trouble than he's worth."

Barilla glared at Zilk. "I mean patient trouble, complications. Look, Joe, you'll learn after a couple of months that the problem with having even one complication is that you have to work extremely hard and for a lot of hours to get out of it. And everyone knows I don't like to work too hard." He smiled. "Gold is the best surgical teacher you'll ever meet. If we have to do some things that are really a bit unnecessary, let me tell you, when I'm out in private practice, I'm going to do those same things. There's too much in medicine that we don't know. The only way to live with that is to do all you can. If you fail, at least you can say you tried. Gold may be slipping a little and he may be crude, but he tries."

"Glory, glory, Dr. Gold. Amen, Barilla," said Zilk. "You just feel that way because you're through next July. If you had to face his bullshit for a few more years you'd see him for what he really is."

"And what's that?" asked Joe.

"A burnt-out old man who just gets in the way." Zilk's lip curled.

"Joe, you'd be wise to ignore our resident malcontent," snapped Barilla. "Look, I just came down to check on things here. Any problems?"

"Nah," said Joe. "I got one more in the next room, then I thought I'd grab a quick lunch."

"Good idea," said Barilla. "You'll need the energy for tonight."

"Why?" asked Joe. "What's happening tonight?"

"What happens every night in this pit? The natives go wild and try to kill each other. Move your ass, Ruskin, instead of your mouth," Zilk snapped.

Joe gave him the dirtiest look he could muster and went into the second suture room.

Benjamin Gold strode past the secretary's desk, his stern eyes set on the administrator's office. "Krauthammer!" he barked, pushing open the door, "Did you know there are only three Senne retractors in our hospital?"

Harold Krauthammer looked up from his work at the large, huffing man before him and sighed.

"I had no idea. That's something we'll have to pay immediate attention to." Krauthammer spoke timorously for he was by nature a quiet man and he also had no idea what a Senne retractor was. It must be important though. He sensed the five-year truce he had with Benjamin Gold was in danger of collapsing.

They had come to Jefferson in the first week of the transfer and they shared a bond as the two most important people in Hirshorn's annex. They had had arguments but each had come to realize the other's limitations and to accept them. Krauthammer understood that Gold was the best surgeon ever to grace the halls of Jefferson and that he held the welfare of the hospital as his only concern. Their arguments were over money and Gold's insistence on acknowledging only factors that directly concerned medical care. The fuel bills alone had doubled in the last year. It wasn't Harold's fault they had been allotted such a small budget to work with.

"I ordered seventeen more." Gold did not blink.

Harold Krauthammer took off his glasses and rubbed his tired eyes. "Are they expensive?"

"Expensive? How the hell do I know? I'm a surgeon, not an auditor. We need them."

"If it's over five hundred dollars, you'll have to write up a formal request."

"It's under that, dammit. That should save two months on the budget director's desk."

"It still has to be okay'd by the board."

"The board!" Gold screamed. "The board at Hirshorn, consisting of Boise and his businessmen. They've refused every request I've made."

"I'm sorry, it's the rule." Gold was now furiously pacing back and forth in front of his desk. "Ben, it's been the rule for all the years we've been here."

"So Hirshorn can continue to treat us as some sort of gangrenous extremity?"

"They put a lot of money into this place."

28

"It's not enough."

"They say some of your requests are out of line. Some of the equipment you've ordered isn't even at Hirshorn."

"It should be. And it should be here. These patients should have the benefit of every modern piece of equipment."

"I'm sorry. It's out of my power. You'll have to make out a request, and I'll submit it."

"We need another resident, also. Dammit!" Gold had stopped and thrown his hands into the air.

"Well, I certainly can't help you there."

"We can't keep working under these conditions." Gold pounded his fist on the desk.

"You're doing fine. Please, Ben," said Krauthammer, rolling back his chair. "Your mortality figures are down from this time last year."

"Sure. That's because the ambulance drivers went on strike for two weeks. The people just died in their homes instead. Pathology has been going overtime. Look, are you going to help me or not?"

"Honestly, Ben, there's nothing more I can do."

"Okay. Go to your goddamn board meeting. That's all you're good for anyway."

"I owe my allegiance to Hirshorn, the same as you."

Gold stared angrily at the uncomfortable Krauthammer. "But you're paid by the city. You have an appointed position."

"Appointed upon Hirshorn's recommendation."

"Look, you're the administrator of this hospital," said Gold. "Jefferson takes care of sick people, a lot of them. These people need care. If they keep refusing, it should be your job to sit in the damn boardroom and not move until they change their policy."

"That's unrealistic."

"You can go straight to hell!" said Gold, storming out the door. "You and Boise and the whole damn board."

Once Gold had left, Krauthammer sat quietly shaking his head. What did Gold want him to be—some sort of crusader who goes out in the streets and pickets city hall? He was an administrator—just a lousy hospital administrator. But he had been around hospitals long enough to recognize Ben Gold's outburst for what it was; the Chief of Surgery was suffering from a chronic case of fatigue and frustration. Krauthammer knew it could only get worse.

*　　*　　*

The choice was between chicken and meat loaf. Elena chose the chicken and Joe, after scanning both trays, decided on three desserts. There was an empty table in the back of the room, and as they walked toward the corner Joe saw the table where Mike Barilla and Matt Zilk were eating. He nodded in their direction.

"Mike seems like a nice guy," he said to Elena once they sat down. "But that Zilk . . ."

"Wait till you know him better," said Elena, "then you'll really learn to hate him."

"What a perverse guy. It's almost as though he doesn't have an ounce of humanity. You should have heard him bad-mouthing Dr. Gold downstairs."

"Save me the details," said Elena, between mouthfuls.

"I hope I never become that callous," said Joe thoughtfully.

"Don't worry, you're not the type."

Joe looked up from his plate, surprised. "And what type am I?" he asked.

"You're the type that asks a lot of questions."

"You gotta ask if you want to know," said Joe.

"You could always look it up in your *Merck Manual*." She smiled.

"Very funny," he said. "I'm trying to understand the situation here, and I'll bet you know plenty."

"Maybe," she said, sipping her coffee.

"When are you going to tell me?"

"Oh, Joe! You certainly do try to get your way. . . . Okay, I'll tell you about Zilk," she said finally, "but believe me, it's not a pleasant story."

"Just tell me."

"I know he's cruel. I know he treats the patients like animals. I know everyone gets really uptight when he's working in the ER." There was a long pause. "And I also know he's probably insane."

"Insane? You mean really crazy, like psycho ward stuff?"

"Yes," said Elena, her dark eyes troubled, "like psycho ward stuff."

"I mean I can see he's a real bastard but he's still a doctor. They wouldn't let him stay if he was really wacko," said Joe quickly, ". . . or would they?"

"He's still here, isn't he?" said Elena, sipping her coffee.

Joe glanced over at Zilk's table. He and Mike were carrying their trays toward the door. Zilk didn't look any different to Joe.

"Tell me what happened."

"He pulled a little stunt about eight months ago," said Elena slowly.

"What kind of a stunt?"

"Well, this beautiful black go-go dancer had taken LSD. She was pregnant and came into the Emergency Room begging for an abortion. Zilk called up to the OB-GYN resident. He found out they were running a small experimental series on salinization abortions. It's really a safe technique where they insert an angiocath into the uterus and infiltrate with about five hundred cc's of saline. They abort within six hours. But Zilk didn't tell the girl about the study. Instead, he gave her the whole bit about how he had a friend in the OB-GYN department, and he might be able to open some doors and get the procedure done, but first she had to do something for him. He said if she really wanted the abortion, she'd better meet him in the staff house after hours."

"Zilk did that? Why didn't she complain to someone?" asked Joe.

"Sure," said Elena, "how would she know to do that? And who would believe her anyway? Well, once he got her to his room not only did he sexually abuse her, but he demanded she come home with him. When they got to his apartment, he made her strip and crawl on all fours. He has a great dane and he made her wear the dog's collar and eat out of the dog's bowl."

"How did you find that out?" asked Joe, stunned.

"They did the procedure down here. The anesthesiologist used ketamine as the agent. She developed an adverse reaction and really started to trip out. I heard her hallucinating. Everyone else dismissed her ramblings as secondary to the ketamine. I didn't think so. I followed it up and went to her apartment a week later. I wanted her to tell me the whole story. She finally did, but she was too frightened and refused to testify. I went to the nursing supervisor, but there was nothing we could do without her." She shook her head. "The word is out on the streets. I wouldn't be surprised if something happened to him."

"You mean they'd kill him?" asked Joe, shocked.

"People have been killed for a lot less."

"You mean someone on the street would just grab Zilk and kill him?" Joe asked again.

31

"That's exactly what I mean. It may seem unbelieveable to you, but here . . . things happen."

"Zilk . . ." said Joe. His face drained of color when he thought of what had been done to the girl. How could a doctor do such a thing? How could any man do such a thing? Elena was right, Zilk sounded like a real mental case. How long could he remain in the hospital without anyone noticing? He didn't hear Elena at first telling him it was time to go. He picked up his tray, walked over to the huge garbage pail, dumped his food into it, and started back down to the Emergency Room, suddenly depressed.

"Sorry," said Elena, "it's not Amherst."

There were eleven patients waiting for them when they got back to the ER; all from one car accident. They jabbered at each other in Spanish; half of them were holding their necks. One overweight woman had fainted and was lying on a bench. Two of her relatives frantically fanned her; her skirt rode up her huge thighs. As they continued to the back area, Joe turned to Elena.

"The only thing that scene is missing is two chickens."

Elena burst out laughing. "We had the chickens for lunch."

"Well, let's hope that we still don't have that crowd here for dinner."

It took them more than two hours to discharge the overexcited occupants. He smiled at Elena. Damp curls fell over her right eye. "How are we doing?" he asked.

"I think that we got them all."

"Where is Arnost?"

"He's over on the medicine side, trying to start an IV. Come, I want you to meet Mrs. Cleveland. She's the best nurse in the whole city. She's been working the three to eleven shift for twelve years."

Joe walked into the nursing station. Bea Cleveland was a six-foot tall, thin, striking, black woman. She was standing against the medicine cabinet with her arms folded. She was about forty and wore her hair in a thick afro.

"Hello, Mrs. Cleveland," said Joe.

She extended her hand. "Welcome, Dr. Ruskin. I know it is going to be a real pleasure to work with you."

"Elena told me that you are the best. I know I'm really going to need your help."

"Now, now, Dr. Ruskin, Elena has already told me that

you're off to a fine start. And I am going to work the same with you, whether you butter me up or not." She smiled. "I think you better go help Arnost. He has already come back here three times for IV needles."

It took them forty minutes to start the IV on the old man. Joe then returned to the nursing station.

Bea Cleveland was just hanging up the phone. "Joe, I just got a call from main X-ray. The patient I sent over has a fracture dislocation of the right ankle."

"Is it badly displaced?"

"It can't be too bad. The ankle itself was only minimally deformed. I have already placed the call to Dr. Morin. He's the second year orthopedic resident." Suddenly, the telephone rang. "Speak of the devil," she said, picking up the receiver. "Hello, ER. Yes, Dr. Morin. We have a patient for you with a fracture dislocation of the right ankle."

"A fracture dislocation of the ankle?" came the thunderous reply. Bea pulled the receiver away from her ear. "A fracture dislocation is an acute orthopedic emergency," continued Morin. "I should have been called immediately. Where is the damn patient now?"

"In main X-ray," Bea Cleveland said into the mouthpiece.

"What's he doing there?" he yelled angrily. "Let me speak to the intern on duty."

"Certainly, Doctor," she said coldly. Bea pressed the receiver against her body. "That ass!" she whispered to Joe. "He wants to give you some heat now. Just mention Gold's name in the conversation. That'll cool him down quick."

Joe took the receiver from her. "Hi, my name is Joe Ruskin," he said. "I'm a surgical intern down here. We have a patient with a fracture dislocation of the right ankle."

"I know that, you idiot," yelled Morin. "I want to know what he's doing in main X-ray."

"Well," said Joe, "our technician was swamped, and Dr. Gold suggested that we send some of the overflow upstairs."

"Dr. Gold?" Morin's tone changed instantly. "Look, I just have to bivalve one cast. If you can get the patient back, I'll be down in ten minutes."

"Okay," replied Joe. "I'll hit him with seventy-five of Demerol on his way back."

"Great. That will really help me out."

Joe put the phone down and turned to Mrs. Cleveland. "Okay, now do you mind telling me what that was all about?"

"You're a quick learner. Morin's absolutely petrified of Gold. And he has a right to be."

"How come?"

"Once, when he was first-year general surgical resident, he accidentally cut a patient's common duct while he was doing a routine gallbladder. Gold reached across the patient and knocked Morin out with one blow, then proceeded to sew up the duct in thirty minutes."

"Dr. Gold did that?"

"Sure did. His rages are famous around here. I guess it's the job. He's aged an awful lot," she said, shaking her head.

"Thanks for the dirt." Joe smiled.

Bea gave him a wide grin. "We try to take care of our own down here."

Joe walked into the second suture room. Arnost was slumped against the stretcher, and Elena was seated in a chair, her feet resting against the top of a metal trash can mounted on three wheels.

"Hey, do either of you smoke? I'm dying for a cigarette. I can't believe I've gone without one since seven o'clock," Joe asked.

"I have a few Marlboros, but I am going to charge you two cents for each one." Elena smiled.

"I left a whole pack in the car, and I had to park miles from here, next to a fire hydrant. Where did you park?" Joe asked Arnost.

"Oh, I park in the lot, but it cost me five dollars. The man at the gate said that I had no sticker."

Elena started to laugh. "There are no stickers for house staff. That's George. Rumor has it he makes a hundred bucks a week selling spaces in the hospital parking lot. He's a pretty smart old bird, though. He makes everyone pay, except the chief residents. He knows the ranks and knows what he can get away with. If the chief resident ever mentioned that to Gold he would have George's job. George has been at Jefferson for fifteen years."

The aroma of steamed meat and vegetables hit Joe and Elena as soon as they reached the cafeteria. Susan spotted them, carrying their trays to a table in the far corner of the room.

"How are you doing?" she asked, sitting at the table.

"Not bad," answered Joe. "I sort of missed a fracture dislocation. The IV line went great. I did bag it by going too deep, but I got it going on the same shot."

"What happened when Morin found out about the fracture?"

"When Mrs. Cleveland told me the story about him and Gold, I just used Gold's name, and he simmered down like a puppy dog."

Susan laughed. "I remember that case. I just came in for the last forty-five minutes. Morin was on the floor and Gold was using him as a footstool. I mean Morin wasn't unconscious, but he was just afraid to get up. Gold kept his shoe firmly on Morin's back, while he was performing this phenomenal repair. Morin has never forgotten. It's funny, but I don't think Gold even remembers who Morin is."

Susan finished her coffee. "Look people, I have to get upstairs. I don't really expect anything bad tonight, but you never know."

As Susan left the room, Joe leaned over to Elena. "Susan is really unbelieveable. She's so smooth."

"Susan is a special person all right. It's just too bad her home life can't match her work life."

"What do you mean?"

"She's basically very unhappy. She grew up in Rochester, and then went to Radcliffe. She was first in her class. Then she graduated AOA from Western Reserve. Now, she's on her second husband. During college she married her hometown boyfriend, who then proceeded to become an alcoholic. When Susan decided to go to medical school, there was no way for that relationship to continue."

"So now she's married again?" asked Joe.

"That's right," Elena continued, "she married the smartest chief medical resident. It was like a hollywood romance. All the administrators and chiefs of services considered it the storybook finish. Except, the guy is really rigid and Susan is a very warm human being. He's on a one-year fellowship in Cincinnati. Frankly, I don't think this one is going to last either."

"It sounds like you don't like the guy."

"It's not that I don't like him, but I really like Susan. She's a great human being. I just wish she could be a little happier."

"What about you?" Joe asked softly.

"You're a funny guy," she said with a puzzled look on her face. "Are you always so direct?"

"When I want to get to know people better, yes, I guess I am."

"And you want to get to know me better?" she asked, folding the napkin into a fan.

"Sure. Look, I didn't mean anything bad by it. It's just that I've never met anyone like you before."

"Why am I so different?"

"Well, you're Spanish for one thing."

"Puerto Rican," she corrected him.

"And you've lived in the South Bronx all your life. I feel like a complete outsider and somehow terribly guilty. You seem to know so much and I want to learn."

"And what exactly do you want to learn?"

"I want to learn about you, and I want to learn about this community. I was assigned to work here, but you're doing it out of choice. How come?"

"It's just the way things happened, I guess," she said. "But now after all these years, I feel like I've made a commitment. Maybe, my staying here will make some difference."

Joe studied her. "No one can say you're not doing your part. Is your whole family this dedicated?"

"Actually," she said, "I only have a younger brother. Both my parents are dead."

"I'm sorry."

"It happened a long time ago. My father died while we were still in Puerto Rico. My mother died here almost ten years ago."

"What became of your brother?"

"He became a brave, strong man. He is going to college, and I love him dearly. He is all I have left." Elena fell silent. Over the last year she had hardly seen her brother and she knew he was back fooling with heroin. "Well," she said, suddenly looking at her watch, "enough about me. It's time to get back to work."

"Maybe we can talk again like this?" Joe asked.

"Sure. Maybe we can."

"You must really be dragging," Joe said, noting her sudden fatigue. She was working a double shift because one of the staff had called in sick.

"No, I'm all right. Anyway, if I'm really dead, I'll pop a Dex."

36

"You mean Dexedrine?"

"I am not a pill freak, but once in a while this grind can really wear you down."

They were in the reception area. Joe stared at the small cardboard sign taped above the double steel door, with the letters painted in black enamel.

"What does AMF mean?" he asked.

Elena did not seem to hear as she walked under the sign.

Outside the doors, backed up to the entrance was a huge boxlike ambulance with "City of New York, Department of Hospitals" printed on both side panels. The back of the ambulance was open, and two empty stretchers lay inside. Elena stopped. Leaning against the ambulance door were two Hispanic men in their late thirties. They nodded.

"Joe, this is Ramon. He likes to boast that he is the fastest ambulance driver in New York. He should have been a race car driver. At least he has a legal excuse to go tearing through the streets. Ramon saves patients, but he has already tipped over two ambulances. And this is Roberto, the ramp attendant."

"How ya' doin', Doc?" said Roberto, extending a strong hand.

"They keep you busy here," said Joe, returning the handshake.

"You know it," replied the stocky Puerto Rican.

"How many come through here?" asked Joe.

"About half of all patients brought to the ER," said Roberto. "Their friends bring 'em in. They drive up the ramp and swing open the car door. Then they drop the sick person out the door and speed down the ramp."

Joe let out a long, slow whistle.

"Usually these injuries are secondary to trauma, or they're overdoses," said Elena. "Their friends care enough that they want them to get to the hospital, so they can be cared for. But they themselves don't want to answer any questions from the police. It's Roberto's job to gather these people off the platform, and get them on stretchers. Roberto also helps unload the patients from the ambulances. He is quite a screener. If the patient is DOA and there is no hope, he won't even take him out. They will drive him down the ramp and make a one-hundred-eighty degree turn. Underneath the ramp is the entrance to the morgue. If the patient is still alive when they make it to the ramp, the odds are in his favor. If they stop breathing within five minutes of reaching the ramp, the odds are still in their favor. We've pulled through some real sickies."

"We sure have," said Roberto proudly. Ramon beamed.

"Yes, but no matter how hard we work, and how lucky we are, the neighborhood always wins. Some of our patients have been admitted four or five times for gunshot or knife wounds. We fix them up, but the neighborhood brings them back."

Elena continued past the ambulance to the edge of the platform, leaned against the railing, and took a deep breath. She scanned the skyline, marked by old brick buildings four and five stories high. The outline was broken by a flattened building or two on each street. Some had been burned, and some had just collapsed. The sun was setting, and there was a strange silence.

"Most weekends, you come out here at midnight, and you'd swear the whole neighborhood is exploding. You can see two or three buildings going up in flames, and the screams and yells in the streets seem to blend into a roar. I look down and I dream I was anywhere else in the entire country. But this is my home. These are my people." Suddenly she was silent.

"Joe, why don't you go over to the staff house and try and get a couple hours of sleep?" Joe started to protest.

"We'll page you if we need you. Better get some rest when you can."

5

The next thing he heard was the wail of the siren, then the phone. It was Elena. "Get down here, stat!"

He ran down to the trauma room. "Is that what I think it is?" Joe asked, trying to peer around Roberto.

"Yeah, he's got an arrow in his chest, and he don't seem to be breathin' too good."

Joe looked down at the young black. He couldn't take his eyes off the long wooden shaft with three green feathers on the end. With each breath, the shaft of the arrow moved.

"Need some help with this one?" asked Mrs. Cleveland.

"You'd better call Susan. Elena, get some oxygen going. We'd better draw a type and cross."

Joe listened to the left chest below the arrow entry. "There are no breath sounds and there's a hiss from around the entry. I need some Vaseline gauze."

Susan came rushing into the room. "What do you have?"

"Arrow in the left axillae. His lung is down. I think he needs a chest tube."

"I'm sure he might, Joe, but let's just clamp that arrow for now, so we can make sure it doesn't move and cause any further damage. We better get an X ray."

Within a few minutes, Susan was reading the X ray as Joe and Arnost looked on. "He has to be explored. His lung is lacerated and air is escaping. Besides, I don't see how we're going to get that arrow out, just by pulling on it. It splintered his rib. We'd better take him upstairs and see what's going on."

Mrs. Cleveland had called ahead to alert the elevator operator and he was waiting as they rounded the corner. They rode up to the fifth floor. Joe led the stretcher out of the elevator. Barilla was at the sink, scrubbing his hands, as the door opened.

"Thanks, Joe. We can take it from here," he yelled from the sink area. "A fucking bow and arrow!" He stood shaking his head. "If they had bazookas, I'm sure they'd use them, too. I've seen machetes, and I've even seen crowbars, but a bow and arrow? Is this the only victim, or did they get anyone else in the wagon train?" Barilla gave a raucous laugh as he continued to scrub his hands.

Joe rode down in the elevator. He wished he could stay and watch the procedure, but he had a job in the Emergency Room; his responsibilities had increased enormously. With Susan and Barilla tied up in the OR, the only senior surgeon in the entire hospital was Matt Zilk.

Joe found Arnost at work on a second-degree burn. "Where are the girls?" he asked.

"In the nursing station. Joe, there is a person in the second suture room with a very big abscess that almost covers his entire arm. He must administer drugs or something."

"Okay, I'll check it out." Joe walked into the nurses station. "How's the young man doing?" asked Mrs. Cleveland.

"Not too bad," said Joe. "His film showed an air fluid level and his lung is down, but it looks like the arrow caught in one of his ribs. Have you seen many of those?"

"About six a year," Bea answered. "Those dudes break into a sporting goods store looking for guns, but the guns are locked up. A hunting bow can really do a job, and on top of that, they're silent. Oh, that reminds me, Sergeant Murray is waiting at the desk. He wants to question you about that patient."

"Arnost tells me there's an abscess."

"Yeah, an addict on six caps a day," answered Elena.

"What does that mean?"

"That's about a two-hundred and fifty dollar a day habit," said Elena.

"How big is the abscess?"

"Big, really big."

"Okay, I'd better go check it out before I deal with the cop."

In the suture room a boy of seventeen was bent over on the stretcher. His right arm hung down. From across the room Joe could see the arm was three times the normal size. He walked back to the nurses' station. "Get me a hundred of Demerol. Does this kid have a fever?"

"One hundred three point two," said Elena.

"Get me Zilk on the phone. I don't know if he can open up another room, but this patient needs an incision and drainage under general anesthesia."

Bea Cleveland looked down at the floor, embarrassed. Elena stood up. "Frankly, Joe, you're just wasting your time."

"What do you mean?"

"Zilk is going to want you to drain that down here."

"Come on!"

"Well, just be prepared."

"Thanks, Elena. I'll be down by the desk if Zilk wants to speak to me."

Joe walked over to the desk. A nervous man of about forty-five was carefully reviewing a chart. He had a sharp, receding hairline and his black hair was combed straight back. He wore a wrinkled seersucker suit. The knot on his tie was uneven, and he had on shiny rubber-soled cordovan shoes.

"Hi, my name is Joe Ruskin. I understand you wanted to speak to me."

"When they brought that kid in, did he say anything?"

"He was almost comatose."

40

"Yeah, but did he say anything?"

"No, he just cried a few times in pain."

"How is he going to be?"

"I think he'll be okay. We have him up in the OR now. He appears to have been lucky. The arrow pierced one of his ribs."

"Hey, ain't that a pisser, Doc? These fuckin' junkies will use anything. It was a holdup in a blind stairwell. The kid was a setup. The guy didn't have more than three bucks on him. These *cucarachas* are like vermin. They will tear your guts out for a couple of bucks.

"So, you think if this guy pulls through, he is going to tell who did it?" asked Joe.

"Bullshit. You haven't been around very long, Doc? The law of the street is simple. Never be a stoolie. I hope they all kill each other. Then we can lock up the rest, and I can go to Florida. Look, if he gets better, and starts talking, give me a call at the Forty-first Precinct. On the job, we call it Fort Apache. Ask for Murray."

Joe felt a heavy hand on his left shoulder. He turned around and faced Zilk. "I took a look at that junky punk with the abcess. I think you better drain it, Doc."

"Drain it down here in the Emergency Room?" Joe protested.

"Why not? That kid doesn't deserve any better. These junk-heads are high as a kite all the time anyway. He won't even feel it."

"Look, Matt, I really think the wound ought to be drained in an operating room under sterile conditions, under general anesthesia."

"Frankly, Ruskin, I don't give a crap what you think. I am the third-year resident around here, and you are a piece of shit intern. With Barilla tied up, I am the chief surgical resident in this hospital, and I give the orders."

"Okay, can I call in a second anesthesiologist? At least if we give him some gas, it won't hurt so much."

"Ruskin, that is ridiculous. Go in there and drain the abscess. Oh, you'd better wear a mask. When you open that pus pocket, it is going to stink to high heaven."

Zilk turned to Murray. "You still chasing ambulances, you dumb flatfoot?" he greeted his friend.

Joe walked back into the treatment room. The hundred of Demerol had quieted the youth down, so Joe could inspect the arm. The abscess began above the top of his shoulder and

41

continued laterally down to the elbow joint. The skin over this area was white and tense. The rest of his arm was also markedly swollen, but here the skin was red and flushed.

Joe walked back into the nurses station. "Elena, I'm going to need your help."

"I am sorry, Joe. I knew that was going to happen."

"Well, get me some Valium, and we'll start an IV line. We'll give it to him slowly and really lay him out."

Joe walked back into the treatment room. "You have a large abscess. It's causing your whole body to be sick. We have to get the pus out. I'm going to start an IV. I'm going to inject some medicine, and you'll feel very sleepy. You won't actually be asleep, but you'll feel very little." The youth moaned softly.

"I am going to put this small needle into your arm."

"Anything, I'll do anything, but don't hurt me," he sobbed.

Joe drove the needle into the small vein and slowly injected two cc's of Valium. Within minutes the patient was half asleep.

"Leave the syringe in, Elena. If he starts to come out, hit him with one more cc."

Joe walked over to the shoulder area. He carefully painted the entire arm with the brown antiseptic soap. Then he opened an I and D tray. One sharp thin number eleven blade was already attached to a handle. There were also several large rubber drains, with safety pins through one end. Joe began to palpate the fluid-distended mass, it was the size of a watermelon. He chose the site for incision over the most prominent portion.

As he drove the blade down a geyser of thick brown syrupy material shot half way across the room. The sulfur-loaded smell caused by the gas forming-bacteria made Joe acutely nauseous. "Ayyy . . ." The young man lifted his arm and pushed ineffectively against Joe. Joe bent over as the spasm gripped his stomach. Elena injected more Valium.

Joe regained his composure and spread open the wound with a long curved clamp; a thicker fountain gushed between the reddened edges. He started to milk the liquid abscess material. As the clumpy, necrotic fluid began to collect on the floor beneath the patient Elena used her foot to roll the metal wastebasket under the draining area.

Joe injected some Xylocaine into the skin above the shoulder and pressed the knife deeply into the thickened white line. As the blade came through into the angry abscess cavity the patient started to rise. Elena injected the last cc of the Valium. Joe made another cut, one inch above the patient's elbow.

"I better irrigate that. Get me a liter of antibiotic solution and a large syringe."

Joe pointed the glass tip into the main opening. As he flushed the fluid into the now empty cavity, the sound of the patient's sobbing was drowned out by the belching exit of the clearing material.

"Elena, get another cc of Valium."

"Joe, you've already given him three."

"If he stops breathing, we'll bag him until the Valium wears off. I still have to insert a Penrose drain to keep it opened, and it's probably going to be the worst part."

Elena administered the Valium, and the patient's breathing became noticeably shallow.

"Well, here goes nothing." Joe placed the tip of the rubber drain beneath the two pointed jaws of the long curved clamp. He introduced the clamp beneath the skin, through the bottom incision. He traced the point to the middle opening. As the tip penetrated the skin, Joe grabbed the edge of the rubber tubing and pulled upward. The young man began to twitch. Joe repeated the same procedure, using the upper incision as the entry wound and bringing the edge of the second rubber drain also through the middle opening. Then he carefully fastened the safety pin, connecting both edges. "Get me a couple of four-inch Kerlix rolls please, and you better drop two grams of Keflin into the IV bottle. We'll keep him down here as long as we can. Make sure we give him a hundred of Demerol every three or four hours."

Joe's face was white. He found himself swallowing rapidly as the acid secretions surged up his esophagus.

"I am sorry," he said, smoothing the matted hair of the now sleeping young man. He opened the door and walked out into the hall.

The two gangs massed on opposite ends of the lot, eyeing each other cautiously across the field. Only a few faded yellow parking lines remained, broken by deep ruts in the asphalt. One stark street light magnified the presence of the milling forces, separated by fifty yards. The usual uproarious street sounds of vendors, laughing drunks, quarreling couples, and screeching cars dimmed.

They stared across the field.

"I don't like it. They must have fifty men," said Paco nervously.

"But we've got Toros," said Ino.

"I'm afraid."

"So are they," said Ino, shoving one of the guns into Paco's hand.

Hernandez, leader of the Five C's, took one step forward and waved a white handkerchief. "Sanchez, I want to talk to you," he said in a challenging voice.

"Talk from here," whispered Paco.

"Man to man," mocked Hernandez, taking a few steps onto the asphalt. His legs were apart, and he placed both hands on his hips.

The rest of the Toros stopped their ritualistic parrying and held their weapons at their side.

"It's a trick," warned Paco.

But Ino had already nodded to one of the Vegas brothers, and he slowly stepped forward. "You come with me," Ino ordered. "Paco, give him the gun."

"Please," implored Paco, "at least take me."

"Shit, he just wants to talk." Ino looked into Vegas's eyes. Paco handed him the gun. "Stay close behind me and watch his hands."

Ino moved toward his rival. Two of the Five C's broke rank and trotted to catch up with their leader. By now, Ino was halfway across the field. From the corner of his eye he saw Vegas several steps behind. "Get up here," he snapped. But before he could look up, he felt a volcanic crushing in his chest and his head snapped down. He saw a stiletto sticking through his jacket, and then he saw nothing as he fell forward, held up by the crook of Hernandez's right arm plunging the knife deeper into his chest.

There were wild gunshots, and Hernandez saw the Toros race forward, crazed. He tried to pull the knife out from under Ino's slumped body, but it was stuck between the ribs. He twisted viciously and felt the knife loosen and drop from the body. He began to run, stopping once he hit the street. He was safe. He turned to see the dazed Toros gather around Sanchez and begin

"Where is the goddamn blade? Get me a ten blade." Joe squeezed the blade between his thumb and index finger. He did not wait to find a scalpel handle. He brought the blade down right at the point of the stab wound and continued curving around the patient's side, until the blade was flush with the black pad on the stretcher. On his next thrust he came down onto the dull white rib. He traced the border of the rib along the path of the original opening. He brought the blade slightly above the rib. The third incision was greeted by a loud hiss of air. Joe put his left index finger in the opening and reached for the tray. Mrs. Cleveland had already switched into gloves and was holding a large curved scissors.

He cut through the remaining muscles. Bea handed him a large metal rib spreader. He took one edge of the bent hook and placed it above the border of the fifth rib. At the same time, she attached the upper edge to the lower level of the fourth rib. Joe turned the handle on the side of the instrument. The chest cavity gaped open.

The lung had collapsed, but there was no obvious bleeding. The heart sac was bathed in a dark blue color. There was no motion. The blood had filled the sac to the point that it compressed the heart itself. Joe grabbed the pickups from the tray and carefully nicked the sac. From the opening poured huge clots of fresh blood. As the clots settled to the bottom of the lung cavity, he spread the leatherlike covering with his fingers.

The heart responded to the sudden release of pressure. It gave two irregular beats, then stopped. In the mid-portion directly below the knife entry wound, was a large opening.

"Give me some one to one thousand solution epinephrine." Joe drove the needle of the syringe into the heart muscle several inches below his finger. Then he began to rhythmically massage the heart against the chest wall.

Arnost yelled out, "IV line." The plasma line was quickly connected to his neck. Joe looked up.

"Great going, Arnost. He has a knife wound in the left ventrical. See if you can start another line in his left arm. We'd better get some bicarbonate into him."

The heart began to contract slowly. The epinephrine was working. Fresh blood poured out from the edges around Joe's finger.

"Give me some 3-0 silk. I'll try to purse-string it."

Bea took the suture with the long tapered cutting needle,

loaded it onto the clamp, and placed it in Joe's right hand. He surrounded his finger with four deep bites of muscle. Arnost had managed to get a second line going, and he too slipped on a pair of gloves.

"Throw down a tie as I slip my finger out," Joe directed.

As Arnost pressed the first loop of the knot downward, the inside edges of the wound folded out. Joe put in a second tie and stepped back.

"We've got a sinus tachycardia, about one-sixty."

The medical resident had heard the commotion and was rapidly scanning the EKG machine. A small amount of bright red blood still pumped from the center of the opening. "I better put one more suture around that," Joe said as he studied the opening.

Bea Cleveland switched positions and now had her hands on either side of the patient's groin. "He has full femoral pulses, Doctor!"

"We've just about got the bleeding controlled up here, too. I think we got him." Joe carefully placed the second suture, making sure to leave a one-inch perimeter around the knot. "Push the knot deep into the cavity," he directed Arnost as he squeezed down. The suture tightened. It had worked. The laceration was now completely closed.

"I don't know what you guys are doing in there, but it's obviously good," responded the medical resident, studying the rhythm strip. "He's got a steady sinus tack, and he's down to about one-twenty."

Joe began to inspect the inside of the lung cavity. He lifted the heart forward. "Back wall is clean. He just missed his left anterior descending artery," pointing to the thick vessel that continued down the entire wall of the heart.

"Luis, stop squeezing on the bag for a second. . . . Good." There was no bleeding from the lung. "Arnost, draw a couple of samples of blood from the line in his neck. Elena, get the blood up to the blood bank."

Joe looked up. Elena was still huddled in the corner of the trauma room. She was bent over and her hands were covering her face. She was shaking. "Elena, I said get the blood to the blood bank." She did not respond.

"Let her be." Luis half sobbed. "I'll run them." Handing Arnost the bag, he ran out with the tubes.

"He has a blood pressure of eighty over fifty," said Bea.

"You better call the OR and tell them to get another room

ready, and tell Susan what's going on down here. Then call up the blood bank and tell Luis to pick up a unit of O negative."

Joe unwound the rib spreader and removed the massive instrument. He placed the sharp edges of a towel clamp above and below the fourth and fifth rib. As he squeezed down, the left chest wall closed. Joe stepped back and removed his gloves.

The stolen Buick peeled down the ramp.

"Park across the street," Paco ordered.

"He looked real bad," said the young driver.

"He'll make it. Nothing can kill him." Paco thought of Ino's cold skin and lifeless resistance as he helped lift him onto the stretcher. He checked himself quickly, remembering the many times Ino had somehow escaped harm. Another sedan, loaded with five youths, pulled up alongside.

"What's happening?" asked Angel, hanging over the front door.

"We got him inside. They're fixing him up now."

"Then let's split. There'll be cops all over this place."

"Not till we're sure he's okay. A couple of you get out and hang on each corner. Tell the other cars to keep circling. No one gets into the cutting room. Not even drunks."

"What about the fucking C's? I think we got one, when we were pulling out."

Paco reached into the glove compartment and brought out two revolvers. He passed one out through the window. "Use this if you have to," he stated coldly. "I said no one gets into that place until Ino is taken care of."

"How we gonna know that?" asked Angel, clutching his gun.

"We'll know. Now keep circling and don't bunch up."

Joe checked the patient's pulse. Nothing to do now but wait for the blood. He was stabilized and would just require formal antibiotic irrigation in the OR before closure.

The room was a mess. The floor was littered with blood-stained clothes, a broken IV bottle, and a mountain of discarded surgical wrappings.

Joe felt an uncontrollable urge for a cigarette. He bent down and began to fish through the blood soaked jeans. In the right rear pocket he felt a small square plastic container. He knew instinctively it was heroin. He slid the container into the palm of his hand and with one swift motion transferred the package to his left shirt pocket. He was still kneeling under the stretcher, and he was sure no one had seen him.

All of a sudden, Zilk was in the doorway. "What the hell is going on?"

"It's a stab wound of the heart. We already have two purse-string sutures in, and the bleeding is controlled. He's got a blood pressure, and we're just waiting for some O negative blood."

"Then, what the hell were you doing on the floor?"

"I was looking for a cigarette."

"You're looking for a cigarette. Ruskin, you really are a stupid shit." He reached in his jacket. "Here," he said as he extended a Camel. "Don't say I never gave you anything."

Sergeant Murray walked in. "Goddamn punks finally did it. They've been threatening this gang war on and off for the last six months. It happened about half an hour ago, in that parking lot next to the movie house on Fox Street. Fifty-five young killer punks slashing each other with knives, pipes, and chains. All over by the time we got there." Murray stepped closer to the stretcher and whistled. "Son of a bitch, that's Ino Sanchez."

"Who's Ino Sanchez?" asked Zilk.

"Ino Sanchez is the leader of the Young Toros. For twelve years, I've tried to get his ass. His gang alone is responsible for at least fifty percent of all the violence in the neighborhood. In the street, they treat him like a god. He don't look so godlike right now. He going to make it?"

"Yes," said Zilk.

Instantly, Murray's attitude changed. "Boy, would I like to get something on that punk. Maybe he still has a weapon. Also, I know he dabs in junk. Where are his clothes?"

Mrs. Cleveland stepped forward, blocking him. "Isn't any place sacred?" she said, pushing against him.

"Police business, hon." Murray brushed her aside and knelt down to thumb through the debris. He was careful to avoid the jellylike clots that had collected directly under the stretcher.

"I found his shirt," yelled Murray, and he and Zilk began to thumb through the pockets. All they found was a small rusty key. "Nothing," summarized Murray.

Zilk stood clutching Ino's blood-drenched pants. They repeated the search. Murray retrieved a leather wallet. In it were two small folded pieces of white paper with telephone numbers on them, a black-and-white snapshot of an older Hispanic woman, and a faded confirmation picture of Ino. The rest of the search was futile.

"Nothing." Murray was disgusted and angry. He addressed Mrs. Cleveland. "I want you to understand that all the contents of this room are police property."

"Not the patient, Sarge."

Joe led the stretcher out of the trauma room, and Zilk was forced to follow.

Luis was waiting in the hall on the fifth floor, holding a unit of typed blood. "It isn't crossed matched, but he is B negative. It'll take another twenty minutes to get two units cross matched."

They pushed the stretcher into the Operating Room. A nurse-anesthesiologist in her early thirties had been called. Expertly, she slid the large plastic tube down the patient's trachea. She connected the tube leading from the anesthesia table and began to turn several dials. Joe slipped on a pair of gloves and removed the towel clamp. He began to wash the outside of the chest with the surgical soap. Small bubbles rose from the surface. Zilk entered, gowned and gloved. He inserted the rib spreader. Joe tried to peer over his shoulder.

"Well, Ruskin, it looks like you finally did something right," he said, as he inspected each area. "That purse string suture is a little crude, but you did the job. Now don't you feel proud of yourself? This punk will be out on the streets in two weeks, seeking revenge, killing innocent people, and protecting his honor. If you had any conscience at all, you would have let him cool."

"I am trying to be a doctor," countered Joe.

"Trying to be a doctor? You're a real asshole."

"Frankly, Zilk, coming from you, I consider that a compliment."

"Ruskin, get the fuck out of here. Get downstairs to the Emergency Room, where you belong, and get back to work. I'm in charge of this patient now."

As Joe rode down the elevator he brushed his right hand against his shirt pocket, checking for the bulge. He slipped into a vacant corridor and transferred the plastic envelope into his right sock. He wasn't sure what to do with it, but he knew that he didn't want Zilk or that Sergeant to find it.

He swung the doors of the ER open slowly. The hall was empty. There were no loud screams, no muffled sobbings. At the nurses station Bea Cleveland had already finished her narcotics count and was relating the problems of the last shift to an older woman, who wore her gray hair tied tightly back in a ponytail.

"Congratulations. Bea was just telling me she thought your young man was dead," the new nurse greeted him.

"How's he doing?" Bea Cleveland asked.

"Not bad at all. We got a unit of blood going on him, and Zilk is just washing him out upstairs. He seems totally stable. Where's the Sergeant?" Joe asked.

"He finally left, but he'll be back. We still have one major problem: Elena. That was her brother on the table."

Joe's chin dropped. "That's impossible. He's in college."

"College? He's been on the streets for ten years."

"And from the looks of his arm into some heavy drugs." Joe paused, stunned. "No wonder. But he's going to be all right. She knows that, doesn't she?"

"Joe, I don't think she knows anything right now."

"Where is she?"

"In the plaster room. Arnost and Luis are with her."

Joe ran down the hall. Elena was seated on a stretcher. Joe grabbed her by both shoulders. "He's going to be all right."

"He was stabbed in the heart," she sobbed. "He's dead." Joe started to shake her. "He's going to be all right." She didn't seem to hear. Joe brought his right palm sharply across her left cheek. Elena looked up suddenly.

"I swear to you he's going to be all right."

"Do you mean that?"

"He had a small stab wound in the left wall of his heart. Once we put a stitch in, the hole was closed. His heart had stopped because of the pressure of the blood filling the outer sac. It was a simple cardiac tamponade."

"A tamponade is never simple."

"This one was. The medical resident said the EKG already looked normal. You know if there was any damage to the heart itself it would show up there. And the wound in the heart wall will heal in no time. Honestly, Elena, he's going to be fine."

"Where is he?" she asked nervously.

"Zilk is just washing him out upstairs. Elena, you just did a double shift. You're exhausted. Why don't you go lie down in my room. I promise to call you if there's any change."

Too tired to argue, she followed him around the mass of people who had collected on the platform and down the covered walkway toward the staff house. Then he quickly bent over and reached for his sock. He handed her the plastic envelope. "Elena, get rid of this."

She stared, then touched him tenderly on the cheek. "You are a dear, sweet man."

"Elena, you can do one thing for me in return."

"Anything, Joe."

"Do you have any more of those Dex on you?"

"I have one more." Elena reached into her pocket and handed him the small yellow pill.

Joe swallowed it. "Thanks. You get some sleep; you've had some day."

Elena walked away. Joe stared at her. She was as lush and soft as a woman could be.

Arnost sat on a stool in the nurses station, contemplating a cup of black coffee. Luis was checking the equipment. They both looked up as Joe returned.

"How's Elena doing?" Luis asked.

"She's sleeping."

"That is good," replied Arnost. "I know she doesn't understand all that I say, but she is a wonderful nurse."

"I'm starting to get the feeling all the nurses down here are top of the line. But where are all the patients?"

"I don't know," Luis looked up. "No one has signed in in the last half hour."

A short disheveled figure with thick glasses, wearing an OR gown, entered the nursing station. "Hi, I'm Bob Kendricks, the intern on the wards. Susan told me to come down and give you guys a hand. I didn't expect you to be sitting on your asses."

"How's that arrow kid doing?" asked Joe.

"We fixed him. Susan's just closing. I can't believe there's nothing happening."

"You have no knowledge of the gang battle?" asked Arnost.

"A gang war!" Kendricks's eyes opened wide. "Like *West Side Story*? That was my favorite show!"

"I don't think they dance," said Joe.

"So where are they?" Kendricks bubbled.

"One's upstairs with Zilk. Stab of the heart."

"Wow! But shouldn't there be more?" He poked his head out the door, searching the hall.

"Don't worry," said Luis, loading an IV bottle. "They'll be here."

"I hope so," said Kendricks. "Zilk told me about some of those gang girls. One came in with a tattoo right above her pubic hair. It had the gang's name and an arrow pointing down here." He moved his hand to his groin. "She had this huge knife strapped to her thigh." Kendricks emphasized by spreading his hands, then adjusted his glasses. "Isn't this place incredible?" Kendricks then noticed Luis, who was studying him guardedly. "No harm meant." Suddenly there was the siren. "What's that?" he asked.

"I think that's the rest of your gang," said Luis.

"Oh, boy! I better run up and tell Susan. . . . And on my first night."

Joe, Arnost, and Luis ran to the trauma room. The studded Toros jacket lay hanging over the stretcher.

"Shit!" said Joe, checking the boy's arm. "He's got a pulse of one-sixty. Get some plasma up."

"You'd better move. I got two more in the hall," said Roberto.

"Thanks," said Joe, pressing down on the oozing wound of the boy's forearm.

Roberto started bringing in the remnants of the gang war, and Joe had no time to think. He just worked as fast as he could:

"It's his belly, left upper quadrant, a stab." Clear yellow fluid poured from the edge each time the boy took a deep breath.

"Where the hell is the blood?" Lap pads covered with clots of blood lay all about the room.

"Get the handkerchief off his thigh. Looks bad." The deep laceration had torn through the muscles. The edges, already taking on a grayish cast, flapped out of the opening, twitching uncontrollably.

"This one's all yours, Arnost."

The little yellow pill was taking effect. Joe was caught up in the rush.

Susan came down from the OR about midnight. "Oh, you sweet pussycat," she gushed in Joe's ear. "Sanchez was a cardiac tamponade. I've only seen three in my life. I lost one, but he had also cut his aorta. You're one for one. Gold will be so happy, he may even go away for two days. I like him a lot more when he's sunburned. It sort of hides his rages."

She started to leave, and Joe grabbed her by the arm. "Remind me to tell you a story about Zilk when we're alone."

"Is it about an addict?"

"How did you . . ."

"I don't know, but I can already believe it. Zilk is weird about addicts. Look, I complained to Gold about him. Gold hates him, but he can't dismiss him. I know for a fact that Zilk is transferring to OB-GYN next year. Don't worry. Everything works out. I have to go feed Barilla another meal."

Cardiac tamponade. This one was impressive. He felt a surge of pride, then a queasy, shaky feeling; the Dex was wearing off.

Sergeant Murray reappeared about two A.M. He barged into the room where Joe was working. "Doc," he called, his cigar smoke filling the room.

"You know what these crazy *cucarachas* did now? Their leader gets a knife in the heart within the first minute of the fight. So the fight stops, right? The Young Toros grab him and head for this place. The car goes all the way up the ramp. One of the members of the other gang was cut up, and they try to bring him in. Sanchez's group intercepts them. War breaks out again right here, at the hospital! There are a couple of shots, and one of the Five C's gets it in the chest. We just checked him into the morgue."

"That's why no one signed in," Joe said. "They couldn't. That's terrible."

"Terrible?" Murray snickered. "You know what the name Five C's stand for? Five *caballeros* who cut ass with knives. So there'll be one less *caballero* to worry about.

"Who do we have here on the stretcher?" Murray looked down at the teenager and began to rifle through the pockets of the denim jacket.

"Sergeant Murray, would you please? We are trying to save this young boy's life."

"Young boy's life, my ass." He took his fist and rubbed it into the boy's chest. "Listen, scum, tell me who knifed you."

"No comprendo."

"Tell me who knifed you, punk!" shouted Murray.

"No te entiendo."

"You're so full of shit it's running out your leg. I hope you all kill yourselves. A bunch of young savages with nothing to do but cut each other up." He spat on the floor.

The boy struggled to sit up. "We fight for our honor," he snapped in English.

"Your honor doesn't mean shit. If you have so much honor, why the hell don't you get a job?" He threw his hands up and turned to Joe. "The old men sit and drink, and the young ones sit and stew, and then about once every six months they fight, and they kill, and then they stew for another six months. Five hundred thousand people, and they're all in my precinct." He shook his head and marched out.

Zilk appeared in the doorway, holding a wet X ray.

"What the fuck is going on down here? It's Wednesday night, and there's not even a full moon. Ruskin, who the hell ever taught you to put in a chest tube?" He glared at Joe.

"The lung's up and there's no hemothorax."

"Well, it's a shitty job, and he needs a chest tube in the right side also." Joe was relieved to see him leave.

By five A.M., Joe and Arnost were finished. There were no more patients. The victims of the gang war had all been treated. Two lay on cold slabs beneath the ramp, and four rested on beds in the crowded Intensive Care Unit.

Arnost staggered slightly as he got off the stool. "You better get some sleep, my friend. You look bagged. I'll take anything that comes in," offered Joe.

Joe took advantage of the lull to check on the patients in ICU. Even before he pushed open the door, he could hear the loud rhythmic groan of the breathing machines and the high pitched bleeps of the cardiogram scanners. A nurse was struggling to adjust the respirator attached to the tube leading down Ino Sanchez's throat.

"He keeps fighting the breathing machine. Dr. Zilk refused to order any pain medication."

Joe evaluated the situation, then pulled the tube. He held his hand against Ino's open mouth. His breathing was even and strong. His cardiogram rhythm was regular. There was little blood draining from the chest tube. He held Ino's hand. Ino squeezed back.

"Can you talk?" asked Joe.

Ino made a shaking effort to lift his head. "The back of my throat is like fire. My chest hurts each time I breathe."

"You were stabbed in the heart, but you're going to be all right. Your left side hurts because there is a tube leading out from your chest. We can remove that in a few days. I'll get you some pain medicine so you can get some sleep. But before you turn in, I'd say a little prayer to your patron saint. You were dead when they brought you in."

6

Joe started for the staff house. His mind was reeling and he was exhausted and confused. He opened the door and saw Elena sleeping fitfully with a pillow under her knee. The headlights from Bruckner Expressway darted about, bouncing off the dresser mirror. Joe could make out the outline of her full bottom under the thin cotton panties.

He lit a half smoked cigarette he found lying in the ashtray. It made him cough.

Elena stirred slightly. "Joe?"

"Yes, Elena?"

"Is he . . ."

"Sh . . . sh . . . he's going to be fine. We're all going to be fine."

"Just hold me."

Torn between arousal and exhaustion, he drew her to him. He could feel her warmth descend over his aching body. He held her like that for a long time until he could feel himself slipping into a deep sleep.

The ringing startled him. He grabbed the phone and heard Arnost's voice. "Joe, are you missing breakfast?"

"What time is it?"

"It's eight o'clock and we have been dismissed for the day. You will meet me?"

Joe glanced over at Elena's body. "No, Arnost. You go ahead without me. I'll see you tomorrow."

She opened her eyes and saw him. The night returned. Her hair was a mass of black ringlets.

"He's going to be fine," he answered before she had to ask.

Elena stood up and the wrinkled sheet suddenly feel to the floor. Embarrassed, she picked it up and wrapped it around herself. She walked over to the dresser and faced him. "I've got to go see my brother now. But thanks," she said softly, touching his arm.

"For what?" he asked.

"For not taking advantage. You're a very special man." He smiled. "I trust you, and besides Ino, you're the only man I can say that about. But all I can ever be is your friend."

"I want to be your friend, too. If I make you uncomfortable o unhappy, tell me and I'll butt out."

They were standing only a few feet apart. "Okay, gringo, butt out." She laughed, breaking the tension, and then she moved closer. Suddenly, he was holding her, and she could hear his heart beating in his chest as his arms surrounded her.

They dressed quickly. Joe's eye fell on the plastic bag lying on the dresser. "We better get rid of this," he said. "Someone might see it lying around."

"That's the problem," she sighed, taking the bag and flushing it down the toilet. "It's always lying around."

They walked out of the staff house and stood on the ramp. It was empty and quiet. "Ino thinks he's stronger than the heroin but it's eating him up. He's changed so. I'm afraid to see him."

Joe put his arm around her. "We'll see him together."

They walked upstairs to the ICU and stood at the side of Ino' bed. He was asleep.

Susan walked in and took Elena's hand in hers. "He's had close call," she said. "We're going to watch him extra careful ly, and he's going to be fine. I know it."

"Let's talk outside," said Joe. "He's going to be out for while." They stepped into the hall.

"I pulled the tube out about five o'clock," said Joe. "Zil hadn't ordered any pain medication."

"Zilk is a total idiot," said Susan emphatically. "In terms of pain medication, I treat all patients, junky or clean, the same way. If they have a heavy habit, I supplement it with methadone. It's strange, though. Most of them never need it. I'm sure there's a bagman in the hospital. One day last year, all four nursing stations began to page me frantically around suppertime. All the patients were screaming for methadone. Somehow the bag man hadn't shown up during afternoon visiting hours and the patients were left high and dry."

"That's incredible," said Joe. "Can't they do anything?"

"Not really. During visiting hours, there are over a hundred and fifty people milling around in the open forty-bed ward. One time, we hid one of the smaller guards. He was intent on catching the dealer, but it was impossible. Joe, Elena, I'm going to get a social worker to look in on Ino. Maybe we can get him enrolled in a drug program."

"Fat chance," said Elena.

"What do you mean?" asked Joe. Elena didn't answer.

"There's one hitch," Susan went on. "The patients have to sign themselves in. Rebirth House has the highest rate of drug cures in the city, but they only accept the patients who really want to stop. They treat them cold turkey and don't let them leave the house for at least three months. The whole program depends on their willingness to surrender to a rigid code. We'll have to see how Ino takes to it." She fingered the pack of index cards in her jacket pocket. "Why don't you both go home and get some rest? If you think last night was bad, wait until the weekend."

"Okay, Susan. Oh, can you make sure Kendricks gets a blood gas on Ino?"

"We'll take care of it."

Joe pushed the elevator button, and they stood waiting for a full five minutes.

They walked down the ramp and continued along the street.

Two men in their twenties, leaning against a wall, were shouting after a young girl with a big swollen belly.

"What do they want?" Joe asked.

"They say they want to make love to her."

"She's eight months pregnant!"

"I know," said Elena, smiling.

"How can they think like that?"

59

"You have to understand the Spanish man. Anything to do with children is beautiful. A woman, ready to give birth, is the most desirable."

"Is that why they keep pumping out kids when there's no bread on the table?"

"A baby is pure—untouched by the environment. A baby is hope for a better future."

"It's another mouth to feed."

"They manage," said Elena proudly.

"I'm not so sure of that," said Joe, putting his arm around her shoulder.

As they approached the car Joe saw something on the windshield. "What's that?"

Neatly folded about the looseleaf paper were three parking tickets, dated about eight hours apart. "The cops thought your car was Rican. And no wonder! Where did you get this paint job?" she asked, studying the designs as she opened the door.

"I let some kids customize it. Do you like it?"

"It's different."

The night began to show on her face; hidden fears began to present themselves. "I don't know if hiding the heroin was the right thing," she said. "If they found it, they would at least be able to press charges."

"Why would you want them to do that?" asked Joe.

"The only way we are going to get Ino to sign up for a program is for him to face a police rap. He would do it then, to avoid being put away."

"Susan says the success of the program depends on the person's willingness."

"You're right. I know my brother. He would go along for several months, then he would cut out." They rode the rest of the way in silence.

Elena lived in a third-floor walk-up in a building that looked ancient, but her apartment was sleek and contemporary. It was painted in bright reds and hot pinks with touches of burnt orange. A mammoth white sofa, flanked by two comfortable club chairs with matching ottomans, dominated the living room. A thick red carpet partially covered the refinished parquet floors. Tossed pillows were everywhere; brightly colored straw flowers stood in an old copper urn. Two large brass lamps that looked like antiques were in the corners. Books and records and knickknacks were arranged on the shelves behind the sofa. "I like your place," Joe said, impressed.

"I kind of like it too." She smiled "Excuse me for a minute. I want to change."

Joe felt strangely at peace as he waited. She returned from the bedroom wearing a terry cloth T-shirt and jeans. Joe stood up. "You look beautiful," he said, holding her.

"There's a lot we have to talk about." Her voice started to tremble.

He relaxed his grip. "Please, don't be afraid. I want to know about you."

She sat down on the sofa, searching his face.

"I'm afraid of you," she finally whispered. She saw the hurt look. "Not you, Joe. All men."

"Luis already told me that. I didn't believe him, and sitting here, I can't believe you."

"Why can't you?"

"Because I have never been attracted to anyone the way I am to you," he said fiercely.

Elena kept her head down. "You don't understand."

"You have never been with a man?" asked Joe softly.

"No. Not really," she shuddered.

"That's not fair. You've never tried."

"Fair?" Elena erupted. "What do you know? You really mean have I ever been fucked? Yes! Oh, God, yes! I have been fucked by over fifteen of your men," she hissed, red-faced. "I was gang raped. I was kept hostage like a piece of meat and dangled as bait for my brother. Ten years later my insides are still raw."

"I'm sorry." Joe swallowed.

Elena began to cry. Joe held her face against his chest.

"You have to tell me. It's the only way it can go away."

"It will never, ever, go away."

"It will between us. That's all that matters."

"I can never go back to that room," she said, agonized. And then a vacant stare came over Elena's eyes, and she was young and full of hope and completely innocent.

The sixteenth year of Elena's life had been an extremely difficult one. The cancer in her mother's body spread rapidly, and she, alone, carried the burden of providing care. That, along

61

with her after-school job, gave her little time to experience the transformation that was shaping her body into a woman of incredible beauty. Still devoutly religious, she prayed for her mother's deliverance and her brother's return.

Ino, at fourteen, was captivated by the strength and camaraderie of the Young Toros. He had been elevated to the Grand Council, serving less than a year as a pledge and then a regular brother. His transfer to a 600 school, as a disciplinary problem, only gave him more time to spend with his brothers. He too, had a part-time job in a gas station, but he viewed his mother's sudden decay with confusion and fear. He stayed on the street, where his bravery was assured, where he already had a reputation; his ferocious instinct clearly marked him as one worthy of notice. And then he fought in his first major gang war.

Ino staggered into the house, his hand still clenching the long stiletto blade. "Elena, help me," he whispered hoarsely and fell into her arms. She brought him into the bathroom and held his head close to her breast.

"What happened?"

"I got one of them, Elena. One of their leaders. He's lying dead in the park. Ayyy." He winced from the pain. "I'm lucky I got out before the cops came."

"Shh . . ." She held him. "Mama will wake up."

She dressed his wounds with bandages. "Why, Ino? Why do you do this? You'll be the next one they find dead in the park."

"They'll be after me. I have to get out of the city." He started to rise, but the pain stopped him.

"Ino, you can go nowhere like this. You need to rest."

"I'll go to Jorge's house in Staten Island. I'll be safe there." She ran to the bedroom, stuffed some clean clothes in a brown paper bag along with a twenty-dollar bill. He stood up and she embraced him. "I'll be okay." Then he was gone.

She was alone. She could not call the police, and she would not disturb her ailing mother. She agonized over her brother's safety. By noon there was still no word.

Elena hurried to her job at the restaurant, which was noisy, hot, and filled with the lunchtime rush. Three hours later, as she bent over to retrieve the dirty dishes from an end table she felt the rough hand of a truck driver under her skirt. She rose angrily and poured the full contents of a glass of ice water into the startled man's face. Mr. Garcia came running over and began to dry the angry customer's shirt.

"I'm terribly sorry," he kept apologizing to the man. He stalked over to Elena.

"What happened?"

"He pinched me."

"If you had moved fast enough, he would not be able. Look, why don't you call it a day? We can handle things now, and you didn't look good when you came in."

She was crying when she left. As she reached her corner the familiar surroundings helped comfort her. She turned into the alley leading to the apartment and felt a hand go over her mouth and a knife stick into her side.

"You Sanchez's sister? Keep you mouth shut and you won't get hurt." They led her into a car and threw her into the backseat. They drove to a condemned building site.

"Get out, *puta*," the men ordered. They led her into a delapidated building, down a flight of stairs, half of which were missing, and into a huge room lit by candles. Five men faced her. The large one in the center spoke to her in Spanish.

"You the sister of Ino Sanchez?"

Elena nodded.

"Where is he?"

"I don't know where he is."

"She's lying," the leader stated impassively. One of his followers slapped her viciously across the face.

"That will teach you to lie to Chico."

Elena gasped. She knew the man who held her, the man who wanted her brother. He was Chico Alvarez.

Chico Alvarez was twenty-nine years old. It had taken him fifteen years, interrupted by two long terms at Manhattan State Hospital for the Criminally Insane, to rise to power. Savage and unpredictable, he managed to instill fear in even the most hardened young men of the street.

His power base had always been precarious, but now he was fighting to retain command of his own small group of twelve. Over the last year he had carefully guided two warring bands together in an attempt to consolidate forces.

Juan and Pedro were stepbrothers. Their father had been shot down in an attempted robbery two years before. Juan blamed his older stepbrother, for he had served as the lookout. They split into rival factions. Each gathered followers and continually fought petty skirmishes for control of a six-block area. Alvarez had gone to the pair and convinced them to give up their long-standing antagonism, in order to wipe the Young Toros from the face of the earth.

The gang war had ended his grandiose scheme. He had had the Toros outnumbered, and after only the first exchange they had broken ranks. They began running down the street. As Alvarez led his men after them he sensed total victory. They reached St. Mary's Park.

Some of the Toros had regrouped and stood on the softball diamond, determined to make a last stand. Alvarez came across the field with his men in their standard double line pattern. Suddenly, there were Toros everywhere. His men held their position, but the Toros had them outflanked. As they squeezed rapidly together his front line broke. Four of his men were badly wounded, and Pedro had been killed by Ino Sanchez, a stiletto-wielding fourteen year old. He had been disgraced.

He studied each of the loyal followers who remained in the room. He had to kill Sanchez. It was his only chance to regain his men's respect and rebuild his battered forces.

Miraculously, he had been handed the only bait Sanchez could not resist. But, it might take days to lure the cowardly killer from his hole. He studied Elena. He had to keep the cunt alive, and he knew that he would be fighting the base instincts of his wounded band.

"Undress her," he ordered. Three men came forward, and within minutes, the waitress uniform had been torn away. She stood totally naked.

"Where is your brother?"

"I don't know. I swear," she repeated.

"I can have you killed."

"I don't know where my brother is."

"Have you ever been fucked, little whore?" He studied her with a half smile.

"Never," she groaned. "I'm a devout Catholic."

"You're a slut. You'll do everything you did with them."

"I've never been touched." Alvarez walked over and brutally squeezed her nipple.

"You've never been touched?" he asked again.

"Once, but only once, when I was thirteen. And just my breasts, I swear to you," she cried in pain. The men stared at her, and when she tried to cover her nakedness, they laughed. Only Alvarez seemed apart.

"I would have had the Young Toros and I would have had the South Bronx. Your fucking brother broke my flank. But I'll get him back. You, my beautiful cunt, will bring him back to me."

"If you harm me, he will kill you."

"We'll see, pretty girl." Alvarez glared.

"Turn her up," he waved his hand. Elena's feet were grabbed high in the air, and suddenly she was on her back, legs stretched apart. Then she heard the whistle and strained to look up. Alvarez had a car antenna in his hand. Suddenly her vagina was on fire, and the torch spread upward. Elena sucked in a huge breath of air as the snap resounded through the room. Then she let out a piercing scream, and her pelvis began to shake uncontrollably.

"Oh, Mother of God, please help me," she prayed as the two men struggled to hold her writhing ankles. She stared at Alvarez; he could continue doing this until she was torn apart.

"Now, little beauty, have you ever been fucked before?" Alvarez repeated his question softly.

Dazed and hurt, now she was afraid to meet the eyes of her tormentor.

"Never," she whispered.

"I did not hear you, little beauty."

"Never," she shouted jaggedly.

"That is good. You will be tight. Now tell us where is your brother?"

"It's no use." She surrendered. "He's left the city."

"Where did he go?" Alvarez again lifted the antenna.

"Staten Island. He went to Staten Island," she whimpered.

"We'll wait for his return." Alvarez led his group away from her slumped figure.

She woke hours later. There were several couples dancing, and the stag boys gathered in the far corner. Every few minutes one would turn and stare, and the others would laugh and begin to jostle him. Her hands were tied behind her.

Alvarez sauntered across the room.

"We're having a party. Your beauty is well known. Look, already you bring ten more followers. And Juan has returned." He smiled at his powerful ally.

"When we get your brother, we'll have fifty more men." His eyes were crazed. He went to the record player and lifted the needle. "Get out, you whores," he ordered. "It's time for her initiation ceremony."

The girls left quickly. Two of the men lifted Elena up, untying her wrists, but still securing her arms. Before sucking the last of the heroin into the modified eyedropper, Alvarez broke open a small red capsule, flaking several grains onto the top.

"Beautiful *bombita*." He contemplated the pure Dexedrine mixture. He'd save the rest for tomorrow. Alvarez twisted his belt around Elena's arm and administered the injection.

As the first wave of spasm tightened over her intestines she rocked forward. The waves began firing off rapidly until the muscular walls clamped down, completely rigid. Alvarez laughed, happy he had not allowed her to be given any food. She continued dry heaving for almost five minutes. As the nausea slowly dissipated Elena felt herself lifted away. She giggled, out of touch.

Alvarez watched with increasing satisfaction.

"She is ready."

The men dragged the mattress into the center of the room and decorated each corner with a candle. There was total silence as Elena staggered about, followed by spontaneous snapping of fingers as the men signified their readiness. Juan, still reeling from the loss of his brother and injuries to two of his best men, was the most aggressive. He took a few heavy steps towards her and pushed her down. The men fought for key positions as Elena fell back, floating on a bed of rippling waves.

The sight of Elena, open and ready, rocked Juan's penis. Crudely holding it at mid-shaft, he drove it into Elena. As he speared forward he was too anxious and managed to only pound the apex of her opening. She froze as his steel shaft slipped downward, tearing through her hymen membrane. Hysterically, she began kneeing at his chest. Juan grabbed powerfully at her buttocks, driving the entire length of his penis deep into her vagina.

Alvarez watched with rising anger. Even as he pushed Elena onto her side and spread her buttocks he thought only of Juan's initiative. He had to retake his cherished prize; his position as leader demanded it.

He eased his penis against her rectal wall and succeeded in forcing the glans through her clinched sphincter. Using his hands to slide deeper into the rocking target, he slipped, and his hands came down against the base of Juan's stiffening column. He marveled at its thickness and power as it relentlessly drove Elena

66

backward into him. He let his hands slide down to touch the swelling scrotum, and with hidden curiosity, he pushed upward to better experience the weight and thickness of each testicle.

Untouched by Elena's cries, captivated by the intensity of the assault, Alvarez savagely hurled forward. Fully embedded, he began pumping, enflamed as each surge brought his distended head solidly against Juan's staff. His brutal fury rose and his onslaught pummeled Elena forward. Realizing the terrible beating Elena was being subjected to, Juan mercifully began cushioning her heaving chest. Finally, the prolonged pressure of Elena's body overwhelmed them.

They rose and began to dress.

"She's all yours, men," said Alvarez, zipping his fly. They descended upon her. Half of them had already removed their pants. They turned her over and over. After several hours she was barely conscious. The underlings seemed more intent on hurting her just to see a reaction from her battered body.

Elena lay on the mattress in a deep, drugged sleep.

"She's out," Juan said.

"Good. We'll need her tomorrow." Alvarez smiled maliciously.

It was morning. Elena was so beaten she could hardly move. There was Alvarez administering this stinging in her arm. She was electrified. They began yelling at her.

"Get up. On your knees."

Elena passed out again.

It was midday before Ino and his men broke in the door. There was a short fight, there was her father's machete, glistening. She awoke in ward 3-D of Jefferson Hospital, where she stayed for a week while the lacerations healed.

Joe had listened to the story without saying a word. Elena's face was white.

"Still want to be with me?" she asked, her eyes lowered.

"More than ever. Alvarez has been dead for ten years. We have our whole lives. I'll make it up to you. I promise!"

Elena looked at him. "You can never make it up."

"Time will. You'll see."

That night Joe went to bed on Elena's couch in the living room. Morning found him drained and uneasy. He had been taken into a world he never knew existed. Elena's pain had become his pain, and he silently chastised himself for being born into the soft luxuries that he had accepted so readily and so often taken for granted.

He studied her as they drove to work. She was looking straight ahead, her hands folded calmly in her lap. Is this how she met all the blows life had dealt her: beauty belying her anxiety, serenity belying her pain? She had remained unprotected for too long. Impulsively he reached over and covered her hands with his. "Try not to worry," he said softly.

She nodded silently, tears springing to her eyes.

"I called the floor before you got up. He's stable."

She looked at him gratefully. "You did? You really do care."

"Why shouldn't I care? You're important to me. Your trouble is not enough people caring about you." He was surprised at the anger in his voice.

"We all have a cross to bear," she said. "Some people's are just greater than others. I see the ones coming into the ER every day. Nice people, good people, and their lives are filled with horrors. It helps me to be thankful for what I have. I can't give up on Ino. If he could just pick himself up, he could do so much."

"I'll do everything I can to help," said Joe "I want you to be happy. You deserve to be happy."

Elena smiled wanly. "Who is ever really happy? Oh, you can be happy for a while, but something is bound to happen to change it. I'm afraid I can't trust happiness anymore."

"Give it one last shot"—Joe grinned as he squeezed her hand—"with me."

7

They arrived just as Arnost and Susan were finishing their eggs and coffee.

"How's Ino doing?" Joe asked.

"Ino is doing just great," said Susan. "I've clamped his tube, and we're sending him down for a film. If his chest stays up, we can pull it this evening. He's already off IVs, so he can walk around. The cardiogram continues to remain normal. He's putting out liters of urine, and all of his lab values are on the line. In a couple of days he'll be as good as new."

"New wasn't that great," said Elena. She averted her eyes from the group.

"How much do you know about Ino's habit?" Susan asked.

"What's there to know? He started like all the kids, sniffing it every once in a while at a party. About three years ago he seemed to change. Skin popping, first on weekends, then every couple of days. I remember," she said sadly, "when it would have been unthinkable for Ino to have carried heroin. He used to sneer at junkies, saying they sold themselves for a temporary escape. Today, he can only deny the fact that he's an addict."

Susan put her arm around Elena, sensing her discomfort. "Why don't you speak to him, Joe?" she asked. "He's already asked for you three times. Try to get him interested in signing himself into a real drug program. It's his only hope."

"It's our only hope," said Elena, looking at Joe.

"Is he still in ICU?" Joe asked.

"We just moved him to ward 2-B. Good luck."

"Thanks, Susan. Elena, I'll be down in half an hour."

Ino sat in the second extra bed placed in the center of the huge forty-bed ward. He was sitting up, reading a small orange pamphlet. Joe sat down on the chair by the bed. "Jessie Jackson," he read aloud. "He can really cut it."

Ino put the pamphlet down. "Yeah, he sure can. And he made it all on his own."

"How are you feeling?"

"I'm okay. I'll be happy when they pull this tube out. It still hurts every time I take a deep breath."

"How bad is the pain?"

"The Demerol is holding me. Thanks for ordering it."

"I didn't order it, Ino. Susan did."

"Well, you ordered it that first night. And I want to say thanks for saving my life." Ino began to stammer. "And thanks for hiding the heroin."

"Do you need any methadone?"

"No, I'm fine. I don't have a habit."

"Ino, I happen to have gotten to know your sister pretty well, and one thing I am sure about is that she doesn't lie. She says you have a habit. I found that envelope in your pocket. Your veins are all scarred up. You can bullshit me, you can go back on the street, but if you do, you are going to be dead in three years."

"Dr. Ruskin, seven-two-oh," bleeped the loudspeaker system. Ino looked away.

"All right, the sermon is over for now. Think about it. I'll be back later to talk with you."

"Why all this interest?"

"I've got an investment in you. You owe me an hour and a half of agonizing fear. That's what I went through from the moment they brought you in."

"That's impossible to pay back."

"You've already paid half of it."

"What do you mean?"

"You're alive, aren't you?"

"You can't con me. That's not the only reason. I heard you're trying to pop my sister."

"Ino, I care about your sister."

"You care about my sister or you care about the challenge? Don't hurt her," Ino threatened.

"You haven't done such a great job. I think I can help a little."

Joe went to the phone at the nurses station and dialed 720.

70

"Hello, Dr. Ruskin here."

"Dr. Ruskin, this is Salina, Dr. Gold's secretary."

"Is anything the matter?"

"No, he wants to give you the intern-of-the-month award. You'd better get up here, as soon as you can."

Benjamin Gold had already been at his desk for over two hours. For the past forty years he had arrived at the hospital every morning at six-thirty, and the habit persisted despite the fact that he no longer had to make rounds on his patients. He was content in this routine. The quiet gave him an opportunity to think, and today he felt more excited than he had allowed himself to be in years.

This new intern, Ruskin, seemed different. He picked up the file that lay in front of him. The kid had a superb record, but Gold knew that a month ago. On his first night he had managed to save that tamponade—a very impressive feat for even a seasoned veteran. Okay, he was good. But Gold had seen a lot of good ones. There was something more, some quality hidden under the brash veneer. He wasn't just another hotshot who would gather any experience he could, ready and anxious to leave once his lessons had been learned. This one seemed to care.

Benjamin Gold remembered when he was an intern. He had been one of the caring ones, too. And then he remembered David. His head hung down, as the pain returned.

Benjamin Gold, at fifty-five, had been at the zenith of his surgical career. A full professor, second in command to a tottering, half-senile statesman who had not performed a major case in fifteen years, the burden and glory of running the Hirshorn Medical Center Department of Surgery had been squarely on his shoulders. He stalked about the OR, supervising, admonishing, and scrubbing-in when things threatened to get out of control. He developed a new procedure for peptic ulcer disease, and the rich and famous, stomachs churning, flocked to be under his care. Once cured, they offered large sums to show their gratitude. Benjamin Gold would not accept.

"I'm sorry, but I'm on salary," he would say.

"Put it in your pocket. No one will know."

"Please, give it to the university. They can use it more than me."

"But we want to thank you."

"I'm a doctor. If I can give relief, that's all the thanks I need."

"What about your wife and son?"

"We are more than comfortable. We have everything we could need."

Benjamin Gold did not want to tempt fate. He was blessed with a good wife and a son who was a constant joy, and he knew he could never be religious like his father. If he was a good doctor, his work was his way of repaying for his good fortune. If he was also to receive great wealth, how would He know? No, it was better to marvel at his son David's disposition and be grateful.

The Golds always spent their summers at Montauk Point, and they had all come to look forward to the solitude and relaxation they found by the sea.

This particular year, David Gold had returned from his finals to spend his summer vacation with his parents at the beach. Premed at Harvard, his scientific background and his hard work had enabled him to stay at the top of the dean's list. The medical schools were already showing interest. His teachers marveled at his papers. His friends marveled at his social grace. His father marveled at his ease and love of life and, miraculously, the respect the boy held for him.

David arrived at the beach house at noon. Both parents embraced him as he got out of the car.

"Mom, I missed you."

"No wonder you missed me, you must have lost ten pounds." She stepped back and studied him.

"You'll fatten me up in no time."

"David!" Gold grasped him and rocked him gently. "I missed you so. How's school?"

"Great."

"How are your grades?" He already knew. He had called the dean that morning.

"Straight As."

Benjamin Gold beamed. "You make us so proud." They walked back to the house, carrying his suitcases.

"How's your roommate?"

72

"Fine, Dad. Everything is fine. Mom, when is lunch going to be ready?"

"It will take a little while. I didn't expect you until three. Why don't you two go out and walk on the beach? I'll have everything ready in half an hour."

"We could help." The boy held his hands to his stomach.

"Go out with your father. You haven't been together since last summer. Besides, you're just making me nervous," she joked, pushing them out the screen door.

They began walking down the familiar beach toward the lighthouse. "You look wonderful." He studied David's lean body as the boy bent down to pick up a shell. He followed the path as it skimmed along the water. "Good throw."

"Remember the time I tried to cut down that runner from third?" They both laughed, remembering the junior high school championship.

"I can still picture the announcer's face when he realized the ball was coming straight at him."

"Yeah. He thought he was safe twelve rows up in the bleachers."

"It was a strong throw."

"That's what you told me then. I still didn't eat for a week."

"Your mother thought you were dying."

"I remember. She told me you were going to start an IV on me." The boy threw his head back, laughing. "And I believed you would. You were hovering all over me."

"Come on, David. I just didn't want you to be so disappointed."

"You told me a story about how you were the high school goalie for Stuyvesant. 'Let the ball go right through my legs.' Three years later, I found out you never played soccer."

"By then it didn't matter." Gold smiled.

"Those were good days." David's eyes beamed.

"Yes, they were." Benjamin Gold shook his head. It was going too fast. "And now look at you."

They sat down on a dune.

"Are you sure you want to be a doctor?" asked Gold.

"Most of the time. It's a grind."

"That doesn't change. I hope you're not doing it because of anything I ever said. I never wanted to push you."

"You didn't have to."

"I don't understand."

"Remember the summer we saved the dog?" asked David. "When I saw that dog walk again, I knew I wanted to be a surgeon more than anything else."

Gold smiled. It had happened on a walk like this one. David was the first to hear the dog's muffled cries coming from behind the dunes. Gold had examined the animal and noted the fractured femur.

"Do you remember walking into the vet's, holding the dog and asking him for an operating room?" laughed David.

"How could I forget?" said Gold. "It was the first time I ever saw you operate."

"You did the operation, Dad." David smiled. "I was just a nervous assistant."

"You did fine," said Gold, remembering his son's quick mind and nimble fingers.

"So you see, you didn't have to push me at all," admitted David. "I always want to be like you."

"You're better than me, David," said Gold, "or at least you will be. Don't ever forget that."

They walked back to the beach house, and Gold's heart swelled with pride.

It wasn't until several hours later, after dinner, that he noticed David looked a little pale. "What's the matter, son?"

"Oh, nothing, Dad," said David. "I just have a bad headache. All the excitment, I'm sure."

Then he slumped against the door to his room. Gold felt his chest. It was warm. He looked into David's eyes. He noted a sudden flickering of his eyes as David turned to face him. Oh, God, the kid was sick.

"Ben! What is it?" asked Dottie, running over.

"He's caught some sort of virus," said Gold steadily. "Nothing to get alarmed about."

They helped him into bed, and for the next four hours Benjamin Gold sat hunched over on the hardwood chair. He would check David's pulse and then his temperature every few minutes. But as he busied himself performing this vigil a dread began to envelop his mind. David's temperature and vital signs were normal, but Gold's long-practiced sixth sense told him David was in fact very ill.

"I can't wait any longer." Gold stood up and began running to the phone.

"Ben, who are you calling?" asked Dottie anxiously.

"The police! We need a helicopter. I want to get David back to Hirshorn now. I don't like the way he looks."

"But, Ben, you said he just has a virus. He's going to be all right, isn't he?"

"Of course, Dottie. I'd just feel more secure having him in my hospital," he lied.

Fifteen minutes before the helicopter arrived, David Gold had a massive grand mal seizure. On the flight to the city he developed a raised red rash on his stomach. They admitted him to the ICU unit and IVs were started.

The spinal tap was free of bacteria. Specialists drove in, and then world famous specialists were flown in. They worked on David in the unit, and they worked on his cerebrospinal fluid in the lab, feverishly trying to isolate the virus causing the fulminating encephalitis.

But David Gold never regained consciousness. Two days after his admission, with his father sitting on a small stool by his bed, rereading his chart for perhaps the thousandth time, hoping to get some clue, David Michael Gold suffered his first and only cardiac arrest. And even as Benjamin Gold pounded on his son's chest in a vain attempt to revive him, he felt his strength and will to live slowly seep from his arms.

Gold looked out the window. The sight of two adults shielding a small boy urinating on the sidewalk brought him back to the present.

In the last five years he had watched the neighborhood collapse. And as urban blight overwhelmed the hospital services Gold, too, began to crumble. Now, suddenly, there was hope. Maybe things were finally going to improve. The resident staff was the key, and Ruskin was a natural. His youthful exuberance was contagious. Gold just might be able to start passing along some of his overwhelming responsibilities.

But Gold wasn't completely sold on his new intern. Yesterday he had looked out the window and studied Joe and Elena as they walked from the staff house. He was shocked. He had known Elena for years and he was sure she wasn't like that. Still, she was a beautiful woman, and Ruskin was just headstrong enough to forget his position. He would never understand these people; they seemed to have no control.

There was a knock on the door. Joe Ruskin stood before him.

"Joe, I want to congratulate you." He started slowly. "Susan told me what you did. Not bad for an intern on his first night."

"I heard you're taking a couple of days vacation," Joe said, embarrassed.

"You know, I might just do that. I'd love to get away if only once this summer."

"The beach should be great this week."

"Oh, one more thing, Joe." There was a sudden sternness in Gold's tone. "One of the aides saw you and Elena walking out of the staff house together. Now, I am not one to play your father, and I am not one to give you lectures on social behavior. I've known Elena for a long time, and I know absolutely nothing could happen. But I don't like to hear things like that about members of my staff. It doesn't look good. Don't get involved with hospital employees."

"Does that mean don't care?" asked Joe, flushed.

"It means don't be seen in the staff house," he snapped, angry at the boy and angrier at himself.

"Is that all?" asked Joe.

Gold turned to the papers on his desk.

"Is that why you called me in here?"

Gold began flipping through the pile, discarding half the letters in front of him. Joe waited.

"I better get back to work," Joe said hesitantly.

Gold finally looked up, nodding.

As the door closed, Gold rose and slowly walked back to the window. How could he begin to daydream that these kids would ever be able to take over? Ruskin's reaction had confirmed his fears. There was no morality left. No wonder this cesspool of a community was disintegrating. He felt so old and alone.

8

Joe met Elena at the door of the nursing station. "How's my brother?" she asked anxiously.

"Medically, he's doing great. That man is strong!"

"But, not strong enough to kick the habit."

"Maybe not today," he told her, "but we'll keep working on him. He's going to be here a while, and he'll have plenty of time to think. He'll change."

"God, I hope so." She sat down on a small bench and held her head in her hands. "I don't know what I was expecting," she said, almost to herself. She looked up at Joe. "You can't know what it means, carrying heroin into a gang war. It shows how far he's gone. Since he was twelve the gang has been his whole life. He would rather die than do anything to jeopardize the Toros. To bring drugs into battle is the worst sign of decay."

"Then we have to get him to acknowledge that," said Joe. "Once he sees what he's become, maybe he'll be ready to change."

"If I could only believe that." She seemed about to lose her composure again, and he sat down and put his arm around her. "I always thought he was different. Not just because he's my brother, but I sensed something special that made him stand out above everyone else. A lot of good it did him," she said despondently. "You don't know him, Joe. If you did, you'd understand what I'm talking about. Did you know he has fifteen credits at college?"

"He does?"

"You wouldn't have guessed it would you? Yes, a while back he got a job as a custodian at CCNY and they let him take courses free. There's lots of things people don't know about Ino. I think sometimes he forgets them too. Like when he studies the

77

ads and gets into his only suit and goes down for a job. But he's either too old or too young or has too much school or not enough. No one wants to take a chance on a spic with a knife scar under his ear. That's all he can see. But I know him. I know what's underneath that tough shell. He's still a scared kid.''

"We're all scared kids," said Joe slowly. "The way I see it, Ino has to be convinced there's another open door. We've got to give him hope . . . hope that things can improve."

"But what kind of future can we offer him?"

"I don't know," said Joe. "We'll work on it."

She looked at his face, saw the concern in his eyes, and found herself moved by his easy sureness.

Luis joined them. "Elena," he said, bending down and holding both her hands in his. "You holding in there?" She nodded and gave him a weak smile. "Good girl," he said, hugging her for a moment. Then he turned to Joe. "Are you coming?"

"Right now. Elena, we'll talk more later. Okay?"

She watched him walk out with Luis. Not since before Mama had gotten sick had she felt so protected.

"I can't figure it out," said Joe. "Why would anyone risk their lives for a gang war?"

"To win," Luis replied simply.

"So what do they win?"

"Respect."

"Respect based on violence?"

"No, respect based on courage. No one thinks about whether violence is right or wrong. It's just there. The only important thing is how a man deals with it. Ino has always dealt with it so intensely and businesslike."

"How do you mean?"

"Well, like for a battle, Ino made sure each man took care in terms of his appearance. That's why the brothers would dress exactly alike. One prepared for the possibility of being killed. If you were hurt, other people would go through your clothes and the Toros would be judged by it."

"You know a lot about Ino," he said.

"I should," he said slowly, "we grew up together. After his mother died he lived at our house. We were like brothers." He held up two fingers.

"Were you in his gang?" Joe asked, amazed.

"For six years."

"Really?"

"Sure," said Luis. "At that time in my life the Toros were everything."

"What happened?"

"I got lucky, I guess. I saw it was a dead end street. Elena helped me a lot."

"She did?"

"Yeah, she would spend a lot of time talking to me and Ino about what we were going to make out of our lives, stuff like that. She was a little older, and I guess, even then she had a better grip on reality. Anyway, all her talking got me thinking. It's just too bad Ino never listened."

"That's kind of ironic."

"Maybe. Mostly, it's sad. He's nothing but an overgrown junkie now."

"Were you ever on drugs?" Joe asked quietly.

"Nah, somehow I never got into it, even though it was everywhere. I guess I'm a lot luckier than Ino all around."

"I'd say you are." Joe looked at Luis with new respect. "You're here because you want to be. You've got a job to do. Ino's here because he has to be. There's a big difference in the way you both came in."

Luis thought about that for a moment. Ruskin was right. There was a big difference between him and Ino, there always had been.

It was the summer of their thirteenth year before they were inducted into the Council, the inner circle of the Young Toros, right after Ino had come to live with them. They had both been in the Toros for a year, and they reveled in the possibility of gaining admission to the elite group. The tests were severe; only those with leadership potential were even considered. Each brother had to display an act of courage, an act of strength, and finally, an act of loyalty. Many didn't make it. Few were even considered. There was Enrique and Paco, himself, Angel and, of course, Ino. Even then, Ino stood out. Angel was usually bragging, showing off, but Ino could manage to put him down. There was nothing Angel could offer the council but trouble. Paco and Enrique were steady and reliable, better at taking orders.

On their first night out they were made to jump the twelve feet from one rooftop to another. Luis broke into a cold sweat when he looked down the thirty-five feet into the busy traffic below. High places had always scared him.

Ino went ahead and easily made the jump to the other side. It was Luis's turn, but he couldn't take a step. The brothers, who lined the jumping pad, were jeering, ridiculing him, pushing their hands in front of his face. "Just look at me, Luis," Ino called. "You'll make it easy."

There was something in the way he said it that made Luis believe he would. As he began running toward the end of the building, the gang stepped back and with a running kick, he landed on the other side. The Toros cheered, and later when they walked back, arm in arm, Luis felt a real sense of satisfaction. They had passed the first test.

The test of strength came the night the brothers took them over to Hunt's Point Avenue. The territory belonged to another gang and the Toros sauntered through the dilapidated blocks, looking for them. They came up against three members standing on a corner. There were seven Toros.

"Whatcha up to, scum bags?" sneered Renaldo, chief of the Toros.

"Keepin' the streets clean of trash like you."

"You're askin' for it, punk."

"You're on, punk. It's one-to-one, hands only." Renaldo quickly eyed his gang. "It's you against Luis."

Luis's heart sank to his stomach. He knew he had to pass the test. The other boy had black hair and was a few years older. Luis jumped into the imaginary circle that formed as the others gathered around him. He tried to look mean. The other boy struck first. Luis swung back. Soon, he was hitting more than he was getting hit. But he didn't notice the blade flash out of the boy's pocket. It was Ino who saw it.

Ino stepped in and spat in his face. "Chicken!" he shouted angrily. "You need the knife." Startled, the boy lunged forward. In one swift movement, the knife slashed behind Ino's left ear. Blood started to ooze out onto the side of his face.

The boy hesitated for a second, unsure of what to do. Luis seized the opportunity. He swung hard and felt the jaw crack as his fist slammed into it. A moment later the boy was down, unconscious. They helped Ino to the car, but there was no celebration that night.

The act of loyalty was the most difficult. Two groups were set up. Ino and Angel and Luis were in one, Paco and Enrique were in the other. They were told to plan and execute a burglary.

Luis struggled with it for days. He wanted to be among the Council of the Toros more than anything else. But he had never stolen before.

They chose a small jewelry store a few blocks out of their territory. An old couple ran it, and the boys watched them prepare to close for the night. Renaldo and two brothers were parked in a stolen car a few yards from the store. Luis was to walk in first.

"I want to get something for my mother," he whispered hoarsely.

"Speak up, sonny, I can't hear you," said the old man. His wife was cleaning the counter with Windex.

"My mother," stammered Luis, "her birthday." He didn't know it would be so hard to get the practiced lie from his lips.

"How much money you got?" asked the man.

Luis looked nervously toward the door as Ino and Angel walked in.

The man looked up. "We're closing—" he started. "Hey what is this?" he asked as Ino flicked the blade toward him.

"Hand over the cash." Ino's voice was hard and cold.

The man turned white. His wife let out a stifled scream. Slowly he walked toward the register as the boys stood and watched. His hands shook as he got the money out and laid it on the counter.

"It's all I got," he pleaded.

"I bet!" yelled Angel. He suddenly took out a blackjack from his back pocket. He started toward the old man.

"Please no," screamed his wife, before the first blow. "It's all we've got, don't hurt him." But her cries were useless, as Angel took his vengeance out on the unfortunate victim.

"It's enough," Luis shouted, dragging Angel off the old man.

"Shut up," snapped Angel. "I know he's got more."

"Cool it," said Ino.

A horn honked from outside.

"Come on," yelled Ino, grabbing the money. They ran out to the waiting car and peeled down Bruckner Boulevard.

"You get it?" asked Renaldo.

Ino handed him the money. He stuffed it in his pocket without looking at it. "How much?"

"Fifty-two dollars and fifty cents," said Ino.

"That's good," said Renaldo. "Our treasury can use it."

At the candlelight induction ceremony that night Luis sat next to Ino and listened as Renaldo welcomed them into the Council. They were the only ones who had made it. "You have proven your loyalty, your strength, and your courage to the Toros. You have gone beyond the deeds necessary for a regular brother. Through your actions you have shown you can not only follow orders but can give them as well. From now on, the only orders you'll take will be from me. You have acted well but it isn't the act so much as what it stands for. In your life the Toros come above all else."

Luis listened closely to the words of his chief. Renaldo was a great man. Luis knew he could never come close to him. He didn't have it in him. He looked at Ino, sitting quietly, taking in every word. Ino could be a Jefe, he thought suddenly. He had that drive, that core of steel that let nothing or no one get in the way. Luis felt privileged to be among the Council. He just wished he could blot out the picture of Angel beating the man with the blackjack.

It was dawn before they got home. In the tiny bedroom they shared with Luis's two younger brothers, Ino whispered, "Now we are real brothers, real Toros, eh Luis?"

"I didn't think the Toros believed in beating up old men," said Luis slowly. His head hurt from all the wine.

"You're still thinking of Angel."

"I can't forget it," whispered Luis.

"You got to. You held him off good. You did what you could. What's it to you anyway? You're on the Council now. And the brothers know. Why do you think Angel didn't make it?"

The following week, he went back. Through the window he could see them waiting on customers. The old man had a bandage over his left eye. He looked up from the counter and seemed to glare out the window. Luis bolted and ran. Only when he was back inside Toro's territory did Luis's stomach stop its erratic churning.

They walked into the second suture room and found a thin ten-year-old black boy clutching a blood clotted handkerchief against his chin.

"Just lie down on the stretcher, and we will have you fixed up in no time."

"What are you going to do, man?"

"Well, I am going to let you lie down on the stretcher, and then Luis is going to wash the wound with a soapy solution."

"It's going to burn."

"Well, not really. Before he washes it, I'm going to drop some numbing fluid on it. But we have to make a deal. Once we wash the wound and I put a towel on your chin, you can't move your hands. You see, we have created a sterile field, and that's the only way to sew the chin wound."

"Sew the chin wound? You ain't putting no needles in my chin!"

"It isn't needles. It's just one small mosquito bite. I inject a fluid that puts the area to sleep. You will feel pressure, but you won't feel any pain."

"You're full of shit, man. I'm getting out of here." The boy tried to break for the door. Luis's hand shot out like a snake and grabbed him by the right wrist. With the other hand he unhooked the papoose board from the wall. He quickly had the child restrained.

"Keep your fucking hands off me, spic."

Luis remained calm. He quickly washed out the wound and then dropped some 4-0 nylon on the tray. "Dr. Ruskin, we're ready."

Joe walked over and began to infiltrate the wound. The child leaped into midair. "You fucking honky cocksucker! You are killing me! You are killing me!"

Joe was getting anxious. As he put in the second suture, the child continued to twist his chin and mouth. The motion was making it much more difficult. Joe stopped and leaned over the small boy.

"Listen, you little piece of shit. You make one more move, and I swear I will break your goddamn arm. I have one suture left, and then you can get out of here. I know it isn't hurting you, so just cool it." With that Joe threw in the last suture. As the dressing was slapped on and the child rose from the papoose board the tears quickly dried.

"Thanks," he muttered.

"Hey, let me ask you something, star."

"Yeah, Kildare?"

"You really kicked up a fuss in here, and I was just wondering, don't you feel a little embarrassed now?"

"What you mean, embarrassed?"

"I mean you cried and screamed and you cursed and you said really bad things."

"I was scared."

Joe knelt down. "Well, I'd be sort of scared if I was laying there also. Now, let's the two of us make a deal. The next time you fall and you get cut and you come in here, I want you to stop and demand that I talk to you for one minute, first, before I even start doing anything. That way I can explain everything I am going to do to you, so you won't have to be scared."

"Solid, Kildare," as they exchanged the palms-up street salute.

"Kildare, how long you been a doctor?"

"Oh, about three days."

"Three days? You've got to be jivin' me."

"Yes, star, I'm jivin' you."

Joe walked the boy out of the Emergency Room and into his mother's arms. "Your young man has some vocabulary."

"I am sorry, Doctor. They learn it on the streets. I try but it's really hard."

Joe stood in the main waiting room and watched as the mother and child approached the large door. She suddenly took her right hand and swung it forward, slapping the top of the child's head. He screamed in protest.

"What the fuck you mean talking to the doctor like that?" she scolded. "He's here to help you—not for you to bad-mouth him." Joe watched the door slam shut, and he looked up to again study the poster taped above the entrance—the letters in black print.

"What does AMF mean?" asked Joe, returning.

"You mean that sign over the door? *Adiós*, motherfucker." Luis laughed. "The guys from the kitchen put it up. Listen, they just brought this kid in. She looks sick as hell."

"Where is she?"

"She's in the first suture room."

The eleven-year-old girl was lying on her left side with her knees drawn up to her chest. She was in obvious pain. Joe reached for the stethoscope. "The kid has no bowel sounds."

He tried to palpate for any specific area of tenderness. "Abdomen's like a board. Get me a glove," he said. As he slipped his index finger into the child's rectum and leaned against the right wall of the distal colon the child let out a loud scream. Joe withdrew his finger and walked to the phone.

"Who is the admitting intern?"

"Dr. Kendricks," answered Luis.

"Well, page him stat. Tell him I have a real present down here for him. She is going to need a routine chest X ray and she is going to need an IV. Make sure that she understands that she can't eat anything."

Joe returned from X-ray with the stretcher, pushing it into the trauma room as Kendricks appeared in the doorway. He was breathing loudly.

"I heard you have an acute appy," he said excitedly.

"I sure do," said Joe.

"And on my third day, this is fantastic! Sometimes you have to wait six months to do your first one." All of a sudden, the magnitude of the moment set in on Kendricks.

"Are you sure it's an appendix?" he asked.

"She has an elevated white count, and her urine is negative. She has a boardlike abdomen and exquisite tenderness on rectal. I am not one hundred percent sure it is an appendix, but I am absolutely positive that it is a surgical abdomen. And I am sure that they will let you do it."

"What do you have in the bottle," Kendricks said looking at the IV.

"I gave her a two gram bolus of Keflin."

"Why the antibiotics?"

"As I said, she has got a boardlike abdomen and no bowel sounds. I think she may have perforated."

"Oh." Kendricks's whole face fell. A perforated appendix was not a routine case.

"Look, they'll at least let you start the case. Even during routine appies they usually steal your first from you somewhere. And besides, this kid needs to be prepped, and you have to get consent. I'm going to lunch. I'm starving. Oh, and you'd better notify Susan."

As he waited in line he scanned the crowded room. Elena was just finishing her coffee at a table with three other women. Her black hair had fallen over her face and had become entwined in the silver chain from which hung a simple cross. Joe could see her deep almond eyes open wide in recognition. She began to wave. Joe motioned to an empty table in the back and she joined him.

"Hi, Kildare." She laughed.

"You already heard the story?"

"It's perfect. The kid read you act. I think you've just been given a nickname."

"It's better than some of the other names he called me." Joe smiled.

"Let's go see Ino together. Maybe we'll have more luck."

"Elena, I'd go anywhere with you."

They walked through the crowded ward to the bed, still sitting awkwardly in the center of the room between the two even rows of patients. Ino was chewing a Milky Way.

"What a beautiful couple," he said sarcastically. "Nice of you to take time out from your life-saving duties."

"Sounds like you're getting better," said Joe, measuring the level of blood in the collection bottle.

"Just get this tube out of my chest and I'll be fine."

"Relax, Ino," said Elena, sitting on the edge of his bed. "You're going to be here for a while."

"Great," muttered Ino. "And what the hell am I supposed to do in this place?"

"Get better, for one thing," said Joe.

"Think about things, for another," said Elena.

"What's there to think about?" Ino asked sheepishly. "I got nothing to think about."

"How about why you're here," said Elena. "How about why you got mixed up with a gang like the Five C's in the first place. They're professional gangsters."

"I had to do something," he said, looking at her. "They killed Jimenez."

"And they almost killed you!" she spat. "Ino, you've got to get off the streets. You've got to get off the drugs."

"Elena, I'm fine. I can take it or leave it. I'm no addict."

"Then what were you doing with heroin in your pocket?" she asked, glaring at him.

"Stop worrying about me so much. I can handle it. Tell her to lay off, Joe, will you?"

"She's right," said Joe. "Why should I tell her to lay off?"

"Ino, you've got to do something," said Elena.

"Like what?"

"Like join a program," she said.

"I'll give it some thought," he replied.

"Ino, there's not much to think about," said Joe.

"I said I'd give it some thought," he snapped. "Will you two bug off? You'd think I was a junkie the way you're carrying on."

"And what are you? I've hardly seen you all year." There were tears in her eyes. "If Mama saw you like this, she'd turn over in her grave."

"That's not true. Mama never gave a damn about me. You were always her shining star," he said bitterly.

"Mama loved you more than life. She was just afraid of your outbursts. She said you were too much like Papa."

"And we know how Papa wound up."

"He just wasn't strong enough," she said sadly. "But you are, Ino."

He looked at her. She was the only one who cared. "Okay," he said finally. "I'll join a methadone program."

"You're running away again," Elena said angrily. "Methadone is just legal heroin."

"It's more addictive and more harmful than heroin," added Joe.

"Okay, okay, so methadone is bullshit. I know that. But I can't just sign myself into a program. What would they say?"

"They'll say you have courage and guts. More guts than it takes to get yourself killed in a street fight," said Elena. "It's the only way," she pleaded. "It's the only way we can ever be close again."

"Looks like you found someone else to be close with," he said, looking at Joe. "You won't be needing me."

Joe put his hand on Ino's shoulder. "Ino, we both need you. Besides, I think your community needs you."

"My community needs fifteen major factories," answered Ino thoughtfully.

By three P.M. things had slowed down. Elena was gone for the day and Joe slipped back to ward 2-B. Paco, Enrique, Angel, and Pablo stood by Ino's bed. They all wore identical denim jackets. The big bowl of fruit they had brought him stood on the nightstand, untouched.

"This is the doctor that saved my life," Ino said, introducing them.

"Glad to meet you," said Joe, extending his hand.

"We're grateful, Doc. You saved our Jefe," said Paco, a thin, small Puerto Rican.

"Thanks, but he's not out of the woods yet. He needs all the rest he can get. Can you guys come back tomorrow?"

"Sure, Doc," said Paco, holding his right fist up to Ino. "*Mañana*, Jefe." The men filed out of the room.

Joe sat down on the bed. "How are you feeling?" he asked.

"Better, but I still can't wait until I get this damn tube out."

"Well, it's only a matter of hours. When are you getting the chest X ray?"

"They're taking me down around six-thirty."

"I'm sure that you can bear with it for another couple of hours. Have you thought about our talk?"

"A little."

"What do you think?"

"I think I don't have a habit."

"If you don't have a habit, I want to know why it was so necessary for you to carry that heroin on the day of a battle? A warrior carries his courage. A coward carries his heroin."

Ino clenched both of his fists. His lips tightened. "You just come here. You do not know the name of Ino Sanchez in the street. I have courage."

"Well, if you have so much courage, you'd get your ass into a program. There is greater courage in doing that, than facing an angry knife."

"What do you know? How long have you been in the South Bronx?"

"You're missing the point, Ino. Your people need you. How much can you do, having to worry every minute about copping so that you can maintain your habit?"

"Well, there's nowhere to lead them."

"There will be if you can get clean. A true leader creates situations."

"How could I lead my people?"

"There are ways. Legitimate ways," said Joe. "Have you ever thought about politics, for instance?"

Ino let out a short, harsh laugh. "Sure. What politician has a five-inch scar under his left ear?"

"We can get rid of that for you."

"What do you mean?"

"We can do a revision on that scar. Plastic surgery."

"Plastic surgery? You could do that?"

"Sure."

"When?"

"Within the next couple of days. I'll speak to Susan."

"Is it a big thing?"

"Not really. I'm sure that it's just a thirty-minute case. They could do it under local anesthesia."

"I'm not afraid of pain."

"I'll work on it. We can clean your face up, but we sure as shit can't clean your veins. You have to do that."

"You're acting like it's so easy to admit that I'm a common junkie."

"You can't get clean unless you do. And you can't lead anyone until you get clean." Joe walked over to the head of the bed. "We'll do it together."

"Just because you saved my life doesn't mean you own it."

"Come on. I'm on your side."

"Just don't crowd me, I get nervous."

"Ino, you're not going to scare me away. And even if you could, you still have to deal with your sister."

Joe glanced into the trauma room. The young girl was still lying uncomfortably on her side. Kendricks was seated by the half desk, feverishly scanning a small red book. Elena was checking the girl's pulse.

"Kendricks, what are you doing?"

"I'm reading how to do an appendectomy. I scrub with Gold in one hour." His eyes did not leave the page.

Joe stared at the patient.

"But she still isn't prepped. Did you get consent?" Joe's brow was wrinkled.

"Her father works in a factory. I called, but no one seemed to know who he was. So I got the administrator to okay a telephone confirmation. Now we just have to get hold of one of her parents."

"How are you going about that?"

Kendricks shrugged his shoulders.

"Kendricks, your first responsibility is to get this patient ready for surgery. No one is going to let you louse this case up. Elena, any suggestions?"

"Get a cop," she stated simply. "The only time the community will cooperate with the police is in a medical emergency." Within twenty minutes the father was found and permission was granted.

Kendricks brought the young girl on the stretcher up on the elevator.

"No problem, kid. I'll have you fixed up in no time," he said, careful to steady his hand against the stretcher. He looked down at the small eyes, staring back blankly.

"Tienes poquito problema. En una hora, estará bien," said the operator, a small gold earring hanging from his brown ear. He pushed the stretcher into the hall.

"Where do I change?" Kendricks asked as the screen door closed.

"Doctor's dressing room is down the hall," he said, already descending.

"Nurse!" Kendricks yelled. There was no answer. "Shit," he mumbled under his breath. The OR staff should be waiting. "Nurse!" Finally, a small dark figure in greens peered curiously out the glass encased wooden door next to the sink.

Kendricks approached as the door swung open. "Nurse, I'm Dr. Kendricks, and I'm the operating surgeon."

"Hello, but I'm not the nurse," she said.

"We'll need a major lap setup," he ordered. "And suction."

"They're already setting up. You'll have everything you need. Let's go," she said, leading the stretcher into the room.

"Where's the anesthetist?"

"I'm Dr. Anna Kaballie. I'll be putting your patient to sleep."

"You?" Kendricks studied her frail Phillipino body suspiciously as she aligned the stretcher with the heavy steel OR table.

"Where did you train?" He was glaring as he helped lift the girl.

"Yale," she said, quickly injecting an ampoule into the IV.

"Oh. What are you doing?"

"I'm putting your patient to sleep."

"Now? Where's Dr. Gold?"

"He's already changing. I think you better join him," she said.

"Sure," he said, trying to recover. "Just as soon as I've positioned the light."

"We'll do that," said the nurse, entering with the tray of instruments.

"I'm Dr. Kendricks, and I'm the operating surgeon," he repeated.

"Yes." She began laying out the table.

"I want to check the instruments."

"Why don't you change first?" Dr. Kaballie interrupted.

Benjamin Gold entered wearing greens. "Kendricks! What are you doing?"

"I'm checking the instruments."

"I did that ten minutes ago. What are you doing in here in whites and without a mask?"

"Sorry. I'll go change. I'll be back in a minute," he said, red-faced, pushing the door open with his backside.

"You'd better call Susan," Gold directed as the door swung closed. "I think this is going to be a long case."

They were at the sink, scrubbing. Gold studied him nervously.

"Don't worry, sir," said Kendricks, noting his concern. "I already checked on that anesthetist. Even though she's foreign, she trained here."

"I thought she trained in New Haven, Connecticut?" Gold had a say in choosing all the members of his staff.

"You're right! . . . I meant here, in the United States."

"Oh," he said, slowly rinsing the soapy water from his arms. "We'd better get to work."

He glanced at the clock. It was a quarter after three.

They began laying sterile sheets around the girl.

"Uh, oh," said Kendricks as he stumbled forward contaminating his right sleeve on the IV pole. "I'd better change into a clean gown."

"Wait! Just use your other hand." He was sure to contaminate himself at least one more time before the patient was draped.

"Hi Susan," Kendricks greeted, lifting his left arm.

Susan looked at Gold. "Do you want me to scrub?"

"I think you'd better," he apologized.

"Dr. Kendricks, I'm sorry, but I think you contaminated your left sleeve on the light," interrupted Dr. Kaballie.

"Damm it. I'm changing my gown, now." He walked over to the nurse's table. "Doctor, what are the patient's vital signs?" he asked, trying to regain control.

"They're fine, Kendricks. Now get over here," Gold bellowed. They were staring at the small square of naked skin.

"I think I'll make a Davis incision. It's more cosmetic. Then of course, I could do a right paramedian. It damages less of the muscle." He looked up at his mentor. "What do you think, sir?"

"I'd make a standard McBurney over the point of maximum tenderness."

"Huh?"

"What's the matter?"

"I forgot to examine the patient."

Gold glared, grabbing two clamps. Susan looked nervously up at the ceiling. "Cut here," he directed in a low voice. Susan recognized the tone and quickly took two lap pads and lined them up next to Gold's clamps.

"You're beveling the skin. Hold the knife perpendicular." He turned Kendricks's hand upright, but the edges were still skewed.

"We're through the skin!" said Kendricks triumphantly. Gold and Susan were already smoothly clamping the small bleeders on each side.

"Should I tie them now?"

"No. Let's just get going. Cut." The knife went unevenly down through the fat to the layers of muscle.

"External oblique, internal oblique."

"Kendricks, what are you doing?"

"I'm identifying the muscle groups. Where do you think the transversalis is?"

"On the bottom! Let's just spread through the fibers. Here. Take the points of two hemostats and find an interval," said Gold, looking at the nurse.

Holding the two instruments awkwardly, Kendricks started to lower the points.

"Together. And not so deep. You'll tear through the peritoneum." Gold gulped. Susan followed quickly with small bent retractors helping to clear the layers as she guided his motion. As the thick blue lucent membrane became clearer Susan stopped, seeing the hole.

"Shit, Kendricks. You just poked a hole in the belly," said Gold, disgusted.

Clear brownish fluid seeped out. "Bad. That fluid looks in-ected. Culture tube!" Gold poked a small cotton swab into the ole.

"I didn't do that," said Kendricks, defensively.

"It's over eight hours old. When did this patient come in? She nust have been simmering for a while. Nurse, we'll need some antibiotic irrigation when we close. Give the surgeon a Metzen-aum."

"I'll have it made up," she acknowledged, handing Kendricks he scissors. He placed it in the hole and started cutting briskly.

"Kendricks, take it easy! You can't see the bottom edge. You ould be cutting a hole in the bowel and you wouldn't know."

"I'm being careful, sir."

"You're doing a fine job, Bob," encouraged Susan. Gold ooked up and Susan winked secretively.

Gold groaned under his mask. "Give me two Deaver retractors."

The abdomen gaped open. A shag blanket of fluffy strands of at and small vessels soaked heavily, outlining the organs, as hin yellow fluid swished over the friable edges in time to the wide breaths.

"That's just omentum. Push it over."

"With what?"

"With your hands, Kendricks. A surgeon is an artist. Use your hands like an artist would. Please, Kendricks. Try," Gold mum-bled, chewing the side of his lip. He started to relax a little as Kendricks gently began to palpate deeply into the hole. Three minutes later he checked the clock. Shit. It was four-thirty and hey still hadn't even found the appendix. The belly already ooked inflammed. "What are you doing?" he asked, impatiently.

"The kidney feels firm and without masses."

"Kendricks, find the goddamn appendix! It's next to the colon."

Three times Kendricks grasped a loop of small bowel and alling. "I've got it," pulled it up out of the wound.

"Okay," Gold said finally. "Trace the small bowel back to he appendix."

"It's stuck down over here."

"Stop pulling like that! Kendricks, what are you doing to this patient?" He swallowed. He had had it. The kid was going to be plenty sick even if her surgery was skilled. This was an on-slaught that would test the very strongest of systems.

He grabbed the curved delicate scissors, studying Kendrick' left hand lying near the patient's umbilicus. He swept down knicking the most distal tip of his glove. "Kendricks, you have hole in your left glove."

Gold's motion had been so quick and smooth and Kendrick had been so absorbed that as he looked at his hand he wa completely surprised. "Now, how did I do that?" He wondere aloud, changing, as Gold's both hands dove into the abdomen and came out with the cecum and the inflammed appendix. H laid it out, packing the borders with four towels.

Kendricks returned to the table. "Oh, there it is!" he calle victoriously.

The appendix lay like a swollen beefy sausage dipped in gray fibrin veil. Its end was black, and speckled brown flui dripped from several small tracts running through the demarcate tip.

"Now, Kendricks. Be careful. It's ready to explode. Put thi clamp across the base." Kendricks put the clamp where he wa directed, further distending the sausage. "Good. Dirty knife Now cut right above the clamp.

"Kendricks, goddamn it! Pay attention. Above the clamp We'll have nothing to tie," he admonished. Kendricks replace the blade and cut across the neck of the appendix.

Gold grabbed the pregangrenous organ and flipped it into metal bowl. He sighed. "We'll need a chronic tie above an below the clamp."

"Tie," called Kendricks, holding his hand out to the nurse As Kendricks's hand moved in long jerky motions he slid th second knot down. It broke immediately.

"Tie," called Kendricks. This time he broke it on the thir knot.

Gold groaned. "Slowly," he urged.

This time as Kendricks's hand went around the clamp, i slipped, pushing the cecum back into the hole. The clamp, unde the twisting pressure, tore off the base. The open end, pouring fecal material everywhere, settled back into the abdomen. Gol looked down, astounded. This was suddenly an emergency. The longer the hole remained open, the greater the chance the patien might develop a devastating infection.

Gold pushed Kendricks aside as his hands leaped back into the belly. This time his efforts were not as quickly rewarded. The traction, clamping, and the spilling fluid had severely trauma-tized the whole area.

"Susan! Get a couple of retractors in here," he barked. "Goddamn it." There were only loops of small bowel. "Wait, I think I got it," he said, palpating urgently. "Wipe." He directed the circulator as sweat collected over his thick eyebrows. "Kendricks, hold this retractor and don't dare move," he said menacingly. He finally pulled the even more swollen cecum up, out of the wound. He took a deep breath as he studied the menacing opening. He looked with hatred at the infected fluid pouring more copiously out from the rapidly filling ballooned large bowel. "2-0 chromic on a needle. Purse-string it, Susan!" Only after the hole was safely closed did Gold allow himself to shudder.

"We'll need at least three liters of irrigation. A couple of big drains. Dr. Kaballie, you'd better start some antibiotics. This kid is going to be sick."

"Joe started some Keflin when she came in," said Susan, not looking up from the intensive washing she was performing.

"That'll help," Gold said flatly. Susan quickly closed the peritoneal wound over the two deep drains. "Susan, don't even close the skin. Just pack it with iodoform gauze. This is an infected case . . . a bad one." His head shook as he removed his gloves.

He staggered out into the cool hall. He leaned, exhausted, against the wall. He felt like driving an osteotome into Kendricks's heart. How many more cases like this would he be forced to endure?

As Susan carefully applied the dressing Kendricks pulled down his mask. "What do you think? Personally I think it went pretty well. All in all."

"All in all, it was a tough case," said Susan, nodding her head unevenly and heading toward the dressing room.

"Thank you, girls. Thank you, Dr. Kaballie. Nice job." He gestured.

Dr. Kaballie checked the clock as she removed the tube. It was five-thirty. She marked it with an *x* on her record and with a deeper *x* in her mind. She would try to change shifts the first moment she got. It was either Kendricks or her. She just hoped she could do it before word got out.

9

Downstairs, Joe was finding the Friday night onslaught impossible to control. Luis brought the first patient in with a large laceration of the scalp. The woman, in her late twenties, had lost a lot of blood. Joe plugged in an IV while Luis washed out the wound. "Find out what happened," said Joe.

There was a rapid exchange of Spanish. "The ceiling collapsed in their apartment."

Joe clamped several of the larger bleeders. Luis wheeled in an unshaved man in his mid-thirties, who was lying on his side, dazed. He recognized his wife, bleeding slowly in the corner. Shaking the crumbled plaster from his hair, he tried to rise, fighting against the cloth restraint that had been secured across his chest. "What are you doing to her?" he yelled in Spanish.

"Get him out of here," ordered Elena. Luis pushed the stretcher back out into the hall. The man's screams were only dulled when Luis slid the steel door shut.

"What's his problem?" asked Joe.

"He thinks he's going to save his wife."

"From what?"

"From us."

"Can't you explain?"

"I tried. He's drunk. I think he's also a little *loco*."

"Maybe he suffered a concussion."

"Maybe. You're the doc."

"Get me some 3-0 nylon." Luis threw down a package of the much thicker number-one kind and ran out.

"Just throw a couple of big sutures in to stop the bleeding," said Elena, looking down at the chart rack. "We got five more waiting."

96

By the time Joe had begun suturing the woman's scalp, Luis was back. "I got two stab wounds. Not too deep. Where do you want me to put them?"

"In the hall. And wake up Arnost. Have him check them out please?" Luis ran into the hall.

"Joe, you'd better not waste any more time," said Elena. "Make two strands out of the hair on either side of the wound. Then just tie them together real tight."

"Will that work?"

"It'll stop the bleeding."

Luis came in with the news. "They'll live. One has a nasty cut on the arm. The other has a superficial stab of the chest."

"Get a chest film on the second one. What happened?"

"A card game. The one with the chest wound was winning too much."

Joe shook his head and finished sewing up the scalp. He would never understand. They wheeled in a motionless patient with a ten-inch Bowie knife sticking in his right side. "He's dead." Joe drew the sheet over his head.

"A bad debt," said Luis.

There were two dog bites, one wino, a hit-and-run fractured femur in a teenager, and a forty-year-old virgin who came in with a mirror mounted on a long stick, complaining her clitoris was getting bigger every day.

He was exhausted. His shirt and jacket were soaked with perspiration. His white pants were now a dull gray, covered with the remnants of the evening. He hadn't slept in thirty hours. Elena came up to him. "You've had it, Joe. Go take a nap. We'll be all right."

"Call me." He gave her arm a tight squeeze.

Joe trudged to the on-call room, barely able to make it to the bed. He collapsed and fell into a deep sleep. His body submitted, but his mind refused to rest:

They kept coming. Long lines of them; men, women, children. He was alone in the old cutting room. At first, they came slowly. They had cuts, bruises, blood was spurting out. Some were missing arms, others faces. He sewed them, he bandaged them. He was working as hard as he could. But they kept coming, faster and faster. A gangrenous leg lay before him. He had to decide. People from the back of the line started to complain of the wait. He chopped it off. He heard shots in the background.

He looked out the door into the hall. But there was no hall, there was no hospital. All around him was open space, smoke, fire, the smell of burnt flesh, cries of pain. He was in the middle of a battlefield, the middle of a war. The victims kept coming. It was no use, he couldn't keep up. He was crying now, he was alone, there was no one else that could help them. And he had failed.

The ringing woke him. His hand shook as he picked up the phone. "Yeah?"

"Joe, it's nine o'clock." It was Elena.

"Thanks."

"Joe, you okay?"

"Sure."

"You sound funny."

"I'm fine. I'll see you in ten minutes."

He took off his bloodstained clothes and dropped them in a pile on the bed. He went to the closet and took out the clean shirt and pants he had brought yesterday. Was it only yesterday? He went to the sink, stuck his head under the faucet and allowed himself a moment under the cold running water. He dried himself off with the last clean towel and watched a spider crawl across the cracked, peeling wall. He dressed quickly, anxious to leave the bleak room and the disturbing dream.

Luis and Susan were in the nurses station when he got there. "What'd I miss?" he asked, joining them at the small table.

"It's been pretty quiet for the last hour."

"Where's Elena?"

Luis and Susan exchanged looks. "We sent her home. She was exhausted."

"Are you going to pull the tube on Ino tonight?" Joe asked Susan.

"Yes, if his chest X ray shows his lung is still up. He's really had no drainage at all. I heard you got a chance to speak to him."

"Yeah, I did."

"How did it go?"

"Not great," admitted Joe. "He doesn't seem to have much hope. I guess it's hard for him to see himself as anything but a gang leader."

"The gang is nowhere," interrupted Luis. "He knows that."

"You were his best friend. How did he take it when you left?" asked Joe.

"He said I deserted him. I guess I did, too. The Toros were our life. Ino had high hopes—he was going to be a different chief, the Toros were going to be a different club. And it was—for a while. We organized a raffle to get toys for kids at Christmas. We helped distribute food to the people after the riots of '69."

"What happened?" asked Susan.

"Too many new guys with dope on their brain itchin' to make a name for themselves. After a while it was war. All the time. I had to work to help out at home. I didn't have the time, and later on, when I saw what was happening, I didn't want to. But the adjustment took me a long time. I guess Ino never really made it."

"Look," said Joe earnestly, "I hear the name Ino Sanchez and I hear some good things right along with the bad. That makes me want to believe in him."

"Sure, he's done some terrific things. He's a born leader," said Luis. "But the real question is can he believe in himself?"

"I mentioned the possibility of a scar revision to him. That was the only thing he picked up on."

"It's because of me he has that scar," said Luis. Joe and Susan stared at him. "It would help. Still, it's only superficial."

"But it's a start," said Joe. "Maybe after looking different, he'd start feeling different. What do we have to lose?"

"Nothing, I guess," admitted Luis.

"Susan, what do you think?" asked Joe.

"It extends beyond his left ear about six inches, right?" Joe nodded. "Technically, it's very easy. We just have to take a small flap and do a Z-plasty. I could get Dr. Whitmore to help."

"Who's Dr. Whitmore?" asked Joe.

She smiled. "Sid Whitmore. He's the Chief of Plastic Surgery at Hirshorn. A very fancy guy. He's one of the only chiefs who refuse to go full-time. He makes an absolute fortune shaping all those Fifth Avenue lovelies."

"Will he come to Jefferson?" asked Joe.

"If I ask him to."

"Whitmore. Isn't he the guy who has hot rocks for you?" asked Luis, laughing to hide his discomfort.

"For me and fifty other women." Susan smiled. "He treats women like they were precious vases. He told me once his whole purpose in life was to create, how did he put it, 'beautiful rosebuds to grace the world's eyes.'"

99

"He sounds like quite a character," said Joe.

"He is. When I was on service with him, we were short two residents. I really had to work my ass off. He couldn't believe that a woman could do something like that or would want to. He was constantly asking me out."

"Did you go?" asked Luis.

"Once," said Susan. "He took me to the Four Seasons. But I was going with Tom at the time, and Whitmore is married with two kids in college. But, I thought about it a lot. If that man performs on a sheet anywhere like he performs on an OR table, it would have to be a fascinating experience."

"How many days do you think it would take to set it up?" asked Joe.

"Three at the very least. We'll have to do it at night. Oh, my, that means clearing it with Gold. He'll have a fit over booking an elective case like that as an emergency. Then when he finds out Whitmore is coming, he'll probably go into a rage. They never really hit it off. They're such opposites."

"But you'll do it?"

"I'll do it." She smiled. "I've suffered through more than one of his rages."

"How did the appendix go with Kendricks?"

"It was such a bad experience I had to laugh. I thought Gold was going to die." She paused. "Then again, maybe I'm being a little rough on Kendricks. Everyone goofs up their first appendectomy."

"I bet you didn't."

"You're right, she didn't. She hit it right on the nail," said Luis proudly. "Twenty minutes, skin to skin. Isn't that right, Susan?"

"It wasn't twenty minutes. When I split the muscle, the appendix popped out. There is one thing that I do remember about that first case, though. At the end, Gold came around the table and lifted me two feet in the air. He hugged me like I had scored a touchdown. I was the first woman surgical intern he'd ever seen. I guess he was afraid I was going to be a stumbling incompetent."

"And it was all downhill after that." Luis smiled.

"Sure, I've seen a change in him," said Susan earnestly. "I'll admit he's more aloof than he used to be. But he still gives the patients the best medical care possible, and I don't think it matters one damn bit if he can't tell the difference between cuchies and rice and beans!''

"That's ridiculous and you know it," Luis snapped. "Gold belongs back at Hirshorn. What this place really needs is a young Spanish-speaking chief who can empathize with people. The most important thing is for the hospital to fill the needs of the community. Maybe if you came from here, you'd know that."

"Luis," she replied seething, "if Jefferson loses Gold, Jefferson loses its heart."

"Okay, okay, end of round one for you guys," Joe said quickly. "Luis, you and I have to go back to work. Come on."

A half hour later, Joe had pushed two people over to X ray, revived a heroin OD, and drawn the bloods on a twenty-five-year-old probable acute alcoholic pancreatitis. He trudged back to the nurses station and saw Luis drinking a cup of coffee. "Still upset over that thing with Susan?" he asked.

"Yeah, I guess I am. Susan thinks Gold is the foundation of Jefferson. As if the strength of a hospital could be one man." He shook his head. "It just shows how little she really knows. The strength of Jefferson is the people. Half a million people, Joe, who live with starvation and rats and no hope of ever getting out. Look, I'm no dreamer. I know Jefferson can't possibly supply all the community needs. But we can still give them the feeling of understanding and concern. That's something that Gold will never give. When I become a doctor, I'll come back here and work, and I hope things will be different."

"I didn't know you were going to med school," said Joe, surprised.

"First I have to be accepted. Then I have to be able to pay for it." Luis shook his head, thinking how hard that would be to pull off.

"Couldn't you get a loan?"

"It's going to be tough. I've already asked. I need someone to sign for me to guarantee it."

"Luis, I'm sure if you get accepted to medical school, you'll find a way of getting it financed."

"Yeah. That's what Susan tells me, and she hasn't disappointed me yet. She talked to Gold and got him to allow the department to cover half my credits for college. That's really helped."

"Gold is doing that?" Joe asked, astonished. "Then how come you're so down on him?"

"You misunderstand, Joe, I'm not down on Dr. Gold. If Jefferson was a three-thousand bed institute, he would be the perfect doctor to head it. But not with only two hundred and fifty beds. The Chief of Surgery at Jefferson Hospital cannot just be a chief. He's got to be much more. Susan thinks Gold's saving this place from medical havoc. What's saving it is Hirshorn Medical Center. Their money, their staff and their political power."

There was a knock at the door. "Come in," yelled Joe.

Roberto stood facing them, his face contorted. "This fucking place is getting to be too much." It was hard for him to speak. "I just checked an eight-year-old kid out five minutes ago. He was shot playing on a fire escape. Some *loco* decided to use him as a target."

"Jesus, no!" whispered Luis.

"One twenty-two long into the right part of his brain. He must have been killed instantly, because he was already cold."

Joe was filled with disgust. "That's sick. Who would shoot a child?"

"Whoever he is, we'll get him."

"Do the police have any clues?" asked Joe.

Luis was pale; he slumped against the stretcher. "Police? This isn't a police matter. This is an insult to our community. There can be no reason. A man like that must be stopped."

"Everyone's meeting on Bruckner and a Hundred Fifty-sixth," said Roberto.

"My shift is over at eleven. I'll join the search then."

The siren started ringing, and Roberto ran out toward the ramp.

"Can't you work with the police?" asked Joe.

"That's how much you know!" spat Luis. "If we were to depend on the police for justice, we'd have no hope." Joe thought of Sgt. Murray. "The code is crude, but it's clear. By tomorrow, the news of this *malo* will be shouted from every corner. We will find him and we will kill him. If there is any meaning to our culture, our children will remain safe."

The blare of the siren continued. Luis opened the window and stuck his head outside. "What is it?" he yelled.

From the back of the ambulance, Roberto's loud wail could be heard. "¡*Por Dios*! Another *niño*!"

"Still want to wait for the police?" said Luis, glaring at Joe. They began running to the trauma room.

As the stretcher came wheeling into the room Joe applied a tourniquet. He was a child, five or six years old, with soft brown hair falling over his forehead. The entire lower portion of his shirt and pants was caked with blood. "Luis, run back to Peds and get a baby blood pressure cuff. It's a gunshot wound of the abdomen," yelled Joe as he cut through the faded dungarees. The small hole and the blackish burnt border contrasted sharply with the blue and red Popeye decal above his navel.

"He has a femoral pulse on the left. Page Susan, stat. You better get a cutdown tray opened," said Joe as he nervously searched for a vein.

"Look out, the kid has no veins. We'd better get a line started." Joe searched feverishly over the pale body.

"What about cutting-down over his ankle?" Arnost started to roll down the crusted sock. The small boy was buried under the two interns.

"No good. If he has an injury to the vascular system in his belly, fluid will just pour in there. He's got no neck veins, either," Joe said with dismay. Susan appeared in the door.

"Help! We got a kid with a gunshot wound. He is shocking, and I can't get a line started."

Susan ran to the drawer and brought out a small CVP catheter. She detached the unit and applied the large hollow needle to a syringe. Then she plunged the needle under the small boy's collarbone. She rotated her fingers slightly and thick blue blood filled the syringe. Joe was already connecting the IV line as she threaded the catheter.

Luis returned, breathing heavily. Joe grabbed the discarded syringe and filled a red top tube, and handed it to him. "Get this up to the blood lab. We need at least four."

"You better get a Foley catheter in him," snapped Susan.

Joe slipped on gloves and began to wash the tip of the child's penis. "I need the smallest tube you have."

He smeared the tip with lubricant and slowly slid the tube through the small boy's sphincter. A column of warm, bloody urine appeared, soaking through the sheet.

"Oh no, the bullet probably got his bladder also. Get some IV Hypaque hung," yelled Susan. "Joe, try and find another IV line."

"His blood pressure is dropping out," called Mrs. Cleveland.

"Forget it Joe. We'd better just take him up. Call the elevator."

Joe and Susan ran down the hall with the boy. By the time they wheeled him into the OR room, Mike Barilla was already scrubbing. Joe lifted the small limp figure onto the table as the anesthetist placed a bag over the child's mouth.

Barilla ran in with soapy water still running from his elbow. "How we doing?"

"No good, I can't get a blood pressure."

"Step back." He grabbed a lap pad and began rapidly drying the soap. Then he threw a large sheet over the middle of the abdomen. Barilla took the scalpel and brought it down over the mid-portion. Susan grabbed two bent retractors and followed the two strokes of Barilla's hand.

"Oh, shit." Barilla gulped. The abdomen was open. Large clots of blood began to flow out.

"Get me some suction," yelled Barilla.

"It's coming from up top."

"You're right, Susan, near the liver." Barilla took a pad and pressed it firmly down against the posterior wall.

"Something is happening. We seem to have better control of the bleeding."

"Yeah, but I still can't find the laceration."

Joe had scrubbed his hands and was fully gowned. Barilla got two large retractors around the three major tubes leading into the liver. He turned to Susan. "I see the hole. It's in the portal vein. We need some vascular clamps."

"I don't have another circulator, yet," stated the nurse.

"Susan, take some rubber tubing and thread it around the regular clamps. I just hope that it won't injure the vessel too much."

Within minutes Barilla had applied a clamp above and below the two-inch laceration in the vein. He expertly excised the necrotic edges, then proceeded to sew the hole with a running 6-0 nylon suture. Barilla's hand did not stop for a split second. Joe was amazed by the smoothness and grace of his motions. He removed both of the clamps. A very small stream of blood was seen pumping from the mid-area of the repair. Barilla pushed another lap pad around the vessel.

"How long did we have the vessel clamped?" he asked.

"Only about ten minutes."

"The vessel looks good. How is he doing, nurse?"

"Pulling up, ninety over sixty."

Luis came running in with the blood. He handed it to the nurse and stood there watching. Kendricks appeared in the doorway.

Susan looked up. "Joe, you and Luis better get downstairs."

"Kendricks, you better scrub," said Barilla. "We still haven't found the bullet and it looks like it knocked a couple of holes in his bowel. Joe, thanks."

Joe and Luis dragged back to the Emergency Room, where Roberto was waiting. "How is he?" he asked.

"He'll be all right, I think," said Joe. "He's stabilizing. The bullet poked a hole in the portal vein. It's funny, but it only nicked one wall. Barilla has already repaired that. The bullet ricocheted once it hit his abdomen. There are a couple of intestinal perforations. I just hope his kidneys are okay." Joe's face was drained.

"That's two in an hour. We have to get this guy now." Roberto started to remove his white jacket.

"Roberto, you just can't leave work," Joe protested. Suddenly all three looked up into the face of Sergeant Murray.

"I understand that a child was shot. How is he going to be?"

"We have him up in the OR now, but the bullet really did a job. We don't have him out of it yet."

"Well, that's too bad."

"Sergeant, are you aware that this is the second case within two hours?"

"What do you mean the second case?"

"The kid in the morgue with the twenty-two through his brain." Joe leered into Murray's face.

"Where did this happen?"

"Around a Hundred Forty-ninth Street," answered Luis.

"You mean you had no idea some sort of lunatic is roaming the streets?" Joe asked, incredulous.

"To tell you the truth, there are fifty thousand lunatics wandering through the streets everyday."

"This is different, Sergeant."

"Okay, okay. I'll check it out. I'm going to call the precinct." Sergeant Murray ambled back to the desk.

He reappeared five minutes later. "You're right. There was another one. What the hell are these kids playing on fire escapes for in the middle of the night?"

"What do you plan to do about it?"

"Round up the regulars. Ask around. Put out a report."

"Sergeant, this is not a routine police matter."

"Shit, Doc. I've seen families machine-gunned, young girls dismantled. I got my captain on my ass. We got the congressman coming down here in the morning. There are four DOAs that haven't even been picked up yet and my shift has been over half an hour ago. I'm not Superman."

"But these are young children."

"No one who lives down here is young."

"Thanks for your cooperation," said Joe with disgust. "You're really a tribute to your job."

"My only job is to stay alive," he said gruffly, moving down the corridor.

By two A.M. the Emergency Room was quiet. Joe hurried upstairs to the OR. He leaned over the anesthetist's shoulder. He looked at the child lying on the table.

"How is he doing?"

"Much better. We had to give him three units, but he seems to have stopped bleeding."

Joe watched quietly at the head of the table. After several minutes, Barilla noticed him. "We got control, Joe. The bullet perforated one area of the small bowel and one area of the large bowel. It must have ricocheted off the liver and gone down into the pelvic cavity."

Susan looked up. "I'm almost through. We just have to sew the laceration in his bladder and we're done. The bullet was lying right in the bottom of the bladder."

Barilla picked it up from the stand, where it was wrapped in a four-by-four gauze sponge and flipped it to Joe. Joe studied the small metal head of the .22.

"It doesn't even look bent. It's lucky it wasn't a larger bullet."

"That's for sure. Forty-five's don't ricochet. It would have exploded the liver and gone out the back. He was lucky."

"Yeah. Real lucky," said Joe, closing the door behind him.

Joe woke up at seven A.M. and had time for a quick shower and shave. Then he went up to ICU. Kendricks was rushing around the room taking morning blood samples.

"How's the kid doing? asked Joe.

"Pretty good. We finished up by three. He started to put out some urine. Maybe you can give me a hand and draw the bloods on him?" asked Kendricks. "I've got to hurry."

"Sure," said Joe. "How come?"

"You know Richard Tanner, the one who's running for Mayor?" Joe nodded. "He's supposed to arrive in thirty minutes for a tour of the hospital "

"I wouldn't want you to miss that," said Joe.

He walked over to the crib. He looked at the clear plastic sheet that was draped around the child's head. He disconnected the line; the boy stirred and looked up. "My belly hurts," he whimpered.

"I know, son. It's going to hurt for a couple of days, but at least you're going to be all right."

A tremendous commotion was coming from the doorway. A short, energetic man in his early forties, with bushy black hair, impeccably dressed in a gray summer suit, began to stride into the unit. He was stopped by another man, taller, younger, and wearing glasses, who walked directly behind him. There were thirty people behind the pair, including two men carrying large portable lights.

"Where are we?" asked the leader.

"We're in the ICU. This place is no good. The people are too sick." The younger man disappeared back into the crowd. In the center was Dr. Gold. He was wearing a new lab coat. They conversed rapidly, then the man returned.

"We made a wrong turn. The wards are down the hall."

"Malcolm, we're wasting time!" stormed the leader.

The large, noisy group reversed their direction. As they left Joe looked at Kendricks. "I guess that's your next mayor."

"Did you see that suit? It must have cost four hundred dollars," said Kendricks, with envy.

"I guess I don't trust a man that wears makeup."

"He's supposed to make a speech."

"I'm sure of that."

"I'm going to listen," said Kendricks. "Come on."

Joe and Kendricks pushed through a mass of people congregating at the entrance to 2-B. When Joe squeezed into the room, he saw Richard Tanner standing in front of Ino's bed. The crowd, about fifty people in all, was standing behind the camera crew, thirty feet away. The crew was rolling the videotape, and the director was yelling at the two men whose job it was to aim the lights at the mayoral candidate. Tanner's right hand grasped the steel railing at the foot of the bed. With his left hand he made large, sweeping gestures.

"And if I am elected," he said, "I promise you, the people of the South Bronx, a brand new hospital, to properly administer to your needs. The South Bronx is a vital part of the great city of New York. The South Bronx deserves the few million dollars necessary to build a suitable medical institution. If I am elected, I promise to dedicate myself to that goal." He spoke directly into the camera. "I have long been a leader of civil rights. I plan to place a Spanish speaking person on the city council. I plan to investigate the housing situation in this area. I am here to help you, but I can only help if you vote for me. My plans and your dreams can be one."

There was a strange echo as the translator finished in a low voice. Tanner had already brought both arms down and nodded to his chief aide. Malcolm began clapping and the rest of the group joined in.

Tanner beamed. The short talk had gone off perfectly. The newsreel should be particularly impressive, for the bed made a great prop. It was fortunate that they had left one standing in the middle of the room.

Tanner walked out with one hand draped around Harold Krauthammer's shoulder. The patients lay staring in wonderment. Joe walked over to the center bed and sat down next to Ino.

"Did you ever hear so much shit?" muttered Ino. "That's the last time we'll see that clown, whether he's elected or not."

"You're probably right," said Joe.

"Sure, I'm right. When he ran for borough president of Manhattan, he became friends with José Moringo, the Puerto Rican middleweight contender. For three days they walked around the neighborhood hand in hand. Once the election was over, Tanner disappeared. The champion of civil rights—Ha! So he hires an equal number of minority groups to work as his domestics. He'll be even worse than our last two mayors."

"He really pisses you off," said Joe, surprised.

"The thing that bothers me is why he feels this place is worth half a day out of his busy campaign. He sure didn't come down to get the people to vote for him. Our turnout is always the lowest of all the boroughs.'' The small vein on Ino's temple began to throb. "He came down here to make a commercial. The fuck!"

"Ino, I didn't know you took such an interest in politics," said Joe.

"I don't. But I do take an interest in con men stepping into my territory. He's probably not even interested in being mayor. He probably wants to be president. He'll use the hype to push his fat face on the cover of every magazine he can. I know the type. I know them all. Politicians are pigs."

"Why don't you do something about it?" asked Joe.

"I'd like to, Ruskin. I'd like to smash this fist right into his face."

Joe sighed. "Don't add to the problems you've already got, Ino. How do you feel?"

"Great, now that Susan pulled that tube out."

"There is a real problem in the neighborhood, that I'm sure you haven't heard about yet." Ino stared at him. "Two children have been shot while playing on fire escapes, within the last twelve hours. One was killed instantly. The other looks like he's going to pull through, but not without a struggle. Luis and Roberto left after the last shift to look for the killer."

Ino was silent for a long time. "Where did the shooting take place?" he finally asked.

"The first occurred near a Hundred Fifty-sixth Street, the second was four blocks away."

"The man must be an outsider. No one from the community could possibly do this."

"I want to help you find him," said Joe.

"Okay." Ino touched his arm. "Call this number and ask for Paco." He wrote a number on a matchbook. "Tell him to come to the hospital. We have to get back in touch with Luis."

"I don't have his number."

"If Susan is still in the hospital, she'll know it. When can I check out?"

"Not for at least twelve more days. We just pulled the tube last night."

"We'll see," answered Ino quickly.

Within an hour, Joe, Paco, and Luis huddled around Ino's bed.

"We've already been through every apartment in a one-block radius of the first shooting. No one is really sure what hap-

109

pened," said Luis. "One of the teenagers swears that he saw someone on the rooftop two buildings down. A guy in his thirties, wearing old army fatigues."

"That might explain it," ventured Ino. "Some of those old vets walking around are crazier than shit. Did you check the second site yet?"

"We haven't had time."

"Paco, get all the Young Toros to help. Find out all you can."

"I want to help," insisted Joe.

"What type of bullet was it?" asked Ino.

"A twenty-two long," said Luis.

"Should be easy to trace. Joe, you call up all the sporting goods stores in the neighborhood. There are only five. See if anyone has purchased a twenty-two rifle within the last week. If we can get some basic description, it will at least be a start."

An hour later, Joe returned. "We may have a break. The fifth call I placed was to a small shop on Fox Street. A guy sold a twenty-two rifle four days ago. I'm going to check it out."

"I'll go with you. You'll need my help."

"But you can't leave the hospital. I've already explained that."

"Can't you sign me out for a few hours on a pass? I'm not afraid. I'll have an expert doctor by my side at all times."

Joe studied him for a moment. "Okay, I'll do it. But just for three hours. Whatever we can do in that time is fine, but you have to be back in bed by four o'clock."

Joe drove his car around to the ramp and pushed the front door open. Ino got in. "This is my first taste of fresh air in five days."

Joe followed Ino's directions, and they arrived at the sporting goods store in a few minutes. Joe's car squealed to a stop. Ino braced his feet against the floorboard. "And I thought Puerto Ricans were supposed to be lousy drivers."

They walked into the store. The old shopkeeper studied Ino, his right hand checking for the small pistol he had hidden behind the counter.

"Hi, my name is Dr. Ruskin. I spoke to you on the phone about an hour ago. Do you remember anything about the man who purchased that rifle?"

"I remember the rifle, a twenty-two long with a really high-power scope. It even had a night light on it. He said he wanted it to shoot rats in the dump.''

"Do you remember what he looked like?"

"Well, he was white, about thirty or thirty-five. He was wearing army fatigues. He was very nervous.''

"Isn't there anything else you can tell us?" asked Joe.

"A scar, something printed on his uniform?" Ino inquired.

"We were busy," explained the man. "The whole sale took three minutes. Wait a minute . . . His leg . . . yeah, something was the matter with his leg. He limped, kinda. Hey, why are you so interested in this guy?''

"We think that he might have used that rifle to shoot two small children," said Joe.

"I heard something about that. Do you really think it's him?"

"I don't know, but we're going to find out."

They returned to the car. "Let's get over to the site of the second shooting," said Ino.

As Joe and Ino arrived Luis, Paco, and four of the Young Toros were just about to enter the four-story red-brick apartment house. Joe held the horn down. The men came running back toward the car, and Ino opened the door. "Any news?" he asked.

"Not really. We've gone through five buildings, and nobody knows nothing."

"Rosita lives down the street. Did you try her?"

"That old *yenta*, what could she know?" Paco asked.

"Maybe a lot," said Ino. "Rosita sees everything. She hangs out that window ten hours a day."

The whole group began rapidly walking down the street. When they got to the corner, they looked up to the second window above the Laundromat.

"Rosita," Ino called. "*¡Abra la ventana!*"

A grossly overweight woman, with no teeth, leaned over the ledge. "Ino, my darling, I heard that you were dead. I heard that you were stabbed in the heart."

"Now, Rosita, you know that it would take more than a little knife wound to kill your Ino. We need your help. Were you looking out the window around nine o'clock last evening?"

"No." She looked at Joe.

"Can we come up?"

"*Sí.* To you my house is always open," she said, tilting her head, searching Ino for some sign.

"He's okay, Rosita. He's the doctor who saved me."

She still looked suspiciously at Joe. "Can we come up?" Ino repeated.

She nodded, and Joe and Ino started up the garbage heaped stairs. Taped above the door was a reflecting bumper sticker that proclaimed "This Is a Catholic Home. Non Believers Are Not Welcome." They entered a small two-room apartment. There was one chair and one plastic covered sofa near a half kitchen with the faucet leaking a continuous stream. The linoleum floor had been scrubbed clean. Against the other wall was a fake mantel, and over this stood a freckled mirror with three different-sized crucifixes precariously taped upright. The single wall was a blaze of reflected neon splendor as tropical-pink wax flowers, purple accordionlike paper necklaces, and a small painting of coconut palms against the blue ocean all vied for attention. The other walls were bare and peeling. She carefully sat Ino down on the sofa, while Joe was free to wander over to the mantel.

There was a four-by five-inch glass encased picture standing between dull brass candlesticks. A thick black rosary was draped over the gilded frame, hanging like a necklace below the neck of John F. Kennedy. Next to the picture was a small vial of holy water. In the corner of the frame was a small yellowed newspaper clipping that began, "In Memoriam 1963."

"You still have pain, darling," she noted as Ino winced lowering himself into the soft cushions.

"I'm getting stronger each day."

"You have to be careful," she admonished. "You're too pretty to lose."

"Rosita, I need your help." She stared at Joe, standing awkwardly in front of the mirror. "I mean we need your help. Were you looking out the window around nine o'clock last night?"

"Sí, ¿por qué?" she said in a lowered voice.

"A small boy was shot. He was playing on the fire escape five buildings down. Did you see anything?"

She nodded slowly and put her hands in her lap.

"I saw a stranger on the rooftop, across the street. I did not see a gun, but he was carrying a large brown bag. He ran down the street, and jumped into a yellow Ford. There were yellow pom-poms hanging from the back window and the car was old. The first two digits of the license plate were 4K. I remember because that was the apartment number of my mother, God rest her soul."

"Which direction did he go?" said Ino, hugging her.

"He headed back to the expressway."

"Do you remember anything more?"

"Not really. I only saw him for a few seconds. . . . Who is the handsome gringo?"

"His name is Joe Ruskin."

"What are you doing on the street? Looking for business?"

"Not really," said Joe. "I came down here to try and stop the killer."

"You take good care of my Ino. He's the best we have."

The men were waiting in the lobby. "Paco, check the roof across the street. Rosita said he was there. The rest of you men get out the word. We're looking for a man about thirty-five years old, probably wearing an army uniform. He has a limp and he's driving an old yellow Ford. License plate is *4K* something. I have to get back to the hospital with Joe. If you hear anything, call me."

They drove back silently. Joe helped Ino back into his hospital gown. He sagged, exhausted.

"I hope we're lucky." Joe stood by the bed.

"If he's in the neighborhood, we'll get him," said Ino wearily. "Let's hope he doesn't decide to lay low for a couple of weeks. We don't know what he'll do. But we got to be prepared for any move he makes."

He dozed off, and Joe looked at him. The dream was beginning to fade. He was no longer alone; he would not fail this time.

10

It was business as usual at Jefferson during the next week. The days were filled with emergencies, and the nights were filled with horrors. There was no news of the sniper.

For the first time, Joe found himself on the inside looking out. He knew Elena was the reason. He didn't see much of her—a quick greeting exchanged in the corridor, a few moments stolen over coffee. Yet, he found himself constantly thinking about her. He felt foolish but knew there was nothing he could do about it.

He discovered she had a passion for old movies, and he asked her to see one with him. She made him drive to Elmhurst, in Queens, where a picture neither one had seen was playing.

The aromas of the neighborhood hit them as soon as they got out of the car. The street was lined with small shops with counters on the sidewalk. The pizza, the tacos, and the knishes were all familiar to Joe, but the *cuchifritos* and *chicharones* were new and strange. "Water!" he shouted in despair, after tasting the hot delicacies. Elena giggled as he drank, and he secretly cherished the sound of her laughter.

A woman was shouting in Spanish at her kids on the sidewalk, and a Chinese family was closing their laundry for the night. A group of hoods stood on the corner, smoking cigarettes. As Joe and Elena passed, the group looked them over. One called to Elena in Spanish.

Elena gave him a livid stare. *"Mi hermano es el jefe de los Toros."*

Quickly, the boys stepped back, and the couple passed.

Impressed, Joe asked, "What did you say to get that kind of reaction from them?"

"I told them to grow up." Elena smiled.

They spent the evening watching an old Carole Lombard

movie. It was romantic and funny, and Joe slipped his arm around Elena's waist as they left the theater. She shivered a little. "Cold?" he asked.

"Nope." She smiled, looking into his handsome face. "Just excited."

He beamed with pleasure. "I take it that has something to do with me?"

"Just a little," she teased. It felt right walking along beside him. He was a man who knew where he was going, she decided. And she was with him. Elena Sanchez, on a date with this man. Like hundreds of other girls did every night of the week. It was nothing unusual, it was nothing extraordinary. Then why did she feel so ecstatically happy and at peace with herself? It was good not to be afraid. And where had all the anger gone?

In her apartment they sipped white wine from champagne glasses. She lit candles, and the room took on a rich, warm glow. Joe stretched out on the sofa, and she curled up beside him.

"I didn't know you were interested in art," he said, noticing the Matisse reproduction hanging on the wall.

"For years now, I've gone to the museums whenever I can. It gives me a sense of peace, a kind of solace. I don't know." She sighed. "Maybe it's my way of running away."

"Come on"—he smiled into her extraordinary eyes—"you're not the kind of girl who runs away from anything."

"Maybe." She shrugged, suddenly embarrassed.

"I saw Ino today after lunch," he said.

"How did he look to you?"

"Never better. Do you know he's up to forty push-ups a day now? His discipline is staggering. He'll probably be in better shape when he leaves the hospital than when he came in . . . The scar revision is set for tomorrow night."

"Susan told me." Her eyes clouded for a moment, and she played with the stem of the glass. "It doesn't change the fact that he's still an addict."

"I know, I know," said Joe. "But God, Elena, give him credit when he deserves it. The man's two weeks out of ICU and he's put himself on a physical fitness schedule I'd have trouble keeping. He's having plastic surgery. Give him time. Show him you're proud of the small things he's accomplished and then, maybe, he'll try some of the big ones."

"Like joining a program?"

"That and maybe even more. Who knows? You said yourself he's a remarkable guy. You're all he's got right now."

"Don't you think I know that?" she asked.

"Sure. All I'm saying is build him up. Don't let him dwell on being afraid, because he is. We're asking him to do the toughest thing he's ever done." He reached over and smoothed her hair. She looked up, and he saw the tears forming in her eyes.

"Why are you sad?" he asked softly.

"I don't want anything to spoil what we have," she said.

He put his arms around her and rocked her gently. "It has taken me all my life to find you. I'll never let anything come between us."

"Not even me?" she whispered.

Joe looked at her, understanding. "Not even you." He smiled. "I'll wait as long as you tell me to wait."

Now the tears were streaming freely down her face. "I love you, Joe."

He thought he would burst from sheer happiness. "If you only knew how I've dreamed of you saying those words."

She rested her head on his shoulder, and he held her for a long time. Finally she said, "It won't be easy. We've got lots of things against us."

"I know," he said, suddenly subdued.

She reached over and kissed him fully on the lips. Her eyes beheld a passion deep within, and he felt a stirring in his loins. He pulled her toward him and held her very tightly.

To be aroused by the caresses of a man was strange and new to her. Later she'd sort it all out. Now, her only desire was to languish in Joe's warm embrace.

Lightly, he traced the outline of her breasts, and she felt her nipples begin to harden. He lay down next to her and unhooked her bra, allowing her massive breasts to spill free. He slipped his hand inside her slacks and felt her damp thighs. He found it difficult to contain his excitement. Her soft moans gave him impetus to move on. Tentatively, he lowered himself and savored the electricity rising from her pelvis.

"I want to, I want to so much," she whispered. His heart pounded fiercely, and he wanted to isolate this moment in time. He kissed her softly on every part of her face. Then he saw the tears. He felt her body stiffen and he knew she was suffering.

"I can't, Joe, I'm sorry." His hardness diminished as he listened to her soft sobs.

"It's all right," he told her gently. "We have our whole lives together."

They sat up, and he stroked her hair as she nestled close to him.

"That's what I like about you," she said with a rueful smile. "Always the optimist."

"When it comes to you, I am."

In her bed alone, long after he had left her, she realized there would never be another man for her as long as she lived.

On Wednesday morning Joe wheeled a stretcher down ward 2-B and helped the man into a bed. Then he went over to Ino's bed, in the far corner.

"Any word on the sniper?" Ino asked.

Joe shook his head.

"Is he sick?" asked Ino, nodding at the new patient.

"Yeah. Why?"

"I know him from the neighborhood."

"He's going to need an emergency operation."

"Now?" asked Ino.

"Within the next couple of hours. Don't get uptight. We'll still do your scar revision at six. Even if we have to open another room. We don't even need a nurse."

Ino swallowed hard. "Wouldn't a nurse make it easier?"

"I'll act as the nurse if I have to. Or Elena will. But, we'll do you tonight, I promise."

"You're sure this guy is coming?" asked Ino.

"He'll be here. You're getting one of the finest plastic surgeons in the world. Relax, nothing's going to go wrong."

"I've just been thinking about it for the last week."

"That's natural. Everyone is nervous before an operation."

"I used to love that scar. I thought it gave me rank. Now I hate it."

"In a week, you'll look like you never had it."

"Yeah, but how much difference . . . ." His voice trailed off, and he turned his face away from Joe.

Bob Kendricks walked into the room, carrying a chart. "Where's the new admission?" he yelled to Joe.

Joe looked up. "Bed twenty," he said. They watched Kendricks begin examining the patient in the bed across from Ino. Joe shook his head in a helpless grimace. "Now, what were you saying?" he asked.

"Nothing," said Ino, embarrassed.

"You're afraid that even with a clear face, you won't be able to make it?" asked Joe.

"I've already made it, Ruskin. And don't start putting what I say into your bullshit words. They come out fucked up."

"I was just trying to get you to understand yourself."

"Come off the mountain, man," said Ino hotly. "Talk to me about the *malo* free to slaughter our children while the police watch. Or talk about winos being set on fire. Or old women being robbed. Or what happened to my sister. I can understand what I can see."

"And you can't see yourself going straight?"

"Drop it, Ruskin. I can't see you giving me a sermon. What time is it anyway?"

"Two," said Joe, glancing at his watch, then getting up. "The nurse will give you an injection pretty soon. It'll really lay you out. I'll see you at six, when they bring you up."

"Ruskin."

"Yeah?"

"Thanks."

"*De nada.*" Joe smiled as he started down the hall.

Bob Kendricks finished his examination on the new patient. Susan had been right. The man had a surgical abdomen for sure. Air under the diaphragm. Pain. No bowel sounds. Now he just had to get consent.

He opened the chart and flicked out his pen. "*Su llama aqui.*" he directed, holding the pen and chart out for the patient to sign.

"*¿Por qué?*" asked the man.

"*Es necesario que tiene un operation.*"

The man started shouting desperately in Spanish and shaking his head.

"*Aquí.*" Kendricks pushed the pen in his hand.

The man looked at Kendricks and threw it across the floor.

Kendricks waved the chart nervously. "*Esta mucho importante.*"

The man spat in Kendricks's face.

Kendricks stepped back. Now what was he supposed to do? A ruptured ulcer would be Zilk's case.

"Excuse me," he said to the patient, already running back to the phone. When he heard the operator begin the page, he breathed a sigh of relief. His senior resident would know what to do.

"Ino, wake up." It was Elena, in her nursing greens, shaking him. He stirred slightly then fell back.

He was running with his machete held high overhead. The water was a deep chilly blue. He stopped splashing, feigned an imaginary opponent and veered toward the dunes. The clean white sand felt warm on his bare feet. He reached the rocks and climbed up. He could see practically the whole northwest portion of Puerta del Mar from this part of the beach. He watched a lizard make its slow exodus toward the treelined shore. He stood in wait, his machete poised, until the animal had reached the rocks where he would have the most trouble gaining footing. The downward sweep came, just as the lizard looked up, catching his scent. The head stayed, splattered against the flat part of the blade, as the legs began carrying the now directionless body forward. He watched the strange form bleeding in the summer sun.

He washed his weapon in the ocean and carefully dried it on his tattered shorts. It was his most valuable possession, left to him when his father's truck, carrying the illegal rum, had crashed brutally into the ravine.

"Ino, can you hear me?" He opened his eyes and saw Elena standing beside him. He smiled at her. She was wearing the iron cross. It was her legacy, from their father, just as the machete was his.

"Ino, they're going to wheel you up to the OR," she said softly. "I'll be there the whole time."

She was always there when he needed her. She had showed him the secret places in the fields until he was old enough to take her to new ones of his own. They had explored the island together, long before either one had ever heard of America. She was the only one left who would never betray him. His mother was gone and his grandmother long before her. He tried to speak but the words never came. He reached for her hand and she squeezed it before she left the room.

Two white uniforms stood at the bed across from his. The big one was yelling. "You understand, you stupid spic. Now I said sign the lousy paper." There was scuffling, and the one with the huge putty ass started to lift the patient by his gown.

"What now?" asked the smaller one.

"You got to know how to handle patients. They won't sign, you make 'em."

"How do you do that?"

"Guy with a surgical abdomen is going to have a tender belly, right?"

Ino watched as the doctor took a forward swing that landed heavily. There was a loud wail. "Ready to sign?" he asked.

Ino tried to get up, but his body would not obey.

"I don't think . . . ." the smaller one started nervously.

"When you know as much as I do then you'll tell me what you think." He dropped the pen and paper on the bed, and the patient made a feeble effort to pick them up. A satisfied smile crossed the doctor's face. "Sometimes you got to talk to them in a language they understand."

It was an effort to keep his eyes open. The last thing he saw were the two white uniforms heading down the corridor.

Sid Whitmore quickly lay the four sterile towels around Ino's ear. "I can't believe you asked me to come do a minor league revision in this hole."

"I can't believe you came." Susan smiled under her mask.

"I never could resist your eyes."

"Sid, I'm a married woman."

"So am I," he said, gracefully excising the scar. "Still some in that corner." He extended the incision at a precise angle. "Two stay sutures 5-0." He nodded to the nurse. The nurse handed him the loaded instrument, which he used to tack two measured sutures. The edges came together perfectly, converting the raised scar into a thin Z. He nodded with satisfaction and looked at Susan. "I heard your husband's on a fellowship."

"He is."

"Well, I'll be happy to take you to dinner."

"Thanks," she shook her head.

"You must be lonely."

"I'm really busy," Susan said.

"With what?"

"With this rotation at Jefferson and with this case," she said, picking up the forceps. "Now maestro, time to close."

*　　　*　　　*

When he opened his eyes in the recovery room, he saw her standing beside him. "It's all over now," said Elena.

"How . . ." His throat burned when he tried to speak.

"It went great." She smiled.

"Do I . . .?"

"You're going to be the Don Juan of the South Bronx."

His eyes closed. "They made him . . ." he started.

"Made him?"

"Punched him . . ." mumbled Ino.

"Rest, my handsome brother." Elena smiled. "You're still dreaming."

"That's the last of them," said Joe, removing the small suture from below Ino's ear.

"How's it look?" asked Ino quickly.

"One of the best revisions I've ever seen," said Joe. "See for yourself," he said, handing him a mirror.

Ino studied his reflection. The scar had faded, and all that remained was a faint red line. He felt a wave of relief as he put down the mirror.

"The redness will disappear in a few weeks," said Joe. "Maybe sooner"—he smiled—"considering your rate of healing."

"So I'm ready to go?"

"Medically, you could have been discharged a week ago. But where do you go from here?"

"I've decided to enroll in a program."

"Which program?" asked Joe warily.

"Rebirth House."

Joe let out a soft whistle. "They're tough. But they're probably the best. They have the highest success rate in the city."

"Let's see if they're tough enough to take me."

"That's some attitude you're going in with," said Joe.

"That's the only attitude I got," said Ino.

"When are you going?"

"Tomorrow, after I check out."

"Really?"

"Sure."

"Ino, this is fantastic," said Joe. "Elena will be so happy. I can drive you over there if you like."

"Okay, Joe, we got a date."

"Is this the truth?"

"I give you my word."

Joe knocked excitedly at Elena's door.

"Where's the fire?" She laughed, unlocking the bolt.

He swept her into the air, spinning her around.

"Joe, Joe, put me down." She laughed. "What's happened?"

"He's going to do it!! He's going to sign himself in!"

"Oh, God! Are you sure?"

"He's asked me to drive him there tomorrow. I guess all the talking paid off." He grinned.

For the first time in months Elena felt as if a weight had been lifted off her shoulders. It was hard enough for her to believe she had met Joe. If Ino signed himself into a drug program, her life would be complete. "I'm so happy," she said between tears. "I can't believe it's going to happen."

Joe hugged her. "This calls for a celebration. Come on, I'm taking my best girl to the nicest place in town." He grabbed her coat from the hook by the door.

"Oh, Joe, I can't go like this." She looked at her dress. "It's too plain."

"Come on, you nut, nothing about you is plain."

They went to a little French restaurant on the east side. Joe blew practically his whole week's paycheck, but didn't care. The look in Elena's eyes as he watched her across the table was worth it. The delicious food, the attentive waiters, the fine wine, in all her life, she had never been treated so royally.

After dinner they took a ride in a horse and buggy through Central Park. The air was crisp, almost cold, and they huddled under the coarse woolen blanket and spoke of new beginnings.

Later, at her apartment, she looked at him lovingly. "You've changed my whole life," she told him.

"I meant to," he said.

She took his hand and led him to the bedroom. She left him, and soon he heard soft music filter in from the other room. He lay back and rested his head against the pillow, more content then he had ever been.

When he saw her, he thought for a moment he was dreaming. She had on a blue silk robe that outlined every crevice of her body.

"Do you like it?" she asked, twirling around the room. "I was saving it for a night like this."

"You're beautiful," he whispered hoarsely, reaching out for her.

She came to him gladly, holding back nothing this time. They moved together in a common joyous rhythm, exploring, caressing. Joe closed his eyes and felt he was drowning in her lovely breasts and her legs and her smooth skin. As he readied himself to enter her she let out a soft moan. For an instant he thought she was frightened. Then he looked deep into her eyes and knew she wanted him as much as he wanted her. Wild primitive explosions overtook them as they burst forth with a surge of power each had never known before.

They lay very still. "We are together," she finally said.

"Forever," he vowed.

It was the happiest moment of Elena's life.

They drove to the hospital. Elena walked up to the nurses' desk on ward 2-B.

"Hi, Joan. We've come to take my brother."

"You're kidding."

"What do you mean?"

"Elena, I thought you knew. Your brother signed himself out of the hospital last night."

Once on the street, it took Inocencio Sanchez less than an hour to connect. Luis located Angel in an alley that served as a shoot-up gallery.

"And you gave him dope?" Luis glowered.

"If Ino came to you looking like he did, you would of done the same. What difference does it make anyway?"

Luis pushed Angel roughly against the brick wall and left.

For the next three days there was no word. Elena, Joe, and Luis searched the neighborhood, but it was as if Ino Sanchez had never existed.

Luis and Joe were in the Emergency Room when the phone rang. Joe walked to the desk. It was Paco.

"Ino told me to call you. I think we may be onto something.

123

A guy with a bum knee has been at the bar on Hoe and a Hundred Forty-ninth Street since the place opened. He's loaded on Scotch. He keeps talking about the One Hundred Twenty-first Infantry and the Tet Offensive. He seems very nervous, and I think he may be our man.''

"Don't go in there, just surround the bar. Luis and I are on our way.''

Luis directed Joe to park the car a block away. Halfway down the street a 1968 Ford Sedan with license plate *4-K208* was parked. Ino was standing across the street with five of his men. He beckoned the group into the hallway of the small run-down tenement building.

He looked haggard, and they could see he hadn't shaved in days. "Ino, where have you been?" asked Joe.

"I'm all right," said Ino.

"You don't look it," said Joe. "But I guess junkies never look too good.''

"Will you lay off that shit for a minute?" snapped Ino. "Right now we got more important things to do. I think we found our man. He's in one of the corner booths. The back door is locked. The only place he'll be able to go is up the stairs to the roof. Give me five minutes. I'm going to try and get on the roof from the next building. If he tries to escape, I'll be waiting for him.''

Ino ran up the three-story stairway to the roof. The building that housed the bar was a story higher than the roof on which he now stood, with a space of about 15 feet between the two. Ino's cold eyes quickly scanned the roof. There was an old clothesline tied to two steel poles, grayish sheets hung from it. There was a stale, putrid odor of rotting food and burnt rubber. In the far corner, near the chimney, was a pile of empty garbage cans. Against the wall rested an old tire, its inner rim charred, huge patches of rubber missing. Ino studied the laundry line. His right hand fell to his pocket. A seven-inch stiletto blade shot out from its ivory handle. He sawed through one end of the rope. Then he wrapped the end and shook it vigorously. The sheets fell onto the dirty roof. He grabbed the used tire, tied one end of the rope securely through it and ran to the edge of the roof.

Two children were playing in the alley below. Their excited laughs and the sound of beer cans being kicked against the wall echoed up to him.

"Get out of the alley!" he yelled.

"We got rights!" they yelled back, running away.

There was nothing to hook the tire onto except for the rounded handles of the fire escape ladder, leading down the side of the other building. Ino coiled the rope in his left hand. With a powerful throw, he aimed the tire at the top of the ladder. He yelled with pain and grabbed the taped side of his chest.

The throw had missed, and the tire lay dangling between the buildings. Hand over hand, Ino pulled the tire back. This time he placed his right hand flatly across the painful area under his shirt. With tremendous effort he threw his left hand up and out. The tire bounced once on the concrete edge of the building and then slid over the curved handrail. Ino jerked the rope down, and the tire wedged tightly over the handle. Wrapping the rope around his left hand, he stepped onto the ledge. With a strong leap he swung over to the opposite side. He landed about twenty feet below the roof edge, using his feet to shield the impact. Then with great effort he began to inch up the rope. He rolled onto the roof edge and landed on his side. He lay there for several minutes, regaining his breath and allowing the sharp pain in his chest to subside.

Joe and the men opened the front door to the bar. The minute the killer saw Joe's white uniform, he sensed something was wrong. He reached under the table and grabbed the large brown paper bag. Then he bolted for the back door. Joe was the first to notice the escape, and he was quickly on his heels. They raced up the dark stairwell. The panicked man rushed through the door leading to the roof, then quickly slammed it shut. Joe tried to open the door but felt only resistance. He took three steps backward and swung his right shoulder against the edge. As the door splintered open Joe stumbled forward on his knees. He looked up to see the killer aiming a pistol directly at his head.

"I have you, Charlie." The whole right side of his face was twitching violently.

Ino lay on his side, hidden against the far wall. He crawled toward them, making sure to stay directly behind the sniper. As he cocked the trigger in his right hand Ino hurled forward and grabbed the gun hand with his left wrist. He brought the razor-sharp stiletto upward into the killer's armpit. The thrust was stopped only when the knife wedged deeply into the bone. The killer's arm jerked inward, then fell limply at his side. The gun fell to the floor. Ino withdrew the knife with a twisting motion and then swept it powerfully backward. The wounded man fell to his knees. Joe pushed between them.

"Don't do it, Ino."

"He was going to shoot you," yelled Ino.

"Please, you don't kill him. Help me take him back. For all of us, don't kill him."

Ino grabbed the sniper by his long, matted hair, dragging him up off his knees toward the stairs.

They drove up the ramp. The car jerked to a stop in front of the entrance. Roberto ran up to meet them.

"We got him," Luis yelled triumphantly.

Joe opened the front door. "Ino, get on the phone and call the Forty-first Precinct. Ask for Sergeant Murray. Tell him we want him."

They helped the captive into the trauma room. He was subdued but bleeding heavily and trying to support his lifeless right arm.

Luis went to the phone and paged Susan.

Ino appeared in the doorway. "Murray will be here in fifteen minutes," he said with a broad smile. "This is going to be a far-out scene."

Susan rushed in and began to examine the patient. "I think we better explore him. He has no reflexes, and he's already forming a large hematoma. Who is he? What's going on around here?"

"This man is responsible for your case with the kid. Ino got him and saved my life in the process."

"You better call the OR and notify them that he's coming up," said Susan. "You can fill me in later. I want to hear this."

Joe watched Luis take the stretcher out, then walked to the phone and dialed "O." "Lucy, get me the *Daily News*."

An hour later two reporters were scribbling on their note pads, as Joe narrated the previous events.

"That's right, Inocencio Sanchez is responsible for capturing this maniac. He has long been a leader in the Spanish community. Hold it one second, please. Only pictures of his right side," he directed the photographer as Ino stood uncomfortably against the far wall.

Sergeant Murray strode into the room. "Who's in charge of this circus?"

"I am, Sergeant Murray," Joe replied calmly. "Oh, gentlemen," he said to the reporters, "this is Sergeant Murray of the Forty-first Precinct. He has served many long distinguished years

126

enforcing justice and protecting the people of the South Bronx. Unfortunately, he's going to retire to Florida. I'm only sorry that your new prisoner can't be presented formally. We had to take him up to the OR. We just have to sew up a little knife hole in his right arm. I'm sure that within a couple of days he'll be safe to transfer.''

"A knife wound?" countered Murray. "Whose knife?"

"Why the sniper's knife, of course, Sergeant. Ino grabbed it from his left pocket.''

"Something smells about this whole story.''

"Come on, Sergeant. Give a little credit to the people.''

Joe and Ino stood on the ramp. "Joe, I'm ready. I'm signing myself into Rebirth.''

"You've said that before.''

"This time I mean it.''

"How come?''

"I think I see a chance. When I left the hospital, I was strung out for two days. Paco and Enrique were looking for me all that time. They'd spotted the guy and needed me. And where was I? Out with a needle up my sleeve. He could have killed ten more kids in the time it took me to come down. I'm fed up with myself.''

"Luckily, he didn't," said Joe, "and we did get him.''

"That's why I think I got a chance. Waiting up there on the roof, I had the feeling it was all laid out for me. Don't ask me how—I don't know. But it was like somebody was trying to show me something—I felt more powerful than I ever felt in my life.'' There was a long silence as they studied the decaying skyline of the South Bronx. "Now that I've made my decision, I'm scared shitless," admitted Ino.

"You've got a right to be," said Joe.

"I'm going to sign up at Rebirth.''

"They won't take any bullshit, Ino. They'll throw you out on your ass if you don't mean it.''

"That's why I'm going there. They got a reputation, and I guess I do, too.''

They drove back toward Elena's. Ino looked out the window. "I wish I knew how it was going to end.''

"We're not going to know that for a while.''

"One thing's for sure." Ino stared intensely at Joe. "I'm tired of fighting wars. Can you understand that?"

"Sure. But I think you've got me hooked. The excitement of catching that killer is still with me. Look, my hands are still shaking."

"They'll shake for a day."

"What a surge."

They knocked on Elena's door, and she opened it immediately.

"Thank God! You're safe," she burst out, hugging them both. "It's on the news every half hour. And the phone hasn't stopped."

"I gave them your number," said Ino. "I had to tell them I lived somewhere. And I'm going to join up. I'm going to join a program."

"You've said it before," she faltered.

"But he means it this time," said Joe. "He really does."

She stood looking at the two men. "I love you both so much," she whispered.

There was a sudden knock at the door. Joe opened it and faced a young man dressed in a poorly fitted seersucker suit. "My name is Cliff Garvin. I'm from the *Post*. Is there an Inocencio Sanchez here?" Garvin ran his fingers through his hair and nervously clutched the small spiral notebook. Joe studied him hesitantly. Garvin opened his wallet, displaying his laminated press card.

"*New York Post*," Joe read. "Cliff Garvin? I never heard of you."

"I'm new, but I've been working the copydesk for over a year. Who are you?"

"My name is Joe Ruskin."

"Aren't you the doctor that helped in the rescue?" asked the eager reporter.

"I guess I am, but in truth, I was more of a burden to Ino than a real help." He motioned for Garvin to come in. "This is Ino Sanchez and his sister, Elena."

Garvin shook their hands. "That's not what the mayor thinks. I hear you're both going to get a gold medal. The whole city is going wild. Everyone's trying to cash in. Richard Tanner has already bought five two minute spots on TV. He has a videotape of himself by Ino's bed."

"I remember when that was taken. He didn't say one word to Ino," said Joe.

128

"That's not what Tanner is saying now. He says that he had a long talk with him right after the killings. He said that his conversation inspired Sanchez's courageous actions."

"Tanner's full of shit," offered Ino.

"I'm sure you're right, but he's going to be the next mayor. Is it true you're a gang leader?" Garvin asked.

Ino appeared momentarily flustered. "Not anymore," Joe offered.

"Is it true you killed two people?" Garvin asked hesitantly.

"Where did you hear that?" Ino's voice was cold.

"I heard it from Sergeant Murray," the reporter said quickly.

"Anything that comes from Murray is bullshit," said Ino. "I have a clean record."

"I know," said Garvin. "I already checked. But they almost got you once."

Ino thought back to the drug setup. "Yeah, but I've never been charged with any crime, and I'd appreciate it if you forgot my scratch sheet."

"Please, Cliff," interrupted Joe, "Ino really needs a friend. We might be able to help you with some follow-up material. Besides, Sergeant Murray has a personal thing against Ino."

"Well," said Garvin, "I do need a follow-up story. That's why I'm here."

"We'll give it to you, and we might help even more in the future," said Joe, placing his hand on Garvin's shoulder. "I'm going to be completely honest. Ino had decided to join the Rebirth House program, and I'm going to drive him over. It's going to take him time to get clean, but then he's going to be out, and the people of the South Bronx identify with him. They need a leader. Ino is the only one that qualifies. You can write your follow-up and expose him as a junkie, or you can write about the good things Ino has done and wait a few months to see how he turns out. I promise you'll have an inside track regarding any future stories."

"Please," Elena whispered.

Cliff Garvin looked at the three of them. "Okay. I'll cover, but only 'cause I need a break too."

Joe shook his hand. "Cliff, we've just become a team."

11

Ino walked into the shabby four-story building and found himself in the center of a well lit, clean lobby. A young black man was seated at the desk, reading a newspaper.

"May I help you?" he asked, putting the paper down. There were scars running up and down his arm.

"I . . . I want to enroll in the program."

The man looked at him for a long moment, then down at the paper, then up again at Ino. "Wait here," he said, motioning to the sofa. He hurried out of the lobby, rolling the newspaper under his arm.

He rushed into the director's office. "Herb," he said, "you won't believe who wants to enroll."

"I'll believe it," said Herb Aquedo, taking a long drag on his pipe.

"Front page of the *Post*."

Herb scanned the paper quickly. "Where is he now?"

"Sitting in the lobby."

"How strung out is he?" asked Herb.

"I didn't bother to ask."

"Why not? He's an addict, isn't he? He wouldn't be here otherwise. Treat him like every other junkie that walks through that door." He pressed the button on his intercom. "Jack, come in for a minute, will you?"

A tall, muscular blond man crowded into the room. "What's up, Herb?" he asked.

"This is what's up. Herb handed him the paper, pointing to the picture of Ino. "He just strolled in . . . says he wants to enroll."

"Well, I'll be . . ." Jack continued reading down the page, then let out a long whistle. "I'm ready, boss, anytime you are."

Ino was led into the small office. "Sit," Herb directed. Ino took the chair facing the two men.

"What's your name?" Herb asked.

"Inocencio Sanchez."

"Why are you here?"

"I want to enroll in your program."

"Why?"

"Because it's eating up my life."

"What's eating up your life? Do you have ringworms? Do you have leprosy? What's the matter with you?"

"I'm a . . . I got a habit."

"How much of a habit do you have?"

"Three years."

"You've been doing drugs for three years? How much have you been doing recently? Like over the last month?"

"Well, I've been in the hospital."

"What does that mean?"

"I've been chippin.' "

"Shit, you really are dumb. When was the last time you stuck dope in your ear or up your ass or in your arm or whatever the fuck you do with it?"

"Three days ago."

"That's a lie."

"How do you know?"

"Because I make it my business to know. If you shot up three days ago, you'd be having the runs right now. So tell me, when was the last time you shot up?"

"I was chippin' a little this morning," admitted Ino.

"Now we're getting somewhere. I asked you a question, and you answered it. So you shot up this morning. Did you bring an outfit with you?"

"No."

"Pills?"

"I don't take pills."

"Great, you only shoot dope. Jack, check him."

Jack quickly pushed Ino up against the wall and frisked him. "He's clean," he said.

"I said I didn't bring anything," said Ino indignantly.

131

"And you expect us to believe you?" said Herb. "A junkie addict who'll sell his own mother for a fix? Your word is nothing here—yet. You're an infant, and I'd be crazy to trust an infant.

"Sit down. Let me tell you how we operate. This is not a prison. There are no locks. You want to leave, day or night, the door is open. You can split anytime you feel like it. As a matter of fact, if you don't follow our rules, we'll make sure you split.

"If you decide it's worth trying to stay, and we decide to take you, you're in one hundred percent. There are two cardinal rules. No chemicals and no violence. You try to sneak dope, pills, alcohol in here, you leave. You try to get someone to help you, he'll turn you in. You won't beat our system, don't waste the energy. You start to push someone around or try to frighten them, you're out. We're a family. You don't push members of your family.

"We'll teach you how to act. In the beginning, we'll even tell you when to shut up and when you can talk. If you don't understand, just go through the motions. In time you will.

"We'll give you a job. You'll start by cleaning the floors or the toilets. It's a job any normal adult could do in less than a few hours. We'll give you a roof, and plenty of food. We'll show you how to act. In return, we expect you to listen and do your job, and we expect you to go to the encounter groups."

"Sounds like jail."

"Shut up, Sanchez," said the director curtly. "These encounters are important. You'll be able to get rid of some of your emotional garbage. Yell, scream, shit on the floor, it's okay. You've got to get through some of the poison you've locked up. But we have a nice family here, and we don't want your anger to carry over into our living room or dining room. It screws everything up. Outside the encounters, we expect you to control yourself."

Aquedo studied him. "You look confused. Any questions?" Ino shook his head slowly. "Okay. Don't worry about it. Wash the toilets. After a while, if you do that real good, maybe we'll promote you. There's no job here you can't have."

"Even yours?" Ino smiled.

"Even mine . . . if you're a big enough man for it. I know what a tough guy you are. You've been fighting all your life. You're here because you've been fighting the wrong things.

"You don't fool us. You're afraid. Everyone here was once

132

like you. Jack made it, I made it, and if you stay, you can make it too." Herb nodded to Jack. "Show him where he'll stay," he said, emptying his pipe. "Oh, one more thing."

"Yes?" said Ino.

Herb smiled. "Welcome to Rebirth House."

Jack led him up the broken stairs into the room that was to become his own. He looked at the coarse plaster walls covered with a fresh coat of pale yellow paint. There was a bed, a dresser, and a desk. Jack eased his enormous frame into the chair, admiring the work the residents had put into the room. "You know," he said, "all the guys put something of themselves into this place. You're lucky to get it."

"Really?" said Ino, half mockingly.

"Sure," Jack continued, "when we first started the program, we had four rooms we rented out of the Metropolitan clinic. It was a dump. Still, I guess I've stayed in worse."

"So have I," admitted Ino.

"One year we were going up to L.A. to play the Rams and—"

"You played football?" Ino interrupted.

"Sure, I was defensive guard for the Chargers. I almost made it to the pro bowl one season. Anyhow, we were going to play the Rams, and we had a chance for the playoffs. The pressure was terrific. One of the guys got a whole bottle of bennies. We started doing them the night before. I don't even remember playing in that game. I woke up two days later in a run-down motel. I got fined a thousand dollars for that one. But, I was still too dumb to get the point. Two years later, Herb found me in jail, recognized me, and I've been here ever since."

Jack watched as Ino put away his few belongings. He unpacked a heavy leather case, old and worn, with elaborate designs.

"What's that?" asked Jack.

"It's a machete," said Ino. He took the knife out of the case, and the silver blade gleamed in the morning light.

"Where did you get it?" Jack asked.

"My father left it to me when he died," replied Ino. He opened the dresser drawer and gently placed the machete inside.

"Ino, I'm afraid you can't keep it here," said Jack softly.

A faint trace of irritation crossed Ino's face. "What do you mean? I thought you guys said this is not a prison."

"It's one of the house rules, no weapons."

133

"I've only used it once in my whole life."

"I'm sorry, Ino, I've got to put it in storage."

"It's my fucking inheritance!" Ino shouted. "It's the only thing I ever got from my father."

"I'm sorry," said Jack. "But we got rules here that can never be broken. This is one of them." Gently he took the machete from the drawer. "Don't worry, it'll be safe with me."

Ino heard Jack's heavy footsteps retreating down the uncarpeted hall. He slammed his fist on the top of the dresser. He felt like a piece of himself had been ripped from his body.

Friday, October 3

In the main living room, a woman was busy dusting the furniture. Soft, cool music filtered through the stereo. Two residents were playing chess at the game table. A woman and child were visiting with a resident in one corner of the room, talking quietly. The child sat on the floor, playing with a doll. From time to time, members of the staff or other residents walked by Ino, sitting on the couch. Some smiled at him. Others came over and introduced themselves and welcomed him to Rebirth House.

Ino had chills and hot flushes and wiped his face continually with his handkerchief. He felt nauseous and went to the bathroom to vomit. When he returned, a thin young man with red hair was sitting on the couch reading a book.

Ino sat down and smiled weakly. A flash of recognition passed over the man's face. "Ino?" he said. "Ino Sanchez?"

"Flaco?"

"Hey, man." Flaco smiled. "It's good to see you." He stood up and hugged Ino. "When did you get here?"

"Two days ago."

"How are you doing?"

"It's rough. I'm still running at both ends."

"How bad was your burner?"

"Not as bad as yours."

"You mean was, Ino. I've been clean for a year now."

"Sure you are."

"It's true. And you know something, I'm a totally different person. That fiend who shot up with you in the street, that dingbat who was always searchin' for a connection—he's gone."

134

"That's . . . great."

"You're gonna do the same thing. You'll do this standing on your head. It isn't so bad. Hey, let me get you a hot chocolate. It'll take the edge off a little."

Ino watched Flaco run into the kitchen for the hot chocolate. Even though he was sick, he had to smile. Flaco had been one of the worst addicts in the South Bronx.

Flaco handed him the mug. "Drink this, you'll feel better."

"The last thing we shared was a hot spoon," said Ino nervously.

"That kind of talk won't do you any good," Flaco said. "It's the kind of thing that got you in trouble in the first place. I'll give you a shoulder rub; it'll ease up your muscle spasms." He began to rub Ino's back. "I just met Herb in the kitchen. I tell him I know you from the outside, and he tells me you're getting a key to the city. Shit—it sounds like you were doing some things right."

Ino nodded and closed his eyes. The shoulder rub felt good, and his tense muscles began to relax.

"You got two, maybe two and a half more days of this at the most," continued Flaco. "After that, you're home free. All the shit will be out of your body, and you'll be able to start to learn what it really takes to be responsible for your own actions."

"I've always been responsible."

"Not for the right things, otherwise you wouldn't be here. Look, Ino, I've been through it. I started in the kitchen and now I'm an administrator. Yeah, little Flaco, an administrator. Just listen to what everyone is telling you and don't split. After you're into the encounters you'll get your head straight. Once you do that, it's something no one can ever take away from you."

Ino didn't know what to say. Flaco didn't even look the same. "You're a different man," he said.

"It's about time," said Flaco with a broad smile.

Monday, October 16

Ino entered a small room off of the main office. Except for eight folding chairs set up in a circle in the center, the room was brutally stark.

"Hey, Gomez," a scrawny youth in a black T-shirt called out. "You see that new motherfucker come in here with his ass in high gear?"

"Who you mean, Ralphie? I don't see no new motherfuckers here," said Gomez, looking straight into Ino's eyes.

Ino took a deep breath and took a seat directly across from the men.

"Yeah, this new motherfucker thinks he's doin' us a favor by bein' here, Ralphie." Both men broke out in long, taunting laughter.

Ino became uncomfortable. He looked to the rest of the group, unsure for a moment if he should respond. He smiled, but their faces were a sea of passivity.

"Yeah, what he don't know is," Ralphie continued, "he spit at us, he spits at hisself. We is all junkie punks here, and we is all the same."

"I'd like to wipe that grin right off his motherfuckin' face but I get satisfaction knowin' he's a piece of chicken shit," said Gomez.

Ino's eyes were blazing. "You calling me a piece of shit?"

"You hear somethin', Ralphie?" Gomez asked with a mocking grin on his face.

"You calling me a piece of shit?" Ino repeated.

Gomez gave Ralphie a broad wink. Then he turned to Ino. "No, I'm not calling you a piece of shit. I'm calling you a piece of chicken shit. There's a big difference, man."

"Nobody messes with me, Gomez," Ino said.

"Why, I wouldn't think of it, your highness," he said with a dramatic twist of his hand. "I'll just tell you you're a piece of chicken shit 'cause you're afraid to face what you really are. You're workin' so hard to keep up that macho image around here we can't keep up with you."

"If we were on the outside, you wouldn't last a minute," said Ino.

"You threatening us? 'Cause if you are, you've just broken one of the cardinal rules and you're out," said Ralphie.

"You got it, Sanchez," Gomez shouted. "If we were on the outside. Only we're not. We're right here and it's the only thing that matters. And you know how you wound up here with the rest of us junkie addicts, 'cause you're a junkie yourself." Sounds of approval emanated from the group. Ino knew he was losing them. "So you better get that through your pretty head, Sanchez. No matter what you were out there it couldn't have been much or you wouldn't have wound up in here. In here each man is responsible for himself. We got nothin' but our dignity and it's a whole lot better than most things out there. But you, Sanchez, you got nothin' but your ego. You fucked up out there and now you're gonna fuck up in here. Only the rules are different here. You fuck up even once and you'll get the worst haircut of your life. I'm puttin' a slip in for you, Sanchez. Do you know what it's gonna say?"

Ino shook his head. He felt sick to his stomach and wished this was over.

"It's gonna say I don't like your attitude. You think that's nothin'? On the outside that may be nothin' but here, in the house, it's enough to get you a haircut. You think you're so tough, the big gang leader. Ha! You're such a baby we shoulda' put a ribbon in your hair and a diaper on your ass. You don't know how to communicate. You've been jailin'. All you know is fight, shoot up, get busted, and fight again. Only it ain't that way here. Here we're a family. Here we tell each other how we feel, and I'm tellin' you. You hurt me, you hurt Ralphie and Chico and Jack and Herb. Your lousy attitude HURTS me, and I'm callin' you on it, Sanchez."

That night he woke up sweating. Gomez was right. He had slid by his first weeks by minding his own business, remaining aloof. He realized he was doing what he had done when he first came to America. Stay in the background, unnoticed, slip by the rough spots. He lay back and lit a cigarette. He was jailin', all right but it was clear that after today they weren't going to let him pull it anymore.

Friday, October 24

"I wouldn't have shot dope if it wasn't for the guys in my gang," said Thaddeus, an overweight black man, summing up his fifteen minute monologue.

"That's bull," stated Jack. "You took it by yourself. They didn't tie you up and shoot it into your veins."

"They might as well," said Thaddeus. "What was I gonna do when everyone was getting high?"

137

"The first thing you gotta do is stop bullshitting yourself," said Jack. "Why do you think we don't allow you to see any of your old friends, your family, or any other motherlovers who've helped screw you up? Because those kinds of influences are bad for you in your present weak state." Jack turned to the group. "Some of you have mothers who support your habit even if they throw you out for it. Some of you have girl friends who shoot up with you. Some of you may have belonged to a gang of dope fiends. You rush back to your secure little environment, and it's a double edged sword. The same things that give you a feeling of security trigger your ridiculous behavior. You have to start to think in adult terms. We're your new family, we're your new friends. Get rid of that gang of dope fiends and you're on your way." He looked directly at Ino.

"All gangs don't consist of dope fiends," said Ino cautiously.

Johnny Fry sat up in his chair. He was a tall, gawky youth with hair the color of wheat. "Look who's finally opened his mouth."

"The famous gang leader speaks," said Ralphie, with a sarcastic smile on his lips.

"Your gang wasn't a bunch of dope fiends?" asked Jack.

"Not really," said Ino.

"What were they then?"

"They were my brothers."

"You mean you had the same mother?" asked Jack.

"No, but we were as tight. My brothers would die for me."

"You mean you could manipulate them," said Johnny Fry viciously.

"Shut the fuck up, Fry," snapped Ino. "It wasn't that way."

"What way was it?" asked Jack.

"We gave to each other."

"What'd you give?" asked Jack. "Speed? Knives? Dope? What did you give each other?"

"We gave each other protection," said Ino.

"Protection from what?" asked Jack. "The police? The other gangs? Stoolies in the neighborhood? You wouldn't have needed protection if you hadn't joined the gang in the first place. You're in here without your gang. Do you need protection now? You only joined the gang because you felt worthless by yourself."

"Yeah," said Johnny Fry. "Either worthless or scared shitless."

Their words scathed Ino. He thought of the time he was a frightened, withdrawn wisp of a boy of nine.

They had called him "dirty spic" and hurled rocks at him on his way home from school. He was ashamed of who he was and where he came from. His insecurity with the customs and the language of the slick natives of the South Bronx left him hiding in the shadows. His mother had no time for him, he had no friends, and at school most of his days were spent in silence. Yet there was little his sharp ears and haunting black eyes did not pick up. Slowly, he learned the ways of the streets and began to take pride in his ability to assimilate.

One of his few joys was to secretly study the antics of the members of the street gang as they joked on the corner. From the moment he first saw them he knew he wanted to be like these Puerto Rican knights with switchblades gleaming from their boots. They were imbued with confidence, exuding a reckless bravery he could only envy.

He had seen the lighter slip from the denim jacket of the leader as they swaggered down the street. No one in the gang noticed and they continued along. Ino knelt to pick it up. He felt a sharp kick in his side. Suddenly, he couldn't breathe. He heard the laughter, tough, mocking, and he felt even more foolish.

"What the fuck you trying to pull?" Renaldo had grabbed him by the back of his shirt.

"I saw your lighter drop. I was going to give it to you."

"Shit. Hock is a lot closer." The boy in his late teens laughed as the gang surrounded them.

"No, honest, I was going to give it to you."

"You little punks are all the same."

"Not me. I'm going to be a Young Toro," Ino ventured.

"You are?" Renaldo dropped his hand. "Do you know who I am?"

"Of course, you're Renaldo Hernandez—el Jefe."

Renaldo was getting interested. "How old are you?"

"Eleven," Ino lied.

"Shit. You can't be more than ten."

"No, I'm eleven. I'm small for my age."

"You're nine and don't ever bullshit me again!"

Now it was Ino's turn to be impressed. "How did you know that?"

"I know everything." Renaldo had smirked as he helped Ino to his feet.

And over the next few years it seemed as if Renaldo had indeed spoken the truth. Ino ran the small errands, never questioning. There were bags to deliver and once a gun. And then he was in front of them, all twenty, and they had asked him to join. He was initiated in a candlelight ceremony as he recited the oath of the Young Toros for the first time. "I, as a Young Toro, give my body and soul to my brothers. I will defend them even if I might die, and they will protect me." He had run through the park, leaping over the broken bottles and dog piles in exaltation. They wanted him. The strongest, toughest, and most powerful Puerto Rican gang in the South Bronx wanted him.

"Well, which was it, Ino? Worthless or scared?" asked Jack.

"Probably a little of both," admitted Ino.

"That's what gangs are made of—frightened children," said Jack.

Ino looked at him. "Not everyone."

"Really? Like who?"

"Like Renaldo."

"And what did this Renaldo do that made him so great?"

"He taught me how to be a man," said Ino.

"When did you become a man?" asked Jack.

"When I was fourteen." Ino's voice cracked as he remembered his life as it had been then.

The fourteenth year of Ino's life was a tumultuous one. He had already been transformed from an insecure school boy into one of the three guiding forces in the Young Toro organization. His explosive emergence into manhood was being controlled and directed by Renaldo, the only man he truly respected. Renaldo taught him everything from how to dress to how to pick a lock. He was the father Ino never had and the friend he would never again enjoy. Ino's responsibility as a member of the grand council was to protect and guide el Jefe. He did his job well.

He was still childlike, thin and gangly, though he was already as tall as most of his brothers and his upper body had begun filling out with muscle. With a stiletto blade in his hand he presented a far more ominous picture. It was not so much his skill and quickness that generated fear. It was his calculated control that set him apart. He had learned the lessons of the street from Renaldo. He was a warrior and gave no quarter.

"Ino!" Renaldo called gesturing to the door.

"Yes, Jefe."

"Let's walk."

"What's up?" he asked hesistantly. Renaldo had never singled him out like this.

"Not here." They walked out of the apartment house and met the glare of the noonday sun. They swaggered down the street. Though Ino was careful to stay one step behind, the shopkeepers peering out studied the pair as a mirror image.

"We'll get a drink." Renaldo led him into the small cafe. They sat down in the corner booth.

"I can't serve him," said the waitress, a pretty brunette in her mid-thirties.

"We only want coffee," Renaldo snapped.

"He doesn't belong here. We could lose our license." She looked nervously around the empty room.

"You could be sent down for pushing smack from your back room," Ino whispered.

"Why you little punk!" She studied him carefully—denim jacket, jeans, greased thick black hair falling over his ears. "I'll say one thing. You're certainly a handsome punk. How old are you?" They only wanted coffee, and her boss had taken off for the afternoon anyway.

"I was just fourteen." Ino looked down.

"Fourteen? Going to be a big gang leader like Renaldo when you grow up?"

"He's already grown up. Now cut the shit, Maria, and get us two coffees."

She hesitated, still staring at the boy.

"How did you get that scar?" She playfully traced the edge up to his ear.

"I told you he's a man. Now stop your whoring and leave us alone." When she was gone, Renaldo said, "Shit, you're only fourteen and they can't keep their hands off of you."

Renaldo waited until the coffee was delivered. "You ever hear the name Chico Alvarez?"

"Yeah. He's crazy. No support. Isn't he on the funny farm?"

"He's out and he's managed to unite the Rivera brothers."

"How'd you get that?" Ino moved closer to the table.

"Don't worry, it's good. I told you I know everything."

"Shit! He'll have forty men."

"Forty-five according to my source."

"They'll come after us first. They surround our territory."

"I know. That's why I had to speak to you. Alone."

"How many men can we get?"

"Not enough. Thirty tops."

"Who's your source?"

"One of Alvarez's own men. He's afraid to split."

"Good. That's one for us."

"Yeah, but we're still overmatched."

"Wait. I have an idea, but it will take at least a week to get ready."

Renaldo now leaned forward. "Why a week?"

"We need to get into shape."

"We can't get any guns."

"I didn't mean that."

"What then?"

"I meant shape. We have to get into physical shape, cut the butts and the dope. We gotta be able to move."

"How are we going to cool it for a week with Alvarez and still look tough?"

"We'll leak it to the fuzz. The Forty-first Precinct will quiet things down."

Renaldo smiled. "That's good. Keep talking. Now why do we have to cut out the smokes?"

"'Cause when we get into that fight, the Young Toros are going to have a sudden loss of heart. We chicken out for say . . . exactly ten blocks."

"Just enough time to wear them out," Renaldo laughed. "I like it! Just enough time to make them think it's a rout. When we regroup and hit them, they'll run like the wind . . . not bad. You sure have come a long way from that rabbit I picked off the sidewalk."

"The Young Toros give me something to believe in. I'm just happy I belong."

"Ino, there's one thing you don't understand."

"Yeah. What's that?"

"You don't just belong. You've become a member of the Grand Council. You'll take over if anything happens to me!"

Ino was taken back. "Nothing's going to happen to you."

"Not with you around, right, brother?" They clasped hands, proud of their friendship and the bonds that tied them.

The gang war had gone off perfectly. By the time the Toros regrouped at the diamond, the confusion among Alvarez's men was turning into panic. Pedro was standing near second base, and none of his followers were within twenty feet. Ino went straight for him. The veteran opened his knife and lunged forward. Ino sidestepped so quickly that as Pedro tried to regain his balance, he felt the cutting steel of Ino's stiletto slide between his ribs; before he fell, he was dead. He lay, sprawled in the dirt, his head twisted over the canvas base, and Ino stood triumphantly over him. The moon cleared some clouds and a stark brightness bathed the field. Everywhere Ino looked, Toros were winning. Soon there were cries of surrender and pleas of mercy from those who hadn't fled. They had total victory!

The harsh siren and swirling lights announced the arrival of the police. As Ino started to run into the trees he felt a catching pain in his back, and he fell. He slid his hand under his shirt and brought it behind his shoulder. He saw blood on his hand and realized he had been stabbed. He looked across the field. They were taking Renaldo away in a police car. He crawled into the trees, sobbing.

"Well, what did your hero teach you?"

"He taught me to be a warrior," said Ino.

The whole group broke out in laughter. They laughed until there were tears in their eyes. Even Jack was laughing. Ino did not understand the humor in what he said.

"And what became of this Renaldo? This teacher of warriors?" asked Jack.

"He got sent up," said Ino. "Three to five at Attica for armed robbery."

"There you have it," said Jack. "And he's still your idol?"

"No one ever told him what to do," Ino stated proudly.

"Listen to him," said Jack shaking his head. "No one ever told him what to do! That's the classic remark of the dope fiend! Every loser who ever comes in here screams the same thing. Well, get this down—NOBODY gets told what to do more than drug addicts. Nobody!"

"Renaldo never let them tell him."

"When they told him to stand up against the wall and spread

his legs, did they tell him what to do? When they took him down to the station for every horseshit heist that went down in his neighborhood did they tell him what to do?"

"Yeah," said Ino, "but he only got three to five."

"You stupid asshole! He only got three to five in the slammer and you think he really pulled it over on that judge for not giving him seven to ten? Do you know what three years in jail is? It's three years, day in and day out, of them telling him exactly what to do!

" 'Nobody tells me what to do'! That's the attitude that got you in trouble in the first place. All this bullshit about the gangs, warriors, battles, you're nothing but a bunch of bullies.

"What do you fight for? You fight for a man's right to live and believe what he wants? No, you fight for the right to hang around a particular pool hall or candy store. You make me sick. The gang is just a kid's way of existing. It's not really living, it's only existing, like some animal.

"You've been here three weeks now, and you've been clean, and you haven't made any connections with your gang. What's going to happen when you do? You've got a brain. You're no moron. Is the highest thing you can aim for—chief executive of the Toros? That's not a job. The job you do washing our toilets is more of a job.

"If you're strong enough to stay here for a year, you'll be ready to get a real job on the outside, or in here, in the organization, if you want it. If you stay straight and work hard and are lucky, maybe someday you'll have a real family—a woman to love, some kids and a nice life. But you're gonna have none of those things as long as you believe the gang is a way of life for you." He paused; there was complete silence in the room; nobody moved.

"You used weapons, didn't you, Ino?"

"It was the only way they understood," said Ino slowly.

"Understood what?" screamed Jack. "Understood not to step into your territory? Understood that you, Inocencio Sanchez, who's got nothing in this world to speak of, owns the concrete between One Hundred Thirty-fifth and One Hundred Fortieth Street? What were you fighting for that was so important? Your image? Face it, you're twenty-five years old and you're still playing little kids' games. I know how you think. You can't manipulate someone, you hurt them. I'll let you in on a little secret. Both ways, you're a loser."

144

"I got off dope, didn't I?"

"Big deal. You expect a basket of flowers or a note of congratulations for stopping something you had no business getting involved with in the first place? You're not ready for a medal yet."

12

Joe parked in front of the dilapidated three-story building that served as the rehabilitation residence. He was ushered into the foyer by a boy of fifteen whose head was completely shaved. Ino came down the stairs, rushing to embrace his friend.

"Ready?" Joe inquired.

"One minute, I just have to check with my Strength. How long do you think this will take?"

"I'll have you back in two hours."

Ino returned with a tall middle-aged man. "This is Herbert Aquedo. He's the director of the facility." They shook hands.

"We don't usually allow a pledge out for a whole month. But considering the circumstances it's been agreed that we can bend a little," said Herb.

"How's it going?" asked Joe, once they were in the car.

"It's rougher than I thought." Joe pulled away from the curb. "You're watched like a hawk. You have to do all the crap around the house. They're constantly yelling at you to pull up after some minor infraction of the rules."

"You've handled worse than that."

"Yeah, but that's not the bad part. They have these long encounter sessions and these guys know all the shit I've pulled." There was a long pause.

"So?" Joe said.

"So, in my life I've managed to break every commandment."

Ino was silent as they turned into a spot in front of Gracie Mansion. He turned to Joe as the car stopped. "Listen, I'm just a junkie and a shitty one at that."

"Hey, take it easy on yourself," said Joe firmly.

"Why?"

" 'Cause that was yesterday and today is today."

The actual presentation took only ten minutes. Mayor Finch looked drawn and defeated. In his office he gave them their medals in a simple ceremony with two other men present. They shook hands and it was over.

Joe and Ino were walking down the polished marble hall, admiring their small gold medals. Suddenly, they heard a tremendous commotion coming from the main lobby. They saw at least twenty reporters and three camera crews milling about. In the center was Richard Tanner, gesturing in sweeping motions. He spotted Ino and started toward him.

"Look out," said Joe.

"I want to congratulate you," said Tanner, his arm sliding around Ino. "I'm extremely proud of your bravery."

Ino smiled weakly. "The talk really helped, sir."

"Our talk!" Tanner's face beamed. "Why, of course. I was just telling the press about it." He studied Ino carefully. "You seem like a really bright young man."

Ino matched Tanner's fixed smile. "I can be a real help to you."

"Well, look, why don't you come visit me in a few weeks, after I've been elected?" he said softly. "I could probably use a smart guy like you in my organization."

One of the reporters rushed over. He spoke into the camera. "This is Mark Robbins from WCBC at Gracie Mansion. I'd like you to meet the two men whose bravery led to the capture of the South Bronx sniper. Tell me, Dr. Ruskin. How did you feel when the mayor was presenting the key to the city?"

"Extremely proud. Some great humanitarians have received this honor. I feel especially grateful."

"Well, the people of New York City are grateful to you. And you, Mr. Sanchez. I understand you're a native of the South Bronx."

"Yes, that's true."

"Can you tell us what was the motivating factor that enabled you to act with such forcefulness and bravery?"

"I did it for my people."

"I understand you also managed to rescue Dr. Ruskin from possible harm during the incident. Why did you do that?"

"Same reason."

"I don't understand. Could you be more specific."

"Dr. Ruskin is one of my people," said Ino. A chill went down Joe's spine. The reporter directed his attention to Tanner "I see that you're already familiar with Richard Tanner, the Republican candidate for mayor."

"Yes," said Ino slowly. "We've had several good talks."

Tanner broke in. "This is just another example of the potential this great city has to offer. If my friendship with Mr. Inocencio Sanchez has in any way influenced him, I can only say that I am proud to play a small part in his achievement. He represents the strength and the power of the people of New York City. We can change things if we want to. In three weeks, you the people of New York City have that choice at the polls. Remember, a vote for Tanner is a vote . . ."

"Cut!" the reporter yelled to the cameraman. "No campaigning on network time, Mr. Tanner, you know that," he said abruptly.

"Completely forgot myself," said Tanner, acting embarrassed.

"Cut the last four seconds," the reporter told the cameraman.

Richard Tanner stalked off. "Damn that station!" he muttered to Malcolm. "They always had it in for me."

Ino was silent in the car driving back to Rebirth House. "Think I'm a whore, bullshitting Tanner?" he finally asked.

"He's going to be the next mayor."

"I hate him, Joe. He's all that's bad in politics. He'll go with the rich every time. But he's not stupid. And he's powerful. Too damn powerful."

"And you need him."

"Maybe. Maybe I need him," Ino admitted reluctantly.

They reached Rebirth House. Joe pulled over and shut the motor off. Ino sat there, studying the small medal. "Not bad," said Joe.

Ino was silent for several minutes. Finally, he said, "There's something I want to talk to you about."

"Sure, anything."

"I know you've been balling my sister."

"I love your sister."

"She's been scarred, Joe, real bad."

147

"I know," said Joe quietly. "I'm going to see to it she'll never be hurt again."

"That's good to hear."

"I want to marry her, Ino."

Ino smiled wryly. "Well, I guess it's time we had some class in our family."

Joe looked at him with admiration. "I'd say we already do."

At ten o'clock that night, Joe and Elena were having cappuccino in a small Italian restaurant on the West Side. The food was good and cheap, and the proprietor, Gino, had come to know them personally.

"Stay until we close," he urged as he brought their coffee. "The way my nephew washes dishes, we may be here all night." A small portable radio stood on the cracked countertop, and Joe and Elena listened intently as the newscaster announced Mayor Finch's presentation.

"Let me see it again." She smiled as Joe took the medal out of his pocket for the tenth time.

"Hey, lady"—Joe laughed—"you're going to wear it out."

"And Ino has the same thing?" she asked again.

"Exactly."

"You can tell me, now that you're officially a hero, Joe. Weren't you frightened?"

"When the sniper was holding the gun to my head, I was paralyzed with fear. But when I was on the street with Ino and his men, their strength was contagious. I understand a lot better how he feels about the gang. Banded together, you feel powerful, immortal. No one can hurt you. But I'll tell you one thing, his courage is unyielding. Any other individual who suffered the injury that he did would still just be limping around a bed. Sheer willpower allowed him to swing twenty feet onto the other building. If he hadn't made it, I wouldn't be here."

"How did he look?" she asked.

"Great. I met the director, Mr. Aquedo, and he seemed as proud of Ino as we are."

"He sounded good?" she asked cautiously.

"He sounded like a politician." Joe laughed.

"What do you mean?"

"Who should we happen to run into, complete with TV coverage?"

148

"Who?"

"The next mayor of New York City, Richard Tanner."

"No! Did he talk to Ino?" she asked excitedly.

"Talked through Ino is more like it. Tanner is really trying to soak all the credit he can for Ino's bravery."

"I hope Ino behaved," she said.

"Behaved?" Joe laughed. "The two of them were so smooth together, I couldn't tell the difference. Tanner even offered him a job."

"A job?" Elena cried.

"Now, don't get too excited just yet. If it happens, it's a long way off. Ino's already got one big job right now—getting straight. But Elena, as sure as I'm sitting here, I know he's going to make it. He even sounds different."

"Joe, I can't believe it." He covered her small hands with his, glad he could share the joy that was in her heart.

Tuesday, December 10

"I was at the top of my profession," said Carol, a striking brunette in her early thirties. "I was clearing fifteen hundred dollars a week, and I lived in a penthouse apartment. My clients were some of the biggest men in the city. They treated me like a queen, and I loved it."

"If you were so happy," asked Jack, "why did you turn to dope?"

"That's funny, I always thought dope turned to me," she said with a soft smile. "A lot of my johns liked to snort and do grass. It helped relax them. I started making connections so I would have it available when they called. I was in it to improve my business. Anyway, a regular of mine threw a big party one night aboard a yacht docked in the East River. The party was important to him, and he was counting on me to entertain his clients. I had been up half the night before working, and I was really dragging. When I got to the boat, he suggested some speed to keep me going. He went into the bathroom and came out with his outfit. Later, I found out he had a really heavy burner. He showed me how to shoot up, and then we went up to the party. I was really flying that night. I did a lot of degrading things. It must have been the next day when I finally crashed in his cabin. I remember him giving me some downers and calling a cab. I started hallucinating and the cabdriver panicked and dropped me off at Bellevue. I was there for a few days, I conned my way out, got back on the street, and immediately tried to score. I was really crazy,'' she shuddered.

"You haven't once mentioned anyone you cared about. Didn't you have any boyfriends?'' interrupted Jack.

"I guess I didn't have time,'' said Carol.

"So the dope became your lover.''

"In a sick way,'' she nodded.

"No, in a very real way,'' said Jack. "Think about it. You go into a quiet room, a bathroom or a bedroom, you inject something into your body, and you feel incredibly euphoric. Until you come down and you start hustling and conning again to make a score. Dope is a jealous lover, it tolerates no one else.''

Ino listened to the exchange, his black eyes darting about the room. This was his first encounter group with a woman, and from the moment she began to speak, her tough attitude reminded him of Margarita.

Margarita was five years older than Ino and had been hooking part-time since she was fourteen. She worked as a go-go dancer in a club called the Avina on Thirty-third Street and Eighth Avenue.

He had watched her dance, entranced as she flung her voluptuous body at the dozen or so broken men huddled around the bar. The music stopped and she slipped into a transparent minirobe. Grabbing a drink that had been left standing at the jukebox, she started over to his table. Her thick red hair bounced about her shoulders as she drew the thin material over her well toned, fleshy body. At twenty she was a terrific looking chick.

"Ino, great to see you! What are you doing down here?''

"Just hanging around,'' he said, hoping he sounded cool.

"Still at the car wash on Eighty-ninth?''

"Nah, I got fired two months ago.''

"I might have something for you,'' she said coyly. "Can you meet me after I get off work? It'll be about two.''

He went home and grabbed a few restless hours of sleep, then took the subway downtown. He saw her walking out of the bar. "Margarita," he called, "over here."

"Oh, you'll like this, Ino," she giggled.

"You look great," he said, meaning it. "What do I have to do?"

"Fuck me for a couple of hours."

He studied her lush frame. "I'd do that for free, Margarita." A big smile lit up Ino's face.

"It's not for me, silly." She laughed. "Let's find a cab, and I'll tell you all about it." She stood on the curb, and in a moment a taxi pulled up.

"Sutton Place," she told the driver.

Ino nervously ran a comb through his thick hair, checking himself in the mirror. "Pretty fancy."

"This rich guy I know gets off watching me screw. My boyfriend got the flu, so you're the stand in. Believe me, it'll be the easiest cash you ever made." Ino suddenly felt very let down. "Come on, silly. I've always been hot for you. We'll just have a nice place to do it."

They pulled up in front of an old brownstone. Margarita went over to a small box on the side of the gate. She spoke a few words, a buzzer sounded, and the gate opened.

A man opened the door as they came through the exotic foyer. He was about seventy, overweight, and balding. He had on a white velour robe with a monogram and a perfect suntan.

"Margarita, my pet, how are you?" He spoke with a slight European accent and kissed her hand flamboyantly. "I see I'll not be disappointed this evening," he said, slipping his arm around Ino's waist. Ino felt himself stiffen. "I've been waiting." His weathered eyes blinked expectantly.

He led them through several rooms, each of which was grander than the last. They entered a small dark anteroom that had a red velvet curtain in place of the far wall.

"Here we are. Be imaginative, my pets." He kissed her hand again, and nodding to Ino, departed.

"Okay, Ino, time to go to work." Ino watched Margarita start to undress. "Come on, come on," she whispered. Ino made no move. "Ino, there's fifty bucks in this for you!" she whispered urgently. "What's the matter?" Embarrassed, he got out of his clothes.

She came toward him, and Ino could feel her warm naked skin touching his. A spotlight switched on from the other side of the

151

curtain. He gave Margarita a puzzled look. "He's ready. Do it good, Ino. If there's something extra, we'll split it."

Margarita led him by the hand out of the curtains to a large settee. She gently pushed him down as the blinding light shone into his eyes. He froze on his back. "Come on," she directed, teasingly running her fingers over her breasts and continuing down to her groin "I always wanted to do it with you," she said, beginning to dance lewdly around the couch. He stared at her, confused. She finally stopped, her back to the curtain, and bending over, took his soft penis into her mouth. Her high heels planted, she continued rolling her hips about, increasing the tempo as she opened herself to the hot, stark light. Ino was having trouble concentrating on her gentle nibbling. Her efforts became more insistent. Finally, almost exhausted, she moved her lips up to his. "What's the matter, Ino?" she whispered.

"Let's get out of here," he said angrily.

"I thought you wanted to fuck me," she enticed in a low, seductive voice.

"Not like this."

"Relax." She giggled. "You've got stage fright."

"I'm no actor!" he spat, frustrated. He felt the fury of his tarnished dreams mount. He wanted to fuck her hard. He glared, then slapped her.

She stood up, slowly resting her hands on her hips as she studied his now stiffening erection. "Get up." She smiled. She quickly exchanged places, wriggling her ass brazenly in front of him. "Harder, but hit me on the cheeks. They're soft," she purred, increasing the digging motion of her thighs. As the harsh slap resounded she began uttering deep grunting noises. She moved her hand down to her opening, steadying the throbbing void of her clitoris.

Ino forgot the lights and the mysterious audience. He forgot his anger over Margarita's programmed actions. Her vagina swelled open and her musky odor surrounded him. He continued hurling her against the edge of the couch. She pressed her finger against the base of his penis, forcing back the wave of semen. She looked over her shoulder, pleased with his arousal. "That's nice," she cooed approvingly. "Can I sit on it?" He nodded awkwardly, acquiescing. He sat on the edge, and she slowly lowered herself onto his lap. She clasped her arms tightly around his neck and began rocking over his magenta organ. As his eyelids closed and his buttock muscles contracted massively, she looked out smiling. Before the last eruption swelled through him, the overhead light flashed on.

"Bravo! Wonderful, children." The old man applauded, walking up to them. His robe caught on a chair, and his limp, wet penis drooped between several rolls of fat. "I must compliment you." He kissed her lightly on the forehead. "And the boy," he continued, his eyes sparkling over Ino's still turgid body, "*magnifique*! You must bring him again!" For a moment Ino thought he was going to be sick.

"But now, an old man like myself must have his sleep. Anton will see you to the door. Until next week, *au revoir*."

They were led out by the house servant. He handed Margarita an envelope as they opened the door. "Have a safe trip, *mademoiselle, monsieur*."

The door closed and Margarita leafed through the bills. "Oh, Ino," she squealed with delight, "an extra thirty! He must have really liked you."

Ino clenched the money and said nothing. He wished his first time with Margarita had been different.

They arrived at her apartment. "Can I come up?" he asked.

"Oh, Ino, I'm bushed. But maybe we can make a date for next week?"

"Maybe," he said mechanically. He pulled the cab door shut and waved.

"Where to, buddy?" the driver asked, pulling away.

"Drop me at the next corner."

"Big spender," the disgusted cabbie muttered as Ino stepped onto the curb.

"Bigger than you know," said Ino coldly, slipping him the folded bills from his shirt.

The driver opened the wad, astonished. "Thank you, sir. Have a beautiful evening, a wonderful evening."

As Ino walked away he decided he, too, would someday be rich enough to buy anything he ever wanted.

"Ino? Ino, are you with us?" Jack snapped. "What were you thinking just now?"

"I was thinking," said Ino, slightly disoriented, "we're all whores."

153

Ino lowered his head. His voice was muffled and strained. "It's true," he admitted. "Elena would be okay today if it hadn't been for me." He thought of her lying on the mat on the floor, her pelvis covered with dried out secretions, her body tattooed with blue and red welts. "I feel like I raped her myself."

"Or maybe you would like to feel that way?" asked Carol.

A horrified look swept across Ino's face. "What are you saying?"

"I'm saying you had the hots for your sister, only you never knew it."

"Are you crazy?" Ino shouted. "She's my sister, for Christ's sake!"

"But maybe you wished sometimes she wasn't," Carol taunted.

"Even for a whore, you're one sick bitch."

"Ino, stop the neck action," interrupted Jack. "This could be important. Think back, were there any times you felt something for Elena that wasn't brotherly? Did she ever turn you on?"

"No!" Ino spat. "She's my sister. She loved me more than my mother!" Then he remembered the time he had caught a glimpse of her in her bra and white cotton panties and how ashamed he had felt. She was just sixteen—but already had the body of a fully blossomed woman. He remembered the stir she had created among the Toros. And how he had worried that he had been brought into the Grand Council just because of her good looks. Renaldo, especially, made a big play for her. It had ripped him apart, and he had been overjoyed when Renaldo finally lost interest in pursuing Elena. But he needn't have worried at all. Elena would have no part of any of the Toros and tolerated them only for his sake.

"How did you think I knew that, Ino?" Carol asked in a soft voice. Ino made no move to respond. "I'll tell you a little secret now. I had the hots for my brother. We used to play all kinds of kids' games." She laughed.

Ino looked at her cautiously. "You did?"

"Sure, all the time," she continued. "I'll bet most of the people in this room have felt that way about someone in their family at one time or another. That's natural. And nothing to feel guilty about.''

There was a general nodding of heads. ''I slept with my kid brother and fourteen-year-old sister in the same bed,'' said Johnny Fry.

Ino clenched his hands in his lap and kept his eyes down. ''I . . . I feel so ashamed.''

Jack could sense what was going on inside him. ''Ino, you've been feeling more guilt about your stuffed bag over Elena than you do for your part in what happened to her. You've got to separate those feelings, put them in the right places, put them where they belong.

''Ino,'' he continued, ''you did what you did and it's over. You have got to accept yourself—for better or worse. Do you know what I say to your guilt—SO WHAT! So what if you've had a screwed up childhood, so what if you've made a mess of your life up until now. Use what you've learned about yourself when you were a fiend. Use what you've learned from your fucked up existence to catapult yourself into something important.''

For the first time in many years, there were tears in Ino's eyes. He looked at the group around him—Carol, Jack, Ralphie, Flaco, Johnny Fry—and he suddenly felt very close to them all. He stood up, and they reached out toward him, putting their arms around him, holding him close. For one ecstatic moment, Inocencio Sanchez was at peace.

Tuesday May 29

Ino stared at the pale youth slouched in the chair. Much to his disappointment, Larry Magdalino still showed little desire to stop thinking like a junkie. Ino saw in Larry the same desperate need to be nurtured, well hidden by the toughness that he himself had displayed in his initial weeks in the program.

He watched Larry flick a comb through his long blond hair. The session had been meandering, and Ino was getting impatient for the right opportunity to open up. As moderator, he was responsible. He searched the faces of the other members, reflecting on his knowledge of each. He wasn't at all sure Larry would be able to handle the all out confrontation Ralphie would relish provoking. To complicate matters, Gomez's aggression would be

155

a problem. It would be hard to direct it to the issue at hand rather than allowing him to use it as a cover for the resentment he knew Gomez felt over his own rapid advancement in the house. No, Ino would have to be the one to lead the assault. If the kid was going to make anything of himself, he would have to be the one to show him how. It would mean some pain, but no one gets a free ride.

Carol had just finished telling a story about working as a maid and being accused of stealing by the woman of the house. "She fired me, even though I was working hard. I never took her goddamn necklace."

"That was a lousy deal," Ino commiserated. "Maybe one of the rest of you had a good job yanked because of prejudice over your bad record. I know I have." Ino held his breath. There was no response from the group. "It hurts to be punished for your past actions and not for what was going down at the time. What about you, Larry?"

"What about me?" the slender eighteen year old shot back.

"You ever have a job screwed up even though you thought you had it together?"

"I used to run numbers," he said, suddenly enthusiastic.

"You're really dumb," said Ino passively. "Numbers is not a job."

"I was making good money," said Larry defensively.

"Making good money doesn't mean you were doing anything decent. They bust you for running numbers."

"Increased my action twenty-five percent in three months," said Larry with a note of pride in his voice.

"Running numbers is like dealing dope. You wouldn't brag about being a big league pusher would you? Didn't you ever have a legit job where you get a regular paycheck and an hour off for lunch?"

"Shit! Like a straight?" Larry smirked.

Ino smiled. "Yes, like a straight."

"Once I was a bricklayer," he said slowly.

"You were a bricklayer? Well, that's a real job," Ino stated approvingly. "What happened?"

"He fucked me."

"Who fucked you?"

"The foreman. He hated Italians."

"Is that all?"

"Yeah," said Larry, remembering the incident, "he was just waiting for me to screw up."

"Oh?" said Ino. "You screwed up?"

"It was my second goddamn day on the job. How was I supposed to know what the fuck he wanted."

"What the fuck did he want?"

"He wanted me to mix two goddamn bags of cement."

"Did you mix them?"

"Yeah," said Larry, uncomfortably, "only I screwed up."

"How come?"

"I mixed them wrong."

"Tell me the whole story," said Ino impatiently.

"For eight months I'm looking for this job," said Larry. "The first day the foreman has me sweeping up. No sweat. The next day I go for the broom, and the foreman tells me come over here and mix this cement. There's these two bags. He tells me to read the directions on the back and mix it in the wheelbarrow. I read the directions. There's some bullshit about wait five minutes for this, add water, wait five minutes for that. I figure screw this. I dump in the concrete. I dump in the gravel. I dump in the water. And I start mixing the shit. It's hard work and it's hot. Some guy comes over and says to me, 'Hey that looks like soup. What're you mixing?' I say what the fuck do you mean? I'm mixing cement. He says, 'What'd you put in it?' I tell him I put in the gravel and the water and the concrete. He asks me, 'Did you mix the sand and the cement first?' I tell him, nah, I just dumped it all in. He says, 'You fucked up. You gotta mix the cement first 'cause the minute the water hits, it starts to bond. That's why you got a big bowl of soup, kid.' I don't say nothing. He tells me to tell the foreman. I figure screw that. I get two big bags of sand and dump them in and start mixing. I get the shit looking real good and thick now. I figure they'll never know the difference. The foreman tells me to lay a row of bricks with the cement I just mixed. I start laying them and I'm really cooking. In an hour, I got the whole wall done. I look at what I made and I feel real fine—proud. You know what I mean?" The eighteen year old's face took on a sudden pain.

"I go over to tell the foreman I'm finished, and he comes back with me to check my wall out. Only now, the cement's leaking all over the place and my whole wall is shot to shit. I wasn't gone five minutes. The foreman is pissed. I tell him the bag of cement musta' been bad or something. He tells me I shoulda realized that before, and I wasted all his bricks, and he tells me to get out.''

"How did you feel then?'' Ino asked.

"I was so pissed off over my wall falling apart, I didn't give a shit about anything else. If I hadn't left to get the foreman, everything would have been all right.''

"What do you mean?'' asked Ino.

"Well, it wasn't falling apart when I was there,'' said the boy.

"Well, that's the junkie mentality for you!'' Ino laughed harshly. "You think just because you were there and the wall didn't fall apart, it was okay? You really are dumb, Magdalino. You think you got screwed because the foreman hated Italians? You got fired because you screwed up. You didn't bother reading the directions. You didn't do as you were told. You didn't have to, 'cause you knew it all. After all, nobody tells Larry Magdalino how to do anything, right? Not some foreman who hates Italians, not some dumb bricklayer, and not some directions on a bag of dirt. You know it all. That's the junkie mentality. That's the kind of thinking that got you into trouble in the first place. So you just keep going, year after year, screwing up and never learning by your mistakes.''

Larry stared bleakly at the floor, unprepared for Ino's assault. He felt betrayed by the one person he had trusted.

"Let me tell you something,'' Ino continued blithely, "you're lucky this happened to you.'' Larry looked at him blankly. "That's right, lucky. You can turn this whole rotten experience into something that could change your life. Call it a new way of looking at things. Okay, you screwed up. Your wall crumbled. You assumed you knew more than the foreman.'' Ino got up and went to the blackboard. In big, bold letters he wrote ASS-U-ME. "When you assume anything, Larry, you make an ass, of you and me.''

Larry's pale complexion turned a bright scarlet. "So, assuming was your first mistake. But, let's say one day, you get another shot at building this wall. You're going to pick up that bag of cement this time and read the directions. You're going to read the directions carefully, and you're going to ask for advice if you don't understand something. You're going to follow the rules, Larry, 'cause you know now, that's the only way that wall is ever going to stand up. No amount of conning, bullshit, or hedging is going to make that wall stand. Now you know that. And that's a very valuable piece of knowledge to have. And you know something else? Once that wall is standing, you're going to feel better than you ever felt in your life. And you're going to get more from screwing up and doing it right the second time than the guy who never screwed up in the first place."

13

Joe, Elena, and Luis were relaxing in the cast room. It was early Friday evening before the rush.

"Shit," said Luis. "I still can't believe Arnost got hepatitis, and we're stuck with Bob Kendricks."

"How long is he going to be down here?" asked Elena.

"At least two more weeks," said Joe.

"He doesn't have a brain in his damn head," Luis blurted.

"Take it easy, he just has to learn the ropes," said Joe. "The funny part is he's really smart. He knows the books cold. He just has trouble applying it."

"I won't be able to take it," moaned Luis.

Even Joe had to laugh at some of Kendricks's misguided efforts. In just three days he had already managed to tie up X-ray for five hours, break three IV bottles, and almost put a chest tube in the wrong patient.

Elena smiled. "Joe, I think you're being overly kind."

"As usual," chirped Luis.

"No, I'm not," said Joe. "Kendricks had the highest med school average in our whole class."

"That doesn't say much for your class," said Luis.

Joe paused for a moment, then broke into a hearty laugh.

"What's so funny?" asked Elena.

"I was just thinking of that last patient's hand that he dressed. It looked like a boxing glove."

159

"It's a pressure dressing developed in Zurich," said Luis, imitating Kendricks's nervous gesture of adjusting his glasses.

"What was under it?" asked Joe.

"Three sutures and four Steri-Strips. This big," said Luis, separating his fingers.

"You're kidding."

"On the dorsum of his hand."

"You're kidding!" The men's laughter continued to grow.

"Come on, you guys. Keep it under control. He's going to be back from dinner any minute," said Elena, going over to close the door.

Luis was still laughing but now more at Elena. "Still giving lectures like a big sister?"

"Why not?" asked Elena, pushing her back against the door. "If it weren't for my lectures Ino wouldn't be in a rehabilitation center. And you probably wouldn't be in school."

"You're right," admitted Luis, laughing.

"Then don't be such a smart aleck."

"What do you hear from him?" asked Luis.

"They've already made him a team leader. He'll be out in a month."

"That's good news."

"He told me to ask you if he could room with you for a couple of weeks. Till he gets settled." There was a long pause.

"Sure," Luis agreed.

"Is anything the matter?"

"No. Why?"

"You don't seem very pleased."

"No. It's terrific."

"But?"

"My place is really small, Elena. Only one bedroom." He seemed embarrassed.

"You just about shared the same bedroom for five years when you were kids."

"That was different."

"I don't get it. What's so different now?" asked Elena.

There was pushing and then a loud knock on the door.

"Open up. The door is locked." Elena moved away, and Kendricks floundered in.

Joe smiled. "How was dinner?"

"Pretty good. Meat loaf. A little too much seasoning. But, not bad.'' Kendricks belched. ''Tonight's the big night. . . . My first weekend.''

''You'll really like it, then,'' Luis said, irritated.

''What do you mean?''

''It's the fifteenth. That's Father's Day.''

''What's Father's Day?'' Kendricks's eyes opened.

''One of the two days of the month the welfare checks go out. It means all hell should break loose.''

Kendricks blinked in anticipation. ''Tonight?''

''Your first Friday,'' repeated Joe.

''I just hope I get to try some interesting procedures.''

''Well, you should have lots of chances.'' Joe patted Kendricks on the shoulder. Kendricks jumped.

''I just got my shot.'' Kendricks winced.

''For what?''

''For hepatitis. I don't plan on getting sick like Arnost. I heard there are a lot of addicts down here.''

''Too many,'' said Luis.

''Over fifty percent,'' said Elena.

''Zilk says they'll do anything,'' Kendricks almost whispered.

''Sometimes.'' Joe started to walk out the door. ''We only want them to do one thing.''

''What's that?'' asked Kendricks, scurrying to catch up and then checking to make sure Elena and Luis were sufficiently far behind.

''Get better,'' said Joe. ''And get out.''

Joe walked over to the chart rack and began to scan each patient to be seen—three lacerations, one second-story jumper, and two acute PIDs. One was hot—over 103 degrees. As he began to usher the young girl into the GYN room he heard the usual siren followed by a shorter more swooping one. The police must have accompanied the ambulance. As he started to run to the trauma room he heard another higher pitched siren accompanied by a bell. Now, what the hell was that? Joe beat the stretcher into the room by seconds. A white male in his thirties, the skin about his cheeks flaking off in patches, was wheeled in. His thick black raincoat had been unsnapped, and his right boot was twisted over, touching his other leg at the knee.

''There's a two station fire out of control. One of the floors collapsed. We got three,'' said Roberto.

''One-ten over fifty,'' called Elena.

''What are the other two?'' asked Joe, nodding to Elena.

"One fell on his back. He seems near shock. The other seems okay."

"Get the second one in here," Joe ordered as he began to check the first patient. Elena and Luis started an IV while Kendricks tried to fold and cut the boot away from the fireman's twisted leg. The man screamed in pain.

"What the fuck are you doing?" he yelled, after Kendricks had released him and the pain had dissipated.

"Relax. You fractured your leg," said Joe.

"Help me!" the man cried.

"Where else does it hurt?" asked Joe, leaning over to hear the indistinct answer.

"Help me. The pain!!" he gasped.

"Vital signs," called Joe as the patient began twisting his head and neck about in anguish.

"One-twenty over seventy."

"His chest and belly are clean. Get me a hundred of Demoral. Then call Ortho," he ordered Luis as he rushed to the cabinet and grabbed a Kerlix roll. Tearing the package with his mouth, he secured the boot with a figure eight hitch. Waiting till Luis injected the IV, he checked the patient. Then, taking several steps back, he put his foot against the stretcher. "This will only hurt for a second," he cautioned as he pulled as hard as he could. The patient screamed again, but now his leg was straight, and Joe secured the ends of the Kerlix roll around the basket underneath.

"How do you feel?" asked Elena.

"Better," he said dazed.

"Where else do you hurt?"

"My leg!"

"You have a fracture. Move your arms." Joe quickly checked him and then turned to face the second stretcher that had just been wheeled in.

"Bob, check his signs again and then get him over to X-ray. Get a chest, also," said Joe.

Elena grabbed another cuff and ran to the opposite side of the room.

"Luis, help me. We got to get this one over to X-ray," said Kendricks trying to push the stretcher through the crowded pathway.

"Watchit, Doc," said Luis as his hand shot out to stop the stretcher from striking the new patient.

The second fireman was on his side, rocking in a tight fetal position. Black mucous dripped from his swollen nose, his eyes were laced with fine ferns of hyperemic venules, and sweat, mud, and chemical foam basted his bull neck.

"He's really shaky," said Elena, cutting the raincoat down the back.

"Look at that bruise. He must've fallen over a stud," said Joe, studying the four-inch band running obliquely down the base of his spine. Joe pressed over the spine, but the tissues held firmly. "It doesn't feel fractured. Let's get him on his back and see what else is going on."

Joe quickly moved the man's head and neck, listened to his chest, and felt his belly. "Not much. Is he still stable?"

"One-twenty over eighty. On the line," said Elena.

Joe reached over, grabbed a reflex hammer, and began tapping on his arms, then his knees. "He's intact. Move your arms," he ordered.

There was only a low, unintelligible groan.

"Are you okay?"

The same groan. Roberto wheeled the third one in. He was seated comfortably in a wheelchair, and he carefully checked out the occupants. He studied the stretcher.

"That's Wheeler. He's been making that sound the whole way over."

"What happened to him?" asked Joe, placing a tourniquet on the stuporous man's arm and slapping his hand to pump up one of the small veins.

"We were on the third-floor landing trying to get a big line down into the center of the fire. The landing just tore off the wall. Wheeler fell over the staircase. They got him first, so he didn't breathe in much. But he wouldn't move and just started making that sound."

Joe slipped the angiocath into the vein and began taping it down.

"That sound . . . what's he got, Doc?"

"I'm not sure; he's basically intact. The only positive finding is a bruise on his back."

"He seems out of it. I've known him a long time. He's a tough man."

"What's going on?" asked Susan, entering the room.

"Problem one: Guy in X-ray with Kendricks. Fractured tib-fib. Stable.

"Problem two: Here. Eight centimeter contusion dorsum L-five. Neurological intact. Moves arms and legs but not to command. Negative Babinski's. Lots of facial signs of smoke inhalation. Chest clear."

"Get a blood gas," ordered Susan.

"He's got good color."

"Get a blood gas," she repeated, taking out the stethoscope.

Four large firemen, one wearing a chief's hat, stampeded into the room, pushing the man in the wheelchair further into the corner. Susan looked up from the stricken man's chest.

"Get them out," she ordered the guard.

"I'm the fire marshall. This is a case of arson."

"Are any of you hurt?"

"No," they said, almost in unison.

"Then get out. We're trying to take care of the ones who are."

"We'll be back," the marshall said, cursing all women under his breath.

Joe carefully put two fingers on the man's groin and measuring down the thigh, he plunged the needle into the pulsing artery. His thrust was followed by a slow elevation of the plunger as blue red blood pushed steadily up the needle. He pulled the syringe out and pressed down on the bounding point of entry. Elena grabbed the syringe, stuck the needle into a rubber top of a red top tube, bending it, and packing the entire assembly in an ice packed emesis basin. Susan rushed over.

"The color's good. He seems to be oxygenating well. Still, send it up to the lab, and get a chest X ray. Get one of his spine and skull. Damn, do a total body. I don't know what he's got either. But keep checking his chest. I don't like the facial findings."

Joe pushed the stretcher out.

He returned five minutes later. Susan and Elena were talking, and the third fireman was seated beside the max cart, facing the cabinets.

"You shouldn't have left him," Susan admonished.

"Kendricks's back there with Luis. The ortho resident came down and has already thrown on some splints. What about the third man?" said Joe, walking over to the corner.

"What man?" asked Susan.

"This man," said Joe turning the wheelchair around.

"I was wondering when you people would get around to me,"

said the thin, sandy-haired man, his fire hat grasped awkwardly in his lap.

"I'm sorry. How are you doing?"

"Not too bad."

"What's your name?"

"Rolf Jensen. My friends call me Nozzle. Has Wheeler come out of it any?"

"Not yet."

"Well, can I take off my raincoat?" he asked almost apologetically.

"Here, let me help you," offered Joe. He helped the man stand. He was only about five feet five and couldn't have weighed over one hundred and fifty pounds.

"Grab the handles on the wheelchair," advised Joe, kneeling down to lock each wheel.

Elena came over to support the man on the other side. They helped him pull his arms through the heavy rubber sleeves. The fireman's arms were firmly toned, well defined, sinewy but powerful, and his legs looked the same. They didn't seem to fit his slight build nor his thick blond eyebrows and ruddy, fair complexion. He was about forty-five.

"What happened to you?" asked Susan.

"I was on the landing humping hose. It was really heavy. When the floor gave, I came down on a cluster of garbage bags piled in the hall. I guess it broke my fall.

"Look, I'm okay," he said, taking a few awkward steps forward.

He slipped, and Joe caught him, carefully setting him back down in the chair.

"You'd better stay put for a while," said Joe, strapping him in.

"No, I'm okay. Take care of the others."

"They're being taken care of," said Joe, staring at his ice blue eyes, framed by deep crows feet. "Open your mouth." Joe checked him with a flashlight.

"It's clear. Did you take in a lot of smoke?"

"A fair amount. On the landing. I had my mask and air pack. But I was still stayin' low."

Joe inspected his face. The whites of his eyes were clear. Aside from a slight singeing of his right outer eyebrow, the man looked clean. He was somewhat red-faced, as if he had just undergone a lot of exertion, but it was normal considering what he'd been through. Joe listened to his chest. It sounded slightly congested. "Cough," he said. The fireman coughed, carefully covering his mouth. Joe listened. The coarse sounds had disappeared.

"You know where you are?" asked Joe.

"What are you—trying to be funny?" his thin lips parted easily, revealing perfect teeth and deep laugh lines. "I'm Rolf Jensen. I'm at Jefferson Hospital. It's about nine o'clock, and I have a wife, Lois, and two children. We live in a two-family house in Valley Stream. Do I make it?" he asked, still amused.

"You make it," Joe smiled back. "We'll need a chest X ray. I'll take you over. We'll have to keep you for at least an hour. When was your last tetanus shot?"

"Three years ago," said the weathered fireman.

"I'm going upstairs," said Susan. "You seem to have everything under control."

"Okay. See you later," said Joe, wheeling the third victim down the hall. As he swung around the corner he saw fifteen people sitting, standing, and lying down in front of the X-ray room.

"Wow, are they backed up. I'll just leave you in the hall for a few minutes while I check on what's holding things up," said Joe.

"Don't forget me again." Rolf smiled.

Joe opened the door. "Hold it!" came Kendricks's voice from behind the glass-encased shield. "We're about to shoot."

"Well, hold it one more second," said Joe, squeezing behind the enclosure. With the busy X-ray tech at the dial, they were crowded into a stuffy area designed for only one person. Kendricks was sweating profusely.

"The guy with the leg is in the cast room. Morin took him back after he threw on the splints. He says he needs help. This guy still hasn't come out of it but all his films so far are negative," said Kendricks, adjusting his glasses.

"Ready to shoot," said the tech. There was a click, and Joe walked out from behind the enclosure. He grabbed his stethoscope and listened to the man's chest. He then turned to Kendricks. "He still has that vacant look. Has he said anything?"

"He keeps making that choking sound," said Kendricks, adjusting the IV flow.

"Well, keep watching him. Luis, why don't you give the

166

ortho guy a hand, and I'll get back and knock off a couple of the walk-ins.''

"I'm on top of everything back here," said Kendricks, now running behind the enclosure.

"There's one more fireman in the hall. He only needs a chest, but I'd check on him every once in a while. He's still unsteady. Nice guy."

"How will I know which one his is?" asked Kendricks.

"He has straw-colored hair and blue eyes. Looks Scandinavian. His fireman's hat is sticking out of the back pouch of the wheelchair. You can't miss him.''

"How old is he?"

"About forty-five. Christ, Kendricks. He's the only white guy out there."

"Okay, okay," he said.

Joe walked back into the trauma room. "What's happening?" he asked Elena.

"The usual. I got one bad dog bite. It's on the face of a pretty little girl."

"Call oral surgery. I can't get involved."

"I already did." She smiled. "Joe, why don't you sit down for a couple of minutes. You look like you're ready to collapse."

"You should have taken it easier on me last night," he teased.

"You started it."

There was a sudden static-filled sound coming over the loud-speakers. "Cardiac arrest. Emergency, X-ray. Cardiac arrest. Emergency, X-ray."

"Oh shit," said Joe, grabbing an ambou bag and racing down the hall. He checked his pocket to make sure he had the large plastic tongue depressor that he would need for the fireman's bull neck. He was angry, chastising himself for having been stupid enough to send the man over to X-ray without tubing him first.

As he pushed through the crowd of people, he gasped. The second fireman had been pushed out of the X-ray room and the stretcher stood, unattended, blocking the door. The man lay bent over on his side but as Joe approached he could see that he was breathing easily. Joe pushed the stretcher aside, confused. He had been sure this was the fireman who had suffered the arrest. If it wasn't him, who could it be?

Opening the door, Joe could hear a few confused shouts, but it

167

took him several more seconds to accommodate to the darkened area beneath the chrome X-ray machine where Kendricks was trying to force air into the mouth of the bloated blue victim. Kendricks was on his knees next to the patient's head, and as he shifted to cover the thin-lipped mouth Joe saw a singed tuft of blonde brow pressed against the white pants. Impossible! It was Rolf Jensen. Joe rushed over to the pair.

"Get some light in here," he ordered the X-ray tech. Joe slid his palm over Jensen's left nipple.

"He still has a pulse. You're not aerating him for shit," Joe snapped, as the skin became an even deeper purple, dusky and cold.

"I'm blowing as hard as I can," said Kendricks, breathlessly lifting his face from the gaping mouth of the dying man. Joe withdrew the curved plastic depressor and sliding his fingers over the teeth, pressed the engorged tongue down and forward against the floor of the mouth. As he engaged the mouthpiece under the gum, thick frothy clear liquid, knotted with yellow clumps of mucus pooled over his fingers and dripped over the stubble of Jensen's chin. Joe positioned the black rubber mask attached to the ambou bag and pressed firmly against the cheekbones. He gave several fierce squeezes. Jensen's chest expanded minimally, and the air belched out from around the curved rubber mouthpiece. Elena came running in.

"Get suction and an oxygen tank. Make up an IV with bicarb. I'll need a trach tray. His larynx is shut off."

"Try to get a tube down him," said Elena, running over with a lighted intubation instrument.

"Line," ordered Kendricks, as thick cyanotic blood poured out of the angiocath, now embedded in Jensen's arm. Elena ran over with the IV pole.

Joe slid the long flat silver blade of the scope over the plastic mouthpiece and down the throat. Hooking it forward against the hyoid bone, he lifted straight up. The glottis was bulged inward, flame red with small pieces of charred debris mixed with continuing secretions pooling at the base. The short elastic pale bands of the vocal cords were clamped tightly together, obliterating the fissure.

"No way," said Joe, throwing the instrument down on the table. "He's clamped off. I couldn't run a pipe through that." He searched for a scalpel blade on the cluttered tray.

Putting the index finger of his left hand against the cartilage, he drove the blade straight down immediately above his nail. Coming down on the firm cap, he turned the knife transversely and plunged directly through the tough membranous attachment. A burst of stale almost pure carbon dioxide gas seeped from the opening in the blocked airway.

"I need a trach tube," said Joe, twirling the blade handle to keep the hole open.

Kendricks started picking up gauze wrapped instruments discarding each in turn. "I've got it," he said finally, handing Joe the metal tracheotomy tube, cloth ties dangling from each side.

"It's too big." Joe grimaced as he tried to push the metal tube into the opening anyway. The diameter of the tube was twice as large as the opening.

"Shit. Isn't there a smaller tube anywhere?"

"I can't find it," said Kendricks, continuing the search. "Make the hole bigger."

"I'm in the cricothyroid space. There's no way I can make the hole bigger."

"I'm going to call for an anesthetist."

"What is he going to do?"

"Maybe he'll have a smaller tube."

"Okay. But this man is asphyxiating. We've got to do something. Elena, get me a twenty-two gauge oxygen cannula. Set the tank regulator at ten liters." Joe fed the supple plastic tube into the incision and then inched it down the windpipe. Jensen's dusky color lightened, but his labored breathing was still sporadic, and the gasps sputtering out with each expiration seemed to be diminishing in volume.

"Open the valve full out," said Joe. "We'll force the oxygen in."

Susan came running in. She stared down at the wound. "He needs a formal trach," she surmised immediately. "Let's get him over to the trauma room."

"I just did a stab laryngotomy. He closed off like that," said Joe, snapping his fingers.

They rolled him onto the stretcher and pushed through the crowded hall. By the time they managed to get back to the trauma room, Jensen was moving one of his arms. Elena poured half a bottle of antiseptic solution over his neck and Susan slid into sterile gloves. She expertly cut down two inches below the original opening and spread the strap red muscles apart, revealing a spongy lobular gland encased in a glossy fibrous capsule.

"That's the isthmus. Retract it up." Joe took the small edge of the blunt Army-Navy retractor and scraping against the stiff base, swept the thyroid tissue away. Blood began to flow down from the pressed off tissue. Susan blindly stabbed at the trachea with a sharp hook and catching it, cut a three-sided trapdoor through the cartilaginous rings. Easily inserting the tracheotomy tube, she could then attach the outer end to the volume respirator. Jensen's chest began expanding rhythmically, and Joe breathed a sigh of relief.

"Get me some saline and suction. We'd better wash him out," she said, throwing a silk suture into the flap and securing it over the cord ties.

Joe walked over to Jensen's head. Air had spread through the subcutaneous tissue, and blisters had formed over his jaw and were beginning to creep up his cheeks. Joe lifted the thin eyelids. *Oh God.* His pupils were dilated. Joe felt his pulse. It was steady and strong. He pulled off one of the boots and dug his nail into the fireman's soul. His big toe went up. Joe shook his head sadly. "Susan, he's stroked."

"How are his vital signs?"

"He's stable, now."

"Maybe he'll come out of it," said Elena hopefully.

"Get a blood gas. Then I'll take him up," Susan ordered, finishing the dressing. Joe walked dejectedly out into the hall. Susan came after him. "It wasn't your fault."

"I should have had an IV in him. I shouldn't have left him in the hall," Joe said painfully.

"I saw him too, Joe. He didn't seem sick."

"I fucked up."

"We all fuck up. What makes you so high and mighty?"

"I should've tried to tube him."

"Joe, get back to work. We do the best we can. Besides, I'd wait a couple of days before I kicked myself. We have a tough man there. I wouldn't be surprised if he came completely back."

"You think so?" said Joe, brightening.

"I've seen a lot stranger things."

"Yeah," said Joe softly, nodding his head. "Maybe he will come back. I'll tell you one thing. I'm going to watch him like a hawk."

"Good. Now get me a blood gas before Kendricks makes him a pincushion." She smiled.

Two days later Rolf Jensen's toes curled downward; the doctors removed the breathing machine. Three days later they removed the trach, and that afternoon they took him back to the ward.

One week later, in the library conference room, Joe presented the case. Gold said nothing while the younger attendings hammered away at each aspect of the presentation. "The chest findings should have been appreciated at the time of the first physical."

"He really didn't show much when he came in," Susan interceded.

"They had to be there. You obviously just missed them."

Gold closed the charts, and slowly walked to the window. "Well, Joseph, what did you learn from this case?" he asked, putting his hands in the pockets of his lab coat.

"I learned you can have a case of severe smoke inhalation without a lot of signs."

"You also learned these patients can close off in seconds," added Gold.

"Yes." Joe nodded.

"If you had checked him over one more time before leaving him in X-ray, you might have been more aware of his impending crisis."

"Yes."

"In those few minutes, he might have demonstrated totally different chest sounds. Do you agree?"

Joe nodded.

"Then again, he might not have."

Joe looked down, confused.

"You're missing the most important lesson this case has to offer."

"I guess I am."

"You were swamped, right? These cases are unpredictable. You should have called for an anesthetist the minute these men hit the door. Even then, he might have missed it. But at least you would have covered yourself. And when you tried to do the laryngotomy, he might have had a pediatric tube. The lesson is don't be afraid to ask for help. Do all of you understand that?" Gold's eyes swept the room. "Good, then grand rounds for this week are dismissed. Mike, I want to take a look at that colostomy patient with you. Joseph, why don't you wait for me in my office? I'll be back from the ward in ten minutes."

"Yes, sir," said Joe softly as the rest of the staff rose.

Joe took the chair on the side of Benjamin Gold's desk. He looked at the mass of papers, notes, and books piled high on top of the desk. To the casual observer, it looked like a massive disarray.

He went over to the beaten-up leather sofa and sat down. Beside the sofa was a small bookcase. He glanced at the books, and his eye caught a fat, tattered green leather volume. He bent his head to read the title on the binding. It was a 1910 *Zabatta Surgery Atlas*. His eyebrows lifted. The book was quite valuable, a real collectors' piece, noted for its magnificent illustrations. Joe reached over, carefully freeing the book from its shelf, and began leafing through it. It was true; the illustrations were incredible. Leave it to Gold to have a volume as rare and precious as this one, he thought.

A small photograph, wedged between two pages, suddenly slipped to the floor. Joe picked it up. It was a picture of Gold, smiling, in an open sport shirt, his arm around a young man. Joe studied the photo and noted the resemblence between the two. It was obviously his son, the one who'd died of encephalitis. He had first heard the story from Elena. Later, others had mentioned it in passing. How awful to have lost a son. Joe looked at the picture of Gold. He could see that at that moment in his life, with his arm around his son, Benjamin Gold had been content. He stared hard at the picture, trying to comprehend this side of Gold—a side he'd never seen. He didn't hear the door open.

Immediately, Gold noticed the book Joe had on his lap. His heart jumped slightly. As he moved closer he saw Joe had already discovered the photograph. It was one of the few remaining pictures of his son he'd allowed himself; it was too painful to remember. Quietly he stood next to Joe and looked at the picture over his shoulder.

Joe started to speak, but no words came. He knew he had trespassed and was embarrassed. He looked at Gold. "I'm sorry, sir," he began. "I didn't mean to . . . ."

Gold continued to look at the picture in Joe's hand. "That was taken at the beach," he said in a subdued voice. "David always loved the beach."

Joe didn't know quite what to say. Gold continued to stand there, staring at the photograph, for a long moment. Then he walked over to his desk and sat down, a look of defeat on his face.

Finally Joe said, "You still miss him."

"A day doesn't go by when I don't think of him," admitted Gold.

"I'm sorry."

Gold looked up at Joe. "I know you are." A sad smile crept over his face. "His soul was filled with compassion; he was a scientist who cared more for people than numbers."

"That's quite a combination," said Joe softly.

"You know," said Gold, leaning forward, his hands clasped on the desk, "you remind me of him."

"I do?"

"Sometimes. You have the same need to help others. It shows through in everything you do." Gold sighed deeply. "David was the same. I only saw it flower right before he was taken away. And I never had time to tell him how rare and beautiful a trait he had, nor how much I respected him for it. Am I making any sense?"

Joe nodded.

"I can teach anyone how to remove an appendix. Technically, I could probably teach an ape. I can't teach someone to take the time to remove a dressing without hurting the patient. That's something that has to be felt.

"You have good hands and a kind heart. You're going to make a brilliant surgeon," said Gold, closing his eyes. For ten years he had been wanting to say that, but there had been no one to say it to. Is this what had kept him in this hellhole?

"I love this job. Does that seem strange? Here I should be thinking of retiring from the worst hospital I've ever been in. And instead, I can only think about Barilla's case at noon. This is the most important job I've ever been given. And I hate myself because I know I'm getting too tired and too old. And then I hate this hospital because it takes my body and my heart and dashes them against these halls, and doesn't it know I don't have the energy anymore?"

"But we could help," said Joe. "Hell, we have more energy than we need. If you were willing to pass some of those jobs down, you'd still be able to teach and that's what we need you for. That's the priceless gift you give us."

"Maybe," said Gold slowly. He cleared his throat and raised himself from the chair. "One more thing before you get downstairs and back to work." Joe stood up as Benjamin Gold once again became Chief of Surgery. "The next time you get someone from a fire down there, make sure the first thing you do is call anesthesia. I haven't seen a stab laryngotomy in twenty years. You really boxed yourself into a corner." Gold give Joe a crooked smile. "No wonder we didn't have the right instruments on the tray."

"Gonna check me out of this hotel?" Jensen asked Joe that afternoon. "The food here is worse than at the station."

His bed was surrounded with a variety of plants, flowers, and fruit. Jensen was sitting on the edge of the bed, and Joe was checking his blood pressure.

"What's your hurry?" asked Joe, removing the cuff. "Didn't you say you could use a vacation?"

"I've been out two weeks already," said the crusty fireman. "That's enough vacation for me."

"They'll survive a week longer without you. You had an arrest, and I almost missed it. I want to make sure you're two hundred percent okay this time."

"You're one hell of a doc, Doc," said Jensen, his blue eyes sparkling. "When I get back to the station, I'm gonna tell the guys everything you did for me. Anytime you need a favor, Engine Company Eighty is at your service."

Joe smiled. "Well, thanks Jensen, that's real nice of you."

"You saved my life, and I don't forget something like that too easily."

Joe checked Rolf Jensen's heart with his stethoscope. The man's attitude was the thing that had helped him the most. "You like being a fireman, don't you?" he asked impulsively.

Jensen thought for a minute, then he said, "It's a job like any other. But sometimes, it's more. When we're in there trying to reach someone in a bad fire and we make it, it becomes more than a job. It becomes almost bigger than life."

"Aren't you afraid?" asked Joe.

"Sure," said Jensen. "But if we don't do it, who's gonna? It's a little like your job, Doc. Someone's got a bad disease. Sure, you might catch it, but if you don't get in there and try, who's gonna?"

174

Joe smiled at the analogy. "I see what you mean, Jensen."

"Twenty years I'm on the force. I'm up for retirement this May."

"How do you feel about that?" asked Joe.

"I'm forty-six, and I can't kid myself. I feel like a big chunk of my life will be missing. Sure, I'll find another job, but it just won't be the same."

"I heard they're giving you a medal for bravery."

"How do you like that?" Jensen's face lit up. "It'll be my third, you know."

"No, I didn't," said Joe. He extended his hand. "It's been a real pleasure treating such a hero."

"In my book, Doc, you're the hero."

"Luis and I are going over to the diner for a quick bite," said Susan. "Want to come along?"

"Thanks, Susan, but I told Joe I'd meet him in the cafeteria."

"Well, go get him," urged Susan. "We'll all go."

"That would be fun," said Elena. "But he's got no one to relieve him. I thought I'd keep him company."

"You really like him, don't you?" Susan teased.

"Well, sure I like him," said Elena, "I like all the interns— except maybe Kendricks." Both women started to laugh at the thought of Kendricks.

"You know what I mean," said Susan. "And I can't blame you. Joe Ruskin is one special guy."

"He really is," said Elena enthusiastically. "He cares so much."

"I think he cares so much about you."

"You do?" Elena asked, obviously pleased.

"I've seen the way he looks at you. You've really got him ga-ga."

Elena laughed. "I wouldn't go that far. But, Susan, I'm happy when I'm with him."

"So we've noticed."

"I never thought I'd be able to say that," said Elena.

"Luis says you look like you're glowing."

"Luis? He knows about me and Joe?"

"Of course. Did you think Luis, of all people, wouldn't notice a change in you? He's known you since you were kids."

175

"Yes, I guess he would," she said thoughtfully. "I just didn't think it would be that noticeable."

"A little love can make a lot of difference in a person's life," said Susan.

"I wish you could be as happy," said Elena sincerely.

"I don't know," mused Susan, "things seem a lot better these days."

"And what does that mean?" asked Elena.

Susan suddenly blushed. "Elena, Luis and I have been seeing each other."

"You and Luis?" she asked. "How long has this been going on?"

"A couple of months now," admitted Susan. "We started out as friends. But now it's a lot more than that." She looked at Elena's guarded expression. "I know, I know what you're going to say—I've already struck out twice. But this time, it's the real thing."

"All I'm going to say is what happens when your husband comes back?"

"That's been over for a long time."

"I sort of guessed," said Elena quietly.

"Luis is the first man I've ever really loved."

"You and Luis," mused Elena. "So that's why he didn't want Ino to stay with him. Well, I'll tell you this. If Luis is interested, it's serious."

"Why do you say that?" asked Susan.

"Luis was never interested in girls, like Ino was. He was too busy working to help his family make ends meet. He's a very devoted son."

"I've met them, you know."

"The Rodrigueses?"

"Yes. Luis brought me over a few Sundays ago. They were great."

"They always are," Elena smiled. "Mr. and Mrs. Rodrigues are two of the finest people you'll ever meet."

"They were so warm. They made me feel like family."

"When Mama died, they took me and Ino into their home and into their hearts. There wasn't enough they could do for us. You're getting into a fine family." She paused, suddenly quiet. "I only wish Joe's family were more like that."

"So it's that serious with you two."

"It's that serious," admitted Elena. "I haven't met them, and

176

he keeps making excuses. I know he goes to see them and cares about them. I'm sure it's because I'm Puerto Rican.''

"In this day and age, come on," said Susan.

"No, I mean it," said Elena. "Joe says they wouldn't care but I don't believe him. They're very old-world, and I'm sure they don't want their son getting involved with me."

"How does Joe feel about it?''

"He's not dealing with it.''

"Are you going to force the issue?''

"Right now, I'm so happy with Joe and the way my life is going, with Ino getting better and all, I find myself going along with him. I don't want to spoil things.''

"Maybe doing that right now is your best way of coping.''

Elena let out a troubled sigh. "I don't know," she said.

"Don't be so hard on yourself," Susan urged. "Enjoy the good times you have together. You know me, Elena. I'm a fatalist. Whatever's going to happen, will happen. Love each other now as much as you can. Somehow the rest will fall into place.''

14

Joe double parked his Mustang in front of Elena's building and left the motor running. He ran into the lobby, pressed the buzzer twice and came out whistling.

The morning was a beauty. They'd still have a couple of hours before the stifling August heat would descend upon the city, but by then, they'd be far away.

She was carrying a small suitcase and wearing cutoff jeans and a black halter top. Her face lit up when she saw him leaning against the car. "You're on time." She smiled. "What kind of doctor are you, anyway?''

"A hungry one." He gave her a tight hug, grabbed her bag

and threw it into the backseat. He made a sweeping gesture with his hand. She laughed and got inside.

One look at her told him it was worth the double shift he had to take last week so they could arrange these two days off together. He switched on the radio and started to drive toward the Taconic Parkway. Once on the open highway, he stepped up his speed, reached over and held her hand. They drove for nearly an hour in silence. Then he veered off the main road, passing small country towns just beginning to wake up. Jefferson seemed a million miles away. They sped on, more and more relaxed as the car swept deeper into the tranquil valleys.

They pulled up to a small white house with a hand painted sign that read "Fran's Kitchen, Good Food."

They ordered a huge breakfast, which Fran cooked and served herself. Joe paid the bill and asked the woman, "Is there a place to stay overnight?"

"There's old man McGrew's," she said, counting her change. "He's got the big farm about a mile up on route four. He rents a cottage, and he was in complaining his weekend just cancelled."

"Then he'll have a vacancy?"

"He sure might," she said, writing the directions on a napkin.

It was a low stone house, built in the thirties, with heavy wooden beams exposing an A-line-shaped roof. The floors were planked oak and a massive brick hearth dominated the center of the room. An old wooden rocker and a love seat faced the fireplace. At the far end of the room was an antique brass bed with a feather quilt serving as a spread. The other end of the room had been converted into a kitchen and beyond that was a bathroom. On the porch stood a locker full of fishing equipment. About fifty feet from the cottage was a small lake.

"Oh, Joe, can you believe this place?"

"Our own private lake! Nobody from the pit will believe this."

They started inspecting closets, pantries, and drawers.

"I don't think they forgot a thing," she said, noting the dishes and fresh linen. They looked out the window at the still lake.

"Let's take a swim," he suggested.

"Last one in is a rotten egg," she called, running toward the bathroom with her suit.

When she came out, Joe caught his breath. Never had he seen anyone look more exquisite. She was dressed in a white jersey one-piece suit that revealed every line of her magnificent body.

The shoestring ties around her neck supported a low-cut bodice that thrust her full breasts forward. Her deep olive complexion was accentuated by the white, clinging fabric.

"You lose," she smiled, grabbing a towel and running out.

He saw her standing on one of the huge rocks that surrounded the lake. She was looking out toward the village. He threw a small pebble to get her attention. She turned toward him, and the sun poured forth from behind, giving her long dark curls a luminous halo.

She smiled and stretched. He watched her move gracefully along the wall of rocks. She came to the last one, pausing momentarily to assume a diving stance, and then jackknifed into the water.

Joe walked into the lake, glad when the water covered his erection. He started to swim toward her. She was gone. He treaded water in the middle of the lake for a few moments. Suddenly he felt a hand give him a gentle squeeze.

"Help, shark attack," he yelled.

Elena came up for air, splashing and laughing. He reached out but she was gone again. She came up a few feet away. "Look, there's a diving board." She pointed to the far end of the lake. Someone had fixed a wooden plank to the rocks. "Let's try it," she cried.

They swam for a few minutes until they reached the board. She tried to get a grip on the rocks to pull herself up, but slipped. Joe grabbed her slender waist and pushed her high into the air. His eyes were fixed on her round behind, and he felt the tension rock through him. He was reluctant to remove his hands from her soft flesh and he held her a moment longer than necessary.

She turned to him. The sun gave a translucency to her suit, and he saw her dark mound fully exposed through the drenched fabric. A rosy haze surrounded her hard nipples. He shimmied himself onto the smooth surface of the rock.

They walked over to the board. It was weather-beaten and blackened from age. He followed her onto the plank. As her arms cut through the water she automatically bent her knees and spread her thighs. Quickly he dove behind her into the clear water.

They swam the half-mile length of the lake side-by-side. Elena did a slow, easy crawl, and her lithe body seemed to glide through the water.

Deliberately he slowed his pace and let her get ahead. Then he pulled at the string of her suit around her neck. She turned, and her lovely round breasts, with their dark plum centers bobbed in and out of the shimmering water. Playfully, she treaded water, covering and uncovering herself.

"They look like melons." He laughed.

"Melons don't feel like this, Kildare," she teased.

"What did you call me, bitch?" He dove toward her, knowing he had to possess her. He embraced her glistening body, gliding with her toward the shore. He felt her smooth, wet skin against his, and he reached for her waist, urgently sliding the white suit down.

He held her close, touching her breasts, circling her full hips. She felt his hardness burrow against her. She held his firm buttocks, allowing the water to slip through her fingers creating small waves as she pressed him closer.

He lifted her out of the water and carried her, naked, to the cottage. She held her arms tightly around his neck, cherishing the moment.

He laid her on the bed, and she reached out for him. When he entered, she let out a soft moan, knowing she would never love like this again. They meshed together until at last, in a single joyful moment, they were one.

It was dusk when they went out to explore the town. They walked along the dirt road, talking.

"Why did you go into medicine?" she asked him.

"I knew I always wanted it. My uncle was a surgeon. He took me to see my first case when I was fourteen. I loved the drama and excitement of it. When I'm in the OR, I'm really alive."

"You seemed pretty alive in the cottage." She laughed.

They found a small grocery store and bought some steaks. Next door was a liquor store. Joe spotted a dusty bottle of champagne on one of the shelves and put it on the counter.

"Champagne?" she said. "It must be quite an occasion."

"It is." He smiled. "We have a lot to celebrate. Not just us, but Ino also."

"What'll it be, folks?" the proprietor asked.

"The champagne," said Joe, getting his wallet out from his pocket.

"Champagne, huh?" said the man, pressing the keys on the ancient cash register. "You folks on your honeymoon?"

Elena blushed. "Not exactly," said Joe, handing him the money.

"You folks from around here?" he asked.

"No," said Elena. "We're from New York."

The man stopped for a moment and studied her. "He may be from New York," he said, "but you sure ain't. You look different. Where you from, honey?"

Elena became uncomfortable. "I . . . I'm from Puerto Rico," she stammered.

"I knew it," he said. "I could tell the minute you walked in here." He turned to Joe with a knowing smile. "Are they as good as they're supposed to be?" he asked, in a low voice, handing Joe the bottle.

Elena turned bright red.

"Shove it up your ass," said Joe, pushing the bottle at him. He grabbed Elena's arm and stormed outside.

He was consumed with rage. "I'm going back in there and punch him in the mouth."

"I knew it would happen," she said numbly.

"Come on, Elena," he argued, "that never should have happened. Never!"

"But it did," she cried, "and it will continue to happen, over and over."

"You're wrong! He's an ignorant bigot, one in a million."

"Oh, no, Joe. He's the rule, not the exception. We'll have to face this all our lives. That's why it can never work for us," she cried miserably.

"Don't say that." He was shaking her now, with all his strength. "Don't ever say that!"

"It's true," she yelled. "You just don't want to hear it."

"What's true is that I love you, and I don't care if the whole world is against us."

"Oh, Joe!" She broke down, the tears refused to stop. "What are we going to do?"

He grabbed her tightly. "We'll make it. I promise, we'll make it," he whispered into her tears. They had to. The alternative was too terrible for him to think about.

*   *   *

Dinner soothed them and afterwards they sat by the fire. "I brought a present for us," Joe announced mischievously. He took a small blue tube out of the side pocket of his suitcase and flipped it up into the air.

"And now, lovely lady, we have here for your special *dee*-light one-percent Xylocaine ointment guaranteed to give you a night to remember."

"What's it supposed to do?" She giggled.

"It keeps you from coming so you can continue to make love for hours. It tingles. You'll feel like ginger ale."

"Sounds yummy." She laughed, rising from the bed. He placed a small drop on each nipple and meticulously spread the ointment outward, completely surrounding her areola.

"Open up, gorgeous." He worked the salve into the walls of her clitoris, careful to leave the tip free. Then he rubbed the underside of his penis at the junction of his glans and shaft.

He lifted her onto the thick feather pillow and watched it slowly envelop her hips. Her pelvis was tilted upward, and he placed his penis against her swollen mons, driving his shaft against her soft flesh. Her skin was a mass of tiny explosions, and she yearned to release the tension.

"I need you," she cried as she slid her hand down and steadied his base. He grabbed her wrist and held both hands above her head, staring into her almond eyes.

"I love you," he whispered. She started to buck, and he held her tightly as the explosion spread outward from their churning centers. He would not enter her, and she began to come, continuously. Finally, almost carelessly, he flipped her over on her stomach.

He wedged a pillow under her pubis, and she dug her sweating face into the sheets, spreading herself invitingly outward. He entered and drove up, and she pushed with a force that matched his.

The powerful ointment held them suspended on a volcanic plateau. They stayed like this for many minutes. While the strength from their bodies slowly dissipated, their sex organs had become electric. They began to grind together, possessed by their savage movements. They both felt the steaming wave break, and they gasped in its power, hurling themselves forward only to be caught in the relentless undertow.

*   *   *

Joe woke to the smell of hot coffee and bacon sizzling. She was at his side.

"Hi," he said sleepily. "What time is it?"

"Almost twelve."

"I was having this great dream about you and me." He smiled, covering his erection.

"That was no dream." She laughed, pushing the blanket aside.

"Had to be. It was the best night in my whole life."

When he went to the table, he saw that she had stuck a wildflower in a cup for a centerpiece. He reached over and touched her arm. "I said I loved you last night. I meant it."

The ride home was slow. A tractor trailer had blocked up traffic for close to two hours. Elena and Joe didn't seem to mind.

"I feel like I missed so much, not knowing you before now. I want to know everything about you."

"Oh really?" Elena laughed. "Where shall I begin?"

"Tell me about yourself, what it was like when you were a kid, what your parents were like."

"Sure you're not planning on doing a psych residency?" she asked.

"Come on," he urged, "I want to know YOU!"

She smiled at him. "I'd say you already know me better than anyone else."

"That's true," he said, "but just for the record."

"What record?" she laughed.

"My own record. Now, speak, woman. What hospital were you born in?"

"I wasn't born in a hospital."

"You weren't?"

"No. I was born in the doctor's back room in Puerta del Mar."

"Is that where you grew up, Puerta del Mar?" he asked.

"Yes, that's where I grew up," she said wistfully.

"What did your father do?"

"He drank," she said sadly. "He ran moonshine too, until he was killed when his truck rolled over a cliff. Mama blamed the revenue officers who chased him and the mountain road and the hundred proof moonshine. She never forgave him.''

The family gathered around the old priest. They huddled together partly for reassurance and partly to form a human barrier against the bleak gray drizzle. Soft sobs emanated from the depths of their despair as they waited for the last bit of earth to cover the casket. The priest made the sign of the cross, closed his book, and led the small procession past all the crumbling markers.

A young woman with two small children stared at the fresh soil. Her kerchief did not hide the thick black curls that fell down her back nor the beautiful almond-shaped eyes.

Slowly they walked toward the iron gate. As the little girl closed the latch behind them a burst of thunder filled the silence and the dark clouds gave way to a torrential downpour. She looked up and knew it was a sign from her father. He would never be at peace, not even in death.

Inside the house the small group sat quietly in the front room. An uncle rose from his chair, uncomfortable in the black suit. ''Carlos loved the *niños* more than life itself,'' he said. ''He wanted them to remember . . . to cherish . . .'' His voice started to crack, ''Elena, Inocencio . . .'' He motioned to them.

The uncle placed the iron crucifix around the girl's neck. She put her fingers around the smooth contour of Jesus on the cross and smiled shyly.

''Ino, your father wanted you to have this so you would be strong and unafraid all your life.'' He took Carlos's silver machete from its case and handed it to the boy. The boy was mesmerized by the intricately carved handle and the sharp blade.

Adeline's eyes blazed with fury. ''Ha!'' she spat. ''Some good these did for Carlos. He lies rotting in the grave.''

''Adeline, Adeline,'' the uncle soothed, ''you are very upset.''

And so she was. Every night, for the next year, the girl heard her mother's anguished cries echoing through the walls of the house.

*   *   *

"When did you come to America?" asked Joe.

"When I was ten."

"This is like pulling teeth," he said. "Why are you so reluctant to talk about yourself?"

"Because it still hurts when I think about it. Besides, I'd rather hear about you." She moved closer to him. "What was it like for you growing up?"

Joe broke out in a broad smile. "High school was the most fun and my senior year was the best. We won the Class A championship in football. I got into National Honor Society. My parents bought me a car. And I got bare tit off of Naomi Epstein."

"That sounds like quite a year."

"What was your senior year like?" he asked.

She was quiet for a moment. "It was the year my mother died."

Elena sat with her mother in the Emergency Room for five hours before their name was called. During that time she watched as the people huddled together on the chairs and benches and finally the floors when there was no more room. She watched the men and women in white scurrying back and forth, speaking a strange language of letters and numbers that seemed to signify the severity of each situation. She heard the loud sirens of the ambulances as they pulled up the huge ramp. She saw the sudden rush of those in white, darting out from the small cubicles where they hid. She smelled the penetrating stink from the filthy drunk who lay stretched out on the floor not ten feet from them. She stared with terror into the crazed eyes of the withdrawing junkies as they tried to warm themselves with overcoats even though the large waiting room was unbearably hot. She sat with her mother patiently, yet her heart was exploding from the excitement that was going on all around her.

Elena's English was much better than Adeline's, and she spoke to the Chinese doctor with as much poise as she could. Where did the pain start? When did it become worse? Did she take any medication? On and on went the questions. They waited in the cubicle.

Finally, he came back with another doctor who was American and much older. The older doctor spoke to Elena. "I am Dr.

Barat. Dr. Chin and I would like to run some more tests on your mother, young lady. We want her to stay in the hospital overnight."

Elena became alarmed. "Are you telling me everything, *Señor* Doctor?"

"They are just tests, Miss Sanchez. They could prove your mother has nothing serious. Do not worry, my dear," he reassured her. She felt his warmth and confidence and knew her mother was in good hands.

That night when she returned without Adeline, Ino became worried. They spoke through the thin wall separating their rooms, drawing strength from each other, reassuring themselves that everything would be all right.

But everything was not all right. Adeline spent two weeks in the hospital, undergoing an exhausting battery of tests. They diagnosed her condition as adenocarcinoma of the colon.

She went to the priest with the news of her mother's illness. When he offered to say the last rites, Elena knew it was the beginning of the end.

"I'm sorry," said Joe.

"So am I. My mother was a good woman." Suddenly she laughed.

"What are you thinking?"

"Before we came to America, Mama told us the streets were paved with gold."

"Come on."

"She really did. So the night before we left, Ino and I packed these little paper bags so we could collect it all once we got here."

Joe smiled. "You were disappointed."

"In more ways than that. Especially after Mama got sick and we had to go on welfare."

"That must have been awful."

"It's the most degrading thing that can happen to anyone," she said coldly.

"You ought to feel very proud of yourself," he said slowly. "You've accomplished so much."

"I do," she said, "but I didn't realize something was missing until I met you."

He smiled at her. "It's funny the way life sneaks up on you."

"What do you mean?"

"If someone told me I'd wind up with a girl like you, I'd tell them they were crazy."

"And what's wrong with a girl like me?"

"You know what I mean," he said. "I come from a totally different background. I mean, if I missed a meal, my mother would think it was a major catastrophe." Elena giggled. "I never met a Puerto Rican until I was in high school. And even then, it was on a field trip, in Social Studies."

She laughed. "You've grown a lot," she said. "How do your parents feel about you working at Jefferson?"

"They start to panic if they don't hear from me every few days. At first, they were so pleased I'd be at a famous place like Hirshorn. They didn't know Jefferson was part of the rotation. They're very nervous."

"They have a right to be," she said. "It's not the greatest neighborhood."

"But it's your neighborhood."

"That doesn't mean it's safe. It's understandable that your parents are nervous. Whenever people don't understand something, they're frightened."

They pulled up in front of her apartment. Elena reached for her suitcase. "How come you're so good at understanding?" he asked. She touched his cheek. "Elena," he said, feeling the heat rise within him again, "I want to move in with you."

"Like hell, *Señor* Doctor," she laughed. "You'll marry me first."

"You got a date."

15

Ino walked into Herb's office. Herb was on the telephone and motioned for him to sit down.

"How's it going, Ino?" he asked, hanging up the receiver.

"Good. I think I may have hit gold with Larry Magdalino. Have you read my reports, yet?"

"Yes. I knew he'd be a tough nut to crack. Everyone knows his record. So I figured you'd find that a personal challenge."

Ino smiled broadly. "You know me by now. I think he's got potential, Herb. He's already been out by himself twice without trouble. I think that shows growth."

"For you as well as for him."

Ino accepted the compliment without embarrassment. Herb was right. In a large way, Larry's achievements exemplified his own growth in the program. He'd been thinking about it a lot recently.

"Ino, remember when you first came in here?"

Ino burst out laughing. "How will I ever live that down?"

"I was baiting you when I told you you could have any job in the house, if you were man enough for it. You asked me if that included my job and I told you it did."

"I was really something, wasn't I?"

"You are really something now. Ino, the work you've done in the time you've been here has been great. I've made a few calls and I want you to stay on, as a staff member. We're offering you a permanent full-time position with Rebirth. You'll have health benefits, social security, a pension plan, and a good salary."

Ino didn't speak for several moments. Finally, he said, "Herb, you've given me more than I can ever repay. Now I'm a member of the human race. But I've already thought about it. I can't stay."

"It's a tough world out there."

"I know," said Ino. "But this is my second chance. I can't afford the privilege of fucking up again. I'm twenty-six years old. It's my last shot, Herb, and I'm going to make it count."

Herb nodded as he doodled on the blotter on his desk. "I understand. But, I'm losing a good man, and I can't afford to lose many good men." He looked at Ino and smiled. "I'll be here if you need me."

"Thanks, Herb. I appreciate that."

"Well, what are your plans? It's obvious you've thought about it."

"I thought I'd start out in one of the worst places in the South Bronx—Jefferson Hospital."

"If there are any changes at Jefferson, you're the man to make them." Herb extended his hand. "I know you'll keep in touch. Good luck."

"Thanks, Herb, for everything. But you don't have to wish me luck."

"How come?"

" 'Cause I figured it out one night. Luck is only preparation meeting opportunity. And this time, I'm prepared."

She clutched the large brass key in her hand and silently led Luis to the door marked "Benjamin Gold, Chief of Surgery." The room was black. She locked the door behind them and deftly found her way around the desk. She switched on the small fluorescent lamp and an eerie glow flooded the corner of the room. She turned and wrapped her arms around him.

"Over here," she whispered as she led him toward the old leather couch behind the desk. She lay down and pulled him toward her. His hands reached under her skirt. His lips covered her face.

"My God. I love you so much." She reached down beneath her skirt, sliding her panties down.

"Oh Luis, please. I need you now." Her legs wrapped tightly around his waist. She explored his body as he powerfully began stroking into her. As his rhythm increased she reached beneath her and ran the nail of her index finger sharply along the under

189

surface of his penis. He came in gripping, jerking spasms. As the warm flow of his ejaculation filled her, she moaned and held him tightly against her body.

At 7:05 in the morning Benjamin Gold was sitting at his desk as usual, going over the patients' charts he would be using during grand rounds. He felt it was important to keep on top of anything the residents and interns might have missed. He saw Kendricks's initials on the chart he was holding and his mind began to wander.

Kendricks was a real pain in the ass. He would get them into trouble for sure. Gold had seen enough surgeons go through the program to have a sixth sense about their future outcome. Quickly, his eyes scanned the page and he noted two tests Kendricks had failed to order in his workup.

As he read the next chart he began to relax. Susan had prepared it in her usual even, round handwriting. He could read the notes easily without the aid of his glasses. Gold appreciated her thoroughness. Everything should be in its place. Her work alone stood above all the others. He leaned back in his swivel chair and chewed on his pen. Rarely had he seen a woman so steel willed. She had guts and drive. Gold knew she had the makings of a great doctor. But experience had taught him not to pin his hopes on her one hundred percent. She was a woman and she was young. Young people had a habit of letting life get in the way of things.

A shiny object on the floor next to the sofa caught his eye. Puzzled for a moment, he walked over to the sofa, bent down and picked up a surgical scissors. It was a gold Swiss Elton, and it had the number eighty-seven on it. Instantly, Gold recognized the scissors. He himself had ordered four of them for graduation presents for the Emergency Room aides.

The Emergency Room Aide Program was Gold's brainchild. He had selected four out of one hundred applicants to train directly under his supervision. He had argued with the administration for weeks over the small salary each aide was to receive. All the aides were Puerto Rican or black and from the South Bronx. Gold grasped the significance of this immediately. He worked them hard, but his intuition had paid off. Now, two years later, Gold could boast of the best ER aides in the whole

Hirshorn complex. The *Daily News* had even run a small story on his program last year.

But how could one of their scissors wind up in his office? The aides never came up to the second floor; all their work was done down in the ER. He went to his old file cabinet and located his notes on the program.

Could one of them have lost it and could it have been accidentally picked up by the cleaning crew? Immediately he dismissed the idea as farfetched. His aides had come to depend on their scissors and knowing how scarce good instruments were, guarded them fiercely. He flipped through the file until he came to the last page. He read: "Graduation Ceremony 7:00 P.M., Sunday, January 12, 1979. Speakers: Robert P. Anderson, President, Hirshorn Hospital; Harold Krauthammer, Administrator, Jefferson Hospital. Presentation of gift: 4 Swiss Surgical Scissors @ $38.00 each.

Juan Martines - No. 84
Frank Krinshaw - No. 85
Jimenez Gondolez - No. 86
Luis Rodrigues - No. 87"

Luis. So it was Luis's scissors. But what was Luis doing in his office? No one had a key to his office except Susan. She was the only one he trusted. He had offered her the use of his office last year so that she might use his extensive personal library for study or his couch to catch a quick nap during her long nights on call. He felt better about letting her sleep in his office rather than having her walk over to the staff house. A woman alone at night, even in the hospital complex, was unnerving. If Susan had used his office last night, what were Luis's scissors doing here? He picked up the phone and had Susan paged.

She walked into his office ten minutes later. He was sitting at his desk and had the scissors in front of him. He could tell from her guarded reaction when she glanced at the scissors that his instincts had proven correct.

"Good morning, Susan, I called you in to discuss a little matter that's been puzzling me." He picked up the scissors and handed them to her. "Do you know what these are?"

"Aren't they the scissors you gave the aides when they graduated?"

"They are, indeed," he answered. "This particular pair belongs to Luis. I found them under my sofa when I got in this morning. Since you're the only one who has a key to my office, I thought you might know how they got there.''

"Well, yes, Dr. Gold, I was in your office last night.'' Susan's mind began to race frantically for an acceptable lie, anticipating his next question.

"Were you alone, Susan?'' He noticed her mounting anxiety.

"Well, actually, I asked Luis to come up for a few minutes to discuss something,'' she stammered.

Gold felt his blood pressure rising. "You asked Luis to come to my office with you?'' he screamed. "I'm not running a coffee shop here. I trusted you, and only you, to use my office, and now I find that you abused that privilege.''

"Dr. Gold, I apologize.''

"I did not offer this office to Luis. I offered it to you. You had no right to allow him in here without my permission. What was so important you had to discuss with him in my office instead of the Emergency Room?''

"I'm sorry, Dr. Gold, really I am. It was a personal matter.''

"A personal matter?'' screamed Gold. "A personal matter in my office without my permission? And what happened during this personal matter?''

Susan's anxiety began to turn to anger. "Nothing happened.''

"Have you forgotten you're a married woman? Have you forgotten your husband is working his tail off while you're shacking up with the hired help on my couch?''

Her voice was brittle and hard. "I'm a human being. And is that what you think of Luis—hired help?''

"You and Luis! Susan, have you lost control of yourself? Luis is a nothing. He'll never be anything compared to you.''

"Why? Because he never had the breaks I did? Dr. Gold, you're a medical snob,'' she sneered.

"You're the best surgical resident I ever trained. I will not allow you to ruin a brilliant medical career over a two-bit Puerto Rican nothing.''

"My career as a surgeon has nothing to do with my life as a woman. And Luis has worked hard to come this far. He's premed, and he's finished in the top of his class. He's going to apply to Hirshorn and is sure to be accepted.''

"Like hell he will! Don't think I won't use every drop of power I have to keep him out of Hirshorn and every other med school in the country as well. Now you either break this off with him immediately, or he can kiss his dreams good-bye.''

"That's blackmail!"

"I see it as taking care of my own. One of my residents is too immature to take care of her own life. I feel it is my duty and in her best interests to do what my wisdom dictates." Suddenly, Gold seemed very calm. He knew he had her over a barrel.

"You're cruel and vindictive," she spat.

"Someday you'll thank me for what I'm doing, Susan."

"You'll be in your grave before you hear any thanks from me," she shouted as she ran out of his office in tears. Benjamin Gold threw the scissors down. First it was Joe and Elena. He had almost accepted that. But Susan was already married and was much more vulnerable. He was furious. He could never understand these people. They carried on like animals.

16

Ino stood in front of the mirror, buttoning the vest to his new three-piece navy gabardine suit. Joe and Elena had gone with him to buy it. The light blue shirt made a striking contrast with his dark complexion. Satisfied with the fit, he straightened his tie and went into the other room.

He surveyed the room with approval. There wasn't much there—a sofa bed, a bridge table and two chairs in the kitchenette, but what was there, was his. It was the first time in his life he could say that. He had rented the tiny apartment on 149th Street with the money Elena lent him when he got out of Rebirth ten days ago. He felt like a new person, and he knew, in a way, he was. He checked the alarm clock. Elena and Joe should be there soon. They had insisted on a celebration dinner. All the pieces were finally falling into place.

*　　*　　*

"We're going to do great things together," said Ino, sated after the big meal at Amalfi's.

Joe raised his wineglass. "To the new Ino Sanchez." He smiled. Elena beamed with pleasure.

Ino raised his glass to Elena. "To my sister, Elena. I couldn't have made it without her."

They drank the red wine.

"So where do you go from here?" asked Joe.

"I've spoken to a lot of the Young Toros. They're going to stand behind me."

"The Toros?" said Joe, disappointed. "You don't need them anymore. You're a new man."

"You're wrong, Joe. I need them. I can't make things happen without them."

"What kind of things do you want to make happen?" asked Elena hesitantly.

"I want to see a real change in the living standards of the community."

"And for that you need a gang?" she asked.

"The Young Toros are no longer a gang. We're a social-political organization now. And we're pledging ourselves to the South Bronx community." He saw the skepticism written on her face. "Elena, it's not what you think. We won't carry weapons or fight wars. The only knives we'll use are ones that'll cut through the red tape. We'll use our energy to help develop new political contacts." He turned to Joe. "It's the only way to make real changes."

"And all the Toros go along?" asked Joe.

"I didn't say all of them. I said a lot of them."

"Ino," asked Elena slowly, "are any of the men with you on drugs?"

"A handful, no more. I've given them a choice. Angel is the worst and he's leaving. Paco and Enrique were always clean. The rest are chippin'."

"How can you be sure?" asked Joe. "You've invested a lot of time at Rebirth. They haven't. Even three or four rotten apples can spoil the whole bushel."

"I made it clear. If they don't stay clean, they don't stay. I'm not interested in support from a bunch of junkies. If there's one slip, I'm going to know about it faster than anyone. But, I need those men that are committed. I've got to have a strong base. Without it, the whole organization is worthless."

194

"What will they do?" asked Elena.

"They'll work," said Ino.

"Where?" asked Joe.

"How about Jefferson?" said Ino. "The community identifies with the hospital." He watched her wary expression. "We'd be together."

Elena looked at her brother, and the flicker of doubt disappeared. "It might work," she said slowly. "The men could carry blood, transport the patients, fill in some of the gaps. I know you'd really be welcome."

"And what about you," asked Joe. "Where will you begin?"

"Me?" Ino smiled, sticking a handkerchief in his breast pocket. "I thought I'd start off with a visit to my good friend, the mayor."

Ino entered the inner office of the newly elected mayor of New York City, Richard Tanner. "Sit down," said Tanner, pointing to the brown suede chair in front of his desk. "How are you feeling these days?" He leaned against the front of his desk and studied him carefully.

"Fine," said Ino.

"That's good," said Tanner slowly. There was a lengthy pause. "Well," he asked, "what can I do for you?"

"I need a job."

"Fine," said Tanner, starting to relax. "Why don't you go down to personnel? They handle the new applicants there. I'm sure we can find something suitable for you."

"They don't know me in personnel," said Ino.

"Well, that's true," said Tanner, shuffling the pile of papers on his desk.

"And you do." Tanner looked at him sharply. "We made a commercial together. Remember?"

Tanner turned a deep shade of scarlet. He cleared his throat. "Exactly what type of job did you have in mind?"

"I want to set up an office for the people of the South Bronx. A place they can come to with their problems and stand a chance of getting something done about them."

A sigh of relief escaped Tanner's lips. "That's a good idea," he started. "I could set you up with a small office right here. We could keep a phone manned twenty-four hours a day, advertise in the papers. I'll even hold a press conference to explain the function of the new office. You can't help the people if you don't listen to them, I've always felt. And we must give them the opportunity to be heard."

"I agree completely," interrupted Ino. "But it can't be here. It's got to be in the South Bronx, where the people live. It should be in a storefront, with a sign over the door, 'People for Progress.' All the people that man the desk will be bilingual. More important, they'll be from the neighborhood. When the people see that you've created a place where they can come to with their complaints, and when they see that they're listened to, then your strength will be insurmountable."

Tanner leaned back in his swivel chair and smiled. The kid just might be onto something. Surely the slogan, "People for Progress," would look great over the Wirephotos. This young man was different from his aides, who were all so eager to say the right thing. He even looked different. He'd come here begging for a job. He would be loyal, and more important, in the hot summer months, when the poor gathered for their now annual outcry, he might even help to keep the streets calm. If New York City remained riot free during the first year of his mayoralty, it would go a long way toward solidifying the middle class behind him. He had just about guaranteed them that their lives would no longer be disrupted by the violent desperation of the poor.

"Use the hospital shot," he had ordered after viewing the tape.

"Who gives a shit about some spics?" Malcolm, his chief aide had countered. But when the private ratings gave the spot an overwhelming score, even his campaign manager had slowly come to understand the power of the simple videotape filmed in the large ward. In the last month of the campaign, they had gone to their strength and forced the speech down the throats of the voting public.

"I like it." Tanner beamed. "From today on, you're on the payroll. You'll report directly to my chief aide, Malcolm. You'll need a title. Have any ideas?"

Ino shrugged his shoulders. "Not really. Whatever you and your people want to call me will be fine."

"How about the 'People's Special Aide to the Mayor'?" Ino smiled. "Ino"—Tanner's voice softened with practiced dramatic effect—"you're one of my people, now. Report to Malcolm in the morning. We'll get you that storefront. Oh, you'll need a salary. Eighteen thousand a year fair?"

Ino gasped. "That's more than fair."

Tanner reached across the desk, and they shook hands. "I want you to know that you're as important to me as any of my other aides. If you have any problems getting through I want you to come straight to me. Together we'll make sure that the People for Progress will be a success."

Within minutes of Ino's departure, Malcolm was in Tanner's office. "What did he want?"

"He wanted a job."

"And you gave it to him?"

"Yes. He wants to set up a storefront in the ghetto. A place for the people to come and air their problems."

"We have enough problems with the goddamn unions."

"I didn't say we were going to do anything. I just said that we're going to set up the storefront. The poor have to believe in something."

"How much is this going to cost?"

"Eighteen thousand dollars."

"For what? What are we buying?"

"Hopefully, Malcolm, we're buying off the South Bronx. If everything stays quiet, I'd say we're getting a real bargain."

Malcolm frowned, "What is Sanchez's position going to be?"

"I gave him the title 'People's Special Aide to the Mayor.'"

"Did you know that your People's Aide has just spent five months in Rebirth House drying out from heroin addiction?"

"No," said Tanner.

"Did you know that your People's Aide has a twelve-year history as the most violent, successful gang leader in the South Bronx?"

"No, again," countered Tanner.

"He's a street rat. At the first opportunity, he'll knife you in the back." He studied Tanner's calm demeanor. "You don't seem very concerned."

"It's nice to know a man has weaknesses." Tanner laughed, and Malcolm succumbed, joining in the glow of their untouchable position.

*   *   *

That afternoon, Ino came rushing into Elena's apartment.

"Ino! What happened?"

"He gave me the job."

"Great! How did he act?"

"Guarded."

"He's going to pay you?"

"And how!"

"I can't believe it!"

"Believe it. It's exactly what I've been waiting for. Now I can come into the hospital with some clout."

"Ino, don't screw this up. This is the opportunity of a lifetime."

"I know that. I also know Tanner just plans to use me. He doesn't realize that I plan to use him first."

"Richard Tanner could be a dangerous enemy."

"This is as high as he'll go. His incompetence will become glaring."

"Why do you say that?" she asked.

"The rich have always gone with Tanner because he's one of them. But the middle class is not such a sure thing. They only went along because they thought the poor believed in him."

"The poor only believe in the hunger in their stomachs," said Elena.

"Exactly, but the illusion has been created, and Tanner is determined to use it to carry him to high places. I'll just string him along until the right time comes, then POW!" He moved his fist through the air. "I'll blow him out."

"Just make sure you don't blow yourself out in the process."

"Be careful with that box," yelled Ino as Paco and Enrique maneuvered through the narrow doorway.

They had been working most of the day to transform the vacant jewelry store on 145th Street into the People for Progress office. Eighteen men had scraped and washed the windows, pulled some useless shelves down and painted the walls a bright orange.

They set up a desk in the center and chairs along the walls of the small square room and wedged a file cabinet in the far corner. Travel posters of Puerto Rico decorated the walls and a rubber plant, donated by one of the street vendors, sat next to the desk.

Paco set the large box down, and Ino, seeing the red mark, ripped at the tape. He pulled open the cardboard sleeve and pushed through the styrofoam packing. Grasping the back, he pushed the box over on its side. He sat in front of it and began pushing his legs against the edge.

"Here, Jefe, let me give you a hand," said Enrique, bending over to grasp the bottom. They pulled hard and the top of the tufted red leather chair appeared.

"Isn't it a beauty?" asked Paco as they wedged the chair out of its tight package.

"It should be," said Ino, getting up and brushing off his pants. "Tanner goes first class."

"He gave you this chair?" asked Paco.

"Not exactly," admitted Ino. "Let's just say he ordered it."

They set the chair up and stood admiring it.

"It must have cost a thou," said Enrique. "How did you get it?"

"Remember Charlie D'Esposito?" asked Ino.

"Yeah."

"He's the foreman of the storeroom now," said Ino. "Tanner ordered ten of these for his boardroom. Only one got lost."

Paco laughed. "You got friends everywhere."

And I'll need every one of them." Ino smiled, looking around the room with satisfaction. "We've done a pretty good job around here," he said.

"This is what the Toros always deserved," said Enrique proudly. The others nodded in agreement.

Ino stared at him. "I never want to hear the word Toros again."

Suddenly the men stopped working. All of them turned to him, startled. "But, Jefe," stammered Paco, "what do you mean?"

Their eyes followed him as he walked behind the desk. He sat down, spread his palms out on the desk and stared at the eighteen silent men. "Sit down," he said.

They sat on the floor and on the folding chairs.

"We're in a new ball game now," said Ino carefully. "We're not a street gang anymore. We are now the People for Progress. We're a political and social organization. We're supported by the city of New York. We dedicate ourselves to helping the people

199

of the South Bronx. This is our headquarters. We're here to do something for the people when they have no place left to go. *Comprende?*''

"But what about the Toros?" asked Juanito.

"The Toros no longer exist, Juanito." He studied the worried expression on the boy's face. "Do not be sad," he said gently. "The Toros were our beginning. But we've grown from our birth on the streets. We can become the voice of the people. As People for Progress, we can have far greater power than the Toros ever commanded. We're finally in a position to do something that will make a difference. But it all depends on you."

"What do you mean, Jefe?"

"You've got to follow my instructions and promise to work your butts off."

"What else?" asked Paco.

"Besides manning this office twenty-four hours a day," continued Ino, "we're going to work at Jefferson Hospital. There's a severe manpower shortage there, and People for Progress is going to help out. We'll rotate the shifts, so we can cover both places. When you get to the hospital, you do what they tell you to do. They want you to empty bedpans, you do it. They want you to deliver blood, you do it. They know where you can do the most good."

"So now we're running errands for the gringos?" came a muffled voice from the back.

"That's just the kind of attitude we don't want," snapped Ino. "We're not running errands for the gringos. We're working our tails off for our own people. If you can't see that, Pedro, you don't belong here. There are going to be changes," said Ino, "real changes. I want every one of you to come to work in this office in a suit and tie."

"What?" they started.

"That's right. We're setting an example for the rest of the community. The first way we show it is by our appearance. Those of you who don't own a suit and tie, let me know. There's money here for that.

"Second, no weapons and no drugs. Those things won't work. Anyone who breaks the rule is out. There are no second chances, so keep your noses clean. They're watching every move we make, remember that always." He looked at their intense young faces. "We are on the threshold of something great. Something that can change our whole lives. Right now, it's a dream, but soon, the People for Progress will have the power. And with the power, comes the reality."

PART II

17

Joe Ruskin drove up the hill to the parking lot in a cloud of smoke. He stopped at the gate and rolled down the window. He already had two bills clenched in his left palm.

"Well, Dr. Ruskin, hello," George greeted him.

"Hello, George. How much is this going to cost me?"

"Standard rate, Dr. Ruskin. Five dollars for two weeks."

"But I'm only on every other day," argued Joe. "I ought to get credit for the times I'm not using the lot. And on top of that, I'm a first-year resident now."

"Well, congratulations," said George. "But I can't do it for you. If word got out, I'd be ruined. Standard rate is five dollars for two weeks."

"I could always tell Dr. Gold." Joe half smiled.

George swallowed hard. He began rapidly wiping Joe's side mirror with his dirty handkerchief. "Yes, sir, Dr. Ruskin. I don't see why we can't make an exception for all the people who work in the Emergency Room. After all, they're only using the lot half the time."

"That's great, George. I only have two dollars."

George sighed. "Two dollars will be fine."

Joe smiled to himself as he rolled up the window. It was better when you knew the ropes. He hurried up the ramp with a sense of excitement. He had spent the last six weeks in a postcardiac-care rotation at Hirshorn, where he had frantically taken care of patients who couldn't talk or smile. It didn't compare to Jefferson. He walked into the ER with a strange sense of confidence. Had a year gone by so quickly?

He ran up the stairs and into the surgical conference room. Gold was leaning out the window. There were four new interns.

The new chief resident was Ed Gordon, a nervous, partially bald surgeon.

Susan was sitting near the door. "Welcome back, stranger." She smiled, giving him a big hug. "We missed you."

"Me, too, Susan. How have you been?" He took the seat nex to her.

"Good. Happier than I've been in a long time."

"That's great," said Joe. "Who's working here this rotation?"

"Would you believe Kendricks?"

"Oh no!" Joe laughed. "How's he doing?"

"He's only been here a few days, so he hasn't had time to get into any trouble yet."

"How about Arnost?" asked Joe.

"He got accepted at the University of Houston."

"He did? Can you picture him in a cowboy hat?" They both laughed.

"The chief there is Hungarian."

"Ah ha! Well, we'll miss him. He had good hands."

"Not as good as yours, Joe," Susan said quietly.

Joe smiled. "And how is Luis?"

"What can I say?" She beamed. "He's wonderful."

"What happened to our old chief?"

"Mike Barilla is now in private practice in Marin County, California."

Joe let out a slow whistle. "That's a far cry from this place."

"He's already bought a house with a swimming pool."

"We'll have to be sure to visit him. What's happening with Zilk?"

"He's still here but he's officially transferred to OB-GYN," she said. "He's Dr. Watel's responsibility now."

"I would hate to have my sister treated by him."

She smiled. "Joe, you don't even have a sister."

"I mean if I did. Gold must be relieved Zilk is out of his department."

"Everyone in Surgery is relieved," she admitted.

"How is Gold?" whispered Joe.

"The same. Maybe a little more tired."

"How come?"

"They turned down his request for a special surgical ICU."

"Did you believe he had a chance?"

"A slim one," she said. "And I guess you know Elena's

206

brother and his organization have been down here giving us a hand.''

"Elena keeps me posted. How's he doing?"

"Great. Best group of volunteers Jefferson's ever had."

Joe beamed. "That's terrific. I knew it would work out. Where's Ino now?"

"I think you'll find him in X-ray."

Gold turned to the group. "Good morning Ed, Susan, Joe, and Team A of the surgical division. Those of you that are new, I'd like to welcome you to Jefferson. Those of you that are still here, it's good to have you back. I'd like to congratulate you, Joe, on your National Board Exam." He turned to the group. "Joe got the highest grade in the internship class."

"It was all that good stuff you taught me, Dr. Gold." Joe smiled.

"Of course, we're not here to get good grades on tests. We're here to take care of patients. What's the schedule for today?" he asked Susan.

"Just two gallbladders."

"Good. It'll give you a chance to take Romano and Goozh down to the ER and get them oriented." The group broke as Gold headed out the door.

Joe looked at Susan. "Nothing ever changes."

Joe hurried over to X-ray. "Ino!" he called from the end of the hall. Ino looked up from the X rays he was filing and smiled. The two men embraced. "We missed you, brother," said Ino.

"I hear People for Progress is doing a great job!"

"We're trying," he said.

"And how's it going at the mayor's job?" asked Joe.

He flipped his palm from side to side. "They gave us a storefront. We got a phone with a special line to the mayor. They've given us five thousand dollars to get things going."

"That sounds great," said Joe.

"It's not enough."

"But it's a start," offered Joe.

"It's a start."

"Well, good luck."

"Come on, Joe. You know that luck has nothing to do with things."

"I don't believe that at all."

"Well, I guess that's one way we're different."

Whether it was luck or not, one thing was certain. People for Progress was making a real impact on Jefferson Hospital. Extra work was getting done, patients weren't waiting as long for routine tests. Morale in the Emergency Room and throughout the hospital had greatly improved.

It was obvious Ino could handle himself in tight situations and he taught his men to do the same. Somehow the big guards leaning against the doors seemed unnecessary. The staff at Jefferson welcomed the enthusiastic volunteers.

Elena was constantly at her brother's side directing, teaching, encouraging him. Joe found that in this second rotation at Jefferson Hospital, he was quickly becoming dependent on the presence of Ino and his men.

One night they wheeled a junkie in. He had taken an overdose and had the familiar milk stains covering the mucous membranes of his nose.

"He isn't breathing. He's got no blood pressure," said Joe, quickly sucking up two cc's of Nalline and plunging the needle into the bloated vein of the addict's neck. Within seconds, the Nalline infused through his system, binding the heroin. The addict began spontaneously breathing. A moment passed, and he was totally awake. He sat up rapidly and wheeled to face Joe, bringing his fist backward. Ino blocked his hand.

"You fucking pig, you blew my high." The man stood, furious.

Ino faced the angry patient. "You had just reached the supreme high. He saved your life. Now get out of here."

The addict stared, slowly understanding. He staggered out without saying another word.

"Well, I guess I'd better keep you around so I stay out of trouble," said Joe.

"No sweat, Joe. I have one advantage."

"What's that?"

"I think like an addict."

"I love you darling. I'll see you tonight," Joe whispered as he hung up the receiver.

"My sister really turns you on." Ino laughed.

Joe became embarrassed. "I'd really like to thank you and your men. You've made the last couple of months a breeze."

"Yeah, but I still feel we're not doing all we can."

"I know what you mean."

"Have you ever looked up at those kids on the Peds ward with lead poisoning? I mean that's something that could really be prevented."

"Look, Ino. There's no doubt that Jefferson could benefit from a preventive medicine program, but we don't have the manpower."

"But my people could do that." Ino jumped at the opportunity. "What would we have to do?"

"Well, you could do a TB screening test, go through the neighborhood putting tine skin tests on everybody. Sickle cell anemia can be screened with a blood test; so could the lead content of the kids. But, that would require training men to actually draw blood."

"Draw blood? Any one of the Toros could hit a small, clogged vein blindfolded."

"I forgot. I guess they could."

They both laughed. "Joe, I would love to do that. That could really link up the hospital and the community, it would help the people. How do we set it up?"

"Well, you're going to have to go through Gold. It won't be easy. Maybe you could get Susan to suggest it."

"Susan to suggest it? Are you crazy?"

"Why? Susan is Gold's pet."

"Didn't you know? Susan and Luis have been having this thing going for months now and Gold is pissed about it."

"Susan and Luis? I must really be blind. Susan and Luis?" He thought out loud. "I'm surprised as hell, but I'm happy for them. Well, maybe I better suggest it."

"Do you think you could?"

"Yeah. If I'm lucky enough to catch him on a good day. He's particularly peaceful after a good case."

"Joe, I'd really appreciate your help."

Susan and Luis walked in. It was obvious they'd been arguing.

"Gold is a super doctor," she was saying. "His patients are his whole life."

"Come on, Susan. He's constantly flying into rages. Face it, he's getting old."

Joe grabbed Luis' arm. "Glad to see you two are still it," he laughed.

"Joe Ruskin! Good to see you." Luis gave him a bear hug.

"What'd I tell you," said Joe, "nothing changes."

The sound of their laughter was interrupted by the harsh whir of the siren, as yet another victim was brought up the ramp.

The fat mulatto man had suffered a twelve-inch wound in the back. They plugged him into three IVs, and Joe began to probe the wound with a small cotton-tipped applicator.

"Shit," said Ino. "Someone really meant business."

"He was sleeping with some woman when her husband came home. He didn't even have a chance to get out of the saddle," said Roberto.

"What did he hit him with?"

"A meat cleaver?"

"Huh?"

"The husband's a butcher."

"He's still shaky," said Susan, pulling the steel door open. "We'd better take him up."

They pulled the stretcher out of the elevator on the fourth floor.

"Luis, you'd better scrub in," said Susan. "Kendricks's tied up on the ward, and we'll need an extra hand."

Joe and Ino lifted the man onto the OR table as Susan and Luis went down the hall to change. Joe pulled on a pair of gloves and began scrubbing the man's abdomen.

Suddenly, the door swung open. A small Puerto Rican man in street clothes entered, waving a stained meat cleaver. Ino was closest to the door. "What the . . ." he started, pushing the intruder back into the hall. He stood braced at the door.

The assailant, now in a frenzy to complete the job, hurled himself back. The door opened several inches before Ino regained his footing and was able to force it closed. Joe was standing by the patient, stunned.

"Give me a hand," said Ino. "I'm not going to be able to hold him alone."

Joe ran over, looked through the glass, and saw the husband take several steps backward, preparing yet another surge. "Where the hell are the guards?" asked Joe, pushing against the door alongside Ino.

The man struck again and managed to force them both backward, far enough to get the hand with the cleaver into the opening. The cleaver began raking through the air. Joe and Ino regrouped and pushed, forcing the hand out, slamming the door shut. The small man slipped, temporarily exhausted, and sat on the floor.

Ino looked through the window. He seized the opportunity and moved quickly over to the OR table, unstrapped the safety buckle, and slid the patient onto the floor. Then he unlocked the table and rolled it up against the door, slamming the locking foot pedal down just as the man hit the door for the third time. This time the door did not move. The crazed husband collapsed with a loud wail on the opposite side.

"That'll hold him," said Ino.

"Help me get him back on the table," said Joe, to the anesthetist, who was furiously bagging the patient on the asbestos floor.

"There's a phone in the sterilization room," said Ino. "Get Susan and tell her to stay put. Then call the guards down at the desk and tell them to round our boy up. Then we'll take care of the patient."

"My God," said Joe, breathing hard. "How did he ever get up here? How did he know where the patient was? How could such a little guy have such strength?"

Ino looked at him and smiled. "That'll teach you not to fool around with Spanish women."

The minute she saw him, she knew something was wrong. He averted his eyes and shoved a wrinkled paper at her. Quickly her eyes scanned the sheet. It was a letter of rejection from Albert Einstein School of Medicine. It was a form letter, cold, impersonal, with only his name typed in.

"Oh, Luis," she started, "I'm sorry."

"You're sorry!" he exploded, turning to face her. The pain of defeat was written on his face. He began pacing back and forth in the small cast room. "I can't understand it. They really seemed interested at the interview. And that was only two weeks ago."

"Einstein isn't the only med school in New York," she said with forced enthusiasm.

"But it's the third school in the city that seemed interested in me and then sent me a rejection slip."

"It could be a coincidence."

"Come on, Susan," snapped Luis. "It's no coincidence. It' Gold."

"I didn't think he'd do it," she whispered, shaking her head

"He told you he would, and he did. That bastard."

Susan sat down on the folding chair and put her head in he hands.

"It isn't as if I didn't get good grades," continued Luis pacing again. "It isn't as if I'm a liability to them. It's only tha I'm Puerto Rican and the great Dr. Gold doesn't like Puert Ricans. At least not for his prize residents."

"We'll fight him, Luis," she said imploringly. "You'll get i somewhere. I'll go wherever you get accepted."

He stopped pacing. "How can you do that?"

"I'll switch residencies."

"In the middle?"

"It's been done before. We'll go someplace where nobod cares who Benjamin Gold is." A cold certainty spread over he face. "We'll start applying to schools outside the city. Let's tr Boston or Washington, D.C. There's lots of good med center there. And if it's not there, it'll be someplace else. But we'l make it," she said, looking at him with new determination "I'm not going to let anyone come between us."

He held her tightly and forced himself to believe her.

Joe got his chance to speak to Dr. Gold two weeks later. I started out as a routine gallbladder. Joe had asked Gold, "D you mind staying late and scrubbing with me?"

The case turned out to be an extremely difficult one; the patient had gallstones through her entire system. Joe's surgery was deft; the case lasted an hour and a half, as they slumped or the bench in the locker room.

Gold turned and said, "Joe, that was a particularly pretty piece of work."

"Thanks, Dr. Gold. And thanks for staying late and helping me. You know sometimes I go in there and I just know that no matter what goes on I can take care of it. Yet sometimes I'n really afraid."

"Listen, Joe. I've been doing this for thirty-seven years and I still get afraid. We try to hide it, but the patients are human

212

beings. You don't want to hurt them." Gold looked at the clock and suddenly groaned. "Oh, no, I'm already late for the director's meeting."

"You have those meetings every week. What do you do there?"

Gold started to dress quickly. "Well, the chief of medicine gets up and gives a thirty-minute talk on how it's impossible to be a GP for five hundred thousand people. Then the chief of radiology gets up and complains that all the other departments are keeping the films on the wards and not returning them to their proper place in X-ray. He then ends up by saying the X rays are the property of the Department of Radiology."

Joe laughed. "And what do you do?"

"I sit back in the corner with my old friend, Dr. Watel. We reminisce about old times."

"How did you get him to accept Zilk?"

"I didn't. Hirshorn decided that matter. When he asked me what I thought, I just didn't say anything."

"That's not like you."

"That's what Bob Watel said. I had to admit I found him unpredictable. I'd still rather Zilk be out of the hospital, but it's sure a lot better not to be personally responsible."

"Dr. Gold, there's something on my mind. Just an idea. In a lot of hospitals, they have a preventive medicine program. You think we could start something like that here?"

"Like what?" Gold asked coldly.

"You know. Start a simple program. Get a couple of the house staff from all the different departments to set up certain guide rules. Then train a couple of people to go out in the community and get the necessary tests."

"Look Joe. I'm already late for this meeting."

"Please, Dr. Gold. Let us try it. If it doesn't work out in a couple of weeks, I give you my word we'll just drop the whole program."

"I can't see how it would hurt. But I don't want it to take away from any of your other duties."

"It won't, Dr. Gold. I promise. I thought we could get the aid of some of the hospital personnel."

"Like who?"

"Well, Ino Sanchez and some of his men have really been helping out down in the Emergency Room."

"Elena's brother?"

213

"He really wants to try it."

"I don't trust him, Joe."

"We can train him in our spare time."

"I don't like it."

"Dr. Gold, please. Just listen to him. It will be a two-week experiment."

"Well, I'm late. I'll think about it." He looked at Joe and suddenly saw his son David's intensity and the urgent determination of his own youth to make things better. "Have him in my office on Monday morning. If we do this, I want to know what we're doing." Joe grabbed Dr. Gold's hand with both of his.

"Thank you, sir. I know you won't be sorry."

"We'll see, Joseph. Time has a way of teaching us new lessons."

"Well, at least you're young enough to accept new ideas."

"Joe, would you do me one big favor?"

"Anything."

"Don't bullshit me."

18

A month later, Ino and Paco were sitting in the People for Progress office.

"I don't think we're doing anything here," Paco stated carefully.

"Hold on, Paco. More and more people are coming in every day."

"What happened to our complaint about slumlords?" asked Paco.

"Nothing," Ino said coldly. "It turns out the slumlords are some of the most respected people in the city."

"What about our complaint about the working conditions at some of the factories?"

"Malcolm said he'd look into it."

"Come on, Ino. You know what they're doing."

"I knew before we started."

"Well, I'm tired of it. I hate wearing this stupid suit, and I hate our weekly meetings with Malcolm. I hate listening to the people and knowing we're part of the con."

"We can't go back to the streets," snapped Ino. "We have to wait for the proper time, and then we'll hit them like we hit Martinez four years ago."

"What are we going to do," asked Paco despondently, "bust up Tanner?"

"Something much worse than that."

"What?"

"We'll seize his power."

Suddenly, Enrique entered in whites, obviously upset. "I've had it," he said challengingly. He threw his short hospital jacket across the floor.

"What the fuck do you think you're doing?"

"Look, Ino, I quit. I'm leaving the Toros."

"We're not the Toros anymore."

"I don't give a damn what name you want to give us. I'm quitting you and your grandstand ideas. I'm tired of your lies."

"You want to go back to being nothing?"

"So we wear suits and hospital whites and we're not nothin'?" asked Enrique hotly. "We look better, that's all. But we're still stooges for Tanner and Hirshorn and any other jerkoff with power. We're losing any trust we had with the people. They're laughing at us."

"You have to cross the water to get to the other side," said Ino.

"Shit. I don't even know what that means. I'm sure no one else does either," said Enrique.

"It means you've got to have faith. You've got to hold in there and trust me. I know what I'm doing."

"That's great," said Paco. "But you've got to let us in on it, too. I feel the same as Enrique. So do the others. Ino, the men are angry. They feel like you're playing us."

"Enrique," said Ino, "I got you that job up on OB-GYN. It took me three weeks to set it up with the administration. It took me five weeks to get the chief of the lab to give Juan and Carlos a chance." He looked at both of them. "We're moving our men into every department in the hospital. We're gaining the staff's support. We're doing good things for the people."

"Carrying bed pans isn't my idea of doing things," said Enrique.

"You get paid. It's a job—the first real job you've had."

"I made more in the streets in a couple of hours than I do there in a week. A real job—ha! They treat me like shit, like I'm a slave."

"And if they want you to do a goddamn dance in the middle of the ward, you'll do it," yelled Ino. "Don't you see, they're testing us."

Enrique moved toward Ino, his fists clenched. "And when do we test them?" he demanded.

"As soon as we have some dirt," said Ino slowly.

"What does that mean—dirt?"

Ino walked over to his desk and lit a cigarette, drawing on it hard. "We need to demonstrate that in this hospital the system doesn't work."

"Well, you already got that," said Enrique.

"How?" asked Ino.

"There's enough things going on in the OB-GYN department alone to close down the whole friggin' hospital."

"For example?"

"Well," began Enrique, "there's this new resident up on the ward. He scares the piss out of me."

"What's he done?"

"What hasn't he done? Just a week ago he had this young girl in the hospital with a hot belly. Her temperature was one hundred and three and she was in continuous shock. I know because I took her vital signs a lot of the time."

"Go on."

"Well, this resident, he didn't do anything for her. Nothing but hang three units of blood. He cared more about getting through the weekend and passing the buck on to the next resident shift. The problem was when they opened up her stomach, there were at least five units of blood in her abdomen. She had a ruptured ectopic pregnancy. Even I knew it. It was a bad scene. Now she's going to be in the hospital two weeks longer. But I guess she ought to be thankful," he said. "She was almost allowed to die on the ward."

"That's disgusting," said Paco.

"It shows what I've known all along," said Ino. "We need a check on the medical activities at Jefferson Hospital."

The two men looked at each other. "And how are you going to do that?" asked Paco.

"With a complaint desk."

"A what?" asked Enrique.

"A desk we set up in the hospital where anyone concerned about a patient in the hospital or the care they're getting can come. We can take these complaints, follow up on them, find out if anyone screwed up, and make sure it doesn't happen again. When the people see that something is being done about their complaints, they'll feel like Jefferson is really their hospital."

"That sounds great," said Enrique. "But I don't know if they're going to let you set up this desk so fast. They're gonna ask where you get off actin' like the high priest."

"If they don't like it, they can shove it," snapped Ino.

"Ino, you don't know what you're sayin'," said Paco. "The honchos are going to fight it."

"Let them. We have Tanner."

"Tanner doesn't give a shit," said Enrique.

"Of course he doesn't, but I know how to handle him."

"Yeah, well, I hope you know how to handle Dr. Watel."

"Who's Dr. Watel?" asked Ino.

"He's the head of the OB-GYN department," said Enrique. "If we follow up on this case, he's gonna explode."

"Let him. He won't the next time."

Paco shrugged his shoulders. "I don' know, Ino. I just don't think you're going to get it going so fast. You don't want to draw too much heat on us."

Ino looked Paco and Enrique squarely in the eyes. "I made a commitment and I intend to carry it out. I was hoping you'd made the same commitment."

The two men looked at each other. "Sure, Ino," said Paco tentatively.

"I'll check with Joe Ruskin," continued Ino. "Maybe he can help us get it started. He helped with the preventive medicine program."

"That's going pretty good," admitted Paco.

"It sure is," smiled Ino. "We've managed to get eight buildings condemned for lead content in the paint already. That's not bad for the first month. And how about the TB epidemic we managed to stop? If Juan hadn't tested that grandmother we'd really have been up shits' creek. We're doing good," said Ino.

"You can see that. You can see the progress we're making, can't you?" He looked imploringly at Enrique.

"Yeah, Ino," said Enrique, averting his eyes. "I guess you're right."

"Sure I'm right," he said, nudging him affectionately on the shoulder. "And I'm right about this complaint desk, too. Now do you remember the name of the patient?"

"No, but I can get it."

"Do you know who the doctor is?"

"Sure," said Enrique. "His name is Dr. Matt Zilk."

Joe and Ino were in the cast room drinking coffee when Ino first brought it up. "We need a complaint desk," he said.

"A what?"

"A place where relatives can come if they're concerned about the treatment of any of the patients in the hospital."

Joe stared at him. "Who's going to man this desk?"

"We are. We're already part of the hospital. We're from the community. And the people respect us. What do you think?"

"Frankly, I don't think it's such a good idea."

"Why not?"

"The chiefs of service are not going to like it. You're trying to set up a group with no medical education to oversee the conduct of the hospital staff. Doctors resent it when other *doctors* tell them what to do. Can you imagine how they'll react to you guys sticking your nose in?"

"Someone has to. Otherwise nothing will change."

"I know that, Ino. It's just that change takes time."

"Are you going to help us or not?"

"I've already gone this far. I'll help you, but I'm afraid this might be a lot more difficult than you think. On top of that, even if you do manage to get it set up, I doubt if it's going to be effective."

"As you told me once, we won't know that for a while."

"What got you started on this all of a sudden?"

"I've been thinking about it for a while. Then I heard about that case Zilk just botched."

"What case?"

Ino told him.

"He really stinks, you know," started Joe.

218

"If you could follow up on this," pressed Ino, "it would help."

"What do you want me to do?"

"Find out all the facts, then go to Gold and he'll have to listen."

"Okay, I'll give it a shot. The first-year resident up there is my friend. He'll tell me the truth."

An hour later, Joe returned. "You were right," he said. "It's worth going into. Since Zilk hit the service, it's been total chaos. He resents being transferred to OB-GYN. He was always a real problem, but now he's actually dangerous."

"You know this guy?"

"Yeah, he was my surgical resident."

"What's his problem?"

Joe shrugged. "Elena thinks he's crazy."

"Elena knows him, also?"

"Everyone knows Zilk."

"What does your friend think about my idea of a complaint desk?"

"Specifically, he thought the idea stunk."

"Well, does he have any better ideas?"

"No. He's just reacting in the normal way. No one likes interference."

"That's the trouble with you doctors. Someone has to watch out for the people."

"Look, I've already made an appointment with Dr. Watel for tomorrow morning. I'll try to make him aware of what's been going on."

"I'm sure he already knows."

The next morning Joe walked into Dr. Watel's office. "I'm Joe Ruskin. I'm a first-year resident in surgery."

"I know who you are," said Watel. "You're Ben's young hotshot."

Joe blushed. "I made an appointment with you because I didn't know where to go and I have a problem."

"And you think I can help?"

"It concerns one of your residents."

"Zilk?"

Joe nodded.

"What did he do this time?"

"He sat on a ruptured ectopic pregnancy."

"You mean he observed a patient and tried to treat her conservatively."

"I mean he sat on her for two days. Her crit was twenty-two."

"First-year residents are the most aggressive people in surgery. It takes some experience to learn to sit on your hands."

"She should have been explored."

"You'd probably want to open every patient that hit the ward. That's why you guys aren't allowed to make decisions. Too hasty. The whole damn lot of you."

"Then how come the minute your chief resident made rounds on Monday, he took her up?"

"Her condition must have changed."

"I don't think so. Why don't you ask him?"

"I'll do better than that." He reached for the phone. "Page Dr. Palmer and Dr. Zilk and get them both up here, stat." He stared at Joe. "I shouldn't be wasting my time on this. But I want to prove to you how dangerous a little information can be."

"Yes, sir," said Joe in a low voice.

"You don't sound convinced."

"Frankly, sir, I'm not sure you are either."

Watel stared at him coldly. "Let me warn you. You're treading on thin ice, young man. I plan to get to the bottom of this. And if you're wrong, you'd better stay the hell off my service. I don't like troublemakers."

"I'm sorry," said Joe stubbornly.

"Believe me. You will be."

There was a knock on the door.

"Come in." Palmer and Zilk entered. "You gentlemen know Ruskin? He's a resident in surgery." They nodded to Joe. "He says you guys screwed up on a ruptured ectopic last week."

Palmer dropped his head, reddening noticeably. "Well?" There was a pause. "Come on, damn it. I want to hear what happened."

"I made rounds early Monday morning. A twenty-two year old, gravida two, had been admitted over the weekend. She demonstrated diffuse abdominal pain, decreased bowel sounds, elevated temp. Pelvic exam was impossible due to severe pain. We took her up. On laparoscopy she had a ruptured ectopic with some chronic scarring over the right fallopian tube. I elected to

220

do a simple ligation and oophorectomy. She's completely stable and ready for discharge."

"Was she transfused?"

Palmer swallowed. "Eight units."

"Eight units?!"

"Actually, I only had to give her four on the table. She had three units over the weekend, and we hung another before we brought her up."

"You didn't think that was strange?"

"She didn't present with a classic picture."

"Goddamn it! She was in shock. Why wasn't she explored before?" There was another pause.

"I wasn't called in."

"You're the chief resident. You're responsible for every patient on your ward."

"I'm fully aware of that."

"Why weren't you called in?"

"Matt thought she was an acute PID."

"Great. Zilk, why wasn't he called?"

"The history was vague. She had been seen in the clinic a couple of months before for acute gonorrhea. I just assumed it was a reinfection."

"How did you treat her?"

"Antibiotics."

"That's it? You also transfused her."

"Three quarters of our patients are anemic. They don't exactly follow a balanced diet."

"Did you think of aspirating her pelvic vault?"

"I did."

"Then why didn't you do it?"

"I was sure she was just another hooker with the drip."

"You were obviously incorrect."

"Yes, I realize that now."

"Yet you almost allowed her to bleed to death."

"Her condition changed overnight. It was a bad weekend, and I was exhausted."

"That's not an excuse."

"She's fine, now."

"Not through anything you did." There was a long pause. "Dr. Palmer, I want the chart on that patient in my office by noon. Now, all three of you, get the hell out of my office." He glared at Zilk as he rose to leave with his chief. Joe stopped at the door, shaking his head.

"He's new. He's expected to make mistakes. I'm sure you screw up more than him."

"Yes, sir."

"But Ruskin, thanks for bringing this to my attention." Joe nodded weakly.

Ino Sanchez had been pacing in the hall next to Watel's office for the last thirty minutes. He stared as Palmer and Zilk walked out the door. He felt a chill over the back of his neck as he watched Zilk's pear-shaped behind. The two men swung around the corner. He knew Zilk from somewhere, and he was sure the experience had not been pleasant.

Joe entered the hall.

"What happened?" asked Ino, rushing up to him.

"He reprimanded Zilk."

"And?"

"He's going to review the chart."

"And?"

"He thanked me for making him aware of the case."

"And?"

"And what? You want him to lift his license?"

"I want to make sure he doesn't do it again."

"I know. So do I."

"But he will. That's what you're telling me."

"Watel is not going to take it any further."

"Great."

"He feels Zilk needs to be given a chance." Joe held his head down.

"But what about the patients? Don't they deserve a chance?"

"I'll speak to Gold today."

Joe knocked anxiously at the door.

"Please come in, Joe," Gold greeted him warmly.

"Dr. Gold, I have to speak to you. I've been thinking it might be a good idea to set up a complaint desk."

"Joe. Not again. Not another . . ."

"It doesn't have to be a big thing. Just a small desk set up a couple hours a day, so that anyone from the community can come in if they're concerned about the care of one of their

222

relatives or friends; so they feel that there's someone in the hospital who's concerned about their care.''

"Joseph, do you realize what you're asking?"

"I think so.''

"You're asking for permission to set up a committee to give the community and lay-people who will have the power to check into medical conduct. That's like asking us to put a loaded gun against our chest. Besides, who's going to man the desk?"

"I think the residents of the hospital could. Or . . .''

"Or perhaps the People for Progress?" Gold exploded, red-faced.

"Why not, Dr. Gold? Even you can see what a great job they're doing on the preventive medicine program. They're really dedicated. Their only concern is improving the standard of the community.''

"No one is going to tell us what the medical standards should be. That happens to be my job.''

"Dr. Gold, the problem is no one in the hospital does their job as well as you. None of the complaints stem from the Department of Surgery. That doesn't mean that the hospital staff would not benefit from outside supervision.''

"Joe, get the hell out of here and get back to work. I'll worry about the supervision.''

"In truth, the complaints concern the Department of OB-GYN.''

"That's Bob Watel's responsibility. He runs a first-class department. First-class.''

"Dr. Gold, a lot of the people in the community feel very strongly about this issue.''

"I don't give a rat's ass what they think. I have a hospital to run.''

Joe began to wonder about the wisdom of sticking his neck out so many times. He also dreaded his next confrontation with Ino; it came late that afternoon, in the coffee room.

"How'd it go with Gold?"

"Piss poor. I told you he wouldn't go for it.''

"Well, we just can't give up. Of course they wouldn't want it.''

"Look, Ino. I'm sorry. I tried.''

"I know that. Thanks, Joe. I guess I'll just have to take this into my own hands."

"What do you plan to do?"

"Go into politics." Ino laughed.

Joe felt the knot of tension in his stomach tighten.

That night he and Elena ate Chinese food in her apartment. He was tired and frustrated and needed to forget. She understood; Jefferson Hospital had a way of doing that. After dinner, Joe started to help clean up. "I'll do it," she said. "Why don't you put on some tapes and relax."

Joe lay down on the couch and tried to lose himself in the music. It was useless. How the hell did Zilk ever get this far? Then he remembered a few students in his classes at med school, scraping by, always looking for shortcuts, never giving a damn. Mix a doctor like Zilk with someone like Ino and you've got an explosion. Ino can't be stopped. Not now. Not after Rebirth and People for Progress. He was a different person, ruthless and headstrong. He had the soul of a radical, and Joe worried he would go too far.

Elena was sitting in the chair facing him. "Where are you?" She smiled.

"I'm sorry, honey. I just can't get the hospital off my mind."

"I know the feeling."

He told her what had happened with Watel and Gold. "I know Ino won't let this rest."

"Never mind. You really went to bat for him. That says a lot."

"Not enough for Ino. But who can blame him? He doesn't like Jefferson's rules."

"I know," agreed Elena. "But People for Progress has been great for him and great for the hospital."

"Sure, it's been good, and everyone's happy as hell with the work they're doing. But I can't help it, I see some kind of confrontation coming. With Ino, it's inevitable."

"Joe, you're overreacting. The worst that can happen is his idea will get shot down and his pride will suffer. That's all."

"I hope you're right," said Joe, unconvinced.

"Sure, I'm right." She smiled, snuggling next to him on the couch. "He's my brother, isn't he?"

She kissed him passionately on the lips. "And you're my lover, aren't you?"

He buried himself in the warmth of her embrace, and she had her answer.

The bar on Second Avenue was hot and crowded. It had its fill of loud music, watered down drinks, and young secretaries and sales managers trying hard to look like they weren't on the make. Ino never would have chosen it, but Cliff Garvin had pressured him over the phone. "It's a great place to meet," said Garvin. "I get all my dates there."

Ino made his way through the thick wall of bodies lining the bar. In the back, there were seven or eight tiny tables squeezed around a minuscule dance floor. Cliff Garvin was sitting at one of them.

"Ino!" he cried, a drink in his hand, a wide smile on his flushed face. "Glad to see you."

"Hi, Cliff." Ino glanced at the two blondes giggling at a corner table. "So this is where the press goes after hours."

Garvin beamed. "The ones who want to score. The real action starts later."

"Good," said Ino, "that'll give us some time to talk."

"What's on your mind?" asked Garvin. A waiter passed their table and Garvin grabbed him by the sleeve. "A drink for my friend, please. What'll it be Ino? It's on me."

"Thanks. I'll have a beer." The waiter brought the drink, and Ino tried to get Cliff's attention away from the sexy brunette dancing on the floor. "Cliff, I have to talk to you."

"I'm listening," said Garvin, his eyes still on the girl.

"I spoke to Mayor Tanner today. We're having problems at Jefferson. He thinks it might be a good idea to set up a complaint desk, but he's afraid to come out and suggest it. It's a political hot potato, and Tanner's afraid to take an official stand. I thought of you. If you could maybe write a piece about one foul-up I have documented and say that some members of Richard Tanner's staff suggested the institution of a complaint desk to help monitor these types of problems, it might go a long way to push the idea through."

"If that's the case, why hasn't Tanner gotten a hold of me?"

"As I said, he's afraid to get involved until we get the ball rolling. I remembered the help you were before, and I think over the next couple of months you'll have a lot to write about Jefferson."

"Okay, I'll try to get it by the editor. If that gets nixed I'll slip it into a small story."

"Anything you can do, Cliff. I'll keep in touch." Ino got up to leave.

"Going so soon?" asked Garvin. "The fun's just beginning."

"Maybe another night. I've got a big day tomorrow."

"You work too hard. You got to learn to relax."

Suddenly, a stunning blonde in a kelly-green dress put her arm through Ino's and started leading him toward the dance floor. Ino looked at Garvin, shrugged and smiled. "Maybe you're right, Cliff. A night off never hurt anyone."

Ino stood in front of Tanner's massive desk, the editorial page of the paper spread out in front of him.

"I thought I told you to clear everything with Malcolm," Tanner said, livid.

"I tried to call him three times. He never returned my calls."

"How in the hell do you have the nerve to release a story like this to the paper?"

"I was sure if you knew the story, you would feel the same as I do."

"But the way this story comes across, I have no choice. I have to follow up on it. Otherwise, I look like a total idiot. You don't think something like this is going to cause a lot of resentment?"

"Mayor Tanner, the people of the South Bronx are as much part of this city as anyone else."

"Look, Sanchez, you pull a stunt like this again and I'll have you back on the streets ripping off hubcaps."

"Mr. Mayor, I only did this because I genuinely felt you'd be as concerned as I am."

"I am. But I also have other problems to worry about. Now get out of here, and I'll try to smooth over your mess."

Three days later Joe was paged in the Emergency Room and told to report to Dr. Gold's office immediately.

Benjamin Gold had been pacing in his office for the last half hour since he received the call. He was still enraged. To think that young snot Boise, who was still wet behind the ears, had ordered him to create a complaint desk in his own hospital. H hadn't even offered an explanation. "The board of directors thinks it would be a good idea." As if the board of directors knew anything at all about Jefferson Hospital. They had never even bothered to come down and visit. There was a knock at the door.

"Well, Joseph. I see you weren't satisfied with our little talk."

"I had nothing to do with this."

"Nothing to do with what?" asked Gold, glaring at him

"Nothing to do with that newspaper story."

"What newspaper story? I just received a call from the esteemed chairman of the Department of Surgery, Dr. Boise. He ordered me to create a complaint desk."

"He did?"

"Look, Ruskin, I don't know what the hell is going on around here, but let me assure you of one thing. I am the chief of this hospital and I will remain the chief of the hospital."

"I never questioned that for a second."

"Well, someone's plotting something around here. I plan to get to the bottom of it. I'm sure it has something to do with your People for Progress."

"No!"

"Joe, you're too trusting."

"Dr. Gold, I'm positive Ino and his men have nothing to do with this."

"Whether they do or not, it looks like we have a complaint desk. You'll be a firsthand witness to the havoc that creates." Joe closed the door quietly.

Gold's prophecy came true just a week later. Joe received a small note in his mailbox. It was handwritten and read: "Please report to the people's complaint desk at 4:30 today. We want to discuss your patient Maria Ruies." Joe read the note, then wrinkled it up and tossed it into the wastepaper basket. Ino wasn't in the hospital, and Elena knew nothing about it.

At four-thirty, Joe walked into the waiting room of the Emergency Room, where the desk had been set up.

Ino sat there, flanked by Paco and two men he had never seen before. Ino was reading a piece of paper.

"Sit down, Joe," Ino greeted him. "The People's Complaint

227

Desk has called this meeting because of a complaint regarding one of your patients."

"Which patient?" Joe said, tight-lipped.

"It seems that you have a patient by the name of Maria Ruies. At two o'clock on Thursday afternoon you were placing an IV in her left arm. All of a sudden you were called away, and you left the IV just sitting in her arm and you didn't even tape it down. Blood kept seeping out of the tube, and it was only ten minutes later that Mrs. Ruies could get a nurse to dress the area."

"You don't understand. There was a cardiac arrest in ICU. I didn't have a choice. The patient had just stopped breathing, he was saved only because I got there so quickly. It took four minutes before another doctor showed up."

"Mrs. Ruies is upset. You have to understand, she only saw that you had stuck a tube into her arm and the blood was draining out of her body."

"Come on, Ino. I tried to explain to her."

"She said you shouted at her. She said, and I quote, 'All you people are so damn sure someone's going to screw you over.' "

"I didn't say that, but I guess I lost my temper a little."

"Well, you can't do that. These people are human beings, and they can't know of your other medical problems."

"I already apologized to her."

"The Desk will explain the situation to Mrs. Ruies. But I hope we don't have any more of these complaints about you."

"Ino, get off the stick."

"You're part of the staff, the same as anyone else."

Joe met Elena for lunch. "Your darling brother is really getting carried away with himself."

"What do you mean?" she asked.

"I was just brought down before the complaint desk. I left an angiocath from an IV because I had to run for an arrest. Ino was acting like he was a combination of Hippocrates and Eldridge Cleaver. I didn't like his tone."

"Be patient, Joe. Even you said you thought the idea of a complaint desk wasn't a bad idea. Maybe you're just getting angry because they dared to question your actions."

Joe stopped and looked at her, shaking his head. "Your brother can be one tough son of a bitch."

*   *   *

Kendricks was talking to Susan in the nurses station when Joe walked in.

"I had to restrain him," Kendricks was saying emotionally. "The man was confused. He pulled the tubes out. I had no other choice, don't you see?"

"I do," said Susan. "The families always come in and see the patient restrained and get all excited."

"But it's for the patient's own good," said Kendricks.

Joe could not help interrupting. "By any chance, were you called down to the complaint desk, Kendricks?"

"Yes," said Kendricks. "They told me I was wrong for restraining a patient. I tried to explain, but they think I wasn't doing all I could to make the patient comfortable."

Joe shook his head in disbelief. "It sounds familiar."

"It sounds like People for Progress is suddenly drunk with power." Susan smiled.

"I told Elena the same thing," admitted Joe. "She disagreed. She said Ino and his men are making a big difference at Jefferson."

"They are. The only question is are they getting carried away with themselves?"

"That's what I'm wondering," said Joe.

"I hope we're wrong," said Susan. "They've become a part of Jefferson—a working part. They could create quite a ruckus if they wanted to."

"Maybe they've already started," said Joe glumly.

On his way down from the lab with two blood samples, Ino saw Luis walking down the hall. "Hey, brother," he said, catching up to him. "How's it going?"

A grimace distorted his usually serene expression. "The truth?" he asked.

"Was there ever anything else between us?" said Ino. "¿Qué pasa?"

"It's Gold. He's sticking it to me real bad. I knew this would happen," he said nervously. "He's going to do everything in his power to stop my application to Hirshorn. He's the worst bigot I've ever met."

"Slow down, amigo."

"I tell you, Ino, there's no way I'm going to keep Susan and

229

get into medical school, too. I got three rejections so far. Ten to one, Gold had something to do with it.'' His head hung down and his eyes studied the worn vinyl tile. ''I guess I overreached this time, huh?''

''You can shove that bullshit, Luis. People like us don't overreach. Let me think for a minute.''

''Thanks, Ino, but there's really nothing you can do.''

''There's always something,'' said Ino confidently. ''We could get rid of Gold. That would take care of your problem.''

''Sure, and how are you going to do that? Gold is practically the whole institution. There's no way to get him out of here. He'll be chief till the day he dies.''

''You've been listening to that woman of yours for too long. Have you forgotten? There's nothing Inocencio Sanchez can't do.''

Luis looked into the fierce black eyes and remembered his friend's careful planning of years ago.

''Stay in touch,'' said Ino, giving his friend the old Toros salute.

19

A middle-aged man with a family of seven appeared at the complaint desk two weeks later.

''Ayee,'' he cried. ''They killed my sister.''

''Take it easy,'' said Ino, putting his arm around the sobbing man. ''Now who killed your sister?''

''The doctor, he killed her. Eighteen years old!'' he cried.

''When did this happen?''

''Today. Not an hour ago.'' The man started to weep once more.

''You want me to help you?'' asked Ino.

The man nodded.

"Then you must tell me what happened. From the beginning."

The man blew his nose and wiped his face. "Yesterday, I bring my sister to the clinic. Her heart is weak. The doctor, he tells her she is with child, that she should have an abortion because of the bad heart. It is simple, a simple operation, he says. It's necessary because her heart can't take the birth."

"So what did you do?" asked Ino.

The man started to cry again. "I take her to the hospital this morning. There was a different doctor, very angry. I didn't trust him. He says we should wait. The operation will take one hour."

"What happened then?" asked Ino.

"We wait, four, five hours. He comes out and tells us something's gone wrong. She has something the matter with her heart. I say, that's why the other doctor say she needed the operation."

Ino looked directly at the man. "Are you absolutely sure this doctor didn't know she had a bad heart before he did the operation?"

"I'm sure," replied the man, "He say to me 'why the fuck didn't someone say something before? You stupid spics is all the same.'"

Ino felt his blood rising. "Then what happened?"

"He goes back in for another hour and comes out shaking his head. 'It is all over,' he says. 'Her heart couldn't take the strain.'" The man started to break down.

"What was your sister's name?" asked Ino.

"Ramona Perez."

"And do you remember the name of the doctor who did the operation?"

"He wore a white nameplate—Malk? Milk?"

"Zilk?" asked Ino, closing his eyes in anguish.

"Yes, that's it!" said the bereaved man. "I'll remember that name to my dying day."

The first person Ino called was Enrique. He had to check out the story. Satisfied with what he told him, Ino sat and thought for several minutes. Then he picked up the receiver and dialed Luis's number.

"Luis, we've got to talk. Are you alone?"

"Yes. ¿Qué pasa?"

"There's just been a major fuck-up here at the hospital. An eighteen-year-old girl, Ramona Perez, came in for a routine saline abortion. Zilk gets ahold of her and fucks up the whole case, and she goes into shock and dies right on the table. I still can't believe it."

"I can. Zilk is a butcher."

"I know. We've got to get rid of him. Now. And maybe . . ."

"Maybe what?"

"Maybe we can kill two birds with one stone."

"What do you mean?" asked Luis.

"Who's going to have to defend Zilk?" asked Ino.

"The chief of OB-GYN, Dr. Watel," said Luis.

"Right," said Ino. "And who's going to stand by Watel?"

"Gold."

"Right again. Well, if we can get something on Gold, we can take him along, too." Ino waited for his words to sink in. "Luis, do you understand what this can mean? We could finally get a Puerto Rican in as chief. And you, *amigo*, will have gotten rid of the worst thorn in your side."

"But how are you going to do it?" asked Luis hesitantly.

"We've got to get something on Gold and fast. Do you know anything?"

"Nothing."

"Come on, Luis, he's got to make a mistake sometimes."

"You don't know Gold. He never makes a mistake. And besides—"

"Can't you help him make a mistake?" interrupted Ino. "Just something so we can make a big stink about it in the papers and on the streets? It doesn't have to be a big thing, anything will do."

"Ino, I can't think of anything. And I don't know if this is such a great idea."

"What's he doing tomorrow?" asked Ino.

"I think he's doing a big case at eight A.M. An aortic aneurysm. He'll be in the OR for five hours."

"A big case?" said Ino. "Isn't there some way you can get him to mess it up? Maybe something with the drugs or the blood?"

"Well, he'll be needing a lot of blood."

"How much is a lot?"

"Ten units."

"What will happen if we only manage to get him five? Carlos is on that lab shift."

"He'd have to sweat it out for a while. But Gold is too good a surgeon. He'll manage to pull the patient through."

"Then it's perfect. We'll have Gold tied up for five hours, and on top of that, we'll have something on him."

"Ino, I don't like it," said Luis.

"Take your choice, Susan or Gold," said Ino coldly.

"But what about the patient?" asked Luis.

"You just said that Gold is too good a surgeon to let anything happen. And by the time he gets out of the OR, we'll have everything set up."

"What do you mean 'everything'?"

Ino was silent for a long moment. "Luis, the People for Progress are going to take over Jefferson Hospital."

"What?"

"On top of that, we may just be able to have Benjamin Gold gone for good. That's what you wanted, isn't it?"

"Hold it, Ino. You're going too fast for me. Now you're going to take over the hospital? Why?"

"So we can show them there are other ways to run a hospital for the people. So we can get them to listen to us."

"I don't know," stammered Luis. "This is not what I was thinking."

"That's your trouble, Luis. Action is the only thing that creates change—not thoughts. This is the break we've all been waiting for, and we can make it work for us. I've got a big job getting the men and the community lined up, and I'm going to need help. Are you in or out?"

"Ino, I . . ."

"In or out?"

"I guess it's in."

"Good. Get over here as soon as you can, we've got a lot to do. Tomorrow is going to be a big day."

Late that night, Inocencio Sanchez sat in the red leather chair behind his desk. All of his men were assembled before him. There was an air of electricity in the People for Progress office.

"Brothers, we have a lot to do in the next twelve hours," said Ino. "First and most important, we have to organize the community. I want at least five hundred people on the ramp by ten o'clock tomorrow morning.''

"How are we going to get that many people?" asked Enrique.

"They murdered one of our sisters. I've written out a small flyer explaining what happened. We've already run off a few thousand copies. Each man is responsible for his own sector. Get these to each block leader and let them take it from there." Ino began handing out the packets. "Paco, we'll need some portable loudspeakers. Try the hospital guard office. It'll be empty at this time of night."

"There's no problem getting in but what if I can't find any?"

"Borrow an amplifier. We have to make up posters. The slogan will be "Seize the Hospital to Save the People." Make sure the letters are painted in red. They'll stand out better on color TV."

"TV?"

"That's right, they'll be there. Shit, we'd better make up a few more posters. Have them say Watel and Gold must go."

"Gold?"

"You heard me. We have the issues. If we show that there's total community support behind this, we won't fail. By tomorrow, Jefferson Hospital will be ours."

"But what do we know about running a hospital?" asked Paco.

"We know as much as they do," Ino said angrily. "Besides, we can always hire someone to help us."

"Jefe, I'm afraid we're going a little too fast."

"We're not going fast enough. This is our opportunity. If we let this slip away, it will be another two years before we have a chance."

The rest of the night was spent performing the various tasks Ino had laid out. As the sun began to rise above the broken skyline they were ready.

"Does everyone know to show up at ten?" asked Ino.

"We divided the community the same way as in the preventive medicine sections. The block leaders have been running their tails off. They'll be there," Paco answered.

Ino continued thumbing through the index cards gathered on his desk.

"We have Watel cold. There are five separate incidents, well documented, of medical misconduct in his department alone, thanks to Zilk. But we still don't have anything on Gold. We

234

have that one instance with Joe and the cardiac arrest, but we need something a lot stronger than that.''

''Maybe Luis will be able to upset him enough with the backup on the blood.''

''I doubt that. Gold is too smooth an operator. Maybe I can trick him. All we need is one good outburst on public television and he'll seal his own fate. Enrique''—Ino checked his watch—''get Malcolm on the phone. We'd better cover our asses with Tanner.'' Enrique handed him the phone.

''Malcolm? This is Inocencio Sanchez. There's been a major screw-up at the hospital, and the people's complaint desk plans to take care of it.''

''Hold everything. I have to clear this with Tanner.''

''There's no time. Tell him we're going to conduct an investigation at the hospital. Tell him I think it would be a good idea if he got down there about twelve noon.''

''No one tells the mayor what to do. Sanchez, I'm ordering you to hold up on this thing until we have a full briefing.''

''I can't do that. No one knows what really happened yet. We have to get the information before they have time to cover up.''

''Sanchez, I want it clearly understood. You're to wait until Tanner gets in touch with you.''

''By that time it may be too late. We're going to the hospital now.'' Ino slammed the phone down. He carefully finished dressing in his three-piece suit.

''You look like you're going to a party.'' Paco smiled.

''I'm going to a liberation. By tomorrow night People for Progress will be known throughout the country. Poor people will look up to us everywhere. We will have taken the first step in returning the power to the people. September fourteenth will become the birthdate of our organization.''

''I just hope we don't screw up.''

''I just hope Gold blows it. Right now he just looks like an eccentric surgeon. The people have to see him as an uncontrolled monster.''

''Which he's not,'' said Paco.

''Never mind. We just have to try to make him look that way.''

At ten o'clock Benjamin Gold looked up from the gaping wound. ''Wipe.'' He ordered the circulating nurse to dab at the beads of perspiration now collecting on his wrinkled forehead. The aneurysm lay on top of the thick psoas muscle, its balloon-thin wall pumping ominously. Each wave distended the twisted pink sac almost a foot as the intestine pressed against the side walls, outlining the fecal liquid within.

"Vascular clamp. Damn, look at the size of that." He clamped directly above the takeoff of the mutilated wall. "Knife." As he cut across the six-inch muscular wall of the aorta, plaques of thick calcium seeped from around the steel serrated edges, and then small pumping fountains of blood joined into a powerful geyser.

"Dr. Gold, his pulse is up to one-sixty and his systolic is down to ninety," the anesthetist interrupted.

"Give him more blood."

"There is no more blood."

"We've only used five units. What do you mean there's no more blood?"

"It's going to take half an hour to get four more units up here."

"Joseph, I distinctly remember when we went over this patient's angiogram, and discussed the case two days ago, my saying that we would need ten units of blood."

"I remember, Dr. Gold. I sent three samples down myself, yesterday morning."

"This guy is bleeding out," said Gold as he pressed down with a lap pad with all his weight.

"There was a mix-up in the blood lab," the circulating nurse tried to explain. "They only had one sample down there, and someone called and told them to type only five units."

"Five units for a case like this?"

"His blood pressure is dropping out, Dr. Gold," said the anesthetist.

"Add some plasma." He looked up to the ceiling for some divine intervention. "I can't believe this. The vessel is falling apart in my hands. We're going to have to put a graft in." Gold fell back on his forty years of reserve as he rapidly started sewing the artificial tube to the diseased vessel at the level of the renal artery.

Ino stood at the foot of the ramp, checking his watch. About fifty of the neighborhood people milled around.

"Where is everyone?" Paco asked uncertainly.

"They'll be here. It's only nine-thirty. Where's Roberto?"

"On the platform."

"Get him down here, now. I want to go over his job one more time. Luis, get up to the wards and explain to the nurses what's happening. All medical treatment will continue as if this was just another day. Tell them we'll even send some of our men up to the ward to fill in just in case some of the staff can't get through. The only area we're taking over is the Emergency Room. Reassure them. Not one patient's treatment will be interfered with in any way."

"Paco said you wanted me," said Roberto coming over.

"Roberto, you're the big man in this operation. I'm trusting your ability to tell us if anyone is really hurt and needs immediate attention. If someone is brought in who needs life or death care, you have to let us know. The signal will be two short blasts on the siren, a pause, then two more short blasts. The ambulance drivers know this?"

Roberto nodded. "I check out everyone who comes in. If their care can wait a few hours, this is as far as they go."

"Good. If we hear the signal we'll clear the way. I don't want anyone to cool; it'll ruin everything."

"I'll try my best."

"I know that. You're not a doctor, and I don't expect miracles."

"I've handled the worst—gang wars, buildings collapsing, major fires. It's Tuesday morning. It should be quiet."

"Ino, look out there. Here they come," said Paco exuberantly as groups of fifteen and twenty began drifting toward the ramp from every direction. Men in beat-up work clothes, street punks, shopkeepers, hustlers, women pushing baby carriages trailed by young ones dawdling behind, priests, and pimps all converged toward the ramp of Jefferson Hospital.

"Paco, get the posters and start distributing them. Don't waste your voice. Use the loudspeaker. Keep them under control. I'm going up. It's time. It's finally time."

The circulating nurse interrupted just as Gold was putting the last suture into the distal end of the remaining vessel. "Dr. Gold, the hospital administrator is out in the hall, and he says he has to speak to you immediately. There's an urgent problem."

"What's that?" asked the weary Gold.

237

"The People for Progress are trying to take over the hospital."

"The People for Progress?" Gold glared at Joe. "You finish closing up," he directed. "I'm going to see what your friends are up to now."

He walked out to the hall, still wearing his gown. He faced a nervous Harold Krauthammer.

"What's so urgent?"

"Ben, you won't believe what's happening downstairs. They have hundreds of people milling around the ramp. They have posters and portable loudspeakers. They're inside the building. They have completely taken over the nurses' residence, and they've blockaded the emergency entrance. They're only letting doctors, hospital staff, and patients enter. They're demanding Bob Watel's resignation."

"Watel is my friend. What could he have done?"

"You haven't heard about Ramona Perez yet?"

"Who the hell is Ramona Perez?" asked Gold as he stalked into the dressing room.

"Here, read this." Krauthammer handed him the mimeographed flyer. Gold quickly scanned the page. In large black letters was the statement, "Ramona Perez was murdered by Dr. Zilk, Dr. Robert Watel, and the medical staff of Jefferson Hospital." In smaller print, "Ramona Perez was an eighteen-year-old female. She was admitted to the hospital ward for treatment of rheumatic heart disease and for an elective interruption of her pregnancy. She underwent a saline abortion, which is a highly dangerous and experimental technique. The introduction of the salt water into her system caused an overload on her heart, and she died within eight hours of acute congestive heart failure. She was a victim of the medical system. We demand the resignation of the people responsible for this murder."

"This sounds like a goddamn indictment."

"There has to be a leak in the hospital," said Krauthammer.

"A leak! You fool! The People for Progress have men in every department. What have you done so far?"

"I did the only thing I could. I called the police."

"Where's Watel now?"

"In his office."

"I'd better go find him," said Gold.

* * *

Gold rushed into Robert Watel's office.

"Bob, what happened?"

"Zilk really pulled a beauty this time. And they want my resignation."

"That's ridiculous. You had nothing to do with it."

"You haven't seen what's going on down there. They're really loaded for bear. Ben, I'm afraid."

"Don't worry. We've been through worse."

"Worse? Sure we have. The entire six years we've been down here have been a nightmare. How can anything get worse? Ten years ago, I was part-time with a private practice netting me over two hundred thousand dollars. I don't know why I ever gave it up to come down here. You warned me about Zilk. Damn, even your resident Ruskin tried to tell me. I guess it was just a matter of time. But I don't know how I'm going to explain this screw-up."

"Don't worry."

"I'm not worried. I'm tired. Tired of begging for supplies and staff. Tired of working my ass off. They don't understand."

"I know. Well, we'll just give them some medical bullshit."

"They know too much medicine already."

"They can't know the medical indications for a procedure."

"They know someone screwed up. And they want me to resign."

"If you resign, I will too. They're not going to push us around. Someone has to take a stand."

Sergeant Murray was cruising past Hunts Point Station when he got the call on his squawk box. "Sector Bobbie. Respond to Jefferson Hospital. Proceed with caution."

"What the hell could that be?" asked Murray.

"Shit. There goes lunch," said the young recruit as he floored the pedal.

"Sector Eddie to Dispatch. Is it a gunshot?" There was no answer. "Sector Eddie to Dispatch," Murray repeated, irritated.

"All units respond to Jefferson Hospital," came the blaring reply.

"Damn. That sounds like a war," said Murray with more excitement as he rolled down the window, tossing out his half-filled cup of coffee. The car began screeching around the corners.

"Where the hell are all the people?" asked the driver.

"There aren't even any kids playing in the street."

When they approached the hill the driver slammed on his brakes, and they both looked out the smudged front window in awe. The driver hitched his belt and started to open the door.

Murray grabbed his arm. "Where are you going? Get on the radio and get the captain. There must be a thousand of them."

The driver got back in, and Murray picked up the receiver. "Captain, this is Sergeant Murray. There is a mob blocking the entrance to the hospital that is impossible to contain."

"Are you kidding me?" came the static-ridden reply.

"Sir, I wouldn't even waste time responding. So far, they're quiet. But there are news trucks and cameras, and there's even a goddamn helicopter. I would notify the mayor immediately. We need the riot patrol or the National Guard."

"He won't like this. Okay, stay put. Over and out."

"Shit," said Murray, settling back, resting his knees on the dash and locking the door. "I wonder who engineered this circus?"

At twelve noon Inocencio Sanchez was seated behind the complaint desk, facing a row of microphones. Ramona Perez's brother had just told his simple, gripping story. Ino proceeded to go through the various complaints that had been registered at the desk over the last month. He explained to the camera crew and the reporters the significance of each medical mistake that had occurred. He looked up at the clock. Gold still hadn't appeared. Luis must have come through. The longer it took for someone from the hospital to come down to defend their position, the better he could get his message across. After each case, reporters rapidly scribbled on pads. The People for Progress stood in the background exchanging power handshakes and nodding to emphasize each significant point that Ino was making.

It was one-thirty when Gold stalked into the crowded waiting room followed by Bob Watel and Harold Krauthammer. Ino greeted them and asked them to sit in chairs that had been placed behind the table.

"Dr. Watel, are you the Chief of Obstetrics and Gynecology at Jefferson Hospital?"

"I am," said Watel.

"We understand a member of your staff is responsible for the murder of Ramona Perez."

240

"No one was murdered," started Krauthammer.

"Dr. Watel, could you tell me why Ramona Perez was admitted to the hospital?"

"She was admitted for an elective interruption of pregnancy."

"I understand she didn't want an abortion. The only reason she agreed to the procedure was because some of the medical doctors on the staff thought that the pregnancy might be too great a strain for her heart."

"That's not true," Watel stammered.

"Are there different methods of performing an abortion?"

"There are several different methods."

"Why was the technique of saline chosen, instead of some of the safer, more tried methods?"

"We've been running an experimental series. We have over two hundred patients, and we've never had one complication."

"Would you call Ramona Perez's death a complication?"

"It was an unfortunate incident. Unfortunate. But medically, everything was done to try to save her."

"You just said the technique of saline abortions is experimental."

"Yes. But four other major centers throughout the country have been conducting studies, also."

"Have they noted any complications?"

"None like this."

"Tell me, Dr. Watel, isn't it true when you infuse the salt water, some of it is introduced into the system of the patient?"

"That's unavoidable."

"Well, tell me, Dr. Watel. You are the chairman of the department. You're a full professor in the Hirshorn Medical complex, and you earn sixty-five thousand dollars a year. Can you think of any instance when the introduction of a salt water load might be detrimental to a patient?"

"Well, if she had a weak heart," Watel countered.

"Wasn't that the very reason she was admitted to the hospital?"

"Yes, but . . ."

"But nothing. You and your staff are responsible for her murder. Your gross negligence has resulted in the death of an eighteen-year-old woman. The People for Progress demand your resignation. The people of the South Bronx deserve better."

"I refuse."

"Dr. Watel, we have a long list of other instances of medical misconduct stemming from your department."

"Hold on, Sanchez." Gold grabbed the microphone. "Just what sort of kangaroo court are you trying to push through here?"

"Dr. Gold is the Chief of the Department of Surgery at this hospital," Ino addressed the reporters. "You don't think there's anything unusual about the death of an eighteen year old after a routine procedure?"

"Dr. Watel is as good a doctor as I know. I wouldn't hesitate to trust the care of my wife to him."

"Would you trust the care of your wife to him at Jefferson Hospital?"

"I'd trust Dr. Watel anywhere. He could deliver my baby in the backseat of my car."

Ino put his hand over the microphone. He whispered, "Or create one, eh, Dr. Watel?"

Gold exploded. "Just what in heaven are you trying to pull? All you His-Spicanos are the same," Gold stammered.

"All us spics are the same. Isn't that right, Dr. Gold?"

"I never used that term."

"You didn't have to, Dr. Gold. During the time I've been working here your attitude toward our people has become painfully clear." Harold Krauthammer wiped his forehead with his handkerchief. Bob Watel was a pale shade of gray.

"I take care of all my patients the same way," Gold angrily retorted.

"How did you treat the man you operated on this morning?" Ino questioned, smiling.

"What do you mean?"

"I understand you had a little problem with the blood. I understand you ordered an inadequate amount of blood for a procedure of considerable difficulty. In truth, the man almost died on the table."

Gold was enraged. "That's a goddamn lie."

"If that's a lie, would you mind telling us how many units of blood you finally wound up using on that patient?"

"Ten."

"But you only ordered five when you began the case. Dr. Gold, I think the facts speak for themselves."

"There are no facts. I refuse to listen to any more of this."

"The people of the South Bronx have a right to know."

"The people of the South Bronx have a right to go to hell.

242

Run your own hospital!'' Gold stalked out of the room followed by Watel and Krauthammer.

Ino smiled confidently. Gold's explosion had been perfect; the baiting had worked. He addressed the assembled people. "Gentlemen, I'm afraid this conference is over. I think we've managed to show you some of the glaring instances of unprofessional medical conduct. The community of the South Bronx has for many years been treated as helpless guinea pigs to a medical system that does not care. Jefferson Hospital must be returned to the people. We demand the resignation of Dr. Zilk, Dr. Watel, and Dr. Gold. Even with their dismissal, there are still major problems facing the community. The People for Progress will not rest until these problems are corrected. We pledge ourselves to the people."

His men started clapping. First Cliff Garvin stood up and then, one by one, reporters from all the different news services slowly rose. Ino beamed. He was almost home.

By the time Joe had finished closing the patient's abdomen, it had been one-fifteen. He walked out into the hall.

Elena was waiting. "Joe, thank God you're out."

"What's going on?"

"Ino and his men are trying to take over the hospital."

"I told you they were planning something," Joe snapped. "What the hell are they going to do with it once they get it?"

"Joe, I swear to you, I didn't know."

"I believe you. But your brother," he said, his voice rising, "he used me. I thought he was my friend. He was just plotting some crazy overthrow." He turned to Elena. "Tell me everything."

"Zilk screwed up a case. Ino has organized the neighborhood and is holding a public conference in the emergency waiting room. The police are outside with riot helmets and shotguns."

They ran down the stairs. They stopped at the bottom, gasping for breath.

"Joe, I'm afraid it's really bad. I think they want to get Gold."

"Gold?" Joe ran down the hall.

They had arrived in the crowded room in time to see the questioning of Watel. When Gold exploded, Joe buried his head. He studied Ino. He looked so different, detached and brutally conniving. He understood Ino's baiting even as it was happening. As Gold rushed past him down the corridor Joe followed. Gold caught the elevator, and by the time Joe arrived at his office, Gold was throwing his cherished books into one of the desk drawers he had removed. He looked up as Joe entered.

"They want me to resign. Can you believe that? All I've ever wanted to be is a good doctor. I am a good doctor."

"You're the best doctor I've ever seen. Sir, you are a great doctor."

"It ends like this? It just can't end like this for me. I've given my soul to this hospital."

"Sir, you could stay and fight."

"Fight?" Gold exploded. "Who am I going to fight? Sanchez? Boise? Tanner? Half a million people? They don't want me. They've made it perfectly clear. And I resign. They can have their goddamn hospital."

"Dr. Gold, please don't do this," Joe pleaded.

Gold stood in front of Joe, breathing heavily. "You, Joe, you're the one who told me to believe. Do you believe now? All your innocent zeal! They got me, Joe, and somehow they got you to set it up."

"Dr. Gold, I swear to you, I had no idea." Joe was close to tears.

Gold put on his coat. "Think of me, Joseph, when you're taking care of the poor and the sick, and remember, they'll take you down. Nothing can feed their hunger. They'll swallow up everything they come in contact with. And they still won't lift themselves up."

"Please, sir—"

"Joseph, listen to me. Get away from here. Take Elena, if you have to be with her, but go away. They'll just hurt you in the end. No one can help them."

"Dr. Gold, please don't go."

"I'm an old man. You have your whole life. Get out of here before they eat you alive. I want you to promise me. I want you to promise me you'll leave."

"I promise, but—"

"Then I forgive you."

Joe watched Gold walk down the corridor for the last time. He went to the phone and called the emergency desk. Paco answered.

"It's me, Joe."

"Yeah, what do you want?"

"I have to speak to Ino."

"He's busy right now."

"Paco, tell him to meet me in Gold's office. You guys owe me that much." Joe hung up just as Elena came in.

"I just said good-bye to Dr. Gold," he said blankly. "He's resigned."

"Oh, Joe, I'm sorry."

"It was the saddest thing I've ever seen. And I . . ." His voice started to break, and he looked away.

She forced him to look at her. "Joe, you have nothing to feel guilty about. You were used. I was used. We were all just trying to help," she said, anguished.

"Yeah, except for your baby brother."

Ino strolled into the room.

"You fuck!" Joe exploded. "You betrayed me. You plotted this whole thing. You treated me like a brother. You saved my life. But underneath it all, you were just planning an overthrow to get Gold."

"We have to fight to change things," said Ino coldly.

"What are you trying to change?" Joe asked.

"The system, you asshole!"

"Explain to me how the dismissal of Benjamin Gold will do that," Joe shouted.

"Sometimes you have to tear down before you can rebuild."

"You didn't answer my question. You've just given me some slogan crap. Save it for the press. I don't understand you! You just made a man, whose entire life has been dedicated to helping people, give up a position where he is vitally needed. You're more dangerous than Zilk. You don't care what you destroy as long as there's change. Well, I'll tell you one more thing your maneuvering has destroyed."

"Yeah, what's that?" Ino smirked.

"It's destroyed our friendship. I'll never trust you again."

"You'll get over this. Wait 'til you see the good that comes."

"Ino, I'm not going to wait."

Paco ran into the office. "Jefe, Tanner is here in his limousine. He wants to see you."

"Let him come up here. This office is perfect." Paco left, and Ino turned to Joe and Elena. "You're both going to have to leave."

"Like hell," said Joe. "I want to hear this. I've earned the right."

"And so have I," said Elena, her dark eyes flashing with anger. "You had no right to put Joe in this position. You had no right to turn everything upside down. What in God's name has gotten into you? And now you want to get rid of Tanner? Ino, what's happening to you?"

"I'm trying to make it better for us—only you're both too blind to see it," he shouted.

Suddenly, Richard Tanner marched furiously into the office. "Just what are you trying to pull, Sanchez?" he gasped.

"With what, Mr. Mayor?" asked Ino.

"Get them out." Tanner pointed to Joe and Elena.

"They stay. They have a right to hear how their hospital is going to be run."

"And you're going to tell me?"

"You're goddamn right I am, Mr. Mayor. Did you take a look at the ramp on your way up here? Did you take a look in the waiting room? Those people don't leave 'til I tell them they can."

"Sanchez, you're through."

"Mr. Mayor, you don't understand me. We're the ones who make the demands."

"And just what are those demands?" Tanner stopped.

"The preventive medicine program needs expansion. We need a free day-care center for the patients and for the workers. We need a free breakfast program for the children."

"You certainly do need a lot of things."

"You're right, Mr. Mayor, and we plan to get them."

"I don't have the power to okay all those demands. You're talking about an outlay of a tremendous amount of money and time."

"If we don't get your okay on these issues, we won't leave the hospital."

"I'll get you, Sanchez."

Ino stalked over to him. In a low controlled voice he said, "You don't understand, Mr. Mayor. We're not playing polo on one of your father's estates."

Malcolm quickly stepped between them. "Gentlemen, gentlemen, we must control ourselves. After all, we're all on the same team," he said nervously.

Slowly Ino stepped back from a white-faced Richard Tanner.

"Are we, Malcolm? Haven't all our suggestions before just been ignored?"

"Things take time."

"Look, Sanchez," said Tanner, trying to regain his composure, "you came begging to me and I gave you a chance. Is this how you pay me back?"

"The people of this community are crying out. You promised us a new hospital."

"We never expected the police to go on strike."

"I have a videotape of you making that promise. That videotape got you elected. That and the five million dollars your daddy wiped your ass with."

"Why you street manure. I promise I'll get you."

"Worry about yourself, Mr. Mayor. We'll meet again. But right now I want one more public announcement from you. Our demands will be met. We need an expanded drug program. Ten percent of the population are on hard drugs."

"You'd know about that. I'll expose you as the junkie you are."

"You can do any damn thing you want. I'm no longer an addict. I'm as clean as you. We also demand the resignation of Dr. Watel and Dr. Zilk."

"Gold will have to resign also." Malcolm interjected, "Calls have been coming in for the last hour. The city thinks he's crazy."

"You don't have to worry about Dr. Gold. He's already resigned," Joe said sadly. "Don't make him an issue."

Tanner knew he was beaten. Malcolm turned his back and sulked in a corner. Nobody shook hands.

"Sanchez"—Tanner rallied slightly—"I demand your resignation!"

"No problem, Mr. Mayor. The Republican party wasn't really my style."

20

Ino leaned back in his big red chair, his feet propped up on the secondhand desk, his arms folded. His eyes were fixed on the portable black-and-white TV set up in the corner of the People for Progress office. Paco and Enrique sat on folding chairs beside him. It was the third time that day they had viewed the news broadcast.

"Beautiful, Jefe. You look beautiful," repeated Paco.

"It was the suit." Ino laughed. Three hours earlier he had entered the office and thrown his tie and jacket triumphantly across the room.

"Look at that motherfucker Gold sweat. Man, you really had him going." Paco pointed to the blurred figures on the screen.

"Yeah, we did it! We pulled it off!" said Ino, waving mockingly at the departing figure of Dr. Gold. He took a deep swig from the wine bottle Paco handed him.

"How sweet it is," said Ino proudly.

"As good as smack, eh Jefe?"

"Better, Paco. On this high you don't have to come down."

Suddenly the scene on the screen changed. They were on live and there was the announcer, and then there was Tanner taking a seat opposite him.

"Look at that asshole. He'd better keep his word," said Paco, fidgeting.

"*Silencio*. I want to hear this," said Ino, slamming the bottle down on the desk.

"Mayor Tanner has been kind enough to come down to our WCBC studio to convey his opinion on the recent developments at Jefferson Hospital."

"Thank you, Tom. I thought it important enough to the people of this city to address them personally on this matter." It was obvious that Tanner was reading from a prepared speech. "We're not going to be railroaded into any major commitment of the taxpayers' revenues. The disturbing events surrounding Jefferson Hospital are just further evidence of the 'Me Decade,' making impossible demands on a system that is dedicated to provide services for all the people of this city. A small group of dissidents have decided to take matters into their own hands. I will not allow it.

"They have illegally come into one of our most vital service areas, a municipal hospital, and they have demanded a controlling role in the running of this institution designed to provide top quality health care for the indigent that they claim to represent. I will not allow it. Without reference to the normal procedures created in the charter of this city for establishing proper changes, they have taken a matter in which they have no training or expertise into their own hands. The actions of this power-crazed band of anarchists and addicts will not be tolerated. I will not allow it. As of two hours ago, with the help of our district attorney's office, I have obtained a court order to prevent the return of this gang to the hospital or any of its affiliate branches. Their presence, for any reason will be met with immediate incarceration."

"What's that shit mean?" asked Paco.

"It means they can lock us up," snapped Ino.

"He fucked us!" said Paco in despair.

"*Silencio*, dammit."

"Let me assure all the people in the five boroughs," continued Tanner, "and especially those inhabitants of the South Bronx area, who are provided first-rate free medical care, that the continued service provided by Jefferson Hospital will not be interrupted. I, as mayor, cannot and will not allow it.

"Thank you, Tom, for the opportunity to express how we—the city council and I—are prepared to handle this incident and assure our constituents that it will not happen again."

"Thank you, Mr. Mayor. If I may take just a few more minutes of your time to ask some questions that perhaps have not been completely covered in your address, questions our viewers have called in over the last few hours."

"Sure, Tom. That's why I'm here."

"Some of our viewers are concerned that this may incite a riot, especially in an area already known for its unrest."

"That would be possible only if Sanchez and his People for Progress did in fact represent the feelings of his community. There is nothing to suggest this. He has little or no following among the decent people.

"However, despite this, I've already phoned the governor and he has assured me that the National Guard will quickly be mobilized if violence does erupt. The people of this city are safe and will continue to be safe. If there is unrest in this sector, we will contain it as always. If a few troublemakers want to set fire to their own dwellings, that's one thing. If they think they can set fire to the homes of the respectable working members of our community, we will meet their violence with force and break their backs."

"The second most frequently asked question expresses concern about Dr. Benjamin Gold, Chief of Surgery. Can he continue in that capacity?"

"More than happy to give you any information I have. I have already been in touch with Walter Daly, director of the board of Hirshorn Medical Center. Dr. Gold is being transferred back to Hirshorn. Dr. Gold has a splendid record, and the interview with that radical was essentially one-sided. Dr. Gold's absence from Jefferson Hospital will be a severe blow. Nevertheless, I have been assured that the same overall quality care will continue."

"Then there's no basis for the rumors that Hirshorn wants to pull out of Jefferson?"

"That's absurd! The care will go on as usual."

"Now what do we do?" moaned Paco. "If he's got a court order, we'll never get back into Jefferson."

"Where's your faith, man? You think Ino Sanchez will let a little piece of paper stop him? After what we've already pulled off!"

"What about this office?" asked Enrique sullenly. "Tanner will kick our asses out of here, too."

"Fuck Tanner," said Ino. "This office will always be ours, one way or another."

"How?" persisted Enrique.

"I don't know yet, dammit!" exploded Ino. "Now shut up and give me a chance to think." His face was bright red, and he glared at Enrique.

The phone rang and Ino lifted the receiver. "People for Progress," he said angrily.

"Ino, Cliff Garvin. Did you hear Tanner's speech?"

"Yeah."

"Any comment?"

"On or off the record?"

"I need a follow-up to his TV talk."

"And I need a job."

"You're a hero. Didn't you read my story?"

"Sure. My phone hasn't stopped ringing."

"I'll bet the Democrats wouldn't mind having you in their corner," offered Garvin.

"The Democrats?" He thought about it for a moment; then he laughed. "It's worth a try."

"Look, I know one of the old-line guys from the garment district. He might be able to get you in to see Tony Coletti."

"Who's Tony Coletti?"

"*Numero uno* on their ticket. He's going to run for Congress."

"I'd give my right arm to meet him. Can you set it up?"

"I'll get on it. But, speaking of time, I got a deadline to meet. What about Tanner's speech?"

"My quote to his statement is simply 'the people will not be denied.' "

"That's good. Thanks."

"Cliff, you'll be back in touch?"

"Sure, Ino. Come down to my office first thing tomorrow and we'll get started on it."

Ino put the receiver down and turned to Paco and Enrique. "What'd I tell you? Something would turn up and it has. If we can get the Democrats to back us, we got someone to pay the rent and a way to get the people back in here. Yeah." He smiled triumphantly, sinking back into the deep tufts of the leather chair. "We're on the road again."

There was a soft knock on the door. Ino checked his watch and nodded. Enrique unlocked the deadbolt and three women entered. They all wore tight skirts and had teased hair.

"What's this?" asked Paco, enthusiastically.

"I thought we all deserved a little victory celebration."

"But, how'd you get them here?"

"I told them to come." Ino half smiled as he sauntered over to the prettiest one. "Going to put on a little show for us?"

She studied Paco and Enrique. "Maybe, later. Right now, I want you to do me. Now," she repeated as her hand began to unbuckle his belt.

251

"Why you little bitch." Ino laughed as he grabbed roughly for her buttocks.

It was almost four o'clock in the morning, and Ino had had it. He had been awake for more than a day and a half. All the reserve strength in his body had been tapped. Those crazy hookers and the last bottle of sangria had seen to that. He turned from the padlocked door and pulling his jacket up around his neck in response to the chilled morning air, crossed 165th Street.

He wanted to crash, but he had one last thing to do. He had to speak to Elena. He had to make sure she understood. Besides the people at Rebirth, she was the only one he couldn't con. And he knew she would be upset.

He rang the doorbell.

"Who is it?" Elena asked, still half asleep.

"It's me, Ino. Let me in."

"What time is it? What happened?" Even in an old bathrobe and with no makeup she was beautiful.

"See me on television?" He smiled.

"I saw you."

"Well, what do you think of your little brother now?"

"I think you're crazy, Ino. And I know you're making me sick." She sat down and looked him squarely in the eyes.

"But we did it!" he exclaimed, oblivious to her anguish. "Now we'll have some clout with the people who matter."

"What did you do? Ino, you just created another war—only this time it's in the hospital instead of the streets. How can a war make anything good?"

"We got Tanner and we got national coverage. We've given the people hope."

"You don't have Tanner. He's still the mayor. You just made the most powerful man in the city your enemy, and he's going to remember. Sure, you've given the people hope, but how long will that last if they're still hungry and without jobs?"

"It's a beginning. We'll finally have some changes. Anything has to be better." Ino looked up, nervously brushing a few crumbs from the table. "I've already touched base with the Democrats. They want me. They hate Tanner too."

"Ino, stop it!" she exploded.

There was a noise coming from the bedroom. "Who else is here?"

Elena blushed.

"Ruskin? When are you going to learn he's not one of us?"

"Maybe she doesn't want to be one of you," said Joe, standing in the doorway, glaring. He was wearing only his white pants.

"Bug out, I'm talking to my sister."

"How can you still trust him, Elena? He'll just keep hurting you." He glared at Ino.

"Shut up, Ruskin. Before I make you sorry."

"You don't scare me. I ought to punch your face in," Joe crouched, moving deliberately towards him.

Elena rushed between them. "Don't, Joe!" She pushed against his chest.

"Please, Elena." He pushed her aside. "It's time you start realizing what a real bastard your brother is," he said as the anger rose. "You had me fooled. I honestly thought you wanted to help, but you hurt the hospital and you knew all along. You don't care about anyone except yourself."

"There are issues here you don't understand, Ruskin. Things you couldn't understand even if you tried." Ino looked at him contemptuously. "Gold was slipping."

"He wasn't slipping that bad. He was a brilliant surgeon. He was just tired. You and your fellow ingrates made him tired."

"The problems of the community made him tired. But we live with those problems, we don't just commute."

Joe put his arms on Elena's shoulders. "Gold isn't the answer, the hospital isn't the answer. We only take care of the waste products, we don't cause them."

"Something has to be the answer. Otherwise, we're just going to shrivel up and die. And even if the hospital isn't an answer, it's a beginning. And goddamnit, we need a beginning."

"Well, it shouldn't have been Gold. You had me set him up, you're a conniving shit."

"You want to see it as a plot, fine. You, with your lily-white hands, could never understand. It wasn't a plot. It was an act of desperation. And we're going to keep acting until something changes." Ino hesitated for a moment. "Or, until we're dead. Gold set himself up. The hospital needs new blood. Spanish blood, black blood. People who care."

"Slogans. You don't really give a shit about the hospital. Otherwise you'd have left Gold alone. You'll use me. You'll use Gold. You'll use your sister. You'll use anyone you can. It doesn't matter that the only pawns in your scheme are the people who try to get close and help you. I feel like Frankenstein."

"Would you be happier if I was still laced out on drugs?"

Elena shuddered. "Joe didn't mean that." She placed her hands on his shoulders. "Ino," she said guardedly. "We're going to be married." Ino pulled back, enraged.

"Like hell you are."

"Like hell we're not. Elena and I are getting married."

"You'd leave me? Just like that, Elena?"

"Not just like that. You're my brother. I love you. But if he wanted me to, I'd go with him anywhere. You've got to understand, I have to."

"You don't have to do anything. You'd give up all we worked for and fought for for this high-class asshole?" Ino shook his head. "I just don't get it."

"Ino, you have to try. You and Joe are the only men I've ever loved."

"Go with him and you're making the biggest mistake of your life. I thought you had more sense. He hasn't been through what we've been through. He grew up with a silver spoon in his mouth. You expect him to be a man for you?"

"Ino, don't do this to me," she whispered.

"You stop at nothing, do you, Sanchez? You will even rip your sister's heart open to get your way," Joe shouted.

"Shut up, Ruskin. I'll never let you take her."

"You've given your last order in this house." They were inches apart.

"Stop it! Both of you!" Elena screamed. "I can't stand it anymore. Is this what it's come to? Am I to find no peace, ever? The only man I ever loved and my own brother at each other's throats, like two animals?" Her body shook with rage.

"Get out, Ino. Leave her alone. Leave us alone," Joe finally told him.

As Ino closed the door he heard her sobs and he remembered her tears of another time long ago when he had held her in his arms for the few short blocks to the hospital. The same sinking feeling reached his gut. She was going to leave him even though he needed her. Ruskin would see to that. He would never stay. He had seen his kind before—the do-gooders. They came and they saw and they worked hard doing penance. But they never stayed.

*.   *   *

At ten o'clock the next morning Paco dropped Ino off in front of the *Post* editorial offices on South Street. He waited impatiently in front of Garvin's small desk where one of the copyboys had set him down unceremoniously. Garvin strolled in at 11:20.

"You don't beat the band to get to work," observed Ino.

"I just got the biggest story of my career. No sense not enjoying it for a day. Hey, by the way, thanks for the tip."

"It was a great story for me, too." Ino laughed.

Garvin pulled open his bottom drawer. He took out a small green metal container and started to flip through the index cards. "Here it is," he said, putting the card on his desk. "Harry Rose." He hit the intercom and· got the call placed with the central secretary.

"So how you been, Harry?"

"No complaints, Cliff. What's by you?"

"Same old thing," said Garvin. "You still working?"

"You still breathing?" countered Rose. "What do you want Cliff? My cutter is sick today, and I got a buyer flying in from Chicago."

"I got a friend I think can help you. In a pretty big way."

"You don't say."

"I want you to talk to him."

"I got no time."

"Harry this is important. It could make a difference."

"Alright. I'm going to take a *schvitz* before I go home. If he's there, I'll talk to him. What's your friend's name?"

"Inocencio Sanchez. Still West Eighty-second?"

"That's right. And remember, Cliff, I'm just talking. I'm not promising anything."

"Thanks, Harry."

Garvin turned to Ino. "Looks like you're going to take a bath tonight."

The steam room at Eighty-second Street was crowded with middle-aged and elderly men wrapped in white towels. Ino undressed and put his clothes in a locker. The attendant handed him a towel, and he wrapped it around his waist. He walked into the main steam room, off to his right, filled with so much steam he could barely see. Slowly the vague outline of men sitting and

255

lying on the old tile benches clad in white towels became clear. Ino began to sweat from the heat. How would he ever recognize Harry Rose?

A short, bald, sixty-year-old man with gray hair and a large paunch waved his hand. Ino walked over and sat down next to him. "Are you Harry Rose?" he asked.

"The one and only."

"I'm Ino Sanchez." Ino looked around. Two more men came in. "How'd you recognize me?" asked Ino.

"Somehow you don't look like one of the regulars." Harry smiled.

"Look, Mr. Rose," Ino began.

"Call me Harry, it's more friendly. Cliff says you want to be friends. With me and with Tony."

"You're right, Harry. I do."

"But, Ino, I'll call you Ino, yes? When people are friends they do things for one another."

"That's right, Harry."

"I know what I can do for you, but I'm not so sure about what you can do for me."

Ino had done his homework. "You got an election for Congress coming up in eight months—I can get you the Twenty-first District."

"The Twenty-first District?" said Harry. "That's the Bronx, for Christ's sake. It's not even my territory."

"It would help the party."

"The party? That's very nice, but my business is in Manhattan. Look, kid," said Harry patiently, "I'm a businessman. I get into politics to help my business."

"That makes two of us."

"You can't help me."

"But I can help Tony Coletti."

"How?"

"I got something on Tanner." Harry Rose's gray eyebrows lifted in surprise. "It's confidential," said Ino. "I'll tell Coletti if you'll call him."

Harry studied Ino for a long moment. "You don't want to trust me, it's okay." He smiled. "Maybe you got something and maybe you don't." He lay down on the tile bench, closed his eyes and began to relax in the heat. "I'll let Tony decide for himself."

*　　*　　*

The day after the takeover was a time of crisis for the board of directors of Hirshorn Medical Center. They massed in a huge boardroom, overlooking Central Park. The room had muted green wallpaper and regal leather-bound books jutting out from oak shelves. The crystal chandelier's tinkling added a high-pitched chorus to the raised voices and fists pounding on the table.

William Boise, Hirshorn's young Chief of Surgery, sat back in his chair, studying the hysteria, careful to express nothing. He knew he carried the least weight of anyone in the room. Secretly gloating that Benjamin Gold, his arch rival, had ignited this explosion, he was still concerned that he might be pulled into its center. He had to protect himself, and he would use the only attribute he alone possessed. He had been trained as a surgeon; he knew how to sit on his hands. He would wait.

Walter Daly, the largest benefactor and Chairman of the Board, banged his gavel. It went unheeded. Exasperated, he lifted the silver water pitcher and banged it back on the desk. A few cubes spilled over and the group sat silent and embarrassed.

"Please, gentlemen. We must have order." The group listened as the chairman continued. "We just can't pull out. The papers are already roasting us over a fire. It'll look like we're jumping out of a sinking ship. And that son of a bitch, Sanchez, will make it look like Jefferson is not only our ship but that we caused the problem."

"Can't we do anything to shut him up?" Jack Osler, the Chief of Medicine and Gold's oldest friend, interrupted.

"I've called Mayor Tanner. He's issued a court order to keep him out of the hospital. But we can't gag him. And he's the TV station's new darling. You saw what he did to Gold. For a street punk, he sure knows how to use the media."

"This is the worst thing ever to happen to Hirshorn," Osler lamented. "Sanchez will just continue to make us look bad. Whether the charges are true or false doesn't seem to matter. People are listening to him."

"What a mess," Daly moaned. "It was a mess from the start, but now . . ." He shook his head grimly. "We take over three city hospitals and only one cost us two million dollars a year. That's two million in the red, gentlemen. Double the cost of the other hospitals. We send over our best men, because Jefferson needs help, and they kick them back in our laps with the

257

community garbage splattered all over. We try to provide them with the best medical care in the country, and they tell us to heal their community. We're a hospital. We're not God.''

'"I say we pull out before this thing really blows up,'' said Osler. "The whole South Bronx is going to collapse. Let's get out now, before we get buried.'' Osler's hand shook as he reached for the glass of water. "Let Sanchez and his People for Progress take care of the patients.''

"Jack, I know what you're saying, but we can't leave Jefferson. Not now. It'll follow us everywhere. We're a humanitarian institution. That hospital needs supervision. Besides, I already told Tanner that we would continue there.''

"Okay, Mr. Chairman, supervise. Tell me, have you thought about getting a new chief of surgery to throw to the wolves? Benjamin Gold was a brilliant doctor. Who in the hell do you think will want to go there now? Oh, and by the way, Walter, it wouldn't hurt if he spoke Spanish. That is if you intend that he stay there at least a year.'' Osler afforded himself a grim laugh at the hopelessness of the situation.

.''We can compromise.'' Boise stood up, finally ready.

"Compromise?'' Daly's brow wrinkled.

"Sure. Who says we have to pick one single chief? Why can't we rotate some of our younger staff men through there as interim chiefs to train our residents? It won't look like we're giving up on Jefferson, while we can still keep training our residents. That was our original purpose in taking over there.''

"I just hope your little compromise doesn't wind up with us being taken over,'' Osler admonished. "I feel time is of the essence.''

"Relax, Jack. I'm not through. We'll give them a year to find some second-rate institution to take over. Then we can announce our transfer, and we're home free. We'll leave them all our equipment, and we go where we can do some good.''

"How do we explain that to the press? There are three reporters outside right now trying to gnaw in here,'' said Daly.

"We say we'll continue to maintain our obligation to the hospital and community. We say we are ready to meet with medical representatives from the hospital staff, the director of hospitals, and the community, to pick a new chief. But that will take time, and we need to continue to maintain 'business as usual.'

"Meanwhile, we'll wait, let everything cool down. We'll

wind up using three different junior men over the next year in four month rotations. That way they won't be able to zero in on any one man."

"What happens to Gold?" Osler was still not satisfied.

"Let him go back to the animal labs where he started. He'll be protected. This thing has been a terrible shock." Boise was still standing.

"We can continue to pay him at his chief's salary," Daly added. "I just wish we could do something more."

"We can name a resident-in-training award after him," Boise suggested.

"But he's still alive." Daly frowned for a second. "I know. We'll get it engraved without a date, and I'll show it to him. Teaching was always his favorite. It will make him happy even if he doesn't admit it." Daly went to the cupboard and lifted a bottle of French wine.

"Then it's decided. To the new chiefs of surgery—whoever you are. '*Buena suerte*,' my young colleagues. You're going to need it."

It was dawn when Ino awoke. He didn't even try to go back to sleep. He lay in his bed, restless, worrying about Elena, thinking of what he had to do. He got out of bed and made himself a cup of instant coffee. He looked in the refrigerator. There was a loaf of white bread, beginning to show signs of mold, and a can of tuna fish. He opened the tuna fish and began eating it from the can. He sat at the small kitchen table and stared out the window, watching the city slowly awaken. Soon, the sun started to come through the clouds. He took it as a sign and decided it was going to be a good day.

At exactly nine o'clock a clean-shaven, immaculately dressed Inocencio Sanchez sat in the People for Progress office and dialed Tony Coletti's number. He reached a secretary, who told him to hold; a moment later Coletti was on the line.

"Hello, Mr. Coletti. This is Ino Sanchez. I spoke to a friend of yours, Harry Rose. He told me to call you."

"Yes, I spoke to Harry. And I know who you are. Now what do we have to talk about?"

"Plenty, as far as I can see."

"Like what?"

"I can help you."

"How?"

"You want Tanner's ass?"

"I'm listening."

"I can get it for you."

Coletti's tone changed. "Look, why don't you meet me for lunch? There's a health food place called Forty Carrots. The food stinks, but I got an ulcer. It's on West Forty-ninth."

"I'll find it," said Ino. The smile disappeared as he hung up the phone.

"So the People for Progress are moving back into politics, eh, Jefe?" said Paco.

"You got it. By tomorrow the Democrats will be paying the rent for this place."

"And the hospital?" countered Enrique.

"We'll return with more power than ever," said Ino. "It's going to take a while, but we'll be back. We need Jefferson. It's our key to the whole South Bronx. Everyone's for Jefferson. When we have enough power to return, then everybody'll be for us."

"How can you be so sure?" asked Paco.

"I haven't been wrong yet."

Coletti was right, the food was awful. Ino, who usually could eat anything, had difficulty swallowing the strange bean sprout concoction. He took a sip of coffee and relaxed until Tony Coletti finished. He had learned a long time ago not to discuss business on an empty stomach.

He watched Coletti finish his milk. "I need a job," he began.

"So?" asked Coletti, wiping the white stain carefully off his waxed mustache.

"I'm interested in politics. The Democratic party represents the common man."

"Sounds noble," said Coletti. He moved his large frame away from the tiny table and smoothed his thick gray hair.

"I can organize the South Bronx."

"Great. No one votes."

"We already have the area split up into sections. We'll get them registered. Your people will show us how."

"We've tried that before. No one cares." Coletti adjusted the brown leather band on his expensive watch.

"They will. That will be my job. If we get them angry enough."

"Even if thirty percent of your voters qualify, elections are won by swaying the working class. That's our strength. You'd wind up hurting us."

"I'll get Tanner."

"You mentioned that on the phone. You have anything concrete?"

"No," admitted Ino. "But he's got to have a couple of loose ends. We'll find them."

"We've looked for six years. Why are you going to succeed where a staff of well-trained lawyers failed?"

"I have an advantage."

"What's that?"

"I don't have to follow the rules."

Coletti considered the point. "I'm sorry, Sanchez, but we can't take the chance." He studied the disappointment on Ino's face. It was suicide. But Tanner was rolling too smoothly. Maybe it was worth giving Sanchez a try.

"We'd have to pay you under the table," he started slowly.

"Okay, fine," said Ino.

"Let's see what you can do. Bring us something good and you're in."

"I just want a chance. I guarantee you'll be the next congressman from the Bronx."

"The election is only eight months away."

"Eight months is a lot of time."

"Sometimes. What do you want if you deliver?"

"I just want to help."

"Look, Sanchez, let's start off right. There's only one rule I insist on. I want honesty."

Ino broke out in a broad smile. "I want to be the new administrator of Jefferson Hospital."

"That's better," said Coletti, shaking his hand.

"How'd it go?" asked Paco, as soon as Ino breezed through the door of the office.

"Like I told you," said Ino, sinking into his chair, lifting his feet onto the desk, "People for Progress is back in politics."

"But what about Jefferson?" asked Enrique. The other men had gathered around the desk to listen.

261

"We're out of Jefferson for a while. For the next eight month we're going to work as hard at getting Tony Coletti electe congressman as we did at Jefferson. Once he's in, we're going t be able to get back into Jefferson with a lot more power than w had when we left. People for Progress will emerge as a unifie bloc. In essence, we'll control the South Bronx vote."

"So why would we want to return to Jefferson?" asked Pacc

"Jefferson is the real power base of the community. Th people identify with the hospital, and no operation in this are will succeed without it. We'll come back and we'll rub Tanner nose in all the shit that he's made us swallow."

"What do we do for bread?" asked Enrique.

"Coletti will cover. But keep it cool, because it's under th table. We'll have enough to operate this office, enough for eac of us to get by on. The important thing is the election. Ton Coletti is our ticket back to Jefferson."

"How you gonna build him up to the people?" asked Pacc "He's Italian."

"Don't worry about building Coletti up," said Ino. "Worr about tearing the Republicans down."

Matt Zilk had plenty of time to think while he waited outsid William Boise's private office in the administrative wing c Hirshorn Medical Center. He'd been in tight situations before but this was getting too close. He was nervous, and he hoped didn't show. Nothing like a scared resident to make these admir istrators think they'd got you by the balls. His heart was beatin fast when the secretary came out and told him Boise would se him.

He shuffled into the large office. It was tastefully decorated rich and understated. Boise was sitting at his desk, "Dr. Boise," he began, extending his hand.

Boise ignored it and motioned to the chair in front of his desk "There's quite a few things we have to discuss, Dr. Zilk."

"That's what I'm here for," said Zilk, sitting back, trying t look relaxed.

Boise scanned the papers on his desk. "There have bee several complaints about your work even before this Ramon Perez thing exploded."

The statement caught Zilk off guard. Well, if that was how h wanted to play it. "Formal complaints?" asked Zilk.

"Informal complaints, Doctor, but complaints, nonetheless. Nurses, Attendings, Aides. Your professional conduct seems to be in question."

"Everyone makes mistakes," started Zilk. "That's what the training is all about."

"True," said Boise, "but not everybody's mistakes start a revolution."

"Those spi . . . people down there, you know as well as I do, they're animals. They're not like you or me," he said confidentially. "They're looking for any excuse they can find to make trouble. They want the world handed to them."

Boise stared at him for a long moment. "Dr. Zilk, in view of everything that's happened, I am reassigning you to Hirshorn for the remainder of the year."

Zilk breathed a sigh of relief. "That's fine with me, Doctor."

"Furthermore, I believe it's best to have you spend that time in the radiology department."

"Radiology?" said Zilk. "There's nothing to do in radiology."

"That's the point. I want you out of the clinical end. I don't want you treating patients," said Boise. "And if I were you, I'd spend some of that time making plans for the coming year."

"*Huh?*"

"Hirshorn Medical Center has reviewed your record, and we have decided not to renew your contract for next year."

"You're making me the scapegoat," sputtered Zilk.

"Bob Watel was the scapegoat. My own esteemed colleague, Benjamin Gold, was the scapegoat. Hirshorn's reputation was the scapegoat. I'd say, under the circumstances, you're getting off easy."

"What about a recommendation?"

"A recommendation? Listen, forget it. In fact, I'd suggest you start applying outside the country."

The following Tuesday afternoon, Joe and Elena waited in the smaller inner chamber of Judge Rudolph Scott's office. Joe glanced at his watch. It was ten minutes before two, and his parents still had time to arrive for the ceremony. He knew they wouldn't come.

Sunday night, he'd driven out the Long Island Expressway to tell them of his decision to marry Elena. He opened the door to

their modest split-level home in Merrick as he had for the pa
twenty years. "Mom? Dad?" he called. "I'm home."

"Joe?" Ida Ruskin came running in from the kitchen, wipin
her hands on her apron. Her brown hair was flecked with gray
and her warm blue eyes lit up at the sight of her son. "Joey!
She hugged him tightly. He thought she looked older. "Com
I've been cooking all day," she said, dragging him into th
kitchen. Joe smiled. Nothing really changes, he thought. "You
father is washing up; he just came home from work. The ma
works like a dog. But you know that already. Here," she sai
placing a bowl of hot vegetable soup before him, "try this."

"Mom, you shouldn't have bothered," Joe said between mouth
fuls. "But it's great."

"Not bothered? If a mother shouldn't bother for a son, the
who should she bother for?" Joe felt sick. Ida Ruskin beamed.
compliment from her son made all the mixing and kneading an
slicing and standing on her swollen legs worthwhile. She watche
him eat and tears came to her eyes. He was a good boy, and he'
always made her and Sam proud.

"Joe!" Sam Ruskin walked into the kitchen, a broad smile o
his robust face. The two men hugged each other. "How are yo
son?"

"Fine, Dad. How do you feel?"

"Eh, some days good, some bad. What can we expect? Tim
doesn't stand still for anyone."

"You look pretty good to me, Pop." Joe smiled.

"Is that the doctor's opinion or the son's opinion?" Ic
laughed.

"A little of both."

He waited until they had finished eating and were relaxin
in the living room.

"Every day, another item in the papers about Jefferson, Joe,
said Ida.

"We're worried about you," said Sam, "It's a dangerou
neighborhood."

"I know, Dad, but the doctors and nurses are the safest one
there. The people have an unspoken code not to harm anyon
wearing a white coat."

"I hope you're right," said Ida. "But your father and I wi
keep on worrying until you're out of the South Bronx."

"Well, there's one good thing that came of it," said Jc
cautiously.

"What's that?" His parents looked up.

"I've met a girl," he started.

"That's wonderful," Ida smiled. "So tell us, who is she? Where is she from?"

Joe took a deep breath. "She's a nurse in the Emergency Room at Jefferson. She's lived in the South Bronx practically all her life. Originally, her family's from Puerto Rico."

Joe watched the color drain from his parents' faces. They exchanged looks. "Joe, am I hearing you right?" Ida asked. "You have a Puerto Rican girl friend from the South Bronx?"

"Mom, she's really a wonderful person. Wait till you meet her."

"How well do you know this girl?" Sam asked.

"Well enough to know I want to marry her."

"Sam," said Ida, gripping the arms of the chair, "get me my pills."

Sam began to fumble through his wife's purse. His face was flushed. "Joe, do you know what you're saying?"

"I love her. I want her for my wife."

"You love her?" Sam's voice grew louder. "What does a kid like you know of love? You live with a woman for twenty-five years, then you talk to me about love!"

Ida swallowed the pills. "Joe, we've never interfered, have we?" Joe nodded. "So forgive us this once. We only care about you. How did this happen to you and . . ."

"Elena . . . Elena Sanchez."

"And Elena. What does her family say of all this?"

"Both her parents are dead. She has a younger brother, Inocencio."

"That name," said Ida slowly, "I heard that name someplace."

"Her brother is very active trying to improve the hospital," said Joe quietly.

"Oh, yes, last week on the television." Ida suddenly remembered. "They were interviewing him with that Dr. Gold."

Sam remembered, too. The young Puerto Rican making a fool out of the older doctor. Right away they knew he was a hoodlum. "Joe, are you crazy? This is the kind of scum you want to get involved with?"

"Elena is not scum," said Joe coldly.

"Maybe she's not, but her brother is. Joe, you have eyes, you can see he's a hoodlum."

"He's not exactly that," said Joe, hedging.

"Then you tell me what he is."

"He's trying to help his people. I guess you'd call him sort of . . . a revolutionary."

"A revolutionary? We used to call them fascists."

"Dad, they're two different things."

"I don't care what you call it—I know what I see. He's no good. And you think that this kind of person, this, this revolutionary . . . this gangster, is going to let his sister leave the only home they have known to go away with you to a nice life? Joe, you can't be that naive."

"Elena wants to leave, too. She's very different than her brother."

"Joe, I'm telling you, he'll never let her leave. If you stay with her, he'll only drag you into the mud too."

"You're throwing away your whole career, your whole life," pleaded Ida.

"I'm not throwing away my career. Elena and I are going to get out of Jefferson. As soon as I finish my training, we'll move to someplace nice. You'll see, I'll be a big success, you'll be proud."

"You marry this girl," said Sam flatly, "you'll never get out of the South Bronx. It will have all been for nothing. All the scrimping, the sweating, all of it—for nothing."

"Dad, you don't—" Joe began.

"Don't tell me about them," snapped Sam. "I've had my shop twenty-seven years. I've been with them day in and day out. I know how they think. Now you say you're in love with this girl? A girl from that world? Joe, you don't know what you're getting into. Believe me, stick with your own kind. Break it off with the girl, Joe," Sam pleaded, "now, before it's too late, break it off."

Joe felt sick. He knew he was losing the battle. Ida touched his arm gently. "Joe, we know what you're going through. Life is so hard sometimes. But, I've lived a long time and I know there is nothing, nothing in this world that time cannot heal."

"I'm sorry." Joe could barely speak.

"Sorry . . . ?"

"I can't leave her," he said in a hoarse, scratched whisper.

Joe shook his head abruptly in an effort to wipe out his father's words. He looked at Elena, calm and serene in a pale blue suit, and took her hand. She had pinned the corsage of violets he had given her to her lapel. His parents were wrong. Every fiber in his body told him so. He just wished the flicker of doubt gnawing at his insides would burn itself out.

Elena was lost in her own thoughts. She knew she loved Joe with a fierceness she had not believed possible. Then why, she wondered, was she feeling so anxious and alone? Luis and Susan would be there any minute to stand up for them. A rush of warmth filled her when she thought of them. They were like family. What's the use, she thought wearily, it wouldn't be the same without Ino.

That last night, he swore he'd never see them married. Painfully and deliberately, he was keeping his promise. She studied Joe and knew he was upset. She wished she could alleviate his fears, the same way she wished she could resolve her own. But there was nothing left to say.

There was a knock on the door. "It must be Luis and Susan," she said, slowly opening the door.

Ino stood facing her. "I can't let you walk down the aisle alone, can I?" he asked sheepishly.

Elena rushed into his arms. "I'm so glad . . . we're so glad . . ."

Joe hesitated, then got up and shook his hand. "For Elena's sake," he said, "let's bury the hatchet."

"I hope we can," said Ino cautiously, "but I got my doubts."

They spent a dreary, rainy weekend in the St. Charles, a second-rate hotel with no hot water and service that was only mediocre. But to them, the food was divine, the accommodations deluxe. They went on to remember it as the most lavish, exciting place they had ever been.

21

Ino Sanchez had been searching hard for an edge against Mayor Tanner. Just as he was desperate for a new hand to play, Paco drew an ace.

Every Sunday, Paco visited his widowed mother in her apartment on 156th Street. He arrived at about one in the afternoon and watched television until she had the meal ready. He always brought her a bunch of flowers, which she placed in a vase on the table. After dinner she told him all her problems, and Paco asked if she needed anything, and she said no, and Paco had a beer and said good-bye until the following Sunday. He usually left his mother's around five o'clock. This Sunday, however, there was much family news, and he didn't leave until six.

As he walked out of the building he spotted a familiar figure just ahead of him. The man was tall, wearing glasses and an expensive coat and hat. He walked to his car, a tan stock Chevy, new. Paco noticed the antenna mounted on the roof. He had broken off enough antennas to know. This man had a phone.

Who was this guy? A cop? Not in those threads. A main man? Not with those wheels. He watched the man open the door and get inside. He studied his profile. Suddenly, he knew. But what was he doing in this neighborhood?

Paco rushed over to the People for Progress office and was relieved to find Ino had not left. "Jefe, do you know who just left my mother's building?"

Ino looked up from his paperwork. "How can I know unless you tell me, eh?" He smiled indulgently and continued writing.

"Malcolm," said Paco.

Ino dropped his pencil and looked up. "Malcolm?" he repeated. "Malcolm, Tanner's aide?"

Paco beamed with pride. "The one and only, Jefe." It wasn't often he got a chance to give Ino news.

"What was he doing there? The slums aren't his cup of tea."

"I've been thinking about it all the way over here. He walked out of the building with his head down and tried to cover his face with his hat. He acted like a man who don't want nobody to know he's there. Maybe he's getting a little piece on the side and wants to keep it quiet," Paco offered.

"Malcolm screwing around in your mother's building?" Ino shook his head, unconvinced. "He's not a bad looking guy. He could afford to get some high-class ass. It doesn't add up."

"I could follow him," Paco offered.

"You do that," Ino told him.

The following Sunday, Paco waited in his mother's front room and watched every person who came into the building. When Malcolm arrived, Paco went into the hall and watched the lighted buttons on the elevator stop at number three. He ran down the two flights and waited on the landing. Soon, Malcolm came out of an apartment. "See you next week, Ann," he said as he started for the elevator.

Paco continued to wait in the stairwell. He knew this Ann had to come out sooner or later. Half an hour later, he heard her door open. He peeped through the railing and saw a woman in a black fur coat come out of the apartment. He raced down the stairs and watched as she left. He tried to remember her face, her walk, but he knew he had never seen her before.

"Jefe," he reported to Ino later that night, "it is a woman Malcolm comes to see."

"Who is she?"

"I don't know. She's not Rican, and she was wearing a fancy fur coat."

"Malcolm and a fur coat in your mother's building?" Ino twisted the pencil in his fingers as he thought. "Something's going down and I want to know what it is. Paco, get a camera and get me a picture of this woman. Sniff around the apartment and see what you can pick up. That shouldn't be too difficult for you," he smiled. Paco had been the Toros number one lock picker.

"What about Malcolm, Jefe?" asked Paco.

"I'm gonna take care of him myself."

*　　*　　*

269

On Monday night Ino parked his car across the street from Gracie Mansion. That night Stewart Malcolm left his office and drove to his apartment on East Seventy-first Street. He stayed till the following morning, when he returned to work. On Tuesday and Wednesday nights he did the same thing. But on Thursday night Malcolm headed up FDR Drive and followed Bruckner Boulevard to the New England Thruway toward Connecticut. He got off at the Darien exit. He traveled on for about two miles, then stopped at a majestic looking Tudor house, surrounded by an iron gate.

Stewart Malcolm got out of his car and spoke into a box at the side of the gate. The gates opened and Malcolm drove up the long driveway to the front of the house. He left his car in the circular driveway alongside a white Turbo Carrera and a dark green 450SL. Then he opened the door and went inside.

Ino parked his car next to the big hedges. He walked over to the gate and read the engraved nameplate. He let out a long slow whistle. *It was Malcolm's house!* Ino walked around the property and saw the tennis court, the swimming pool, and the servants' quarters in the back. He wanted to jump the fence but saw the wires. What the hell, he thought, he had seen enough anyway.

On the ride back he had time to think. Malcolm was living like a fucking king on the salary the city was paying him as Tanner's chief aide. It didn't add up. Malcolm had no claim to wealth if he was working for Tanner. He snapped his fingers in a gesture of impatience. It had to be a cover. For months now he had searched for something, anything, he could get on Tanner. Why hadn't he thought of Malcolm before?

By nine o'clock the next morning Ino was in the Darien city hall. By ten o'clock, he had located the plat number of Malcolm's property. He dragged the large, leather-bound book off the shelf and rifled through the pages until he came to the right number. He held his breath as he read: "Title to this property contained in Winding Acres Estates, Subdivision 4, Section 12 or Plat #3862 deeded to Stewart Malcolm and Anita Malcolm, his wife, on this 19th day of May in the year 1979." So he hasn't been living like this for long, thought Ino. Just about as long as he'd been working for Tanner.

Two hours and several volumes later, he discovered more. The mortgage to Malcolm's house was held by Wholesale Food Corporation, 8915 Canal Street, New York, N.Y. Now what was a wholesale food operation doing in the mortgage business?

Early Saturday morning Ino stood across the street from the large warehouse that comprised the general offices of the Wholesale Food Corporation. He studied the brick building, sitting innocently between a coffee shop and a tire exchange. A few workers, their white uniforms smeared in blood and animal fat, walked out onto the sidewalk to smoke a cigarette and get some coffee at the shop next door. A large company truck honked its horn in front of the garage entrance. As it rolled in Ino studied the carcasses of beef hanging from the steel rod running down the middle of the back of the truck. A vegetable truck pulled up and honked, then entered the garage.

Ino could pick up nothing unusual about the scene. People were doing their jobs, just as they did on other days. Suddenly, another truck pulled up to the garage entrance and honked its horn. Only this one was different. Immediately, Ino noticed the orange and white emblem on its side panel. It belonged to the Department of Hospitals-City of New York. The door opened and the driver waved to one of the workers, obviously recognizing him.

What was a hospital truck doing at the warehouse along with all the vendors?

By the time he got back to his office, it was noon. Paco was waiting for him. "Jefe, I got a picture of Malcolm's girl friend getting out of her car." He handed Ino the snapshot.

Ino sat back and studied the picture, and a slight smile crept over his face. "This is getting interesting," he said. "That's a Jefferson parking sticker on her window."

"Jefe, you know her?"

"I'm not sure, but I know someone who might."

"Who's that?"

"Luis," said Ino, grabbing the picture and heading for the door.

Luis opened his door with a big smile on his face. "Come on in, Ino, if you can find a place to stand."

Luis's apartment was a mass of cardboard boxes, clothes, and books strewn all over the place. Empty beer cans and a bottle of wine stood on the kitchen counter.

"Looks like the aftermath of a Toros's party." Ino smiled.

"Yeah," Luis said, folding his shirts and packing them in an old leather suitcase. "Susan and I did some celebrating."

Ino pushed aside a carton and sat down on the old sofa. "I still can't believe it, you're gonna be a doctor."

"Sometimes neither can I. I keep rereading my letter of acceptance to med school every day." He laughed.

"You've worked hard for this, Luis," Ino said sincerely. "Nobody deserves it more than you do."

Luis smiled at his old friend. "I guess we've both come a long way," he said. "Did you know Susan's coming to Boston with me?"

"No, I didn't. When did this happen?"

"A few days ago. She got a letter from her lawyer, and her divorce will be final in two months. She's gonna finish her residency at Mass. General. We'll get a small place there, and with her full-time pay and my part-time pay, we ought to make it."

"No way you can lose. Like always, you got it all mapped out." Ino smiled. "I'll really miss you, Luis," he said suddenly.

"I'm gonna miss you, too," Luis said, "but you know we'll be back."

"We're counting on it," said Ino.

"Sure, after I graduate, Susan and I will come back to Jefferson."

"That's great. We need more doctors like you guys. Keep in touch with the old neighborhood." He smiled warmly.

The two men shook hands. "Anytime you need me, just call, Ino."

"As a matter of fact, I could use your help right now."

"I'm all yours." Luis smiled.

Ino took out the snapshot. "Do you know this woman?" he asked.

"Sure," said Luis, returning to his packing. "She's the chief dietician at Jefferson Hospital."

Ino wasted no time. He called the *Post* and set up an appointment with Cliff Garvin as soon as he got back to the office.

"This may be big," he told him over a cup of coffee.

"How big?" Garvin wanted to know.

"Front page."

Garvin was interested. "Fill me in," he said anxiously.

Ino related his findings. When he finished, Cliff asked, "How do I fit in?"

"See if you can get a date with Ann Marshall. Find out anything you can on her."

A week later, Cliff Garvin sat in his car and checked his watch for the third time. He pulled down the visor and straightened his tie.

"Not bad." He admired himself. He checked the address, 29 East Sixty-second Street, written on the top page of his spiral notebook. He tilted his head jauntily and opened the door of his car. As he walked down the block he smiled. It could be his first real story and if he followed through, maybe he'd be able to write a book. Then he'd show his city editor and maybe, just maybe, he might become famous like those guys from Washington and have lots of girls. He had hurdled the first step easily enough and since he was usually so clumsy in terms of dating rituals, he felt this to be a positive sign.

Warned by Ino, he had been careful. He made the appointment with her on the premise of doing a story about one of the cafeteria workers who had retired after fifty years at Jefferson. "Human interest," he had repeated several times while looking straight into her eyes and hoping she was attracted to the fact that he was six or seven years younger than she. He had taken enough information to catch her off guard and then had asked her to dinner. At first she refused, but was unprepared for his surprising pressure; she agreed to the date.

He had checked her through the Jefferson records that night, with the help of Paco supplying a key. She was thirty-six, divorced, had two children, graduated from CCNY fifteen years ago, one service award, eight years head of dietary.

She lived in a three level brownstone, obviously costing top dollar. He'd know soon enough, he thought, as he knocked on the door. He felt his pulse race and sprang into her foyer.

She was dressed and waiting for him. "That's what I like" —he smiled—"a woman who's on time." He was just able to scan the contents of the hushed living room, but it was enough.

He waded through a boring dinner, gaining little.

"You've got a nice place," he said as they approached her house. "Must cost a pretty penny."

"It does," she replied.

He knew from her guarded behavior she wouldn't invite him in. "Where'd you get the money for it?" he plunged.

"My aunt died." She laughed. "And thank you for a lovely evening."

Garvin stared at the closed door and headed straight for the People for Progress office.

"Let me tell you," said Garvin, "whatever she's doing, she must be doing it right."

"What do you mean?" asked Ino.

"You should see her apartment," said Garvin. "Real orientals, fine old antiques, she's got a Chagall hanging in her foyer. We're talking about big bucks here, Ino. I don't know where the lady's getting it, but it sure ain't from her weekly paycheck, I'll tell you that."

The reporter's information convinced Ino. "You're doing a great job, Cliff, but we need more. We'll have to corroborate what Paco's seen at his mother's apartment. Snoop around there, but remember you'll only be getting circumstantial evidence. Malcolm is the key. Put out some feelers on his financial situation. That's one spot I'd have trouble scouting."

"Then what?" asked Garvin.

"Then you're the hero." Ino smiled.

"How?"

"You got the scoop on the biggest scandal in the city."

For Joe and Elena, Sundays were the best of all. They'd lie in bed, on those wonderful days they didn't have to work, until one or two in the afternoon. They had breakfast and sometimes lunch under a blanket of pages from *The New York Times* and tried to forget Jefferson and the problems that waited for them. But by eight o'clock Monday morning, the weekend was a distant memory.

Joe walked into the large open ward and grabbed a chart from the rack. He passed quickly over the first ten post-op beds and their uncomfortable occupants. He stopped in front of a thin Island man with a huge swollen abdomen.

Large varicose veins bulged into his navel. Joe knelt down and tapped his side. He felt the fluid wave bounce against the palm of his other hand laying flat against the skin. He frowned. He checked the chart. Lytes, BUN, okay. Protein was still down. His hematocrit had stabilized. It was a far different picture than the stormy night two weeks ago when the man had arrived.

He had come into the Emergency Room bleeding internally

from his stomach. Joe had started three IVs and rinsed his belly with four liters of ice water. He put him on a cooling blanket and watched him turn a faint blue. He administered the sedative that kept him from shivering. He placed the balloon pressure device down the man's esophagus, hoping to stop the flow. But nothing helped, and the man was bleeding out.

On Joe's insistence they had taken him up. When they opened his belly, even the young attending had gasped. His portal pressure was over 600, and huge dilated vessels that crisscrossed everywhere gave each organ a blue-red spongelike cast. They decided he had only one chance, and they connected the two major vessels from the drainage system together. The surgery took over seven hours and they wound up giving him sixteen pints of blood. But he stopped bleeding.

Joe looked down at him again. "Mr. Rivera, how are you feeling?"

"It's getting hard to breathe."

"I know. We're going to tap some of that fluid out of your belly. That'll help."

"No more!"

"Please," Joe said sympathetically. "I know you've been through a lot already. But just hold on. We'll pull you through."

"My weight?" The old man was being weighed three times a day.

"You've gained another two pounds. That's from the fluid. The water pills aren't doing it."

"*Dios*, what can I do?"

"You've got to keep eating. You've got to get some protein into you."

"I try. This food tastes funny."

"It's a special diet. All hospital food stinks. You're not missing anything." He tried to joke.

"I eat almost everything on my tray. Even though I can't stand it."

"We've got to get you strong. Then you can sink into some hot fish and sauce."

"My wife used to make the best *cuchifritos*. Now she's gone," he said sadly.

"My wife is Spanish and a great cook. You'll be our guest."

"I would enjoy that," he said, smiling for the first time.

"I'll be back in a while." Joe waved.

He went to the nurses station, frustrated over the old man's stagnation. Rivera was a real fighter. If he made it, he and Joe would both have performed a major accomplishment.

"Miss Kelly, how many grams of protein is Mr. Rivera getting in his diet?"

"One hundred and fifty. Just as you ordered."

"How much salt?"

"Less than a gram."

Joe nodded. "Do any visitors bring food in?"

"He has no visitors. He's alone."

"I don't get it. He keeps gaining weight."

"I'm sorry, Doctor. Maybe he'll be better tomorrow."

"Maybe. I'll be back after lunch. We'll need a thorancentesis tray. I'll have to tap him."

Joe returned an hour later. Mr. Rivera had dozed off, and Joe didn't have the heart to wake him. He looked at the almost empty tray. It was true he was eating almost everything they gave him. There were only remnants of the cottage cheese and custard left. On impulse, he stuck his finger into one of the small piles. The cottage cheese had a strange aftertaste. Joe tried it again. No wonder Rivera complained. There was a definite metallic flavor. Joe rinsed his mouth with some water. He tried the custard. It made no difference. He scraped the remainder of the meal into a small plastic cup and carefully laid it on a shelf in the refrigerator in the doctors' lounge.

At two that afternoon Joe knocked on the door to the office of the chief dietician. He faced a dark-haired woman in her late thirties, wearing a white lab coat. She wore heavy makeup and looked as if she'd just left the beauty parlor. "Hi," he began, extending his hand. "I'm Joe Ruskin, first-year surgical resident on ward 2-B."

"Glad to meet you, Joe," she said, matching his firm grip. "I'm Ann Marshall. What can I do for you?"

"I want to check on the diet of one of my patients, Enrique Rivera."

"Yes, what seems to be the problem?" she asked cautiously.

"He's a post-op portacaval shunt, and the low salt, high protein diet is imperative to his recovery. He's gaining weight. I checked some food he had on his tray for lunch and it tasted funny."

"Funny?" Ann Marshall suddenly found herself perspiring. "How so?"

"I tasted some cottage cheese and some custard. Both had an unusual aftertaste. Could the food be spoiled?"

"Impossible," she said smoothly. "I can't imagine what it was you tasted. All our food is prepared under strict supervision by my assistants and checked by myself before it goes up to the wards. Our foods are the highest quality and USDA inspected. Proper storage facilities and adequate refrigeration are provided. An inspector from the mayor's office comes through the premises periodically. If you would like me to show you the kitchen facilities, I'd be glad to, Dr. Ruskin. I'm glad you're interested in your patient's diet. But to suggest that the food prepared here is spoiled is not fair to me or my staff." Her face had turned very red while she spoke.

"Mrs. Marshall, I'm sorry. It's just that both dishes had the same aftertaste. I was just wondering if you had any idea why."

"Other than noting the food reacts differently to different tastebuds, I can't say. That's a very special diet Mr. Rivera is on. One you're not used to tasting. Also, have you eaten recently?" She seemed to have resumed her cool demeanor.

"Yes."

"Well, that's something else that could affect the aftertaste."

"I wasn't aware of that," said Joe. "Perhaps that could be the reason after all."

As soon as the door to her office closed Ann Marshall was on the phone.

"City Hall, may I help you," said the operator.

"Stewart Malcolm, please," she spoke softly into the receiver.

"Stewart Malcolm here."

"It's me, Ann."

"Why are you calling me here? I told you never to do that!" he whispered angrily.

"This may be important, Malcolm, so shut up. Some young resident just marched into my office. He wanted to know why his patient's food had a funny 'aftertaste' as he put it. You know these liberal save-the-world types. He could blow our whole operation."

Malcolm was stunned. "Wha . . . what did you tell him?"

"I tried to double-talk him, but he seemed like a bright kid and I just don't know."

"Well there's nothing we can do about it now," said Malcolm, thoughtfully. "Anyway, what's he going to do? Have the food analyzed? We have Dick in the lab. Better put him on guard. In the meantime, just try and stay cool. I'll meet you Sunday at the apartment."

"Malcolm," she said coldly, "don't forget my full share this time."

"The lady doth protest too much," Joe told Elena over dinner.

"What do you mean?" she said, taking a bite out of her sandwich.

"She got all excited when I suggested something might be wrong with the food. Too excited. I think she was trying to con me."

"It could be nothing, Joe. Just regular bureaucratic feather ruffling. Maybe Mr. Rivera's lunch was sour. It does happen every once in a while, even with the best precautions."

"That's just it, Elena. I've tasted food that was spoiled. This food was not spoiled. It had some kind of chemical aftertaste, something like diet soda."

"Why don't you have it analyzed? Then you'd know for sure."

"I've already thought of that. The problem is I wouldn't want to do it at Jefferson."

"Isn't there some other lab you could use?"

"Dr. Gold works in a lab," Joe said, trying to sound nonchalant. Elena smiled. "You'd find any excuse to see him, wouldn't you?"

A shy grin swept over Joe's face. "You really got my number."

Joe had a hard time finding the lab. It was sandwiched between two modern clinical towers of the Hirshorn complex. The faint smell of formaldehyde hit him as he walked inside. No attempt was made to make the place anything more than the research area it was. The dull green walls and linoleum floor badly in need of repair comprised the entire three stories. There were animal noises in every corridor. Joe stood before the door marked "Benjamin Gold, M.D.-Surgical Research." He knocked lightly. "Come in, it's open," came the familiar voice.

'Dr. Gold.'' Joe smiled, extending his hand. ''It's good to see you, sir.''

"Joseph.'' Gold smiled. ''I'm glad to see you, too,'' he said, really meaning it. ''It's been a while.''

"Four months,'' said Joe sadly. Joe looked around the office. There were boxes still unopened with the names of companies specializing in scientific equipment. On his desk was a microscope and several burettes stood on the windowsill. Everything looked new. ''You've got some setup here,'' Joe said, looking around the room.

"You can't find out anything unless you've got the right tools to do it, son.''

Joe guessed Gold was probably buying equipment here too. ''What kind of work are you doing here, sir?''

"Mostly I just operate on dogs,'' said Gold. ''My emergency days are behind me.'' He seemed rather subdued.

"You're the best surgeon I've ever known, sir,'' Joe said impulsively. Gold seemed a little embarrassed, but Joe knew he was secretly pleased. ''What are you working on?''

"I'm trying to find a cure for ulcer disease. We've got a project going on at the moment and the early work looks really impressive.'' Joe smiled. ''I know. Here I am trying to find a method of preventing a surgical procedure that I, in many ways, developed.''

"I think that's terrific. You once told me time has a way of teaching us new things.''

Gold was silent for a while, lost in thought.

"You know Elena and I are married now.''

"Yes, I heard. Congratulations. I hope you'll have a long and happy life together. How is she?''

"She's great. I don't know how I got along before I met her.''

"She was the best ER nurse Jefferson ever had.''

"Still is, sir,'' Joe corrected him.

"How's the hospital?''

"Treading water. . . . Barely.''

"How are the new chiefs doing?''

"Terrible. You and I both knew they wouldn't stand a chance. They're unsure enough about themselves medically. As administrators they're nonexistent.''

"It's a big job.''

"Too big, I'm afraid. I mean they try. It's not like they don't care. It's just that supplies, residents, aides, everything seems to be shrinking up."

"I've heard."

"Rumors are flying that Hirshorn is just waiting for the right moment to pull out. Is that true?"

"I don't know. Money is tight."

"You know. You just won't tell me," insisted Joe.

"I have no idea. No one talks to me about Jefferson. Do you blame them? I see that bastard hasn't gotten one of his demands met. I knew it."

Joe closed his eyes. "The only thing he accomplished was to hurt the hospital."

"No, he also managed to hurt me and Bob Watel. I'll never forgive him. He's getting everything he deserved. He sure led his people down a dead end. I hope they just stay there and rot."

"I'm sorry you're still angry."

"I'm sorry I gave in so easily. I should have fought that son of a bitch. I knew it would be the worst thing that could possibly happen. Was I hurt? Sure. Was the hospital hurt? Sure. But it was the people, his people / . . my patients who were destroyed. What kind of leader is that?"

Joe shook his head sadly. There were no answers.

Gold cleared his throat. "Tell me how I can help you. Over the phone you said it was a private matter."

"I want to use your lab to have some food analyzed."

"Food?" Gold was puzzled. "Sure. I have the equipment. It's no problem. But why, if I may ask?"

"I did a portacaval shunt on an eighty-year-old patient. His early post-op recovery was fine. He progressed to solid foods, and I put him on a low salt, high protein diet. He hasn't responded. In fact, he's gaining weight and has developed severe ascites. I tasted the food and it had an aftertaste to it. I want to check it."

Gold raised his eyebrows in surprise. Ruskin was still top of the line. "Do you have it with you?" he asked.

Joe took the container out of the brown paper bag he was carrying.

"Do you want to taste it, sir?"

Gold put his finger in the container. It tasted unusual. Not salty, not sour, but not normal. "Let's go into the lab and see what we can find out."

Joe followed him into the large lab next door to his office. There were twenty technicians working over microscopes, Bunsen burners, and foaming beakers of chemicals. Gold tapped a young Chinese woman on the shoulder. She looked up from what she was working on. "Can you analyze this for me?"

"I'll have the results in ten minutes," she said cheerfully.

Later, as Gold stood reading the technician's report his eyebrows furrowed in dismay.

"What is it, sir? What does the report say?"

"Joe, you sure you ordered the low salt diet?"

"Of course, I'm sure."

"Because the food you brought is loaded with salt."

"That's impossible!" Joe cried. "May I?" He reached over and read the report himself. It was true. The food had a dangerously high level of all the minerals. "But it didn't taste salty," Joe said. "You tasted it yourself."

"Look at the RQ-three column. See that spike."

"Yes. What does that mean?"

"The RQ-three column is a measurement of a type of preservative. It has a strong binding property. It's presence will cover any salt taste. Joe, this food has been treated!"

"So that's the aftertaste."

"Joe, there's absolutely no protein in this food. I'll bet they just use starch fillers and needed the RQ to disguise it. I'm sorry but that's what it would seem to me."

"But why?" Joe was stunned. No wonder Mr. Rivera was getting worse.

"It's cheaper. Doesn't cost the food wholesalers a quarter as much to produce. This kind of stuff is usually reserved for livestock who are being force-fed before slaughter. In a few countries it's illegal."

Joe sat down, still holding the report in his hand. "I just can't believe it," he said.

"You can't fool color spectrophotometry. I'm just surprised you're able to pick it up by taste." Joe told Doctor Gold about the dietician. "Looks like you've opened a Pandora's box. What are you going to do with it now?"

"I don't know." Joe looked at him, distressed. "I just feel sick. Sick that people would sell health care for a buck. Taking advantage of patients. And I'm sure it's just at Jefferson. They know the chances of getting discovered are negligible. I'd like to see this slop being passed off as food in Hirshorn or Presbyterian."

"I'm sure you won't find it there," admitted Gold.

"I discovered it and I'm outraged. But I'll go home tonight and Elena and I will continue to make plans for the next year, when we're out of Jefferson Hospital. And things will go on just like always."

"Maybe you shouldn't leave," Benjamin Gold stated simply.

Joe looked up at him. "It's been tearing me up inside ever since you left. I made a promise and I respect you more than any person I know. I gave you my word."

Gold said nothing for a long time. Then he spoke softly. "I know I asked you for that promise. I didn't want them to hurt you like they hurt me. But we're different people. In many ways I'm happier here in the lab than I was at Jefferson. You have your whole life to live. What's right for me doesn't mean it's right for you. I had no right to ask such a thing of you. You have to live your own life." He put his arm on Joe's shoulder. "Go Joseph, be happy with Elena and do what you know you have to do."

Joe let himself in and collapsed on the white sofa. Elena wasn't home yet and the apartment was dark and quiet. He lay there thinking about his conversation with Gold and the implications it presented. The next thing he knew, Elena was standing over him. "Hi, honey." She kissed him on the nose. "Were you taking a nap?" She walked around the apartment switching on the lights.

"No, just thinking."

"In the dark?"

"I hadn't noticed," he answered despondently.

"Hey, you're in a great mood."

"I went to see Gold today."

"Okay!" She smiled. "What did you find out?"

"Sure you want to hear?"

"I'm sure."

"Mr. Rivera's food is treated. It's ninety-five percent fillers."

"No!"

"It's true. A special preservative is used to hide the taste. Now I know why he wasn't getting any better."

"Joe, that's criminal!" Elena's dark eyes flashed with anger. "How could the hospital allow such a thing to happen?"

"Maybe they didn't know about it."

"But somebody had to know. Somebody had to authorize the purchase order for Mr. Rivera's food."

"That somebody is Ann Marshall. She told me that herself."

"What reason in the world would she have for doing such a thing?"

"Who knows." Joe shrugged his shoulders. "But it's happened, and my patient is getting sick from it."

"What are you going to do?"

"That's what I've been thinking about."

"What did Dr. Gold say?"

"I'll say this for him, he took it better than I did. He told me each man had to make his own choices in life. I have to do what I feel is right."

"And what do you feel is right?"

"I don't know about the future, but I know what's happening now is wrong—dead wrong. It goes against everything I've ever believed in," he said with an anguished look.

"If you know it's wrong, the question is do you want to do something about it?"

"I do and I don't," he mumbled.

"What's that supposed to mean?"

"Of course I want to do something about it," he snapped, "but what? I don't want to break open another hornet's nest."

"You mean you want to help, but you don't want to get too involved?" she asked.

"Can you honestly blame me?" he exploded. "Sure I'm afraid to get involved. I'm afraid of what I might find. I'm afraid of dropping a bomb. When bombs go off, innocent people get hurt. Look what's happened to Gold. And that's all Hirshorn needs is more embarrassing publicity," he said, shaking his head.

She got up and walked over to the window. She studied the traffic jam in front of their building. "Joe," she said slowly, "I think you should tell Ino what's happened."

"Ino! That's exactly what I don't want. He gets hold of this news, he'll turn it into a circus and make himself star of the

283

show. And once again, the only ones that will get hurt are the people."

"And you don't think the people are being hurt right now?" she shouted angrily. "You don't think Mr. Rivera's being hurt? Come on, Joe, you've got your head in the clouds. This situation will never get better by itself. You've got to do something about it."

"And what do you suggest I do," he asked sarcastically, "go tell your darling brother?"

"Yes," she cried. "That's exactly what you have to do. It's the only thing you can do," she pleaded. "And I'll go with you." She was close to tears now, but couldn't stop the rush of words pouring out from her. "Don't let him turn this into a circus and he won't. You can say what you want about him, but he stays and he cares and he tries. And right now, he's the only one who can help us," she said desperately.

They were silent for a long time. Finally, she knelt down beside him and held his hands in hers. "Joe, you can't let your feelings about Ino get in the way of doing the right thing. We've got to go see him. Tell him everything you've found out. It may make no difference, I'm not sure, but I'll feel better just knowing you talked."

He looked into her clear eyes, and he knew there was nothing in this world she could ask him that he could ever refuse.

It was obvious both men were uncomfortable. They hadn't really spoken since the bitter fight in Elena's apartment. Cordially, they shook hands, neither knowing quite what to say.

Finally Ino asked, "Well, what brings you down to the humble People for Progress office?"

Elena looked at Joe hesitantly. "Joe's discovered something that I . . . we think you ought to be aware of."

"Really?" Ino swung his feet on top of his desk and motioned for them to take a chair. "I'd like to hear about it."

Joe began his story. When he got to the part about Ann Marshall, the dietician, Ino sat forward in his seat. "That's it!" he shouted even before Joe had finished. He slammed his right fist into his left palm. "I got him," he said in slow exhaltation.

Elena and Joe were confused. "What's it?" asked Joe.

"Who did you get?" asked Elena.

"Look, Ruskin . . . Joe, I've been doing a little investigating

284

of my own. I've been checking into one Stewart Malcolm, Tanner's chief asshole, and one Ann Marshall, Jefferson's dietician.''

Joe glanced at Elena. She had been right about Ino's hotline. ''What did you find out?'' he asked.

''It seems that the two of them are living high off the hog. Malcolm's even got two addresses. One apartment on East Seventy-first—respectable, well within his means—and then he's got a second little home, a mansion in Connecticut, which I'm sure his constituents know nothing about.''

Ino continued to tell Joe and Elena all about the Wholesale Food Corporation. ''So Malcolm and Ann Marshall are living off the kickbacks they get from the Wholesale Food Corporation.'' Joe was stunned. ''And the Mr. Riveras of Jefferson Hospital are the only ones that suffer.''

''My God,'' said Elena, incredulous, ''that's murder.''

''Dammit!'' hissed Ino, slamming his fist on the desk. ''Ten to one odds this slop is rampant throughout Jefferson. We've all probably eaten it ourselves. The wholesalers make a huge profit and can siphon the legitimate food into the class hospitals.''

''We've got to stop them,'' said Joe.

''We've got to get more proof first,'' said Ino. ''We don't have enough yet to break it to the media.''

''Media?'' Joe turned to Elena, enraged. ''There he goes again! Using situations for his own ego trip.'' The muscles in his face were taut as he faced Ino. ''Remember,'' he said, ''I'm through being a patsy for your political schemes.''

Ino looked at his brother-in-law carefully. ''You know, Joe,'' he said calmly, ''that may have been true at one time. But right now I'm doing a job that I think I'm good at. It's the only thing I know how to do. If you want to call it an ego trip, that's fine. I see it as making a contribution to a place I care about a lot. I did not create this situation, you know that. It's an injustice we both discovered together. When I see something like this, I can't let it die. I'm just doing the best I can, the only way I know how, to change the odds so they work out a little better for us all.''

Elena watched Ino as he spoke. She couldn't help it, she believed him.

Joe felt himself weakening. Elena was right. This thing was too big to let old wounds get in the way. He prayed this time it would be different. He'd have to trust Ino. In the end, he knew it was the only way they could make it work.

*   *   *

Cliff Garvin had an old army buddy who worked at the IRS office in Staten Island. On Saturday, he called him up and after discussing the old days for a while, asked him for a favor.

"No problem at all, Cliff," said the friend. "Now that's Stewart Malcolm, with an e, right?"

"Right, Charlie. It's probably a joint return and his address is Forty-one East Seventy-first Street. As soon as you find it, give me a call, will you?"

"I'll do better than that, Cliff. I'll send you a copy."

Elena and Joe had been busy that Saturday, too, even though it was their day off. They had sampled the meals of ten patients restricted to a special diet and ten patients on a regular diet. They carried these samples over to Gold's lab where he had been waiting anxiously for them to arrive. When the last specimen was tested, there could be no doubt. All of the patients' food had been treated.

"It's a sad commentary on society," Benjamin Gold said wearily as they were preparing to leave.

"We think so too, Dr. Gold," Elena said gently. "That's why we're going to do something about it."

Like any good reporter, Cliff Garvin spent the next two days on his feet. He spoke to everyone he saw coming or leaving the apartment house on 156th Street. He showed Malcolm and Ann Marshall's pictures to the superintendant, the newsboy, and every tenant on the third floor. Two of them, a teenager and an elderly woman, recognized the couple.

"Yeah, I seen 'em," said the straggly youth, chewing a wad of gum. "They only come on Sundays."

"What else do you know?" asked Garvin.

"There ain't no furniture in that apartment."

"How do you know?"

"Me an' my friends bust in."

"Would you be willing to testify in court if you had to, son?"

"What's it worth to you?"

"Plenty," said Garvin.

286

The old woman corroborated the teenager's story. She lived next door to the apartment.

When Garvin received Malcolm's IRS report in the mail, he raced over to the People for Progress office.

"I got it all," he said, shoving the return on Ino's desk.

Ino studied the papers quickly. "He only claimed thirty-six thousand dollars last year. I'd say it's time for your presses to roll."

The dismissal of Stewart Malcolm and Ann Marshall from their respective positions made the first page of the *Post*. There was a photograph of a furtive-looking Malcolm and another of Ann Marshall, in kerchief and sunglasses, being whisked into a courthouse. They were each sentenced to two years in prison. The food scandal at Jefferson was relegated to page three. A federal investigation of the Wholesale Food Corporation was pending.

The papers had a field day with the story, and Cliff Garvin did an additional piece on the "country club" atmosphere of the prison where there were no bars on the cells and two tennis courts for the inmates' use. In a prepared statement to the press Mayor Tanner expressed his shock and disbelief. "It is difficult for me to comprehend the enormity of the crimes committed against the City of New York by people I thought I knew but now find I never really knew at all." He concluded his statement by saying that he still had the greatest belief in the integrity and honesty of civil servants. Privately, he cursed Malcolm's stupidity for getting himself mixed up in the scandal and for getting himself caught. He knew that Malcolm's mistake would cost him dearly.

Ino came over to Joe and Elena's with a pile of newspapers. They were in a festive mood, and Elena was beaming as Joe set the table and Ino scrambled the eggs for their breakfast. She'd waited a long time for a reunion like this.

"Garvin finally got his scoop," said Joe, looking again at the paper. "I'm glad for him."

"Don't be glad for him. Be glad for us," said Ino serenely standing at the stove. "We've got the ammunition now."

"Who are you planning to gun down?" asked Joe with a slight edge.

"Relax, Joe. Only constructive things, right?"

"Right." Elena smiled.

"If we put a push on, right now, the people of the Bronx will come out in force. We've got three months. If we work hard, we'll have a Democratic congressman."

"How's that going to help us?" asked Joe.

"Coletti just about promised me the job of Administrator of Jefferson."

"He did? You don't know much about running a hospital," said Joe.

"I've got some time to learn," smiled Ino. "And besides, I've got some good people to help me."

"We'll give as much as we can," said Joe.

"We're family now," said Elena.

"We're family," repeated Ino.

"What do you want us to do?" asked Joe.

"You stay in the hospital. I'll be fine. I'm on my own territory."

Joe laughed. "Ino, how come your territory keeps getting bigger?"

22

In the next three months Ino's territory advanced to the very edges of the Twenty-first District, and People for Progress were everywhere. In an all out effort to elect Tony Coletti to Congress, Ino Sanchez emerged as the true spokesman for the Democratic party. His name became synonymous with Coletti's. After that, there was no way to stop him. He had the backing of a major party squarely behind him. He was no longer an outsider; he was one of them and the American dream was being ushered in, to the din of steel bands and Columbian reefer.

Tanner, in support of his candidate, came on television to

reveal Ino's past history as a heroin addict. Ino appeared on the evening news two days later demanding a new drug detoxification unit. Tanner asked for a crackdown on crime; Ino was quoted in the *Post* saying "if that happened, there would be no present administration left." Tanner demanded a curb on welfare frauds; Ino appealed for day-care centers and free abortion clinics.

He never flinched. He wore his past as a badge of courage, and he surrounded himself with the people of the street. Every day, he and his men would canvass the community they knew so well. There wasn't a person over eighteen that Ino didn't try to convince to vote for Coletti.

They set up a folding table in front of the Fox Street Supermarket and were giving out free balloons and bubble gum to the kids. Posters and signs written in Spanish were pasted to the walls and taped to parked cars. An elderly woman, carrying two heavy bundles, stopped at the table. She looked quizzically at Ino.

"Can I help you?"

"What is this?" She rested her bags on the side of the table.

"We're People for Progress. We want people to go to the polls and vote."

"For what?"

"Not for what. We're voting for a man."

"Okay. So, who's your man?"

"Tony Coletti, the next Democratic congressman from the Twenty-first District."

"Is this him?" She picked up a flyer with a photograph of Coletti.

"Yes. If you want changes made, right on your block, you let me know and I'll tell him."

"Looks Italian."

"He is. And he's good people."

"You know him?"

"Very well. I know he really wants to help."

"I need help all right. I got a letter. They're tearing my building down in six months. Where will I go?" she asked, biting her lower lip.

"Where do you live?"

"Simpson Street."

He was familiar with the project. "You vote Democrat and I personally guarantee that provisions will be made for you and for everyone else that lives there."

"Are you sure?"

"Positive. I've seen the plans. We can't put them to work unless we win the election."

"What's your name?"

"Inocencio Sanchez."

"Inocencio Sanchez?" She looked at him then started to smile. "I didn't recognize you all grown up. You've changed in fifteen years." There was a twinkle in her eye. "You still don't know me?"

Ino shook his head.

"I'm Mrs. Pacino from the Bay Towers."

"From next door?"

"You do remember." The woman laughed. "I remember you and your sweet sister and your mother, before she died, God rest her soul." She crossed herself. "So now you're a big shot, right?"

"Right." Ino smiled. He remembered her. She was a nice woman.

"And Elena?" she asked. "How is she?"

"Fine. She's a nurse now."

"That's good to hear. You send her my regards. Okay, little Ino"—she laughed, picking up her bundles—"for you, I will vote."

"Great, Mrs. Pacino. I'll see you at the polls. You know where it is?"

"Sure, sure I know where it is." She laughed, walking off. "I should be taking you there."

People for Progress, with Ino at the helm, did not let up. They moved into the Grand Concourse and Ino joined hands with the old block leaders.

He stopped men on their way to work. "You read the papers?" he asked a construction worker.

The man nodded.

"You see what the mayor and his gang do for the people. You want men like that to take care of you?"

"You got a point."

"You want to be ripped off again?" asked Ino.

"No, but how do I know you'll be any better?" he asked.

"Because we can't be any worse."

More doorbells were rung, more candy given away. Inocencio Sanchez was fighting for the gold ring on the political merry-go-round. Whether he got it or not depended on Coletti winning this election. Ino made speeches through a loudspeaker perched on top of a station wagon. At the end of each day, he and his men stood in the subways, greeting the returning hordes with flyers and buttons. It was a con and he knew it; yet not for a single moment did he ever doubt it would work. They covered the Bronx systematically, block by block, day by day, right up until election night.

Ino sat in the hotel room, slowly getting drunk with Tony Coletti. The last returns were trickling in, but it didn't matter anymore. The victory was theirs and they knew it.

"I gotta hand it to you, Ino," Coletti said through the haze of his cigar, "you certainly do have a flair for timing."

"It's my specialty."

"I've never seen the South Bronx turn out like this for an election, and I been in this business thirty years." He let out a loud laugh. "After the Malcolm-Marshall story broke in the papers, the Republicans didn't stand a chance. Yes, sir," he said, putting his arm around Ino's shoulder, "you and I are in business."

"I was hoping you'd feel that way."

"You name it," said Coletti, "and it's yours."

"I already did."

"You did? What do you want?"

"I told you before I got involved in this election. I want to be the administrator of Jefferson Hospital."

Coletti stared at him for a moment then burst out laughing. "You were serious?" He looked into Ino's cold black eyes and had his answer. "But, Ino, be reasonable. I'd have one hell of a job getting you through. The others would vote it down; you have very little experience. Hirshorn is already itching to pull out. You'll start off great without a medical staff."

"Look," said Ino roughly, "I didn't work my tail off for a pat on the behind. I'll get another medical center if I have to."

"But the administrator of Jefferson . . ." Tony shook his head.

"That's right, Tony. I want it, and you're going to see that I get it."

When Tony Coletti woke up the next morning, his ulcer was killing him. He took a long swig from the bottle of antacid

sitting on his nightstand. It would take a lot of pressure on a lo
of people to get Ino what he wanted. He knew Daly and the res
of the board would shit over this one. What the hell, he thought
grabbing his cigar, he'd been through worse. Besides, he owe
him. And if anyone could say anything about Tony Coletti, i
was that he paid his debts.

The mood in Coletti's small office that afternoon was festive
despite the fact that it was too crowded for the eight men and
two women that sat around his desk. They comprised his first
string lineup, the group he never made major decisions without
and they were basking in the glow of the upset. Smoke filled the
room, and a sea of paper coffee cups decorated the desk and the
windowsills. Harry Rose had just finished telling one of hi
famous stories and had gotten a big laugh.

Coletti felt the time was right. "Everyone here is responsible
for the victory," he started. "You've done a great job and you
know it. You also know you couldn't have done it alone. Al
those party workers running their tails off deserve to share in the
credit." Coffee cups were raised and Coletti was cheered again
"For the first time in thirty years, the South Bronx has been
organized. It has become a viable voting power-bloc. The person
responsible for that is Ino Sanchez." The group nodded their
heads in agreement. "Not only did he get us grass roots support
but he managed to get Richard Tanner twice in the bargain
Tanner comes up for re-election in two years and let's hope this
time we strike him out."

Coletti lit his cigar but didn't inhale, silently cursing the
doctor who forbid him to smoke. "I think such work needs to be
rewarded." He put down the cigar. "I propose Ino Sanchez for
the new administrator of Jefferson Hospital."

Bedlam broke loose. "Administrator?" "But, Tony!" "You're
kidding!"

Coletti raised his hands, and the group quieted down. "Now
before you all fly off the handle, let me explain why I think
Sanchez would be a good man for the job. First of all, he's
Spanish and he can relate to the people in a way the usual
white-collar administrator can't."

"That's all well and good," said Harry Rose, "but what's he
know about running a hospital?"

"Probably nothing. But he wants the job."

"*What?* It's going to be chaos. Hirshorn will definitely pul out. They're just waiting for an excuse. And we'll be blamed," said Rose.

"They're going to pull out anyway. They've been quietly looking around ever since Sanchez's takeover," said Coletti.

"I don't think this is a good idea. I don't think we should just agree to whatever he wants if it can make the party look bad," said a small dark-haired woman. "What does he want to be administrator of Jefferson for, anyway?"

"Think about it," said Coletti. "The hospital is the only damn thing in the whole South Bronx that works. People are hurt, they're brought in, they're taken care of. The people can see that and Sanchez understands that."

"But can he run it?" asked Rose.

"Don't underestimate him. He and the People for Progress were an integral part of Jefferson until Tanner kicked them out. Besides, he learns fast. And besides that, we'll be calling the shots; we'll be controlling the purse strings."

"So, Sanchez becomes a puppet?" asked Rose. "I don't know if he'll go for that, Tony."

"He doesn't have a choice. And neither do we. We need Ino Sanchez in our corner."

It was midnight, the following day, before Coletti reached Ino. "Did I wake you?" he asked.

"How'd you do?" asked Ino.

"Take it easy, Sanchez, I got something to say to you."

"What's that?"

"Congratulations, you're the Chief Administrator of Jefferson Hospital."

"Great!"

"Don't thank me, yet. Hirshorn Medical Center is going to be your first casualty."

Ino walked through the ancient corridors and into the over-crowded green wards. He felt a deep sense of pride; he had returned. All along he believed the time would come, but when it actually did, it caught him by surprise. He saw the Emergency Room with its graffiti-marred walls and its bleeding patients left on stretchers in the halls. He had lived with the squalor and the poverty all his life; only now, he had the chance to change it.

His black hair was thick and full, and the same haunting eyes peered out at him each morning. He noticed the small scar on his face as he shaved and he knew very few remembered the way he had looked before the revision. Joe had seen to that. It had been an eyesore, the mark of a loser, but it had been wiped away, just as the traces of his old life had been. Now, only the faint scars remained.

He reorganized hospital procedures to help eliminate waste and free up available funds. He called Joe Ruskin and Tony Coletti for advice on things he was unfamiliar with. He called Herbert Aquedo at Rebirth House for moral support. He went to hospital meetings and community rap sessions and listened. He spoke to doctors and nurses and patients and patients' families. There weren't enough beds to treat the five hundred and fifty thousand people in the South Bronx. A drug rehabilitation program was desperately needed. Old problems—but did he have new answers? The demands the People for Progress had made during the takeover were still just that—demands. He reinstituted the complaint desk and the preventive medicine program. He put Paco in charge of running the People for Progress storefront office. He told him, "any complaints, any hint of medical misconduct, I want to know about it."

He did all that he could do; still the inevitable transpired. Hirshorn Medical Center announced its resignation. Osler didn't have to do much convincing this time; the board voted unanimously to pull out.

"I've already called Harold Krauthammer," said Daly, sitting before the group. "He'll be reassigned back to Hirshorn."

"Why do we have to get rid of Krauthammer?" asked Boise. "Why can't we kick Sanchez out?"

"We've already gone over all this, Dr. Boise," said Daly, trying to remain patient. "The administrator is a political appointment. The Department of Hospitals has gotten the word from Tony Coletti, and there's nothing we can do about it."

"What about our approval?" asked Boise. "Why not refuse to give it?"

"It makes no difference," said Daly. "It's a mere formality, a courtesy, that's all. They'd like our approval of their appointee, but legally they don't need it. Our problem now, Dr. Boise, is not trying to stop Sanchez—it's too late for that—our problem is trying to find a polite way of washing our hands of the whole mess. Now, I beg you to address your thoughts to that issue and that issue alone." William Boise sat back in his chair.

"The only humanitarian way I believe we can bow out gracefully is to find another institution crazy enough to take over the running of Jefferson Hospital. Meanwhile, we'll phase out gently."

"And quickly, I hope," said Osler.

"It should take no more than six months. We'll start the beginning of next month eliminating all ancillary services. After that, we'll drop all the subspecialties. By the following month, we'll have each of the major departments phase down. Then we'll drop Pediatrics, and we'll leave Radiology, Medicine, and Surgery for the last month. By the summer, we ought to be completely out of Jefferson."

"Too bad we can't just leave them holding the bag," said Boise coldly. "It's what Sanchez deserves."

Hirshorn's resignation added new pressures to Ino's life. Almost immediately, he began the arduous task of soliciting help from another hospital. He went from the richest institutions to the not so rich. He spent nights in his small office on the second floor of Jefferson, reading, studying analysis sheets of previous years and past directors. His own reports were detailed, carefully presented. But all viewed this rough talking Puerto Rican with suspicion.

Over the weekend he talked to Joe and Elena in their apartment. "I think I got the plague," he told them. "Seven out of the seven hospitals I went to don't want any part of Jefferson"—he swallowed—"or me."

"It's only been one week since Hirshorn announced its resignation," said Elena hopefully. "We still have six months."

"To tell the truth," confided Ino, "I don't think I'd have any better results if I had six years."

"I think it's obvious," said Joe, "They're so scared of Ino and all he represents, they're not giving any consideration to the precarious position Jefferson is in."

"What do I represent?" asked Ino angrily.

"You have an image as an activist. Don't get pissed; it's well earned. Do you think it would help if someone else went to them?"

"I never thought of that," said Elena.

"Anything could help," said Ino. "But who's going to go?"

"I could," offered Joe.

"Go ahead, give it a try if you like. I just don't think you have enough clout to make any difference. Now, don't you get pissed."

295

"What if we don't get someone?" asked Elena. "What happens to Jefferson then?"

"There is no Jefferson then," said Joe.

"Look, let's try and stay cool," said Ino. "Like you said, we still got six months. Something will come up. In the meantime, Joe, you try to get another hospital, even if it's a shithole. I'll use my influence with the press to keep Jefferson considered top priority. We still have a month before they pull the ancillary services. Elena," he asked suddenly, "what's the first thing scheduled to go?"

"I heard it'll be the home-care unit," she said.

"How many people do they have working the unit?"

"Three—two R.N.s and a P.A."

"What's going to happen to those patients?"

"Most of them are just follow-ups. But a few are really too sick or too old to come to the hospital."

"Okay." Ino decided quickly. "We'll have to phase out all the follow-ups. Do you think one nurse could take care of the really bad cases in the unit?"

"If she worked her tail off, she could." Elena smiled.

"Then that's what it's going to come down to," said Ino.

"But there's some danger involved," said Joe. "You'd need a nurse who was medically trained in all aspects of trauma as well as home care."

"No doubt about it, it's a big job. Only a really qualified person could make it work." Ino looked at his sister. She was sitting on the sofa, knitting. "Elena," he said suddenly, "you'd make a good administrator for the program."

"Me?"

"Sure, why not?" Ino asked, suddenly enthused. "You could do a great job."

"I don't know about that, but I'd do whatever I can to help."

"What do you think, Joe?"

"If she has to take over when home-care phases out, she'd better spend some time there now, to prepare herself, don't you think?"

"It's our only protection, if we don't get anybody by then."

"I'll spend my days off there. I'll start Monday and get acquainted with the cases," said Elena. "No matter how hard it is, I'm sure it can't compare to Emergency Room duty."

"You've never been afraid of hard work, Elena," said Ino "Why are you concerned with that, all of a sudden?"

A funny smile crept over her face. She looked at Joe and they started to laugh. Evidently, there was something Ino had missed. He looked from one to the other, confused.

"Because all of a sudden, Ino—" said Joe.

"You're going to be an uncle," she grinned.

Over the next month and a half, Ino made the support of Jefferson Hospital his personal crusade. He spoke to the philanthropists and the politicians. He spoke to the priests and the scavengers of the streets. He spoke of Jefferson to anyone who would listen. He appeared on Public Television and audiences were suddenly attracted to this handsome dynamic speaker—even if the hospital boards weren't. He spoke of the problems of Jefferson, but he knew the solutions would have to wait. They needed someone to pour money in, lots of it. So far, nobody wanted the job. Ino was discouraged, but he was damned if he'd give up now.

He requested an emergency meeting of the Mayor's Committee of Hospitals. He came to the meeting with a fixed smile on his face. It wasn't much different from the Grand Council of the Toros. The stakes were bigger and the rules more defined. The men dressed better and used bigger words, but they were just as callous and conniving as any gang he'd ever faced. It was the streets all over again.

"Gentlemen," said Richard Tanner, standing in front of the large conference table, "I know you would like to get home, but we do have one important item on the agenda: Jefferson Hospital and its future." He shot Ino a supercilious look. "In view of Hirshorn's decision to phase out of Jefferson, I believe we have two alternatives. One is to rezone the specialties to other hospitals closest to the area. The other is to sink money into Jefferson and at the same time look for another institution to take over. Both alternatives have their drawbacks. I'd like to throw this item out on the floor for open discussion."

The administrator of Bronx General waved his hand. "I'm all in favor of trying to save Jefferson. It's a depressed area and they need their own institution." His hospital was in Riverdale, the upper-middle-class community lying on the northern edge of the borough. Just the thought of the residents of the South Bronx streaming through his emergency room would have the exclusive community up in arms. "It's going to put a far greater burden on the rest of us if we try to shoulder Jefferson on a permanent basis."

"I couldn't disagree more," snapped the administrator of Morrison Hospital. "Do you know what kind of financial responsibility we're talking about if we decide to keep Jefferson afloat when and IF we can find someone to take over."

"I think Mr. Sanchez's viewpoint is clear to the Committee, but just as a matter of record, I'd like to hear his comments. From a professional point of view, of course."

Ino ignored the dig and stood up. The administrator of Morrison leaned over and whispered to his neighbor. "Sure, Jefferson folds, he's out forty thousand dollars a year." It was loud enough to be heard. Tanner smiled and quickly took his seat.

"In going over the annual budget," started Ino, "I discovered that one-point-one million dollars are earmarked for ancillary services at Morrison Hospital. The running of their satellite facilities alone cost two hundred fifty thousand dollars a year. That's a quarter of a million dollars more than Jefferson is receiving in one area alone." He turned to the administrator of Morrison.

"That's right," said the administrator, "and it's money well spent. The satellite facilities are important. If people are too far from Morrison, we can offer them a close care center to handle the minor outpatient emergencies. Those satellite facilities are located in some of the most depressed areas."

"Jefferson is located in the most depressed area."

"What has one thing got to do with another?"

"Plenty. We provide services for many of the people in that area anyway. Why not spend the money where it's needed more?"

"Certainly, you're not suggesting stopping those services?" interrupted Tanner.

"That's exactly what I'm suggesting, Mr. Mayor. We have to cut back where we can. I'm asking the administrator of Morrison to cut back a little on the satellite facilities and give the money to Jefferson. That way, both of us can continue to exist."

"You can fend for yourself, Sanchez," snapped the administrator. "None of Morrison's money is going to go to save a drowning ship."

"Look," pleaded Ino to the rest of the Committee, "all I'm

298

saying is that Jefferson needs money to continue on a day-to-day basis. Morrison has that money.''

''The money is earmarked for Morrison and it stays with Morrison,'' said Tanner brusquely. ''If there's not enough money for Jefferson, then it will simply cease to exist.''

Ino flashed Tanner a deadly stare. ''I promise you, Mr. Mayor, Jefferson will never cease to exist.''

Hirshorn kept to its schedule. All ancillary services were dropped. Elena took over the home-care unit, and Ino put a skeleton staff on the other services. Still, he wondered how long they could exist this way. Next week the subspecialties were scheduled to go. No big deal, the hospital could still run without them, but this was only the beginning. Unless another hospital came through with funds, Jefferson was doomed. He felt like the boy who was trying to plug up the dam with his fingers.

Ino drove up the ramp and saw Roberto. ''How's it going?''

''Quiet this morning,'' said Roberto.

''I'm glad it's quiet someplace,'' said Ino. ''Can you keep an eye on my car for a few minutes? I should be coming right out.''

''Sure, Ino.'' Roberto smiled. ''But you don't have to worry about getting ripped off.''

Ino looked at the '73 Dodge with pride. The hood was scratched, the right fender dented, but it was the first car he had ever owned. ''That's why I bought it.'' He smiled, running into the building.

He met Mrs. Cleveland at the nurses station in the ER. ''How are we doing?'' he asked.

''No problems here, Ino. Everyone's showing up, but for how long, I can't say. There's lots of talk.''

''What about the wards?''

''I've got enough to keep me busy down here. You'll have to find out yourself.''

He walked to the elevator and let out a small sigh of relief. As long as the Emergency Room was still fully staffed, things were all right. On the second floor he checked with an attractive blond nurse on duty.

''It's a good thing we're slow today,'' she told him. ''Two nurses called in sick. They were fine yesterday. Between you and me, I think they're out looking for new jobs.''

"As long as you stay, we'll be okay." Ino flashed her a brilliant smile and she blushed.

Enrique was carrying blood to the ward. Ino caught up with him. "This place is as nervous as a cat in heat," said Enrique. "Everyone's wondering when they're going to get the ax."

"I know," said Ino miserably.

"They cut Central Supply back. We're washing the Ace bandages and using them twice, but the patients are really bitching."

"How can they tell?"

"They looked frayed. Ino, what are we going to do?"

"Hope for a miracle," he said glumly.

Joe returned from dinner to find Kendricks huddled over a young black man in the trauma room. He was lying face down on the stretcher with a two-foot wrought iron rod sticking through his thigh. Between his short labored breaths, his deep moans could be heard outside the room.

"What happened?" asked Joe.

Kendricks looked up, relieved. "He's a criminal."

Joe felt his pulse. "Did you give him any Demerol?"

"No. Sergeant Murray wanted to cuff him, but he agreed to leave him alone if I promised not to sedate him."

"The man's in pain," said Joe, disgusted.

"That's the point. We figured he couldn't run with that rod. It would hurt too much."

"Terrific." Joe filled a syringe with 10 mg of Valium and started to inject it into the man. "How did it happen?"

"He tried to mug somebody and a patrol car saw him. He tried to escape over a fence and slipped. They had to call the rescue squad to torch the picket off."

"Is he ready to go up?" asked Joe, noting that the sedative was beginning to work on the man.

"I guess so. X-ray shows it missed the femur."

"Let's go," said Joe. They maneuvered the stretcher down the hall until they reached the elevators. The gates were closed. "We should have called ahead," he said, banging on the steel-mesh gate. There was no response. "What the hell is going on?"

After a few minutes, a guard came strolling down the hall. "What's wrong with the elevators?" asked Joe.

"Something electrical. They haven't worked in two hours."

"Two hours! How do we get this man up to the OR?"

"Beats me," said the guard, continuing along.

"Hold it! Kendricks, get back to the nursing station and get a hundred milligram syringe of Demerol. You," he said, pointing to the guard, "stay here and watch the patient."

"Where are you going?" asked Kendricks, adjusting his glasses.

"I'll get Ino. Maybe he'll know what's happening."

Joe ran up the stairs and swung left, entering the administration wing. He ran into Ino's office, out of breath. "The elevators aren't working."

"Beautiful," said Ino, reaching for the phone.

"We have a man in the hall who has to go up to the OR."

Ino dialed a number and waited. "Shit." He slammed the phone down. "Engineering doesn't answer. Come on."

They ran back to the elevator. The man was still lying on his stomach, but he had risen out of his stupor and was crying out hysterically. Kendricks came running down the opposite hall, holding the syringe. Ino started to bang on the gate.

"I already tried that," said Joe.

"Where the hell is the operator?"

"He's obviously not around."

"Stay here," said Ino. "I'll run downstairs and check the boiler room."

Joe administered the injection, which calmed the patient almost immediately. Then they stood waiting until Ino reappeared from the stairwell.

"The starter is jammed."

"We'd better transfer the patient," suggested Kendricks.

"That'll take thirty minutes," said Joe.

"More than that," said Ino. "I called from downstairs. All three ambulances are out on call."

"How about a police car?" asked Joe.

"They'll refuse," said Ino. "I went through something like this two weeks ago when one of our wagons broke down. They said they can be sued if anything happens to the patient, and the captain has passed down an order."

"What do we do now?" said Kendricks, looking at Joe.

"Don't ask me," said Joe. "He's the administrator of the hospital."

Ino stared at the patient. He grabbed the sheet and began covering the man, wrapping his legs tightly together. Then he lifted both feet. "Take his head," he ordered. "We'll carry him upstairs."

301

"What about the stretcher?" asked Kendricks.

"It'll never turn the corners," said Ino.

Struggling with their strange cargo, they finally reached the third-floor landing. "I'm exhausted," said Kendricks, sweating profusely as he supported the man's back. "Let's lay him down for a minute."

"We'll rest when we get him on the table," snapped Joe.

Slowly, laboriously they continued until they reached the fourth floor. As they carried the patient into the Operating Room a nurse appeared. "Haven't you guys ever heard of elevators?" she asked.

Ino glared at the nurse. "The elevator is broken."

"Oh no! What'll we do with him once the case is over? My shift ends in two hours."

"Don't worry. I'll get that elevator working if I have to drag Tanner down here to fix it," said Ino, running down the stairs.

An hour later he reappeared with grease all over his shirt and hands. "It's fixed."

"Great, how'd you do that?" asked Joe, looking up from the open wound.

"Enrique hot-wired the motor. He's always had a knack for anything electrical."

"That's not a solution."

"I know. But we'll have a new motor installed by tomorrow."

"I've heard that before," said Joe, continuing to explore the wound.

"I guarantee it. The head of supply has already signed the invoice."

"How'd you do that?"

"He and I share a secret."

"What's that?"

"He likes young guys."

"So?"

"His wife wouldn't be too happy to know it," said Ino, finally allowing himself to smile.

When he got back to his office, two attendings were waiting for him. One was Dr. Trotman, from the ENT department, and the other was Dr. Flaisher, from Hematology. Dr. Trotman was holding an envelope. From the expressions on their faces, Ino could tell it was not going to be a happy meeting.

"Mr. Sanchez," said Trotman, "I received this letter from

Hirshorn Medical Center today." He handed Ino the letter. "I'll save you the trouble. It says as of next Wednesday, they can no longer guarantee my paycheck." His face was a bright red.

"I got one, too," said Dr. Flaisher. "Only I have two weeks."

"What's going to happen?" demanded Trotman.

"We're doing the best that we can," faltered Ino, "under the circumstances."

"What does that mean?" asked Trotman. "Who's going to pay me after Wednesday?"

"I'm sure something will be settled by then," said Ino.

"I got a wife and three kids to feed. I'm not doing this for the glory of it."

"I understand your position completely, Doctor."

"Then you'll understand why I'm resigning tomorrow," said Dr. Flaisher. "I've advised Dr. Trotman to do the same. We've got to start looking for work that will pay."

"Now wait a minute, gentlemen," began Ino. "You're jumping to conclusions. We may be in a whole different ball game by tomorrow. If you leave, others will follow and Jefferson will fold. If you stay, we've got a fighting chance."

"I care about Jefferson as much as anyone," said Trotman. "It's just that I have to take care of my family."

"Dr. Trotman, I will personally guarantee your paycheck if you promise to stay. At least give it a couple of weeks."

"I can't survive for a couple of weeks without eating."

"I will pay you out of my own pocket if I have to," urged Ino. "You have my word on that." He turned to Dr. Flaisher. "The same goes for you, Doctor. We're in this together." Ino extended his hand. "Deal?"

The two doctors looked at each other. Reluctantly, they shook hands. "But only for two weeks," said Trotman.

After they left, Ino slumped into his chair and loosened his tie. What a mess. He reached over to the buzzer on his desk.

"Could you get Tony Coletti on the phone for me?" he asked the secretary. A few moments later, his buzzer sounded and he picked up the phone.

"How are you, Tony?"

"Working my butt off. You think it's easy being a congressman? I haven't had a good night's sleep since I got into office. What's up?"

"We've got problems."

"How much is this going to cost me?"

"It won't cost you anything."

"When is Hirshorn going to pull out?"

"Three months. But from the way things are going around here, you'd think it was tomorrow."

"That bad, huh?"

"They've cut the ancillary services. ENT and Rheumatology are scheduled for next week. It's not good."

"Have you gotten any nibbles from the big medical complexes?"

"Not one."

"I figured as much, because I heard Hirshorn has been trying to convince some of these hospitals to do it. And if they haven't had any luck . . ."

"There's something you can do right now."

"Here it comes."

"Look, Tony, Jefferson is sure to fold unless we can sink some money in right away."

"And where do you suggest getting this money?"

"Morrison Hospital. They have two hundred fifty thousand dollars earmarked for satellite facilities. I want to take that money and use it at Jefferson. We can handle the patients; we already handle a lot of them and they don't amount to that many in actual numbers. Ninety percent of the money goes for salaries, anyway. We can stretch it pretty far if we have to. Morrison just won't have the extras, but it'll have enough to live on."

Coletti thought for a moment then he said, "So now you're the Robin Hood of the South Bronx." He let out a loud laugh. Ino was afraid to breathe. "Okay, Ino, I'll see what I can do. I don't like to see Jefferson go down any more than you do. Just remember, this is it. No more siphoning off and rearranging. You just bought yourself a little time."

"About a month's worth," said Ino, elated.

23

She came to look forward to each day as she never had before. For the first time since she was a small girl, her life had reached a high plateau of serenity. Each morning, as she watched Joe get out of bed, she felt blessed. Their love had grown and expanded beyond anything she believed possible. So much had happened over the past year, and now it was finally all right. If only another hospital would take over the responsibility of Jefferson, life would be perfect. Ino had proven himself a man of his word; he was devoted and concerned. And when she noticed her thickening waist and the small bulge in her belly, she knew at last they had become a family.

Right from the beginning, Elena enjoyed the home-care nursing unit. After years in the Emergency Room, it was refreshing to work with patients who weren't so sick. The nurses in the program were old friends, only too happy to show her the ropes. She'd have little trouble, she decided, taking over the unit herself.

Early Tuesday morning she and Joe sat in the surgical office. He slammed the phone down in disgust. "That's the third time I've been told, 'He's in a conference and will be unavailable for appointments.' I'm going to have to go down and sit in each bastard's office until they have to see me."

"Something will come up," encouraged Elena. "I just feel it."

"It better be damn soon. The Department of Medicine is scheduled to vacate in five weeks. Once that happens, we don't have a hospital."

Elena scanned the home-care list of patients who were scheduled to be seen that day. "Right now, the only thing we don't have is a home-care program. I can carry on for a while, but maybe we ought to cut back and just staff the major sectors. We're never going to be able to provide all the services we used to."

"Call down to the ER and get Mrs. Cleveland. She said she'll be able to give you a hand."

"That's fine for today. But then what?"

"Maybe I'll have gotten something going by then."

"I hope so."

"I just wish I didn't feel responsible. Somehow I knew the food scandal would explode in our faces."

"We have to keep going with what we have. At least we're all together." She smiled.

"We might soon be the only ones left." Joe frowned, as he put on his jacket. "I'm off to Presbyterian. Board meetings can't take forever."

"I'd take something to read," she said.

"Shit. I'll throw a seizure in their office. Then they'll have to see me."

"They'll probably admit you to the psych ward." She smiled.

"Would you visit me?"

"I'd bring you cigarettes every Friday."

"I'll call when I'm through." He planted a quick kiss on her forehead.

"I'll be back by noon," she said. "Only two patients have to be seen. One's Enrique Rivera."

"Mr. Rivera? He didn't show up for clinic last week. I hope he's all right."

"After what he's been through? I'm sure he'll be fine."

"Tell him I asked about him. Also better draw an amylase and SM-twelve."

"Good luck."

"I love you," said Joe, rushing out.

Elena began the three-block walk down Intervale Avenue to Rivera's apartment. She passed two young mothers in sleeveless dresses sitting on a bench, rocking their carriages. She smiled to herself as she hurried by. In six months or so she, too, might be out on a sunny day, giving their baby some fresh air. She was filled with a sense of anticipation.

Enrique Rivera lived in a run-down building that was scheduled for renovation within the year. It had broken windows and missing fire escapes. Scattered glass and paper bags of trash lay on the sidewalk. Three boys, twelve or thirteen years old, sat on the crumbling steps in front of the building, bored and restless. She climbed the six flights to Mr. Rivera's apartment. Small piles of decayed garbage met her on each landing. She covered her nose and mouth with her hand and wondered if she'd ever get used to the smell. She reached his door.

"Elena?" The wrinkled face offered a crooked smile. "What did I do to deserve such a treat?"

She laughed at his flattery. Even at eighty, he was a lady's man. His home was a single large room with a bed pushed to one side and a stove and sink at the other end. There was a small crucifix hanging on the wall above the table and two chairs. Amidst all this, something good was cooking in the old pot on the stove. She sat him down on the bed and took his pulse and blood pressure and drew the blood.

"How am I?" he asked.

"You're doing fine." She smiled.

"So the examination is over?"

"The examination is over."

"Good"—he decided—"now we will eat." Slowly he made his way to the stove.

He was pleased when she sampled his chicken.

"You take good care of yourself," she told him. He was glad he had the strength to do that.

"Doctor Ruskin said I should come to your home and you will cook for me."

"We'd love to have you as our guest," she said. "We owe you a lot." She stared at the back of his leathery brown hands and watched the arthritic fingers grasp the handle of the fork.

"You seem happier than when I saw you last," he said.

"I'm going to have a baby." She smiled.

"Then we must make a toast, yes?" He raised his glass to hers. "May it be the first of many."

"Thank you," she replied, pleased.

"I'm a great-grandfather now, three times. My sons are old men. My wife is gone. Yet I am not alone." He looked at the crucifix.

The boys outside the building passed a joint between them.

"Shit," said the leader, "nothing's happening."

"Let's get some action going," said the one with the pimply face.

307

"Like what?" asked the youngest.

"How about the firemen?" offered the pimply face. "We can always get them to move their butts."

"We can pull the alarm up the street," said the leader.

"We can blow a little smoke around this building," said the young one, nodding back against the wall.

"We can block their path, line up some garbage cans in the street," said the pimply face. Electricity charged the air; the boys had found their kicks.

Rolf Jensen sat on his bench in the corner of the crowded kitchen of Engine Company 80, greeting each arriving member of his shift with a short nod of his head. The younger men, "Johnies," would nod back respectfully and quickly seat themselves at the long tables. The two shifts intermingled easily, discussing the problems of the day and the inspection tour planned for later. Jensen's stature had been gained through countless campaigns. Half the men in the room, at one time or another, owed their lives to the plucky veteran, and among the young, tales of his bravery were exchanged and added to daily.

A swarthy man wearing a soiled T-shirt entered the room and stalked over to the corner where Jensen sat. "Hey, Nozzle, how you doing?" he asked, sliding down the bench to face his friend.

"Hello, Eddie. How come you're not eating?" Jensen broke into his slow, easy smile. "The slop Smith cooks . . . it's bad enough going down. But each time it comes up, it tastes worse." He laughed.

But neither man was in the habit of eating for the first few hours after coming on duty. They joked around the issue, never acknowledging their pattern, as if they were afraid to admit to each other that after all these years, they were still nervous.

"How's the addition coming?" asked Eddie.

"I've already studded out the walls. Lois's brother is going to give me a hand with the plasterboard."

"Should be beautiful, if you ever get it done."

"I'll finish before spring. Now that the kids are older, they each need a room of their own."

Eddie nodded. "I heard we're up for inspection," he groaned.

"Not this week. It's Ladder Company Twenty's turn."

"So we get to shine brass. I don't know which one is worse," said Eddie.

"Whichever one we're up for." Jensen smiled.

"You're right." Eddie laughed. "Shit, Nozzle. If I was in your shoes, I'd have checked it in a long time ago. You could go out on a disability."

"Come on. For what?"

"Your throat."

Jensen swallowed. "I'm fine. I've been back five months. I never notice it. Besides, live on half pay? I couldn't manage," admitted Jensen.

"You could always get another job."

"I'm a fireman. What else could I do?"

"Shit, with your pull you could make out just selling insurance through the union."

Jensen's blue eyes closed painfully. "I would never do that, take advantage. No, one more year and with my promotion points we'll just be able to make out."

"You've been saying that for three years. Face it, Nozzle, you're just a mangy firedog who can't exist without eatin' smoke."

"You're different?" asked Jensen. "I thought you were going to transfer to a quieter company."

"I withdrew my request," admitted Eddie.

"I know." Jensen smiled.

"As long as I have to put in the hours, I may as well be working."

"Yes. Of course," Jensen said politely.

"Well, I've been here for over ten goddamn years!"

"Yes."

"Shit, Nozzle. Okay, so we're both just a couple of mangy firedogs who need the action. We don't deserve better."

"We are what we are," replied Jensen philosophically. "I just hope it's a quiet day."

The oldest boy slouched against the brick wall, peering down the alley. The pimply boy appeared and began swaying toward him, carrying a large gasoline can in both hands.

"You got it?" The leader checked.

The boy nodded, setting the can down. "High-test. I figured it would add some color."

The leader smiled. "Where's Miranda?"

"We found some cartons behind the liquor store. He'll be back in a couple of minutes."

"Good. I want to get the street blocked off before we send it up. Leave the can here, this won't take long."

The thin boy appeared and leaving the gasoline and cartons in the alley; they walked down the block.

"Fuck. They're all loaded with junk. I'm not bustin' my balls liftin' one of these."

"Maybe we can roll it," said the leader, tilting one of the overflowing cans on its edge. Together they began rolling the garbage can toward the street. Attracted by the harsh, scraping sound and garbage splattering all over the sidewalk, several passersby stopped to study them.

"Fuck. Everyone's looking. Besides, it'll take half an hour to get enough of these shit piles moved to do anything," complained the youngest one.

"Just stay cool. Set it down. Here, let's have a smoke."

The trio was still being scrutinized by a middle-aged couple who had stopped thirty feet away. "Son of a bitch squares. Why don't they just keep movin'?"

"They won't report us?"

"What they goin' to report us for? Livin' here? Movin' some of this crap off the sidewalk?"

The couple gave one last glance and then proceeded on their way. "See, I told you they'd split."

"Still want to block off the street?"

"It sure would be something to see those hot dogs' faces when they'll come barrelin' down the street, lookin' so fuckin' high and mighty on their big fancy wheels. They'll look like big jerkoffs if they're stopped by a few kids."

"I got it. We'll block them off with a car. They can't move a car too easy. 'Specially, if there's no tires left."

"Where we goin' to find a car?" asked the youngest.

"They keep some of the cabs on that lot on a Hundred and Thirtieth."

"There are gates."

"What about the hospital lot?" asked the leader.

"No good, they have a guard."

"That old piece of shit? He spends half his time at the diner."

"Then let's go. I could use a hamburger," the pimply one joked.

310

"How about one well done?" said the leader, pushing his friends and joining in the laughter. "Real chaarrrcoaalbroiled."

Elena and Enrique Rivera had finished eating. "Delicious. And I was worried that you'd have no one to take care of you. When you come visit us, I'll let you make the meal." She laughed.

"Thank you," he said humbly. "But you still haven't told me why you're here. I was expecting the old nurse."

"She won't be coming anymore. For now, you're looking at the entire Jefferson Hospital Home-Care Nursing Service."

"The trouble at the hospital? I heard. But you shouldn't be wasting time here. There are sicker people who need you."

"We were worried when you didn't keep your clinic appointment."

"Last week? It was raining. And I'm not as strong as I was. Three blocks is a long walk for me now." He sighed.

"You look better than I've seen you."

"I do?" He laughed. "Well, I feel better. But when I was young . . . ah, I was like a bull. I carried the sugar on my back fourteen hours a day. And still, at night I danced with all the pretty girls."

Elena knew she should be leaving, but she wanted to do more. He had so little, yet, indirectly he was the reason Joe would remain here, in her community, with her. She walked over to the counter and turned on the radio. "Would you like to dance with me, Mr. Rivera?" She smiled.

"I would love to," he said, leaning his gnarled weakened body against her.

They parked the car at the end of the block, leaving it running.

"We shoulda' copped that Lincoln. That's a boss car. It's got stereo," said the pimply boy.

"Big fuckin' deal. This'll do for what we need. We're not goin' cross country. Let's get cookin'," the leader said with a cruel smile.

They dragged the cartons and gasoline can into the main lobby of the apartment house.

"Stack 'em behind the staircase. We'll see if the firemen can fly."

311

"What about the people?" asked the youngest, suddenly frightened.

"This blaze isn't going anywhere. The only thing we're going to fry are some shit-eating rats. Come on, pour the gas."

The pimply one took the can and began to douse the cartons.

"Don't use all of it," the leader warned, grabbing the can and pouring a thin trail out to the entrance.

"You wait here," he ordered. "We'll set up the roadblock. Torch it when I give the signal," he said throwing him the matches.

The two boys ran back to the car. The leader slammed the gearshift into reverse and the car swerved into the center of the narrow street and continued backward up the block.

"This'll be fine." He laughed, seconds later cutting the wheel. The Ford now stood across the center of the street. He pulled the ignition wires apart. The car coughed twice and then stopped.

"How we goin' to yank the tires?" asked the youngest, opening the door to his side.

"Shit. Just pull the pins on the valves. They'll be flat in a minute."

They knelt down on either side of the car and began twisting the fine steel pins. After several turns, their efforts were met with the high-pitched rush of escaping air. They shifted to the rear tires. As the car settled they began running back down the empty street to the entrance where the pimply boy waited.

"Now!" the leader yelled.

The boy struck the match, looked up and down the block, and then dropped it face down into the pool at his feet. Red yellow flames shot up, and he watched, hypnotized as a low hedge of fire crept, serpentine, back into the lobby.

The song had finished, and the old man leaned over Elena, exhausted.

"Thank you," she said graciously. "You dance beautifully."

"Thank you. It's been long. If I was younger, I would sweep you around the room. You're a beautiful young woman. Strong. Kind. I feel the life in your body. And I am happy for you. I've lived a long time," he said. "Perhaps too long."

"Life strengthens, you know," said Elena, her eyes clouded.

"Yes," he said.

"Let me help you."

"I am tired," admitted the old man.

"Would you like to lie down for a while?" she asked. He curled up contentedly in the bed, and she covered him with the rough woolen blanket.

She had just started washing the dishes when she smelled the smoke.

As the two short bells began to ring out, Rolf Jensen was already off his bench and running towards the apparatus room. By the time the ninth bell of the fourth group had ended he had already grabbed his favorite hooked crowbar from the wall. The voice alarm blared, "Twenty-one-forty-nine . . . Twenty-one-forty-nine Intervale Avenue. Engine Company Eighty. Chief goes." He should have known. It was one of the busiest boxes in one of the busiest companies in the city. Jensen was already reviewing in his mind the location, with the liquor store on the corner and the two hydrants, as he slid down the pole. He grabbed the rubber-covered rear crossbar with his right hand and began to slide into his left boot as the driver gave one short warning blast on the air horn and began moving out. The other men leaped on the rear and the pumper began roaring down the street.

"I bet it's a false alarm," yelled Eddie over the roar of the air horn and the sirens.

"You never know," said Jensen, scanning the sky over the sector.

"It's too damn early in the day. Five to one it's a false alarm. Nothing burns now." He slipped on his turnout coat. "The people only want to see fire against the night sky."

"Get your helmet on. This looks like a beauty," said Jensen, suddenly icy voiced, as the heavy cloud of smoke became visible. As the pumper turned around the corner the brakes began to screech and the men were tossed against the piled hose as the fire engine came to a sliding stop. Jensen leaned over the side and was the first of the men in the rear to view the crippled car. "My Lord," he said, grasping the full implications as he began to run to the obstacle. The driver had gotten out also and together they pulled open the door.

"It's been hotwired. They got the tires," said the driver. Jensen looked down the street and saw the flames shooting out the second-story window. He reached inside and released the brake. He grabbed the shoulder of the driver. "We'll blast through it with the truck."

"And fill out twelve reports if there's a dent? Like hell! Let's get the Chief."

"I'll take the responsibility," Jensen said in a measured voice. The driver stared into Jensen's cold blue eyes and nodded. They ran back to the engine cab.

"I'm gonna' back it up. I need more speed," he said grinding the gears. As the pumper reversed direction it just missed the chief's car as he came racing around the corner.

"What are you doing?" he yelled out the window as Engine 20 shifted into first and began screaming down the street toward the parked car.

"Try to slide by," said Jensen, leaning to his right.

"There's no room. Hold on, Nozzle. I used to drive figure of eight demolition." He laughed as the engine bore forward against the lowered left rear panel, lifting the car up and over. The firemen cheered and within two minutes the pumper churned to a stop in front of the apartment. Two fifty-foot hoses had already been attached, and Eddie darted through the shaking, coughing tenants who had made their way out of the building. He crossed the street to make the connection at the hydrant space.

Jensen dropped the bridge to the two and one half inch hose and ran into the lobby. He carefully scanned the room, assessing each area. The main blaze was coming from behind the stairway. Already high flames were licking around and eating into the second landing. Part of the side wall had caught on, and the beams above were heating up quickly. He glared at the can lying against the wall. He ran back to one of the younger men who was carrying the walkie-talkie. He pushed the transmission button.

"Engine Twenty to Battalion Three."

"Battalion Three responding," squawked the chief.

"We're on the fire, Chief. It's bad. We're going to need a ladder company and a couple of extra lines. Get someone to run my haligan tool in. I left it on the truck."

"Ten-four," came the reply as the smoke gathered. Jensen felt the scar in his neck tighten into a sharp spasm, and he gasped. He dropped to one knee, slipping on his air pack. Why was he still doing this?

"Think anyone is up there?" asked the Johnny, lifting his mask.

Jensen studied the fire, now covering over the beams. "I hope not," he said, grabbing the outstretched crowbar from the panting aide and hurdling up the stairs.

Elena ran to the bed.

"Wake up! Please!" She shook the old man.

"¿Por qué?" he asked, still half asleep.

"Fire! We have to get out of here," she screamed, helping him stand up. They walked to the window, and Elena set the old man against the wall. She tried to force the warped frame up, futilely pushing with all her strength. She ran to the nearest chair and grabbing it by one leg hurled it through the bottom pane. There was a shattering of glass and she pushed her head through the opening. The fire escape was three windows over. As she traced its path down the building she cried out in dismay. The lowest two levels had broken off, and one of the rusted landings twisted loosely, banging against the brick. Someone was running down the alley towards the street. She tried to call out. The blare of the air horns and sirens filled the air, and the man continued, never looking up. She took one deep breath of the clear fresh air and pulled herself back inside. The top layer of the room was now completely filled with smoke and her eyes began to tear against the irritation. The firemen had been called but the alley was empty. Even if they were discovered, the old man would never survive a four-story jump. The stairway was the only answer.

She half-carried Enrique Rivera to the door, and they pushed through. There was a blast of heat, and a curtain of black, thick smoke made vision impossible. Leaning against the wall, they edged forward. The old man began to cough and sob and fell to his knees. Elena knelt down and began to lift him by the shoulders. There was a muffled gurgle deep in his throat and vomitous sticky secretions poured out, over her hands. She felt his pulse. It was thready. She began crawling along the landing to the staircase. She looked down. A wall of exploding flames, the red yellow peaks scorching up against the hissing ceiling, was all that remained. Her eyelids were swollen half shut. Frantically, she began crawling down the hall and dragging the old man by his feet, back into the apartment. She slammed the door shut. She ran to the bed. Stuffing a blanket under the crack where acrid smoke was still drafting into the room, she collapsed onto the floor.

Rolf Jensen had somehow managed to make it to the third-story landing. He looked up. The entire staircase was totally consumed and the flames were shooting up to the ceiling. Methodically, he checked each corner with his flashlight. Then, he saw something moving against the far wall. A huge cloud of smoke enveloped his mask, and he pulled it down, rubbing his eyes with his grimy worn gloves. There was something moving. *Father in Heaven! Someone was up there!* He wheeled around and began running down the staircase. He tripped against a broken step and fell, sliding on his back, to the second landing. Eddie had dragged the big line up and with two aides securing the hose, was cascading water against the scorched far wall. They looked down and saw Jensen, who had already made it to his knees. He was jabbing his index finger, pointing upstairs. Eddie transferred the hose and came running over. "Are you okay, Nozzle?"

"Someone's up there!" he cried. "Where's the ladder company?"

Eddie shrugged his shoulders. Jensen ran over to the man carrying the walkie-talkie.

"Engine Twenty to Battalion Three."

"Battalion responding."

"There's someone up on the fourth landing. Get a ladder up there. There's no staircase left!"

"Company Twenty has just arrived. Ten-four." Jensen threw the squawk box angrily on the floor and began running down to the lobby.

Elena lay sprawled over the old man, blindly inching up his legs. It was cool on the floor, and she was able to breathe easier. She felt his neck and then his open mouth. There was a small gasp—then silence pierced by the steaming hiss of the water being pumped from the three hoses working beneath them. She felt his chest. There was no motion. She leaned over his mouth and gave three short bursts, breathing her life's air down his throat. He did not move. She kissed him quickly and began crawling desperately back toward the open window. A singed beam, already gnawed in half, collapsed, pinning her leg. Ferociously, she began kicking out, scorching her arm as she tried to free herself from the heavy stake.

Rolf Jensen ran out of the building, stumbling towards the large hook and ladder. The ladder was perched against the third-floor corner window, and the nozzle man was already flooding the area. Jensen leaped up on the truck and pulled off his air pack.

"It's the fourth floor," he yelled to the man at the swivel control.

The man looked at him blankly. Jensen began running up the ladder and finally reaching the fireman holding the hose, grabbed at his ankle. "Step back," he ordered. He waved his hand, and the control man extended the ladder.

"Let's go. There's someone up there," said Jensen, scurrying up to the next level.

The deepening fumes began to suffocate her, and she gasped from the toxic smoke collecting in her chest. She regained consciousness, taking deep slow breaths. She thought of her baby growing inside of her, and she worried the smoke would effect him. *Please, God, he shouldn't be damaged.* She closed her eyes as the hungry flames continued forward, devouring everything in their path. She thought of Joe as the noxious gas began to disseminate through her bloodstream. She wanted to tell him . . . a low moan, half human, half animal formed on her lips. She was with Ino in Puerta del Mar, playing in the open fields. As the heat thrust it's heavy blanket against her, forcing the last breath from her lungs, she knew nothing could hurt her ever again.

Rolf Jensen swung the haligan tool through the window. He scanned the floor and saw Elena lying on her side. He put one leg up on the ledge and grasping the windowsill, lifted himself up. There was a sudden, deep, horrible tearing sound, and as Rolf Jensen was about to put his boot down the entire floor opened up in a brilliant white burst and then disappeared into the

317

searing inferno. Jensen grasped the windowsill and looked down into the crater. He felt the arm of the fireman grasp him around his chest. He began to cry. Maybe everyone was right. Maybe it was time to give this up.

24

Joe got into his car and sat there, staring straight ahead. The meeting with the two administrators had been a total bust. They listened to what he said, but he knew he was wasting his time. How did they ever think they could pull this off themselves? It was obvious. They needed more clout to make themselves heard, and they just didn't have it. Better break the bad news to Ino now, he decided, before heading home to Elena.

He pushed down hard on the clutch and smiled to himself. Somehow, he still couldn't get enough of her. The honeymoon had never worn off, and he didn't believe it ever would.

Traffic was heavy at that hour, and he was afraid he'd missed Ino. He pulled into the hospital lot and stuck his head out the window. "Hey, George," he called to the attendant, "did Ino Sanchez leave yet?"

"About twenty minutes ago," the big black man told him. "You missed him, Doc."

Shit. Now he'd have to get Ino over to the apartment tonight. There goes the nice quiet evening with Elena. He checked his watch. It was close to five and he decided to call her and tell her he'd be late.

He walked into the Emergency Room and started for the phone. Suddenly, Mrs. Cleveland stopped him. "Joe," she asked quietly, "where have you been?"

"I was over at Presbyterian, why?"

"Could we talk for a minute?" She looked drawn and nervous.

"Sure," replied Joe. "Anything wrong?"

"Why don't you sit down?" she said.

Joe took the chair facing her. "What is it?"

"Joe, I hate to be the one to have to break this to you," she began in a halting voice.

"What is it?" Joe asked, his heart suddenly beating very fast.

"There's been an accident, a fire, a really bad one." Bea Cleveland took a deep breath and braced herself. "Joe, Elena died in the fire."

"Elena? Died?" he repeated dumbly. What was she saying? Elena was on her way home, probably right this minute.

"Joe, I'm so sorry. They did everything they could to save her. It was too late."

Why was she telling him this? There was some mistake. There had to be. "How do you know it's Elena?"

"The police called the hospital. The medical examiner checked her dental charts."

A switch seemed to click off in his brain. "You're lying," he shouted, "you're a filthy liar!" Suddenly, Roberto was there. "Steady now, Joe."

"I want to see her," he screamed. "Where is she?"

"She's in the morgue," Roberto whispered, still holding Joe's arms. "I'm afraid there's nothing to see."

Joe looked up and saw Kendricks and the medical resident running toward him. A young nurse was coming off the elevator, a look of horror across her face. There was a sudden hush in the usually busy emergency room. Could it be true, this lie they were telling him? Joe put his head between his hands and let out a wild cry of despair.

There was a record-breaking crowd at Miller's Funeral home. Mr. Miller himself had assured Ino that everything would be done with the greatest speed in order to ease the family's grief. Only Joe and Ino sat in the first row during the service. Ino had made most of the arrangements himself, never breaking down once. Her body was too charred to have an open casket, and he thought it just as well. He wanted to remember her as she lived, as he knew her. Now he sat with large tears falling down his cheeks, unashamed and unable to stop. He held Joe's arm.

Joe could not cry. He was too numb. He heard nothing of the eulogy. He kept thinking it had happened because his life had been so good since he had met her. He felt that his heart had been ripped from his body and all that remained was a huge, gaping hole.

When he heard the cold thump of the casket dropping into the ground, he had a strange desire to jump in and open it, to shout to all these people that his beloved wife was not dead at all. He left in the black limousine with Ino.

When they arrived at his apartment, people were already there. Bea Cleveland came over to him, didn't say anything, just cradled him in her lean, strong arms, rocking him back and forth. Someone had brought platters of cold cuts and soft drinks and put them on the table. The door kept opening and bereaved friends kept coming to pay their respects.

Joe moved as if in a daze, talking, hugging, shaking hands, yet remembering none of it.

"Go lie down for a while," Susan told him. She and Luis had driven back from Boston as soon as they heard the news. They had not left him for a minute. He didn't know what he would have done if they had.

Their bedroom still smelled of her—her uniforms, her dresses in the closet they shared, her nightgown hanging on the hook behind the door, her makeup strewn over her dresser. He didn't want to move any of it, as if to do so would take her further away from him. He lay down on their bed and closed his eyes. He prayed it was a hideous nightmare from which he would soon wake up.

He walked back to the living room, now swelling with well-meaning people. Luis got up and gave him his chair, one of the few that was left. "Sit down, Joe," he said softly.

He looked around and each new face conjured up a torturous image of the times they had all spent together. Arnost walked in and embraced Joe. "I'm so sorry," he said. They were all sorry.

Ino sat in a chair in the corner, a blank stare on his face. Herb Aquedo sat next to him. "It was the neighborhood," Ino was saying in a shaking voice. "The neighborhood killed her. I can't believe it." Then he broke down again, and Herb tried to comfort him the best he could.

Joe shook his head abruptly. He couldn't believe it either. She was buried in the earth, and he never would hold her in his arms again.

Sam and Ida Ruskin, looking pale and old, tried to comfort their son. "We made a mistake, Joe," said Sam, "and now it's too late." Ida cried in her son's shoulder. "We caused you pain, our own flesh and blood," she said. "We hurt you. And now it's too late to make good." Joe saw they were suffering and said, "You're here now, and I know that would have meant a lot to her. She only wanted peace in the family. She only wanted for us all to be happy."

Roberto, wearing his only black suit, came with his wife and son. A subdued Kendricks came and Paco and Cliff Garvin and Tony Coletti. The whole ER staff—residents, nurses, interns, aides—all of them were there. It could almost have been our wedding party, Joe thought with remorse.

There was a knock at the door. Cliff Garvin got up to answer it.

"Is this the home of Dr. Joseph Ruskin?"

Garvin's jaw fell open at the sight of Benjamin Gold. "Yes, sir, it is," he sputtered.

"I'm Benjamin Gold. I'm a friend of Joe's. I know it's a bad time," he began.

"Dr. Gold," said Garvin, extending his hand. "I'm Cliff Garvin, from the *Post*. I'm a friend, too. Here, sir, come in," he said, opening the door.

"Well," Gold hesitated, "actually I'd rather not. I was wondering if I might see Joe, alone?"

"Certainly," said Garvin, "I'll get him." A moment later he brought Joe out and stood guarding the door while their hushed voices continued down the vestibule.

"Joe," said Gold, extending his arms, "I'm so very sorry."

"I know, I know," said Joe, fighting back the tears.

"She was a good woman," said Gold. "One of the best. I know what it is to lose someone you love very much." He was trying hard to control himself.

"I have this awful pain in my chest," said Joe. "When will it go away?" He cried openly now, and Gold put his arm around his shoulder.

"It'll take a long time, Joe. Maybe a year." He did not tell him it would never go away completely.

"You had a great love in your life and you lost her. But it should be a comfort to you to know that you had that much, even for a little while. Some people go their whole lives without having ever come close to what you and Elena had." Joe nodded numbly. "She cared so much, Joe. About you, about the hospital. I know about Hirshorn pulling out and the trouble Jefferson is in right now."

"It doesn't matter anymore," lamented Joe.

"Of course it does," said Gold. "Wasn't that how Elena came to be killed? It mattered to her, and I know, in time, it's going to matter to you." He paused. "She called me three days ago."

"She did?" said Joe.

"We talked for a long time. She was the one who told me what was going on. She pleaded with me to help. I thought about it for several days, and in truth, I was undecided. Then when I heard about the fire, I knew I had to do something. I made several phone calls and went down to see Leo Bergman over at Long Island Presbyterian. Seems they're looking to expand. I convinced him to take a chance on Jefferson."

Joe looked at Benjamin Gold, astonished. Cliff Garvin, not sure he had heard right, moved closer.

"How did you do that?" asked Joe.

"It wasn't easy," Gold said haltingly. "I had to make one minor concession."

"What was that?" asked Joe.

"I had to agree to become Chief of Surgery."

"You agreed to go back?" Joe was flabbergasted.

"Well, I'm not as young as I was, and I'm sure I won't be able to work at the same pace. I'll have to hire extra attendings to give me a hand," admitted Gold.

Joe shook his head in disbelief. "After what they did to you, you'd still go back?"

"I always cared; I just couldn't show it. You and Elena taught me how to do that."

"I only wish I could tell Elena," said Joe suddenly.

Benjamin Gold put his arms around him and whispered softly, "We have."

Cliff Garvin, unable to control himself any longer, walked over to them. "Is what I heard true? Is LIP going to take over Jefferson and you're going to be the new chief?"

Gold turned to Cliff Garvin. "If the administration okays it."

Joe opened the door and looked across the crowded room at Ino. "I don't think we'll have any trouble along those lines. I'll talk to the administration right now."

They looked down at the floor. Finally, Garvin said, "This means a second chance for Jefferson."

Benjamin Gold turned away. "And maybe for us all."

Epilogue

Two years later, on Thursday morning, July 5, Jefferson Hospital was pulsating with excitement. At noon the new wing would be dedicated. It had actually been in operation as soon as the paint had dried, but the official ceremonies were not to occur until lunchtime, when the greatest portion of the staff could be on hand for the festivities. The ceremonies were to take place outside, on the old ramp, which had been extended to lead to the new wing. A podium had been constructed two days before to seat the important philanthropists that Long Island Presbyterian had managed to entice and the political dignitaries who hoped to have their pictures in the paper.

Inocencio Sanchez had been assigned a middle row, center seat for the proceedings. The event held much personal significance, and he had worked on his speech for two weeks. It was after his speech that Tony Coletti would cut the ribbon, officially dedicating the new building. Folding chairs for the chiefs of staff were placed to the right of where Ino sat. Benjamin Gold had been notified that he would sit in the first chair, closest to the crowd. Joe Ruskin would sit with the other residents and attendings behind the chiefs of staff. The people of the South Bronx had waited a long time for this day and promised to turn out in full force.

Another ceremony, smaller and more private, had also been planned. At ten o'clock, Ino stopped by the doctors' lounge. "Just checking, Joe." He smiled. "I want to make sure you're here on time. You doctors have a reputation for being late." He was carrying a small box and a screwdriver. "Have Susan and Luis arrived yet?" They were coming in from Boston, the first time in two years, for the day. "We wouldn't miss it for the world," Susan had told him over the phone last month.

323

"Not since I last checked," said Joe. "But, come on down with me, maybe they're here by now."

The two men made their way down to the Emergency Room. Susan and Luis were just coming in the door. "Joe!" she called out.

He ran toward her. "It's been a long time," he said, hugging her tightly.

"Too long," said Ino, embracing Luis.

"You both look great!" said Joe enthusiastically. Susan and Luis seemed healthier and more relaxed than he had ever seen them. They seemed to exude contentment.

"I guess Boston agrees with you," said Ino.

"I'd say marriage agrees with us," said Luis, looking affectionately at Susan.

"How's Elena?" asked Ino, still smiling.

"I thought you'd never ask," said Susan, pulling out a long plastic accordian of snapshots. Joe and Ino looked at the pictures. "She's walking all over now," continued Susan happily. "I need eyes in the back of my head."

"I'd say she's the spitting image of her father," said Ino.

"Don't you think so, Joe?"

Joe felt a small pang and thought of what might have been. "Without a doubt," he agreed.

"Where is Dr. Gold?" Susan asked excitedly. "I want him to see her too."

"Speak of the devil," said Joe as he watched Benjamin Gold lumber down the hall.

"It's still hard to believe, him back working here," said Luis.

"Let me tell you," said Ino, "he's done one hell of a job. More than anyone else, he's turned the new wing from a dream into a reality. He's a great surgeon."

"He always was a great surgeon," said Luis. "It's just you who've mellowed, Ino."

"These two years have taught me a lot," said Ino. "I wanted him to be a spokesman and also to take care of the people. Now I realize that's a two-man job."

"And now two men have it." Luis smiled. "Two good men."

Ino looked at his friends around him. "This is like the old days, having you guys back," he said suddenly.

"It is, it really is," said Susan.

But Joe knew the old days were gone for good.

Benjamin Gold held his arms out to Susan and extended his nd to Luis. "Good to see you," he said warmly.

"We're glad to be here," said Luis.

After a while, they moved to the Emergency Waiting Room. few doctors and nurses joined them. Ino opened the box and wrapped the tissue paper. "Well, what do you think?" he ked. He held a small gold plaque before them. It was in-ribed:

In Memory of Elena Sanchez Ruskin/Jefferson Nursing School/Class of 1971.

Susan held Joe's hand and squeezed it. "It's beautiful, Ino," e said.

"I wish she could be here today," said Ino.

Joe knew who she was.

The plaque was hung in the Jefferson Emergency Waiting oom, in full view of all who passed through the ancient doors d sat on the rickety benches.

Directly opposite, on the far side of the waiting room, was other sign. Its edges were worn and frayed. In chipped black ters it said: "A.M.F."

Later, in the cafeteria, they drank coffee. "Congratulations on ur research award, Dr. Gold," said Susan. "I can't believe at one of the discoverers of Wondertron trained me," she said, ughing. "You're a real celebrity in the medical world."

"Not for long, I'm sure," he laughed. "That's the last research vard I'll win. I've got my job back, and my job is taking care patients. But I'll tell you one thing about the research. At least 've been able to grab off some decent residents because of

"How are things at Mass. General?" Joe asked Susan.

"Okay, good. But Luis and I still miss Jefferson."

"Your third year of med school and you have time to miss ything?" joked Joe.

"Luis made AOA, the top ten percent of his class." She amed proudly.

"Congratulations," said Gold. "That's quite an accomplish-ent."

"When I finish med school, we want to come back here," id Luis.

"You do?" Gold laughed. "The place is worse than ever."

"It hasn't been the same without you," said Ino, looking at san and Luis.

"We thought I could work as an attending while Luis does h
residency—that is, if the chief of staff wants to hire us," sa
Susan, smiling at Gold.

"I always ask all new applicants the same question," sa
Gold. "Do you have any special experience that would prepa
you to work in a place like this?"

The whole group broke out in a warm, deep laugh.

Ino checked his watch. "Hey, it's almost noon. This is
friends," he said, straightening his tie. "We'd better get moving.

A large crowd had gathered, and the nurses and doctors a
patients who couldn't go outside stood by the windows a
watched with anticipation. Dr. Benjamin Gold took his seat. F
Susan and Luis the moment was mingled with bittersweet mem
ries as they watched Ino and Joe walk arm in arm toward t
podium.

ABOUT THE AUTHOR

ETHAN BARNETT is a pseudonym for a husband and wife team. The husband is a famous orthopedic surgeon, and the couple resides in Maryland